DISNEY MASTERS

MICKEY MOUSE:
THE ICE SWORD SAGA
BOOK 2

by Massimo De Vita

Publisher: GARY GROTH
Senior Editor: J. MICHAEL CATRON
Archival Editor: DAVID GERSTEIN
Production: PAUL BARESH, CHRISTINA HWANG, and KEELI McCARTHY
Associate Publisher: ERIC REYNOLDS

Storyboard drawings on page 154 courtesy Disney Publishing Worldwide.

Disney Masters showcases the work of internationally acclaimed Disney artists. Many of the stories presented in the *Disney Masters* series appear in English for the first time. This is *Disney Masters* Volume 11. Permission to quote or reproduce material for reviews must be obtained from the publisher.

Fantagraphics Books, Inc | 7563 Lake City Way NE | Seattle WA 98115 | (800) 657-1100

Visit us at fantagraphics.com. Follow us on Twitter at @fantagraphics and on Facebook at facebook.com/fantagraphics.

Cover and title page art by Marco Ghiglione and Stefano Attardi, color by Digikore Studios.
Thanks to Francesco Spreafico

First printing: August 2020
ISBN 978-1-68396-250-2
Printed in The Republic of Korea
Library of Congress Control Number: 2017956971

The stories in this volume were originally published in Italy and appear here in English for the first time.
"The Prince of Mists Strikes Back" ("Topolino e il ritorno del 'principe delle nebbie'") in *Topolino* #1517, December 23, 1984 (I TL 1517-A).
"Sleeping Beauty in the Stars" ("Topolino e la bella addormentata nel cosmo") in *Topolino* #1936–1937, January 3 and 10, 1993 (I TL 1936-AP).
"The Secret of 313" ("Paperino e il segreto della 313") in *Topolino* #2071, August 8, 1995 (I TL 2071-1).
"Arizona Goof and the Tiger's Fiery Eye" ("Indiana Pipps e la tigre dagli occhi di fuoco") in *Topolino* #2744, July 1, 2008 (I TL 2744-1).

TITLES IN THIS SERIES

Mickey Mouse: The Delta Dimension (Romano Scarpa) (*Disney Masters* Vol. 1)
Donald Duck: Uncle Scrooge's Money Rocket (Luciano Bottaro) (*Disney Masters* Vol. 2)
Mickey Mouse: The Case of the Vanishing Bandit (Paul Murry) (*Disney Masters* Vol. 3)
Donald Duck: The Great Survival Test (Daan Jippes and Freddy Milton) (*Disney Masters* Vol. 4)
Mickey Mouse: The Phantom Blot's Double Mystery (Romano Scarpa) (*Disney Masters* Vol. 5)
Uncle Scrooge: King of the Golden River (Giovan Battista Carpi) (*Disney Masters* Vol. 6)
Mickey Mouse: The Pirates of Tabasco Bay (Paul Murry) (*Disney Masters* Vol. 7)
Donald Duck: Duck Avenger Strikes Again (Romano Scarpa with Carl Barks) (*Disney Masters* Vol. 8)
Mickey Mouse: The Ice Sword Saga Book 1 (Massimo De Vita) (*Disney Masters* Vol. 9)
Donald Duck: Scandal on the Epoch Express (Mau and Bas Heymans) (*Disney Masters* Vol. 10)
Mickey Mouse: The Ice Sword Saga Book 2 (Massimo De Vita) (*Disney Masters* Vol. 11)

COMING SOON

Donald Duck: The Forgetful Hero (Giorgio Cavazzano) (*Disney Masters* Vol. 12)

ALSO AVAILABLE

Walt Disney's Uncle Scrooge: "The Twenty-four Carat Moon" (Carl Barks)
The Complete Life and Times of Scrooge McDuck Volumes 1 and 2 (Don Rosa)
Mickey Mouse: The Greatest Adventures (Floyd Gottfredson)

Walt Disney
MICKEY MOUSE
THE ICE SWORD SAGA

BOOK 2

FANTAGRAPHICS BOOKS

SEATTLE

CONTENTS

This content has been reprinted in its entirety as first created in 1937–2014.

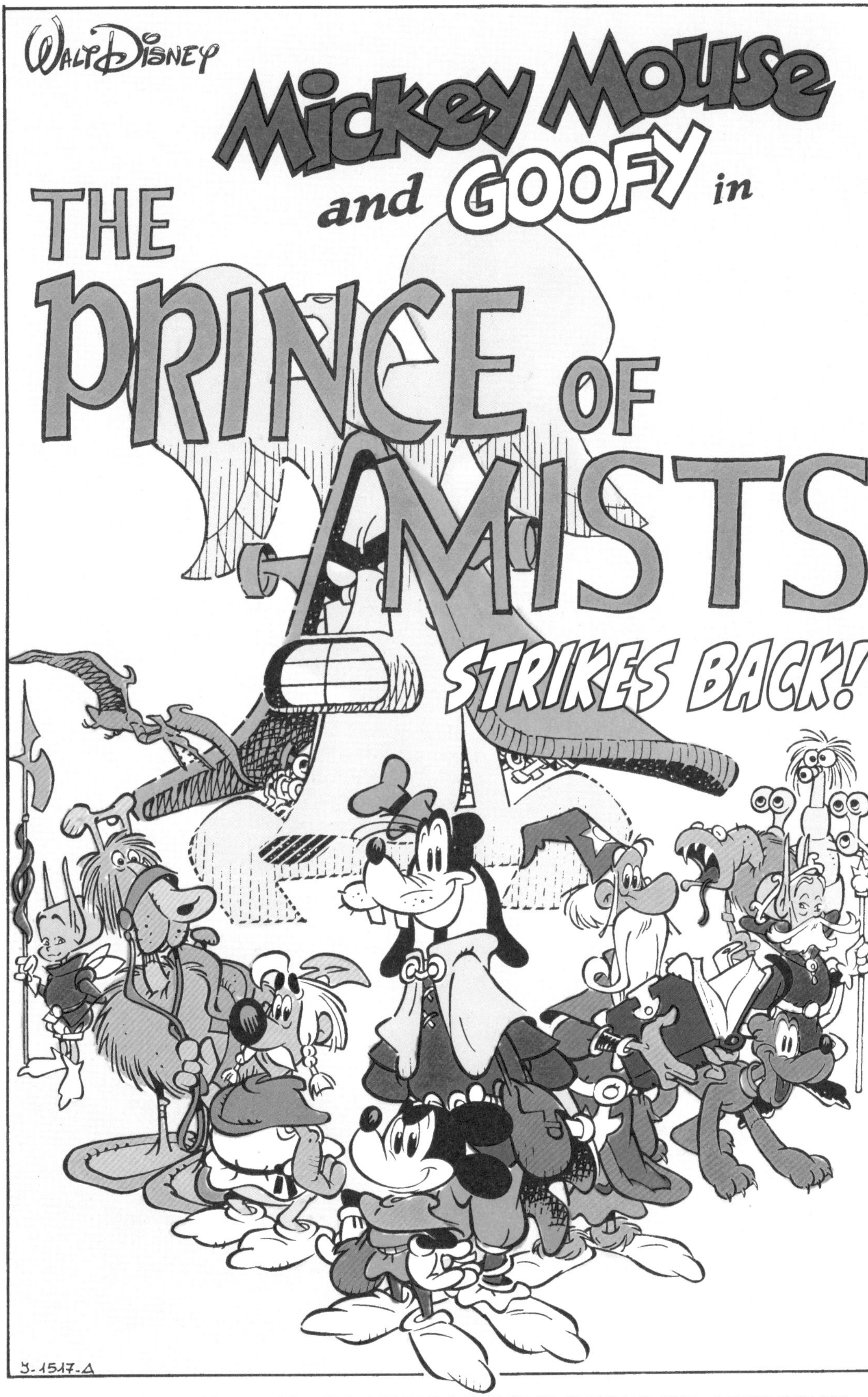
Walt Disney
Mickey Mouse and Goofy in
THE PRINCE OF MISTS STRIKES BACK!
I-1517-A

STORY AND ART BY MASSIMO DE VITA • TRANSLATION AND DIALOGUE BY JONATHAN H. GRAY • LETTERING BY PAUL BARESH AND CHRISTINA HWANG • COLORING BY MONDADORI • EDITING BY DAVID GERSTEIN AND J. MICHAEL CATRON

The Premise

Call them what you will, different dimensions -- parallel or otherwise -- exist beyond our own! And in one of those faraway realms, you'll find the fantastic lands of Argaar ...

WELCOME BACK, FRIENDS! I'M *YOR*, THE SAGE! LET'S TAKE A TRIP DOWN MEMORY LANE, EH? THE 13TH YEAR OF THE *ALDEBARAN STAR ALIGNMENT* WAS A *DISASTER* FOR THE PEOPLE OF *ULULAND* ...

UTGARD

VALLEY OF SHADOWS

RAINBOW BRIDGE

LAND OF THE TROLLS

ENCHANTED FOREST

ELVES

DWARVES OF MUNZE

THE LANDS OF ARGAAR

YARNONI

YETIS OF YORBALINDEN

MOUNTAINS OF THE MOON

ULULAND

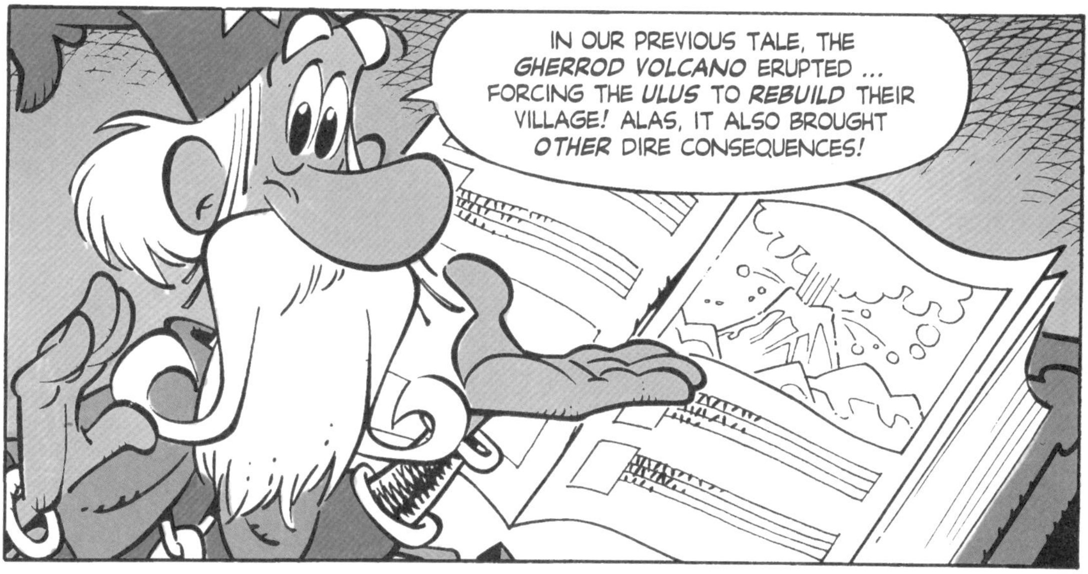
IN OUR PREVIOUS TALE, THE GHERROD VOLCANO ERUPTED ... FORCING THE ULUS TO REBUILD THEIR VILLAGE! ALAS, IT ALSO BROUGHT OTHER DIRE CONSEQUENCES!

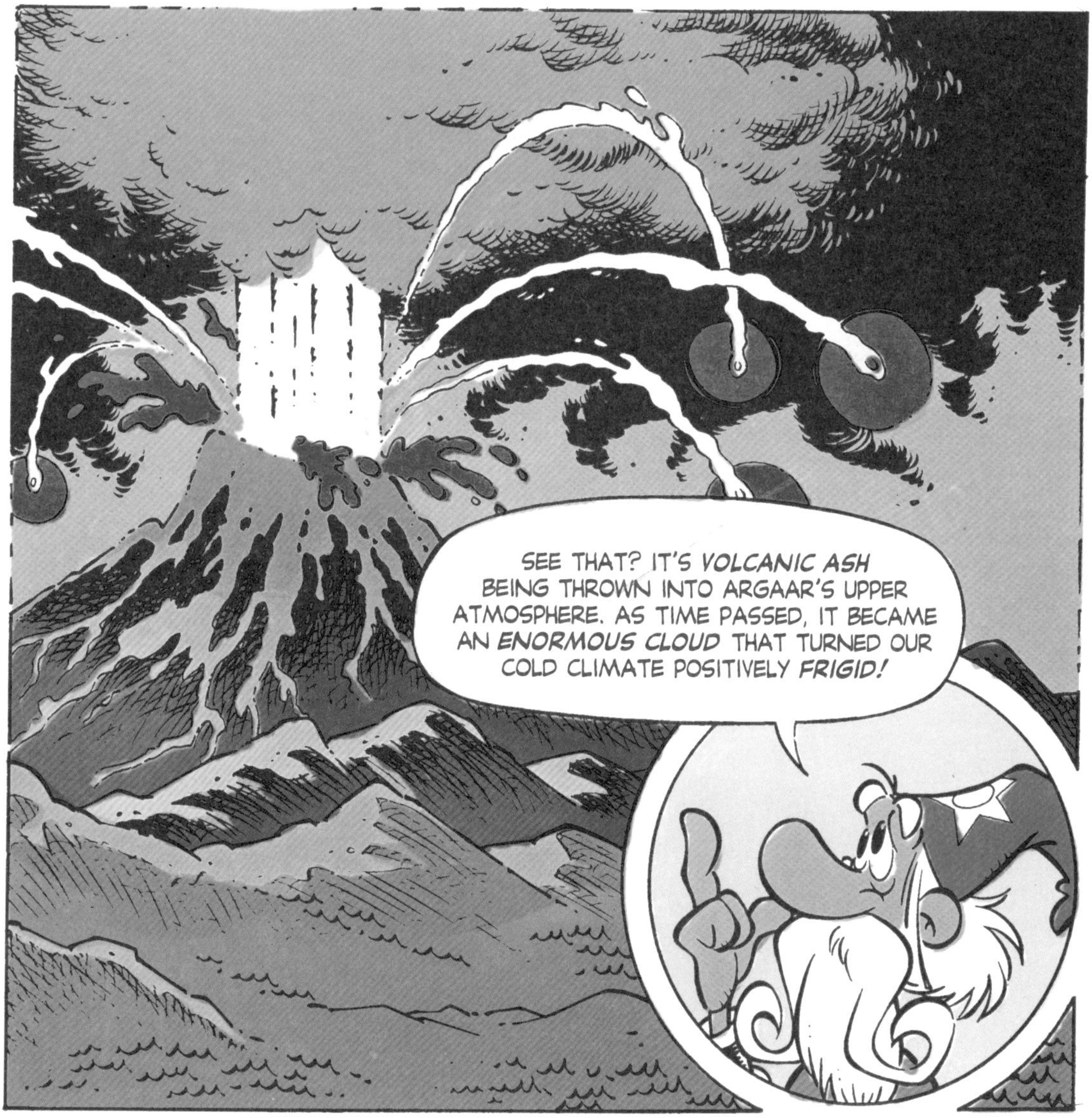
SEE THAT? IT'S VOLCANIC ASH BEING THROWN INTO ARGAAR'S UPPER ATMOSPHERE. AS TIME PASSED, IT BECAME AN ENORMOUS CLOUD THAT TURNED OUR COLD CLIMATE POSITIVELY FRIGID!

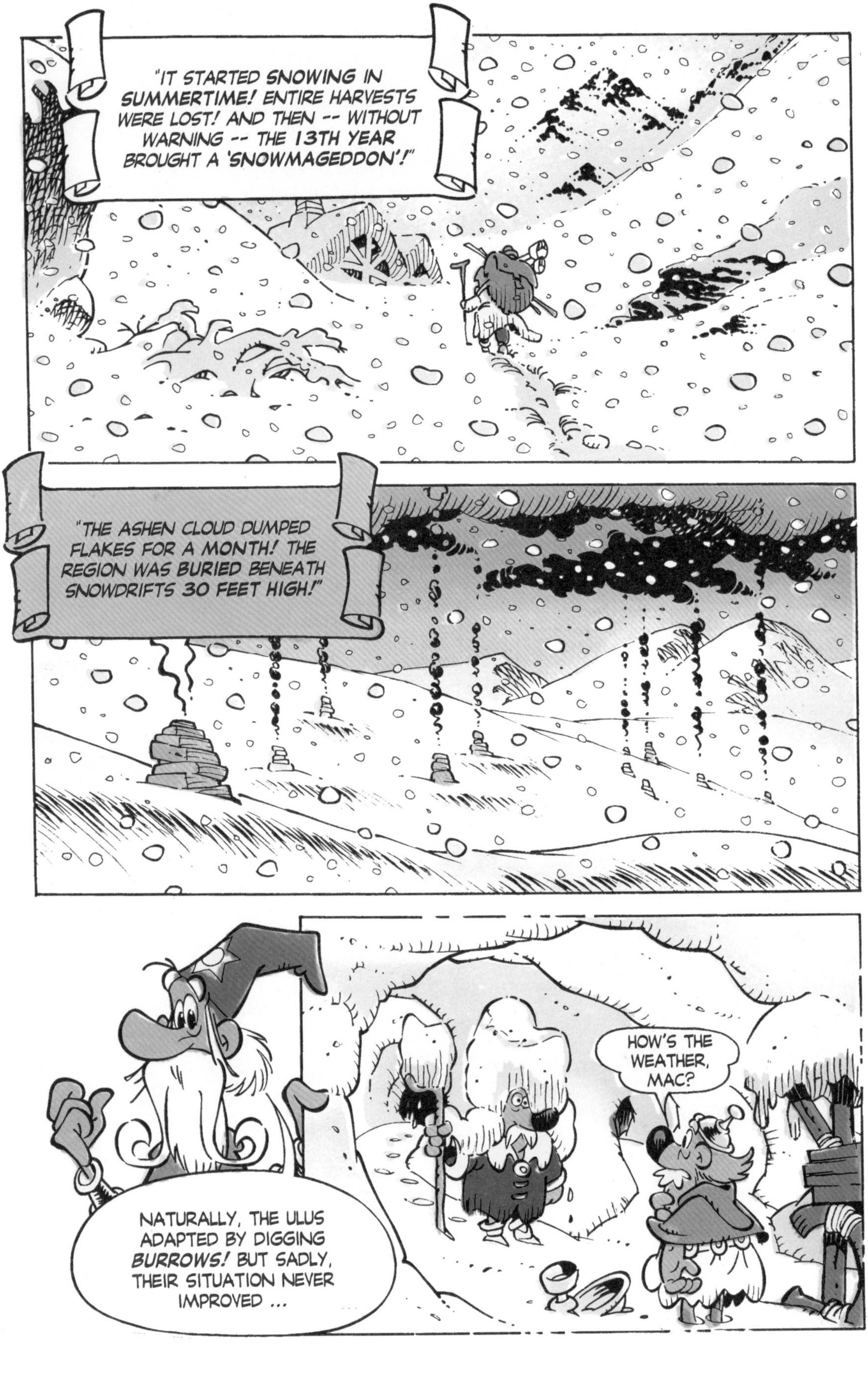
"IT STARTED SNOWING IN SUMMERTIME! ENTIRE HARVESTS WERE LOST! AND THEN -- WITHOUT WARNING -- THE 13TH YEAR BROUGHT A 'SNOWMAGEDDON'!"
"THE ASHEN CLOUD DUMPED FLAKES FOR A MONTH! THE REGION WAS BURIED BENEATH SNOWDRIFTS 30 FEET HIGH!"
NATURALLY, THE ULUS ADAPTED BY DIGGING BURROWS! BUT SADLY, THEIR SITUATION NEVER IMPROVED ...
HOW'S THE WEATHER, MAC?

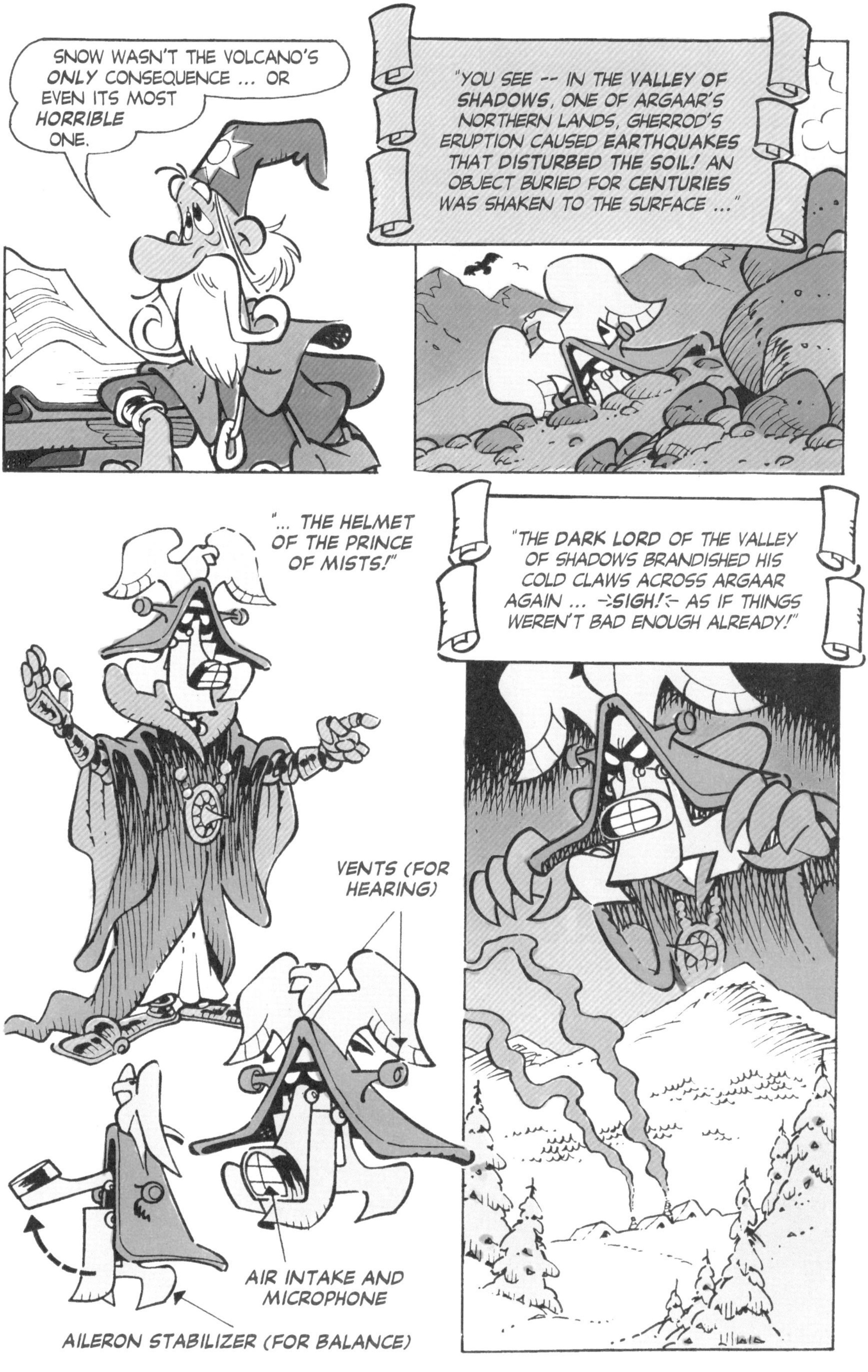
SNOW WASN'T THE VOLCANO'S ONLY CONSEQUENCE ... OR EVEN ITS MOST HORRIBLE ONE.
"YOU SEE -- IN THE VALLEY OF SHADOWS, ONE OF ARGAAR'S NORTHERN LANDS, GHERROD'S ERUPTION CAUSED EARTHQUAKES THAT DISTURBED THE SOIL! AN OBJECT BURIED FOR CENTURIES WAS SHAKEN TO THE SURFACE ..."
"... THE HELMET OF THE PRINCE OF MISTS!"
VENTS (FOR HEARING)
AIR INTAKE AND MICROPHONE
AILERON STABILIZER (FOR BALANCE)
"THE DARK LORD OF THE VALLEY OF SHADOWS BRANDISHED HIS COLD CLAWS ACROSS ARGAAR AGAIN ... -SIGH!- AS IF THINGS WEREN'T BAD ENOUGH ALREADY!"

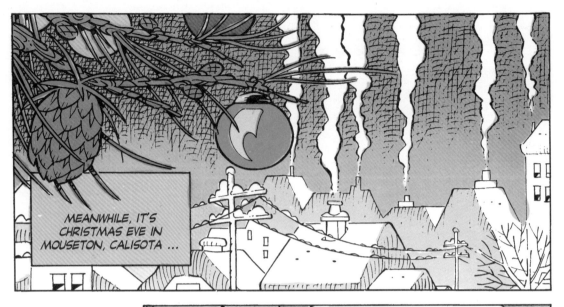

MEANWHILE, IT'S CHRISTMAS EVE IN MOUSETON, CALISOTA ...

... WHERE WE FIND A CHARMING YOUNG LADY CHEERFULLY CLEANING HOUSE!

I'M THE GAL THEY CALL LITTLE MINNIE MOUSE!

FR-RR-RR-RR

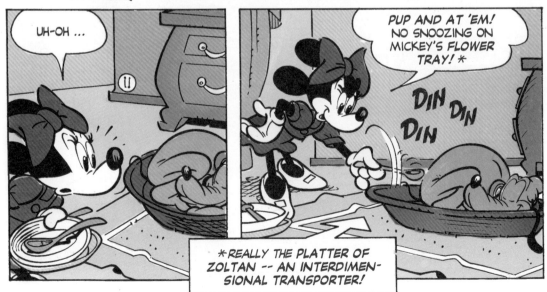

UH-OH ...

PUP AND AT 'EM! NO SNOOZING ON MICKEY'S FLOWER TRAY! *

DIN DIN DIN

*REALLY THE PLATTER OF ZOLTAN -- AN INTERDIMEN-SIONAL TRANSPORTER!

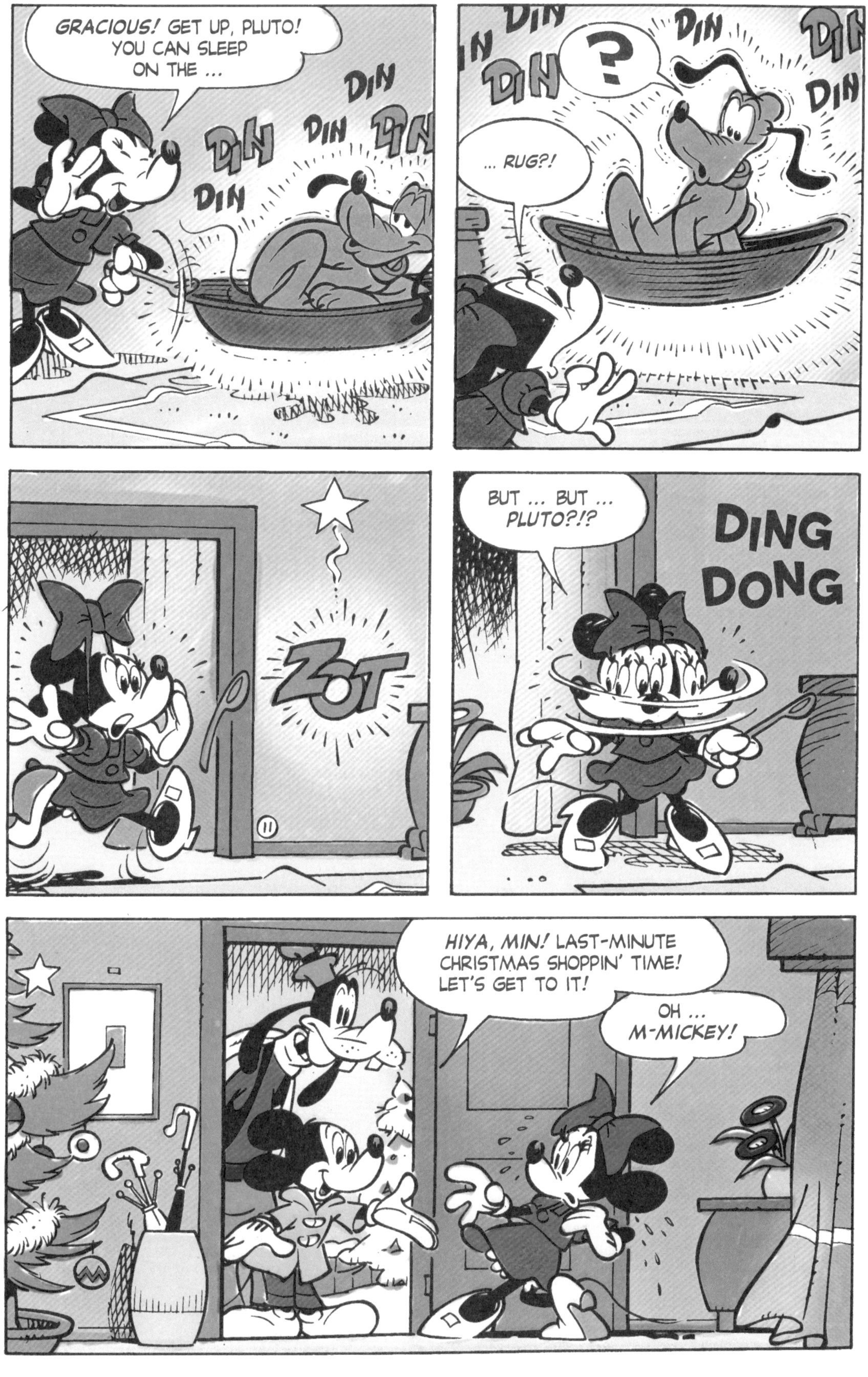
GRACIOUS! GET UP, PLUTO! YOU CAN SLEEP ON THE ...
DIN DIN DIN DIN DIN
?
... RUG?!
DIN DIN DIN DIN DIN
ZOT
BUT ... BUT ... PLUTO?!?
DING DONG
HIYA, MIN! LAST-MINUTE CHRISTMAS SHOPPIN' TIME! LET'S GET TO IT!
OH ... M-MICKEY!

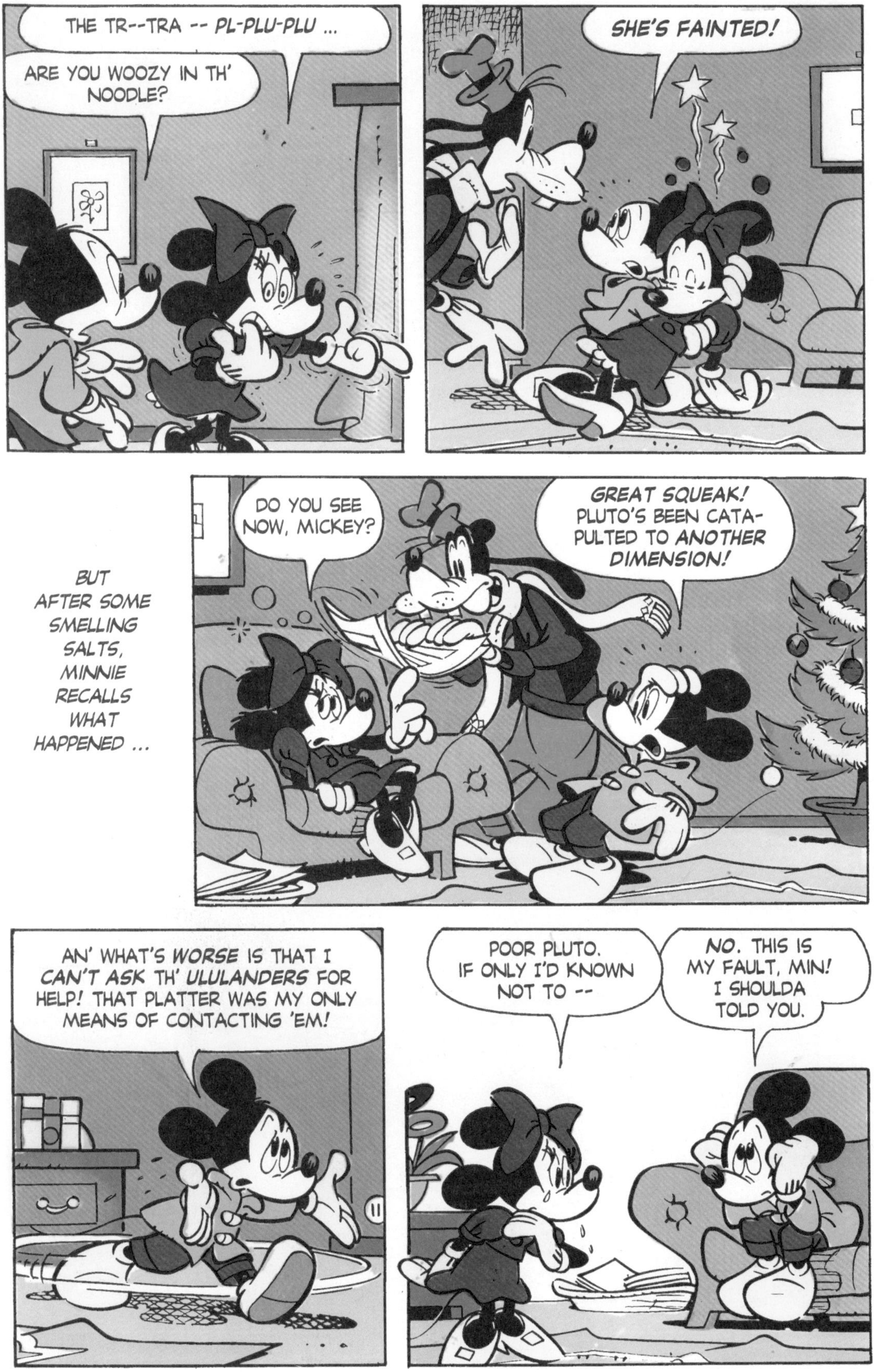
THE TR--TRA -- PL-PLU-PLU ...
ARE YOU WOOZY IN TH' NOODLE?
SHE'S FAINTED!
BUT AFTER SOME SMELLING SALTS, MINNIE RECALLS WHAT HAPPENED ...
DO YOU SEE NOW, MICKEY?
GREAT SQUEAK! PLUTO'S BEEN CATA-PULTED TO ANOTHER DIMENSION!
AN' WHAT'S WORSE IS THAT I CAN'T ASK TH' ULULANDERS FOR HELP! THAT PLATTER WAS MY ONLY MEANS OF CONTACTING 'EM!
POOR PLUTO. IF ONLY I'D KNOWN NOT TO --
NO. THIS IS MY FAULT, MIN! I SHOULDA TOLD YOU.

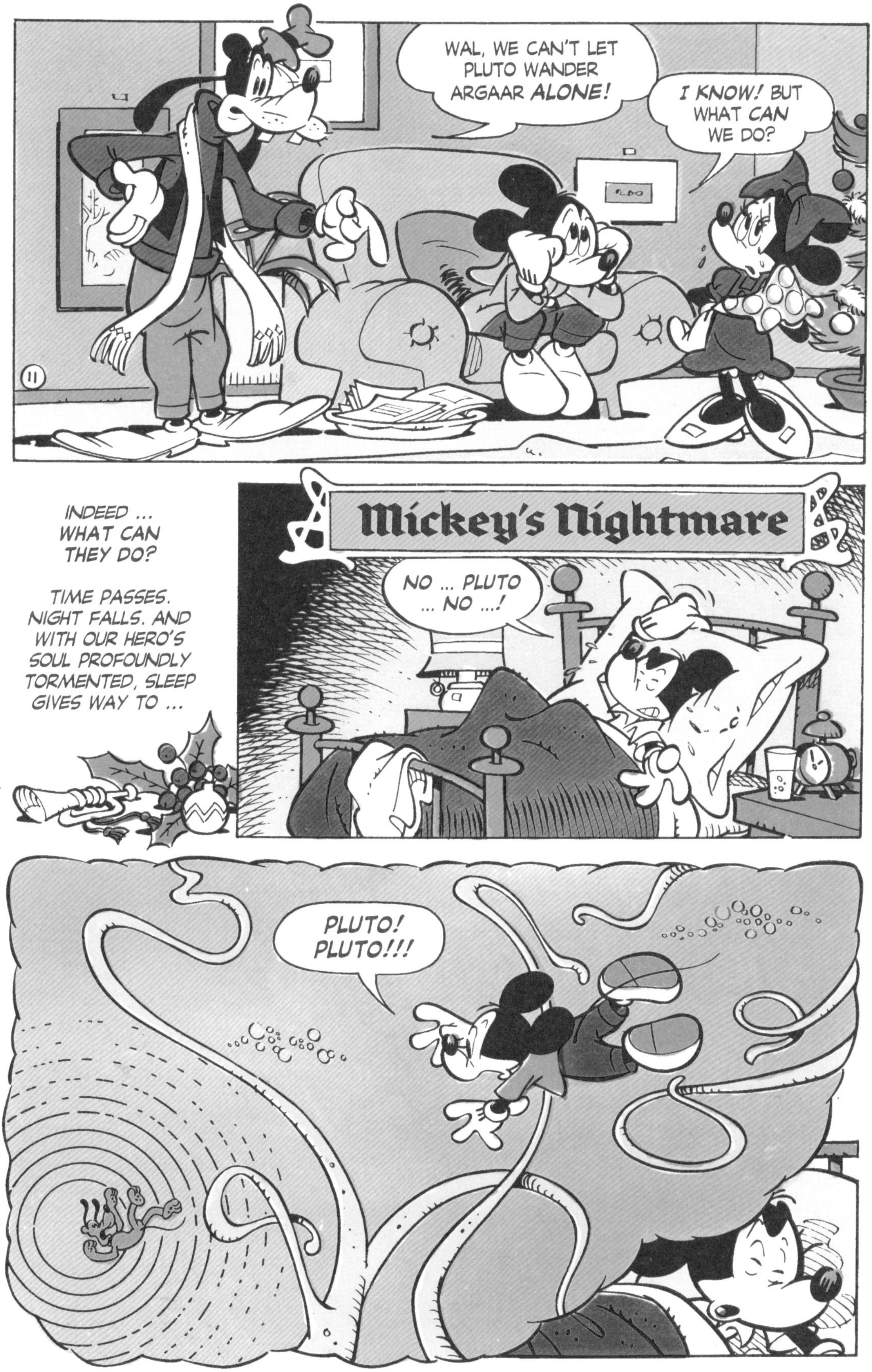
WAL, WE CAN'T LET PLUTO WANDER ARGAAR ALONE!
I KNOW! BUT WHAT CAN WE DO?
11
INDEED ... WHAT CAN THEY DO?
TIME PASSES. NIGHT FALLS. AND WITH OUR HERO'S SOUL PROFOUNDLY TORMENTED, SLEEP GIVES WAY TO ...
Mickey's Nightmare
NO ... PLUTO ... NO ...!
PLUTO! PLUTO!!!

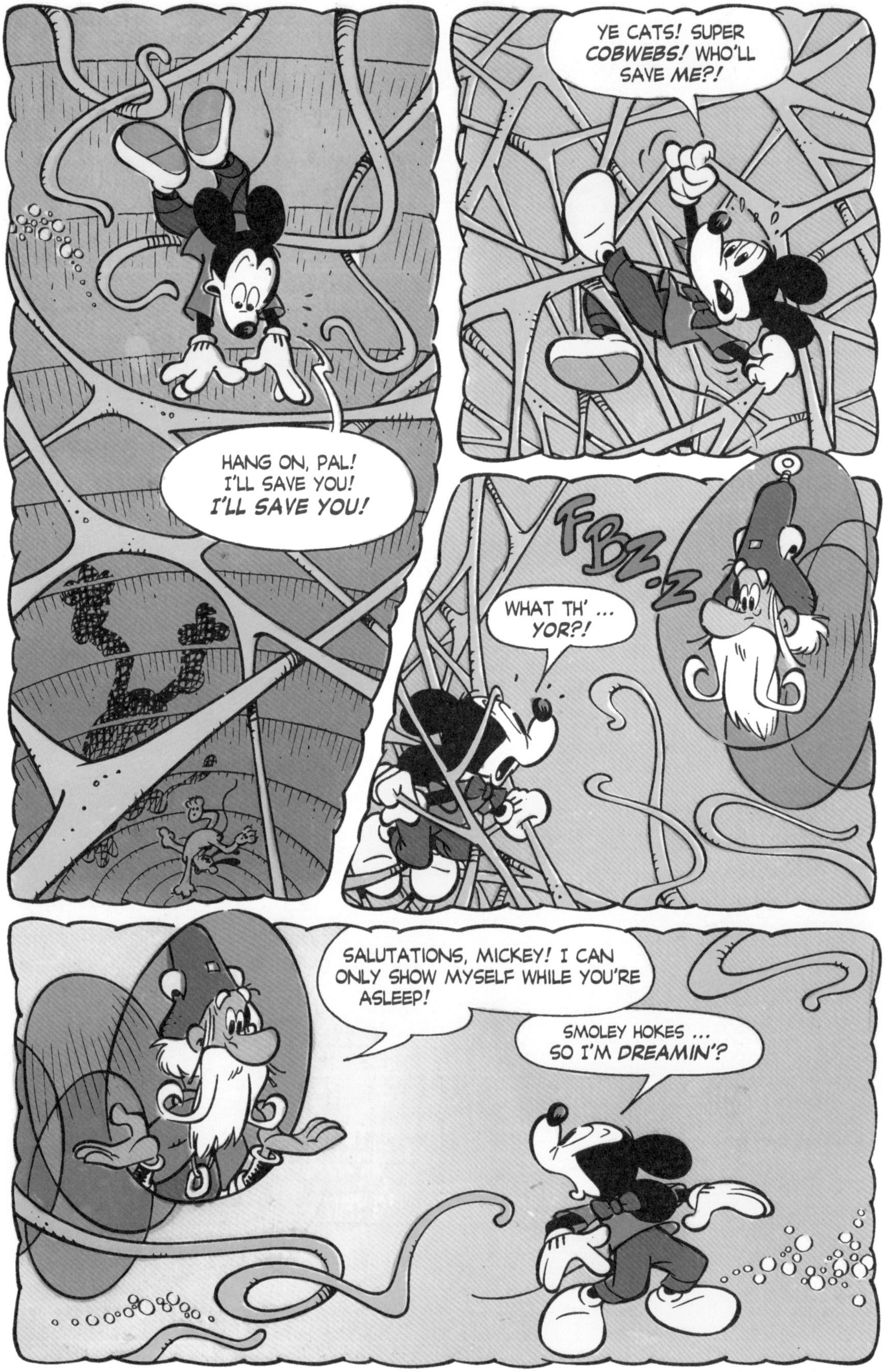
YE CATS! SUPER COBWEBS! WHO'LL SAVE ME?!
HANG ON, PAL! I'LL SAVE YOU! I'LL SAVE YOU!
FBZ-Z
WHAT TH' ... YOR?!
SALUTATIONS, MICKEY! I CAN ONLY SHOW MYSELF WHILE YOU'RE ASLEEP!
SMOLEY HOKES ... SO I'M DREAMIN'?

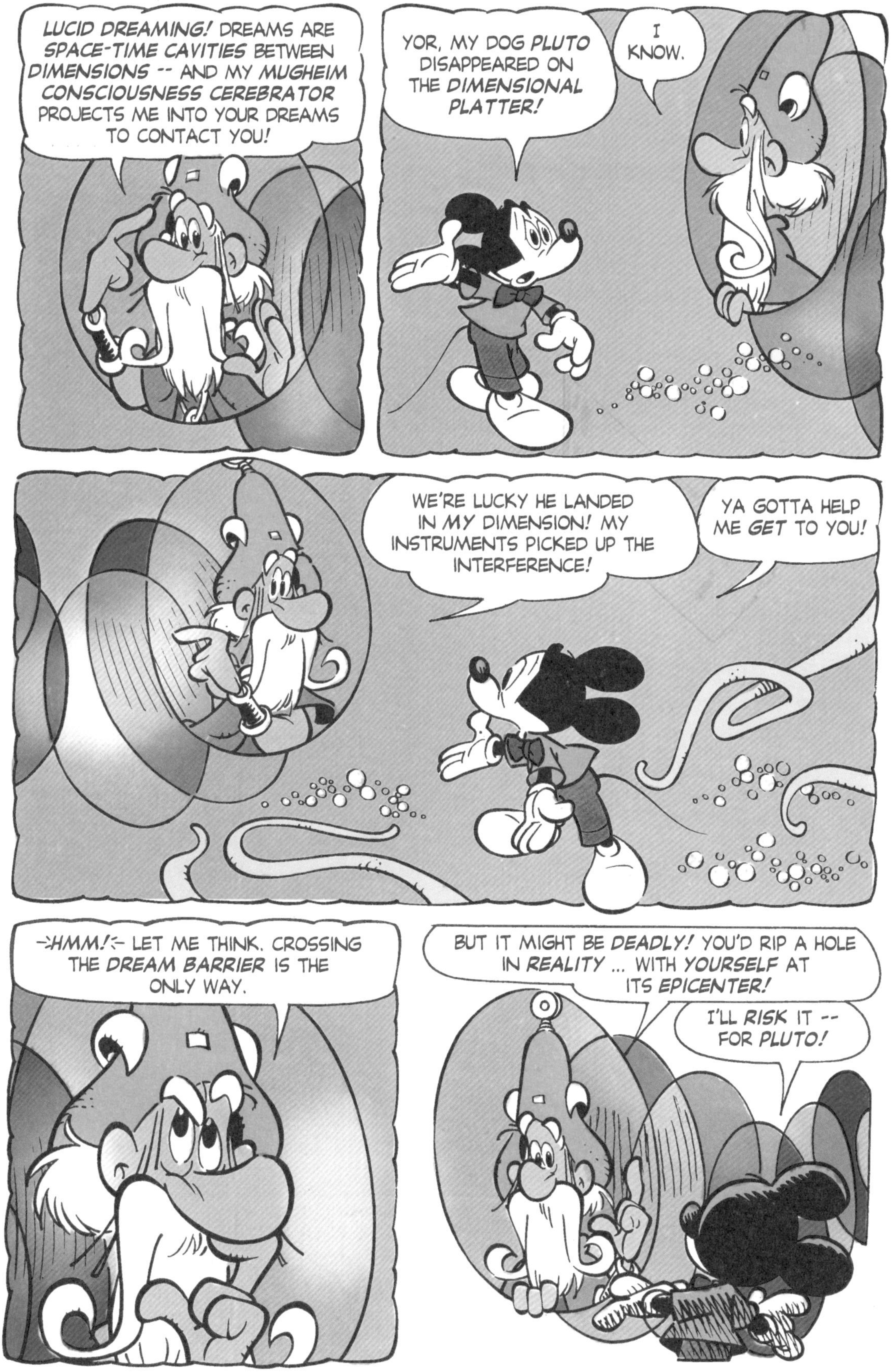
LUCID DREAMING! DREAMS ARE SPACE-TIME CAVITIES BETWEEN DIMENSIONS -- AND MY MUGHEIM CONSCIOUSNESS CEREBRATOR PROJECTS ME INTO YOUR DREAMS TO CONTACT YOU!
YOR, MY DOG PLUTO DISAPPEARED ON THE DIMENSIONAL PLATTER!
I KNOW.
WE'RE LUCKY HE LANDED IN MY DIMENSION! MY INSTRUMENTS PICKED UP THE INTERFERENCE!
YA GOTTA HELP ME GET TO YOU!
-HMM!- LET ME THINK. CROSSING THE DREAM BARRIER IS THE ONLY WAY.
BUT IT MIGHT BE DEADLY! YOU'D RIP A HOLE IN REALITY ... WITH YOURSELF AT ITS EPICENTER!
I'LL RISK IT -- FOR PLUTO!

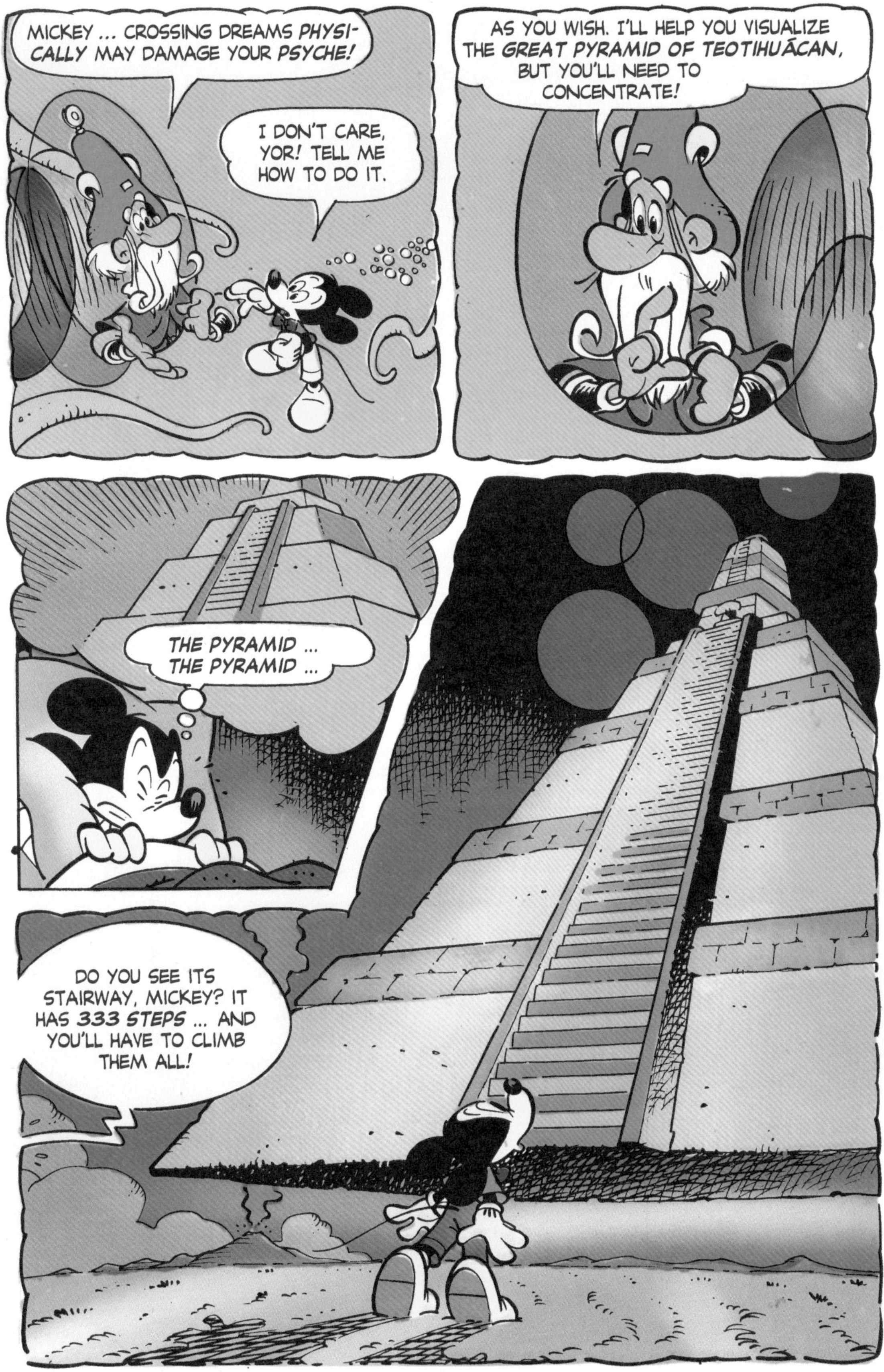
MICKEY ... CROSSING DREAMS PHYSICALLY MAY DAMAGE YOUR PSYCHE!
I DON'T CARE, YOR! TELL ME HOW TO DO IT.
AS YOU WISH. I'LL HELP YOU VISUALIZE THE GREAT PYRAMID OF TEOTIHUÁCAN, BUT YOU'LL NEED TO CONCENTRATE!
THE PYRAMID ... THE PYRAMID ...
DO YOU SEE ITS STAIRWAY, MICKEY? IT HAS 333 STEPS ... AND YOU'LL HAVE TO CLIMB THEM ALL!

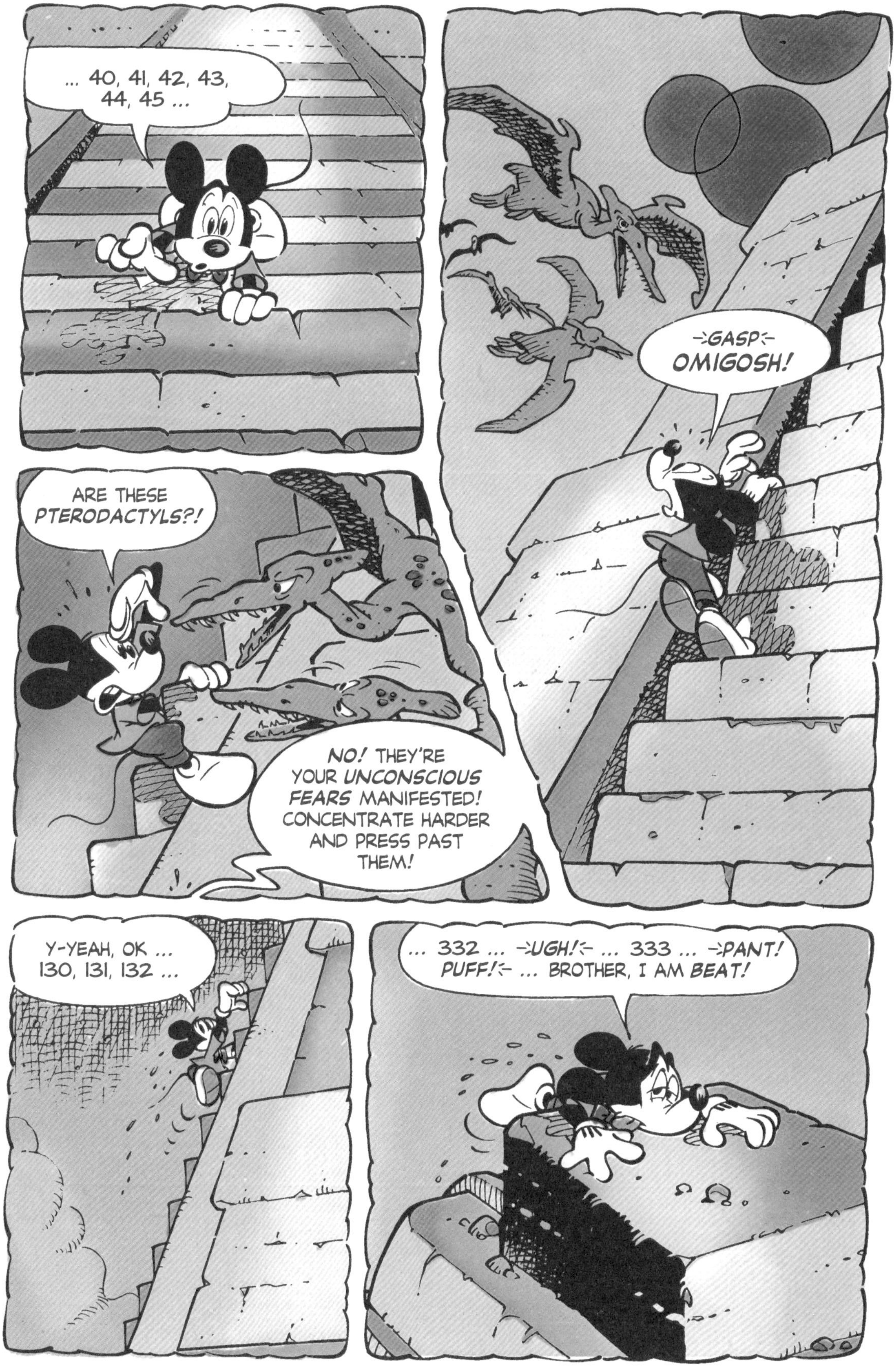
... 40, 41, 42, 43, 44, 45 ...
-GASP- OMIGOSH!
ARE THESE PTERODACTYLS?!
NO! THEY'RE YOUR UNCONSCIOUS FEARS MANIFESTED! CONCENTRATE HARDER AND PRESS PAST THEM!
Y-YEAH, OK ... 130, 131, 132 ...
... 332 ... -UGH!- ... 333 ... -PANT! PUFF!- ... BROTHER, I AM BEAT!

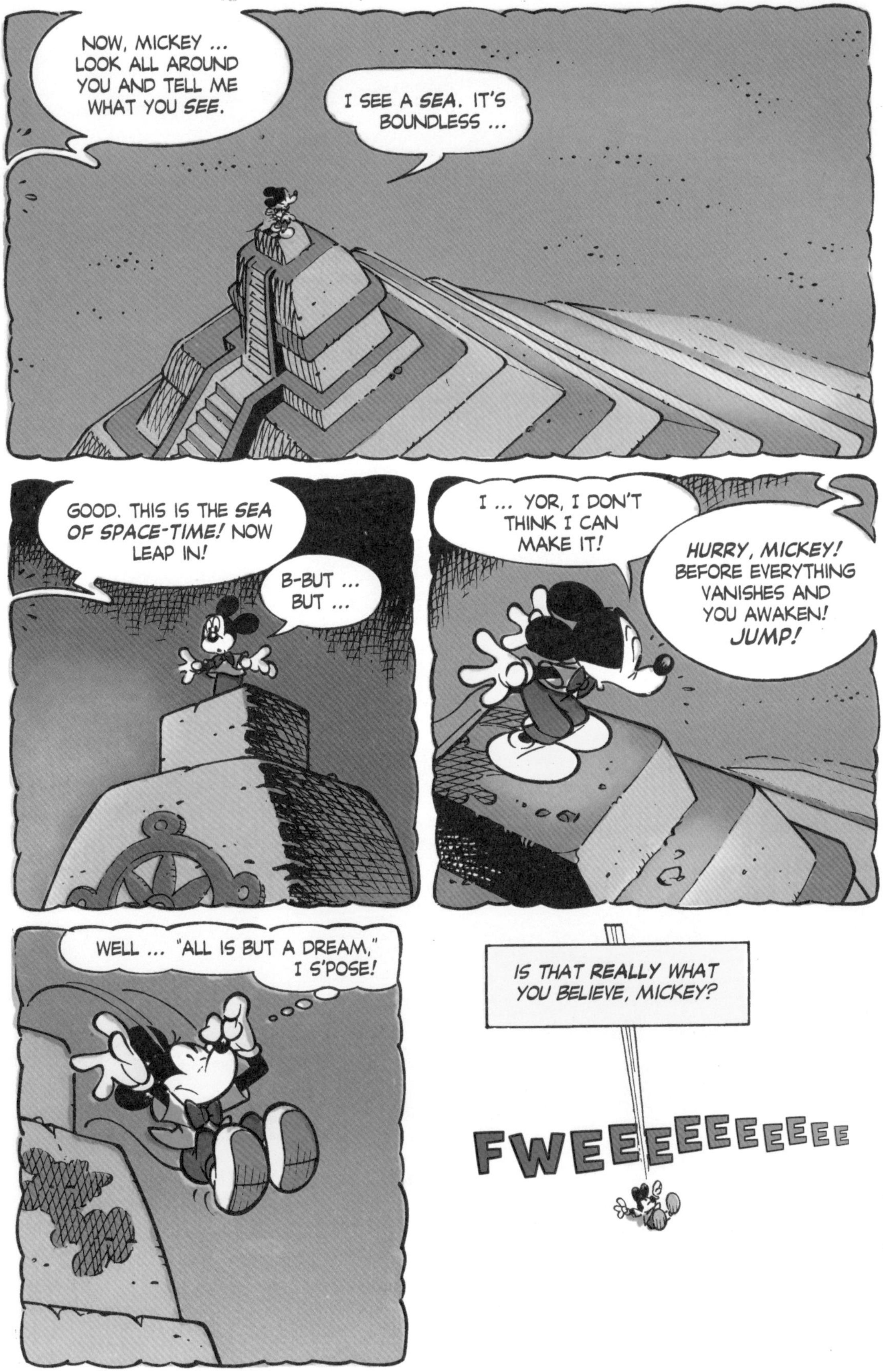
NOW, MICKEY ... LOOK ALL AROUND YOU AND TELL ME WHAT YOU SEE.
I SEE A SEA. IT'S BOUNDLESS ...
GOOD. THIS IS THE SEA OF SPACE-TIME! NOW LEAP IN!
B-BUT ... BUT ...
I ... YOR, I DON'T THINK I CAN MAKE IT!
HURRY, MICKEY! BEFORE EVERYTHING VANISHES AND YOU AWAKEN! JUMP!
WELL ... "ALL IS BUT A DREAM," I S'POSE!
IS THAT REALLY WHAT YOU BELIEVE, MICKEY?
FWEEEEEEEEEE

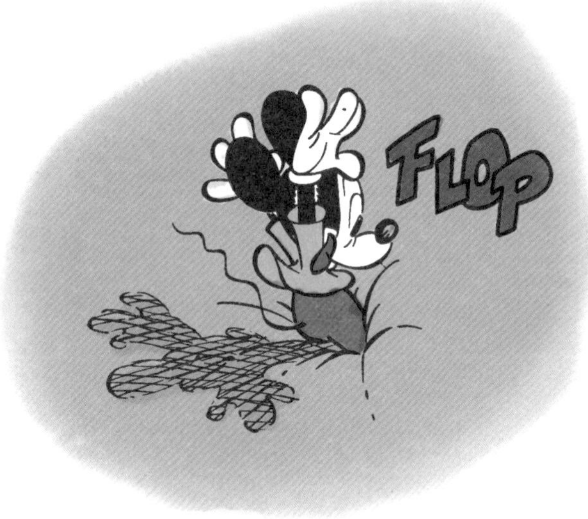
FLOP

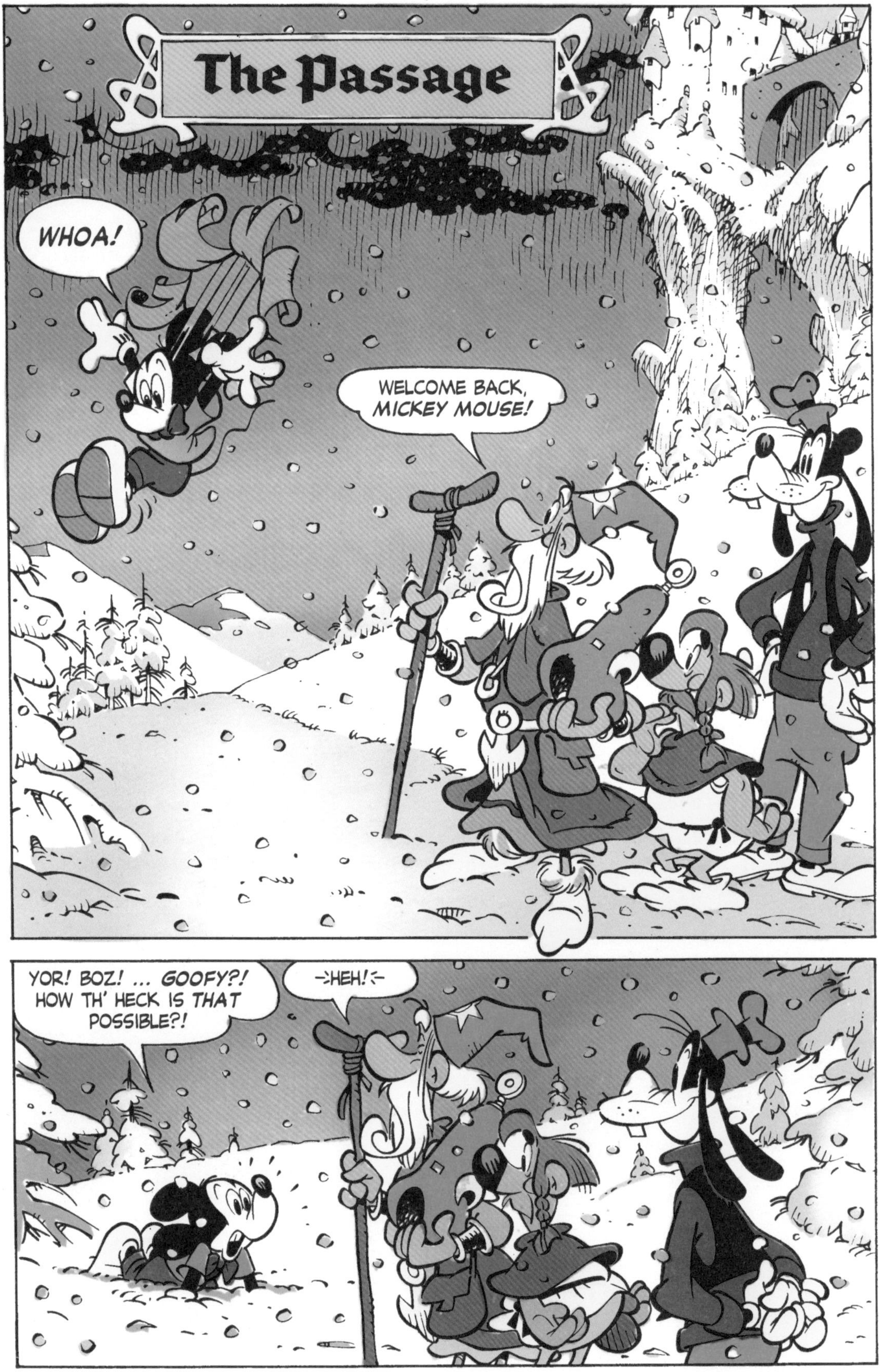
The Passage
WHOA!
WELCOME BACK, MICKEY MOUSE!
YOR! BOZ! ... GOOFY?! HOW TH' HECK IS THAT POSSIBLE?!
HEH!

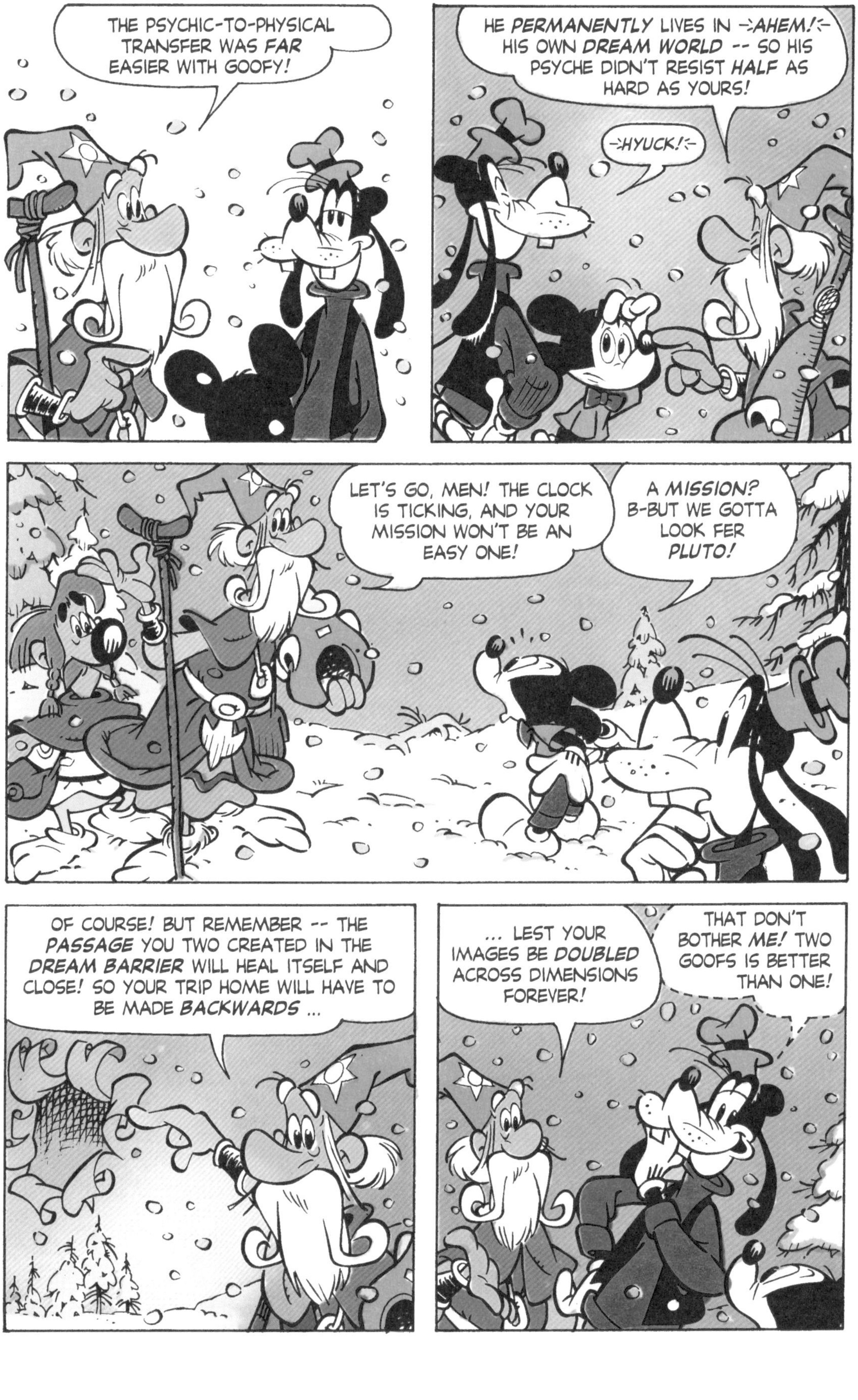
THE PSYCHIC-TO-PHYSICAL TRANSFER WAS FAR EASIER WITH GOOFY!
HE PERMANENTLY LIVES IN -AHEM!- HIS OWN DREAM WORLD -- SO HIS PSYCHE DIDN'T RESIST HALF AS HARD AS YOURS!
-HYUCK!-
LET'S GO, MEN! THE CLOCK IS TICKING, AND YOUR MISSION WON'T BE AN EASY ONE!
A MISSION? B-BUT WE GOTTA LOOK FER PLUTO!
OF COURSE! BUT REMEMBER -- THE PASSAGE YOU TWO CREATED IN THE DREAM BARRIER WILL HEAL ITSELF AND CLOSE! SO YOUR TRIP HOME WILL HAVE TO BE MADE BACKWARDS ...
... LEST YOUR IMAGES BE DOUBLED ACROSS DIMENSIONS FOREVER!
THAT DON'T BOTHER ME! TWO GOOFS IS BETTER THAN ONE!

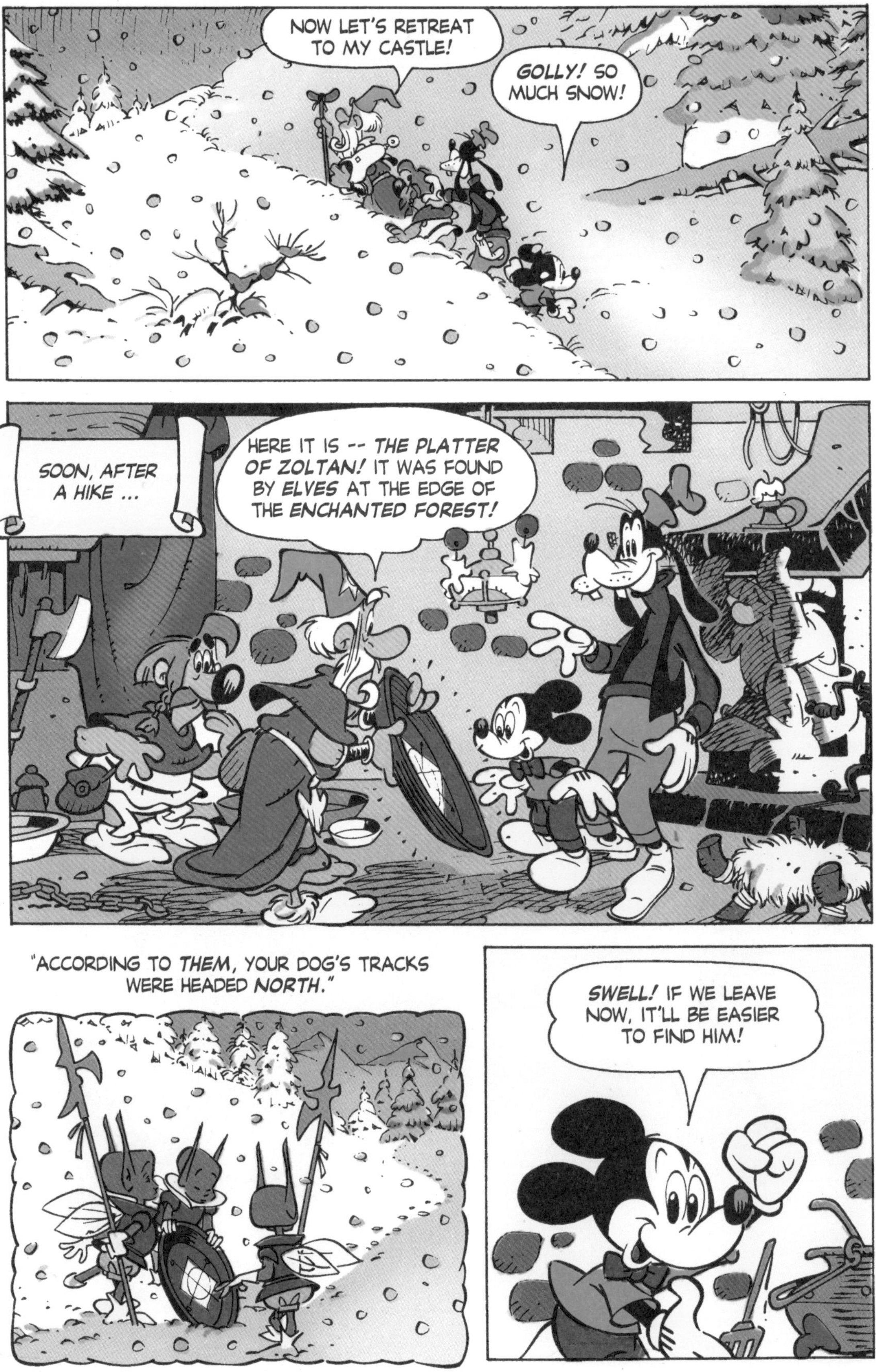
NOW LET'S RETREAT TO MY CASTLE!
GOLLY! SO MUCH SNOW!
SOON, AFTER A HIKE ...
HERE IT IS -- THE PLATTER OF ZOLTAN! IT WAS FOUND BY ELVES AT THE EDGE OF THE ENCHANTED FOREST!
"ACCORDING TO THEM, YOUR DOG'S TRACKS WERE HEADED NORTH."
SWELL! IF WE LEAVE NOW, IT'LL BE EASIER TO FIND HIM!

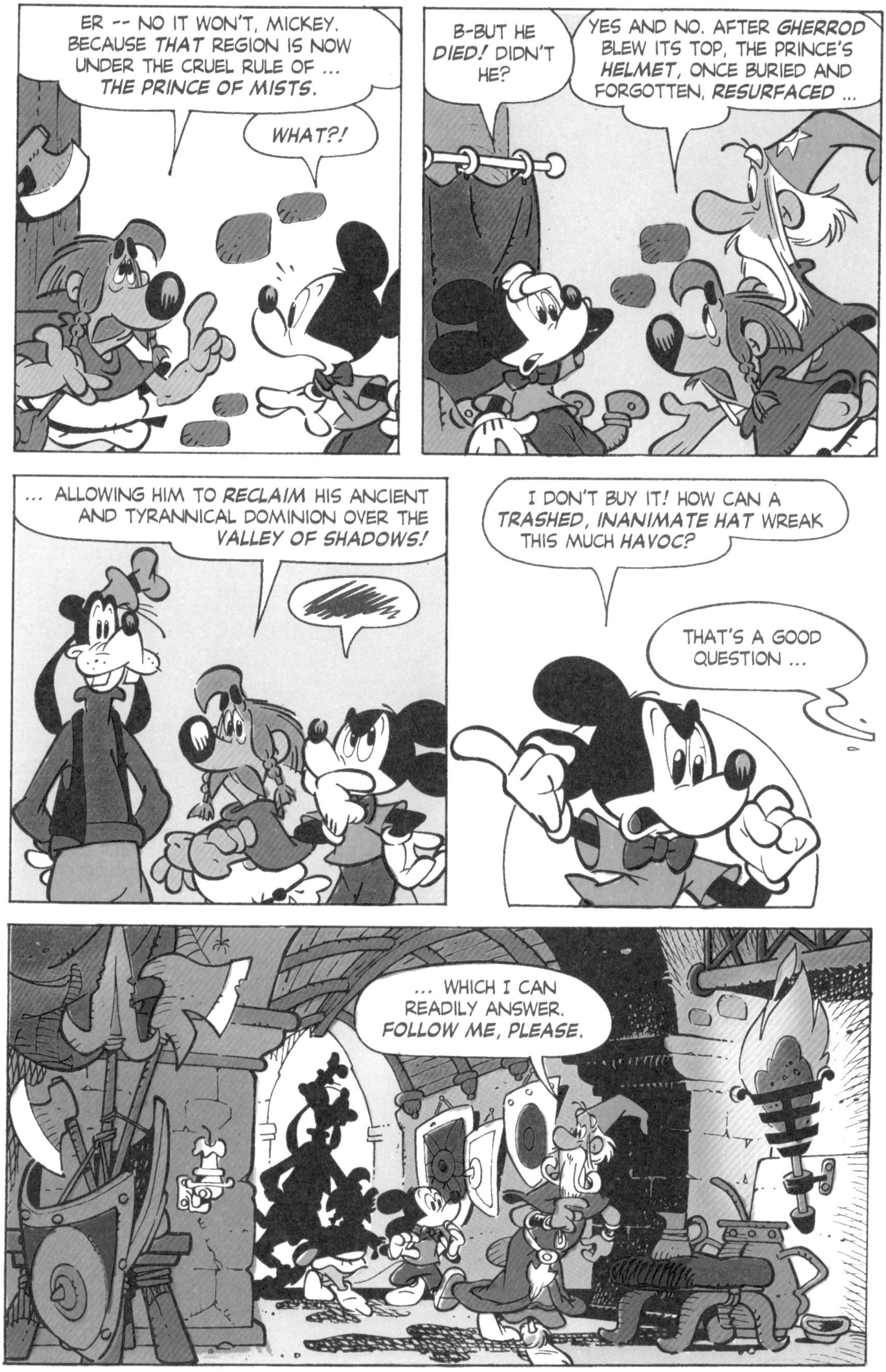
ER -- NO IT WON'T, MICKEY. BECAUSE THAT REGION IS NOW UNDER THE CRUEL RULE OF ... THE PRINCE OF MISTS.
WHAT?!
B-BUT HE DIED! DIDN'T HE?
YES AND NO. AFTER GHERROD BLEW ITS TOP, THE PRINCE'S HELMET, ONCE BURIED AND FORGOTTEN, RESURFACED ...
... ALLOWING HIM TO RECLAIM HIS ANCIENT AND TYRANNICAL DOMINION OVER THE VALLEY OF SHADOWS!
I DON'T BUY IT! HOW CAN A TRASHED, INANIMATE HAT WREAK THIS MUCH HAVOC?
THAT'S A GOOD QUESTION ...
... WHICH I CAN READILY ANSWER. FOLLOW ME, PLEASE.

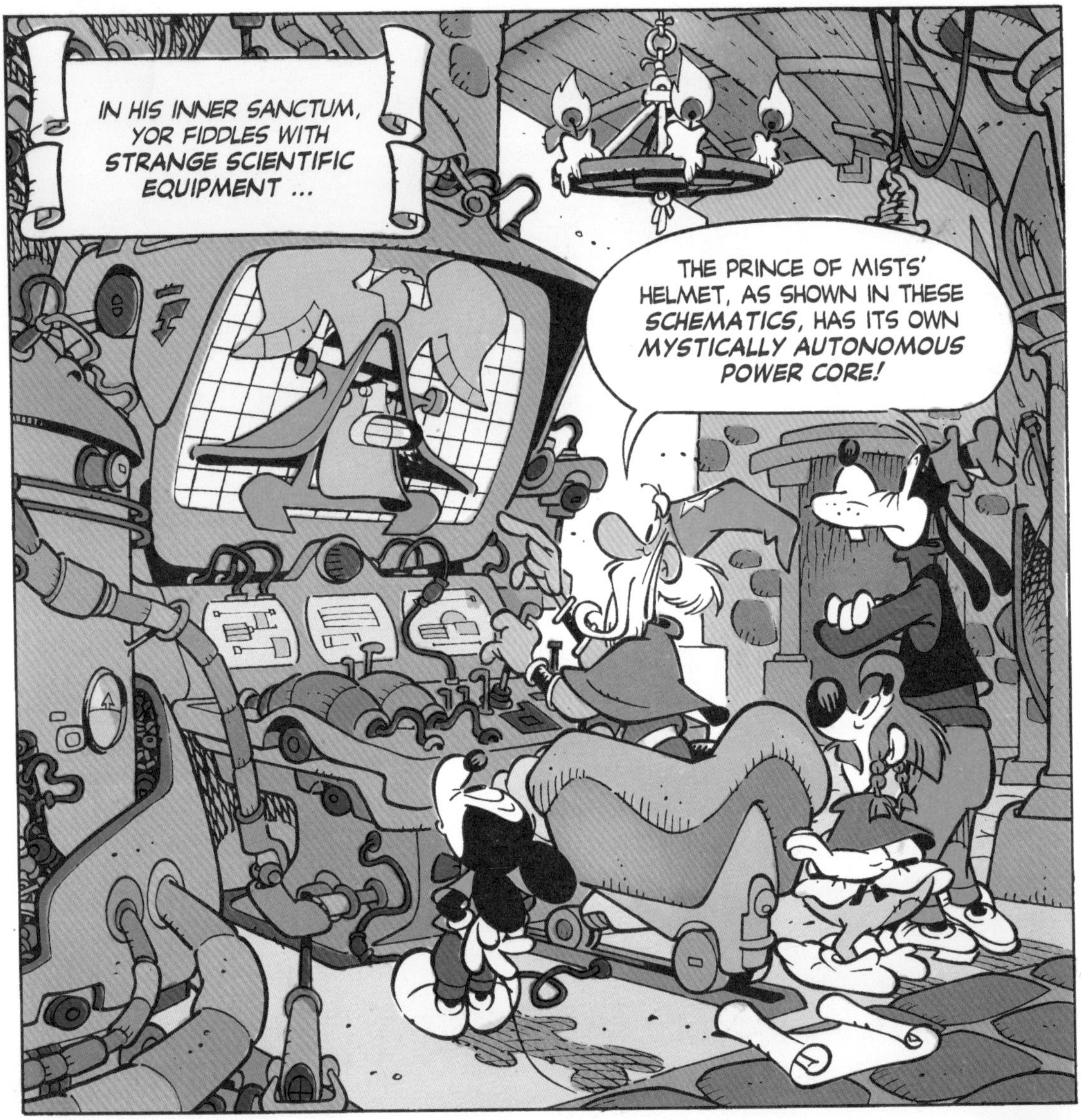
IN HIS INNER SANCTUM, YOR FIDDLES WITH STRANGE SCIENTIFIC EQUIPMENT ...
THE PRINCE OF MISTS' HELMET, AS SHOWN IN THESE SCHEMATICS, HAS ITS OWN MYSTICALLY AUTONOMOUS POWER CORE!

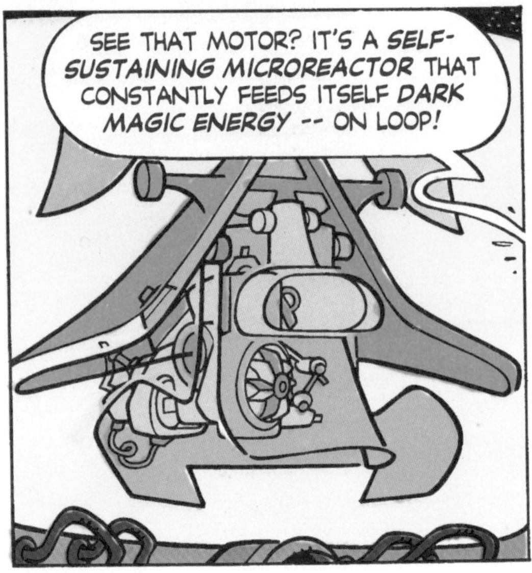
SEE THAT MOTOR? IT'S A SELF-SUSTAINING MICROREACTOR THAT CONSTANTLY FEEDS ITSELF DARK MAGIC ENERGY -- ON LOOP!

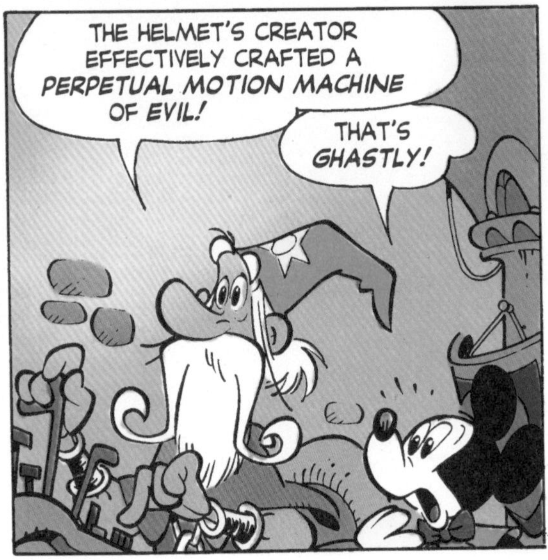
THE HELMET'S CREATOR EFFECTIVELY CRAFTED A PERPETUAL MOTION MACHINE OF EVIL!
THAT'S GHASTLY!

AYE. BECAUSE WHOEVER *WEARS* THE HELMET BECOMES *CORRUPTED* BY IT!

SO ... DOES THUH *PRINCE* HAVE MAGIC POWERS, OR IS IT THUH *HELMET?*

THE PRINCE'S *"PERSUASION POWERS"* -- PROJECTING SOLID ILLUSIONS AND MINDREADING -- WERE GIFTED TO HIM AND AMPLIFIED *BY* HIS HELMET!

THAT'S *BANANAS!*

INDEED. LOOK HERE ... INSIDE THE CORE'S NUCLEI, SUSPENDED IN A TRANSPARENT *CATALYTIC LIQUID,* ARE TWO *MINERAL STONES.* NOW IF I ZOOM IN ...

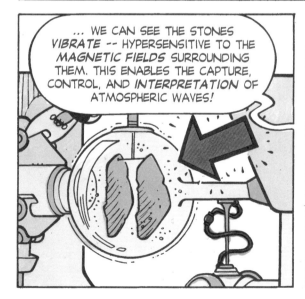

... WE CAN SEE THE STONES *VIBRATE* -- HYPERSENSITIVE TO THE *MAGNETIC FIELDS* SURROUNDING THEM. THIS ENABLES THE CAPTURE, CONTROL, AND *INTERPRETATION* OF ATMOSPHERIC WAVES!

AN' THAT'S HOW THE HELMET WEARER *WARPS REALITY* TO CREATE *SOLID ILLUSIONS?*

PRECISELY!

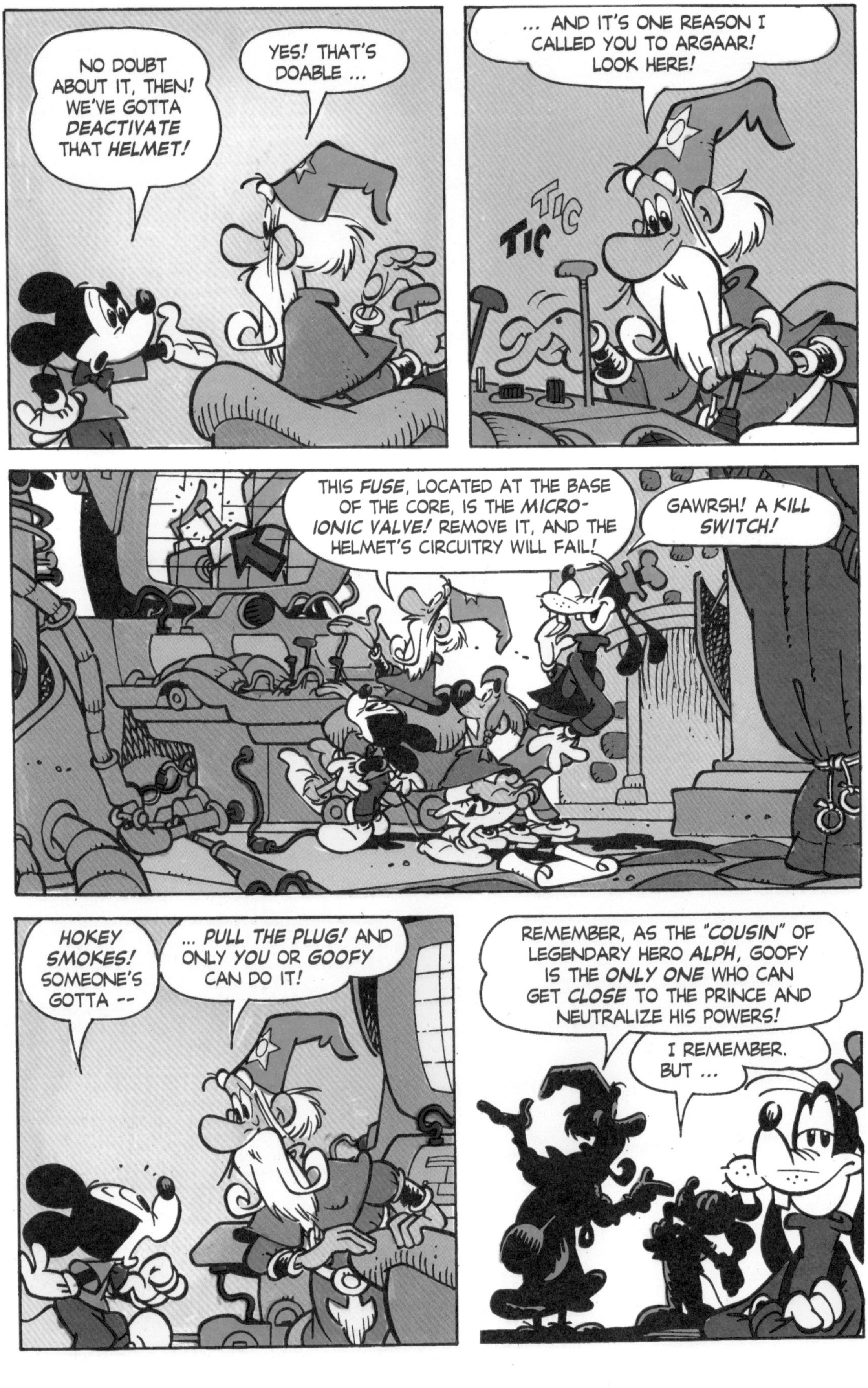
NO DOUBT ABOUT IT, THEN! WE'VE GOTTA DEACTIVATE THAT HELMET!
YES! THAT'S DOABLE ...
... AND IT'S ONE REASON I CALLED YOU TO ARGAAR! LOOK HERE!
TIC
TIC
THIS FUSE, LOCATED AT THE BASE OF THE CORE, IS THE MICRO-IONIC VALVE! REMOVE IT, AND THE HELMET'S CIRCUITRY WILL FAIL!
GAWRSH! A KILL SWITCH!
HOKEY SMOKES! SOMEONE'S GOTTA --
... PULL THE PLUG! AND ONLY YOU OR GOOFY CAN DO IT!
REMEMBER, AS THE "COUSIN" OF LEGENDARY HERO ALPH, GOOFY IS THE ONLY ONE WHO CAN GET CLOSE TO THE PRINCE AND NEUTRALIZE HIS POWERS!
I REMEMBER. BUT ...

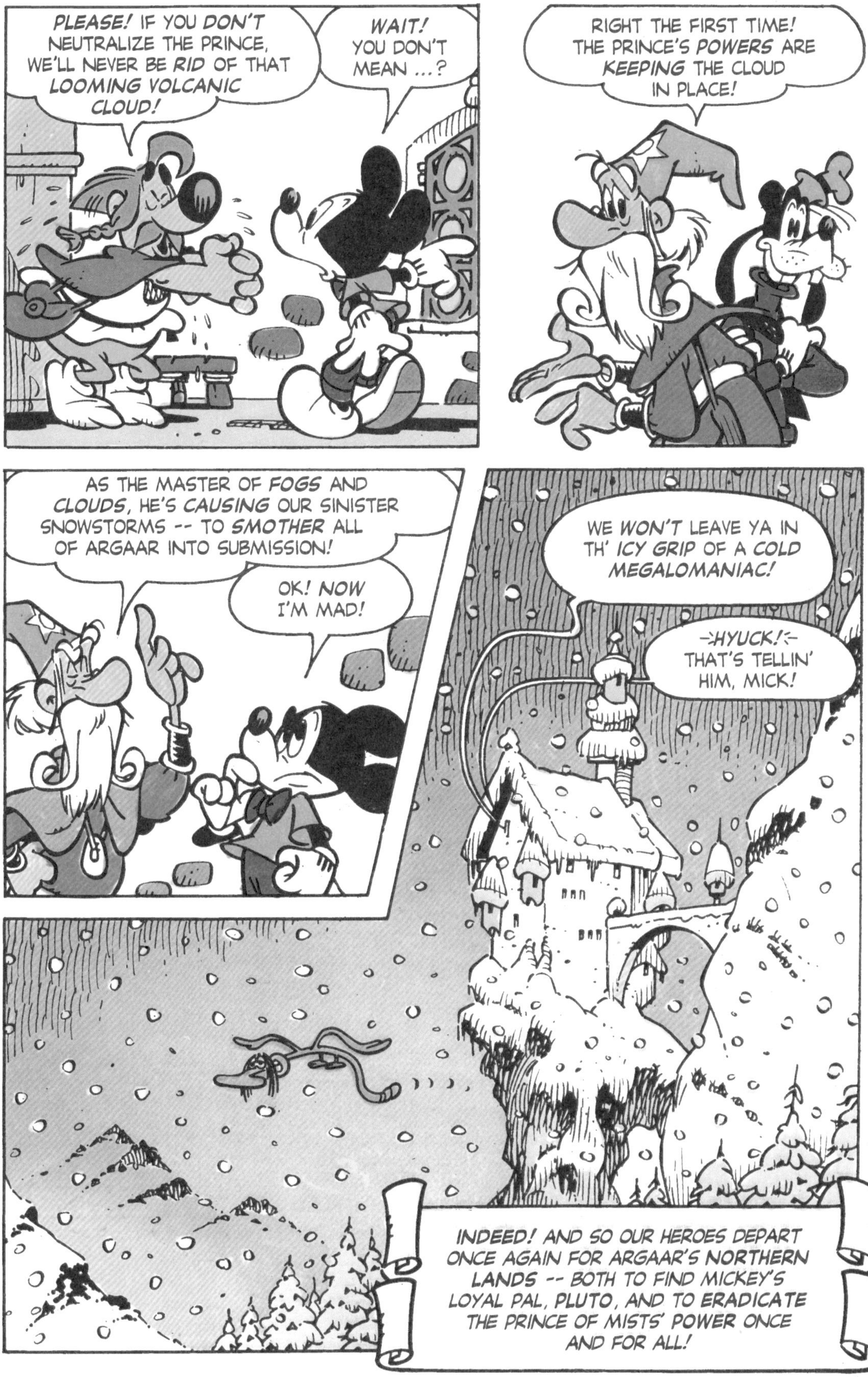
PLEASE! IF YOU DON'T NEUTRALIZE THE PRINCE, WE'LL NEVER BE RID OF THAT LOOMING VOLCANIC CLOUD!
WAIT! YOU DON'T MEAN ...?
RIGHT THE FIRST TIME! THE PRINCE'S POWERS ARE KEEPING THE CLOUD IN PLACE!
AS THE MASTER OF FOGS AND CLOUDS, HE'S CAUSING OUR SINISTER SNOWSTORMS -- TO SMOTHER ALL OF ARGAAR INTO SUBMISSION!
OK! NOW I'M MAD!
WE WON'T LEAVE YA IN TH' ICY GRIP OF A COLD MEGALOMANIAC!
HYUCK! THAT'S TELLIN' HIM, MICK!
INDEED! AND SO OUR HEROES DEPART ONCE AGAIN FOR ARGAAR'S NORTHERN LANDS -- BOTH TO FIND MICKEY'S LOYAL PAL, PLUTO, AND TO ERADICATE THE PRINCE OF MISTS' POWER ONCE AND FOR ALL!

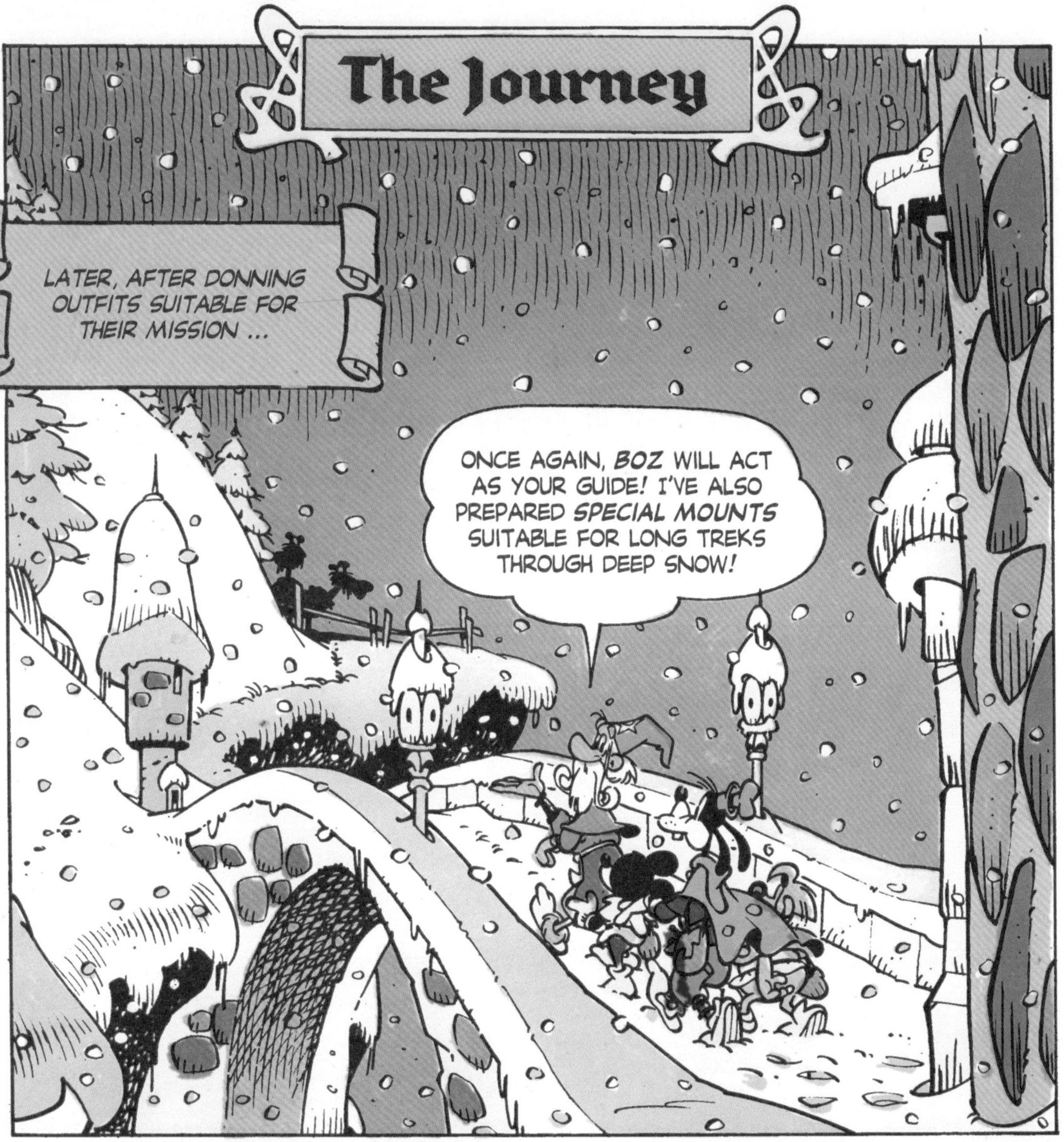
The Journey
LATER, AFTER DONNING OUTFITS SUITABLE FOR THEIR MISSION ...
ONCE AGAIN, BOZ WILL ACT AS YOUR GUIDE! I'VE ALSO PREPARED SPECIAL MOUNTS SUITABLE FOR LONG TREKS THROUGH DEEP SNOW!

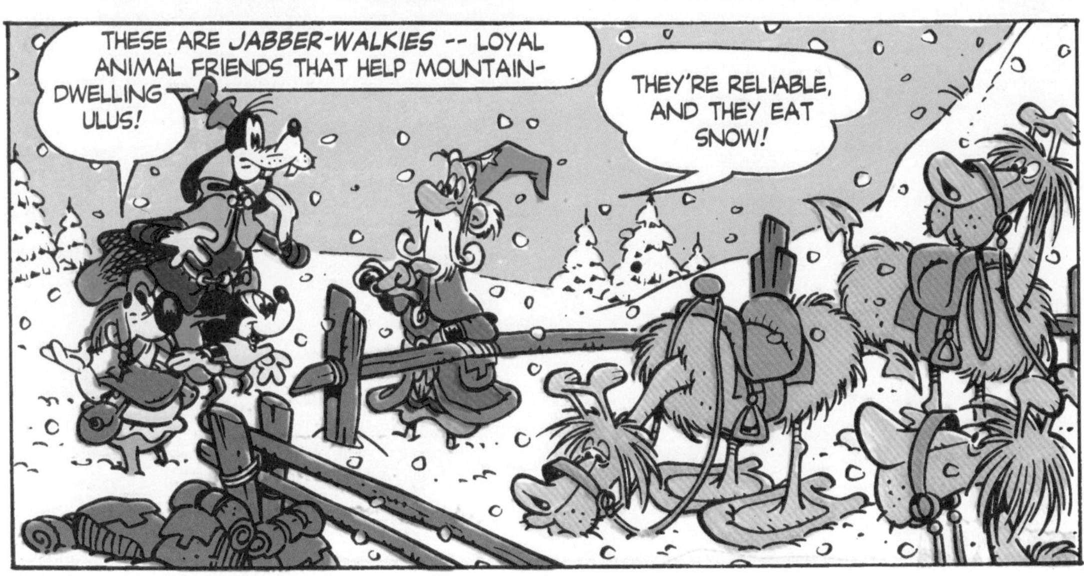
THESE ARE JABBER-WALKIES -- LOYAL ANIMAL FRIENDS THAT HELP MOUNTAIN-DWELLING ULUS!
THEY'RE RELIABLE, AND THEY EAT SNOW!

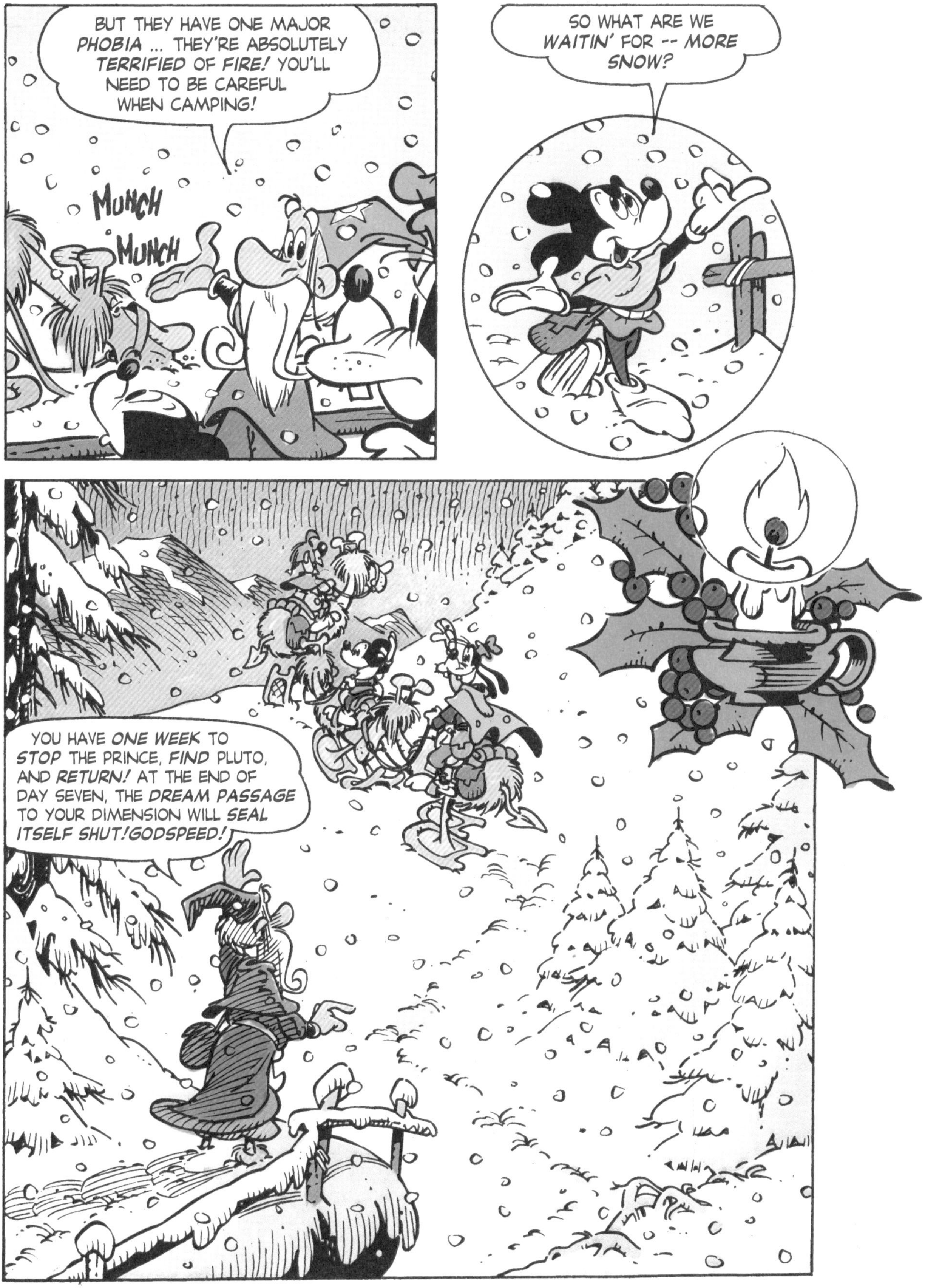
BUT THEY HAVE ONE MAJOR PHOBIA ... THEY'RE ABSOLUTELY TERRIFIED OF FIRE! YOU'LL NEED TO BE CAREFUL WHEN CAMPING!
MUNCH
MUNCH
SO WHAT ARE WE WAITIN' FOR -- MORE SNOW?
YOU HAVE ONE WEEK TO STOP THE PRINCE, FIND PLUTO, AND RETURN! AT THE END OF DAY SEVEN, THE DREAM PASSAGE TO YOUR DIMENSION WILL SEAL ITSELF SHUT! GODSPEED!

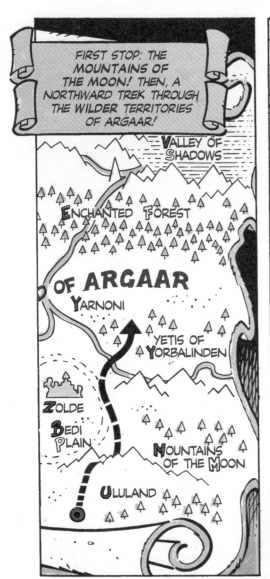

FIRST STOP: THE MOUNTAINS OF THE MOON! THEN, A NORTHWARD TREK THROUGH THE WILDER TERRITORIES OF ARGAAR!

VALLEY OF SHADOWS

ENCHANTED FOREST

OF ARGAAR

YARNONI

YETIS OF YORBALINDEN

ZOLDE

BEDI PLAIN

MOUNTAINS OF THE MOON

ULULAND

A LIMITLESS PERMAFROST OF ICE AND SNOW HAS SEIZED THE REGION ...

... BUT THE BEDI -- AND OTHER ARGAARIAN KINGDOMS EAGER TO END THE PRINCE'S TYRANNY -- BRING HELP TO OUR HEROIC TRIO, URGING THEM TOWARD THEIR DESTINATION!

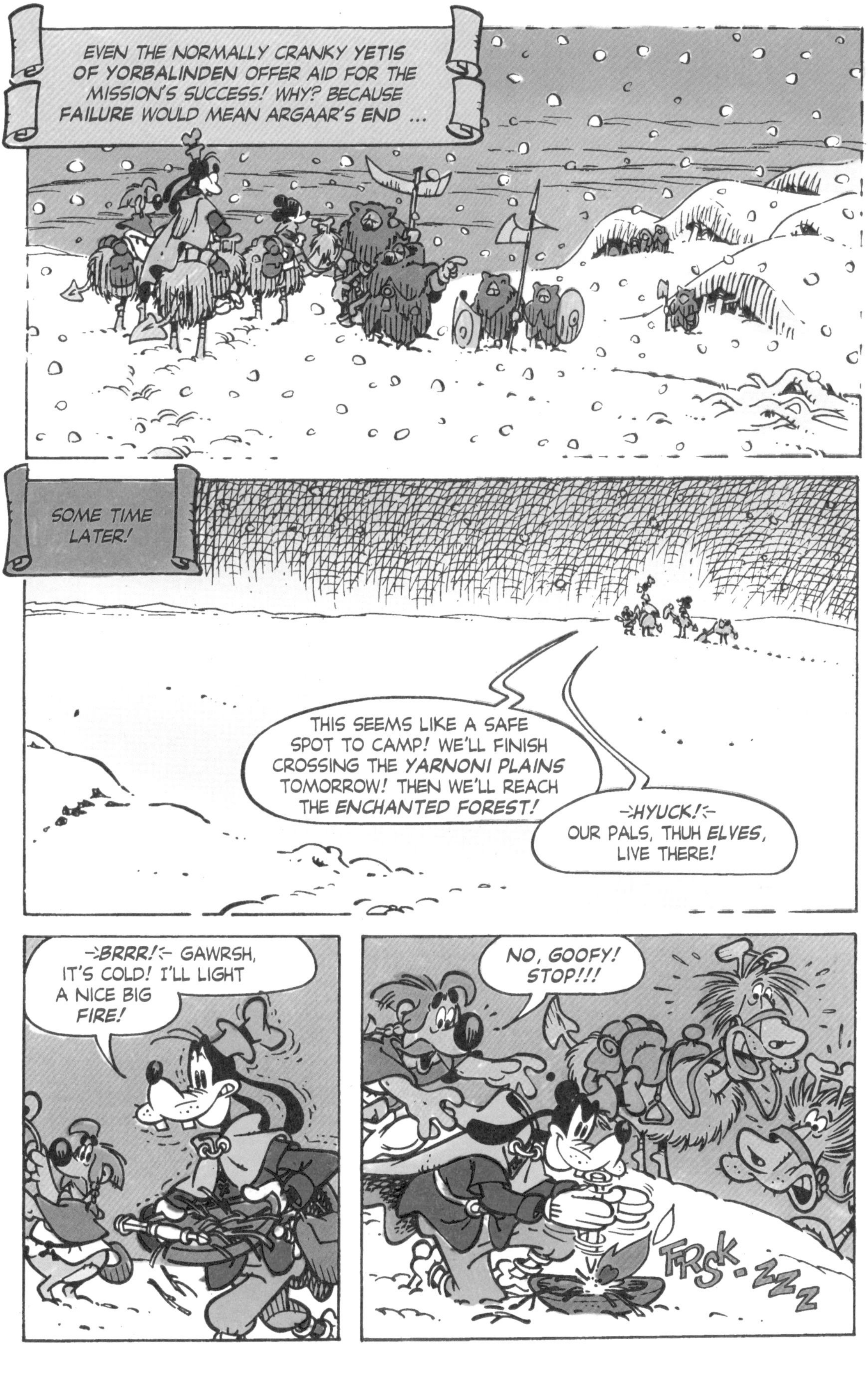
EVEN THE NORMALLY CRANKY YETIS OF YORBALINDEN OFFER AID FOR THE MISSION'S SUCCESS! WHY? BECAUSE FAILURE WOULD MEAN ARGAAR'S END ...
SOME TIME LATER!
THIS SEEMS LIKE A SAFE SPOT TO CAMP! WE'LL FINISH CROSSING THE YARNONI PLAINS TOMORROW! THEN WE'LL REACH THE ENCHANTED FOREST!
-HYUCK!- OUR PALS, THUH ELVES, LIVE THERE!
-BRRR!- GAWRSH, IT'S COLD! I'LL LIGHT A NICE BIG FIRE!
NO, GOOFY! STOP!!!
FRSK-ZZZ

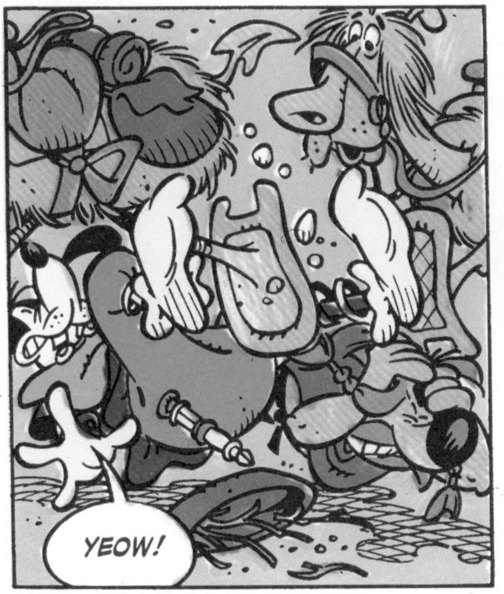
YEOW!

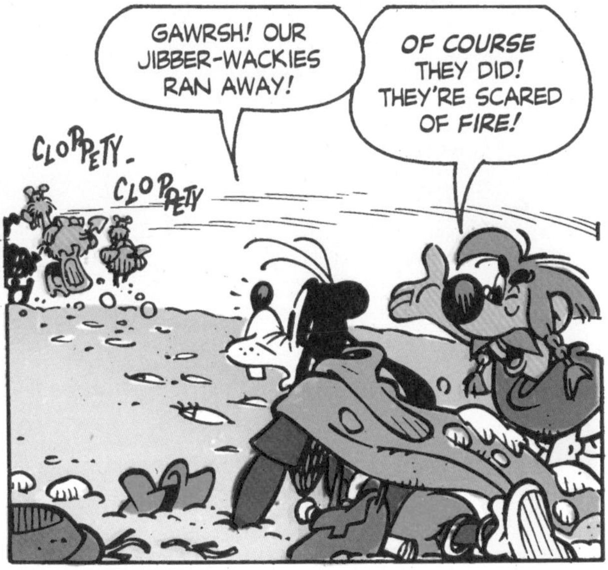
CLOPPETY-CLOPPETY
GAWRSH! OUR JIBBER-WACKIES RAN AWAY!
OF COURSE THEY DID! THEY'RE SCARED OF FIRE!

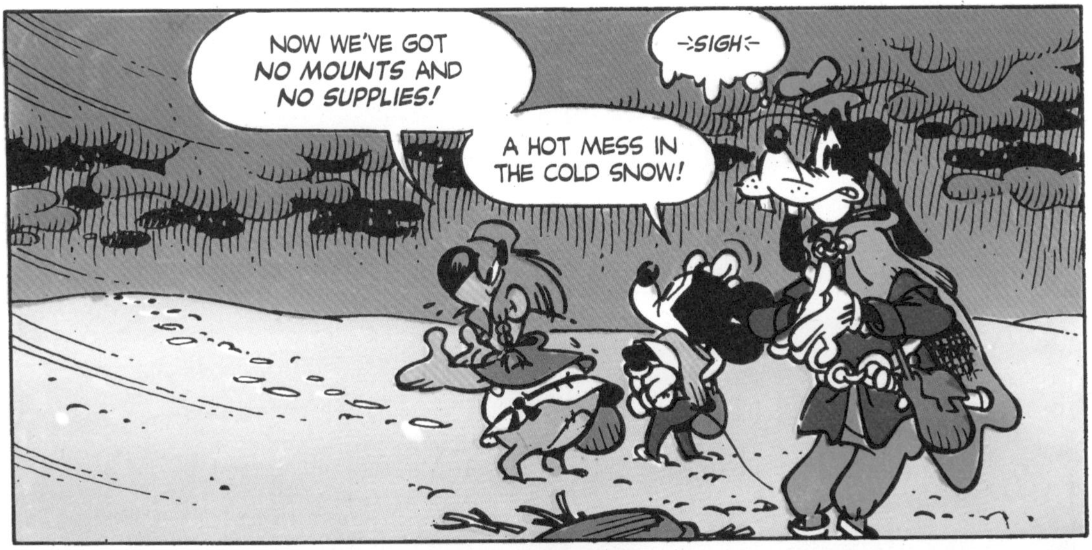
NOW WE'VE GOT NO MOUNTS AND NO SUPPLIES!
SIGH
A HOT MESS IN THE COLD SNOW!

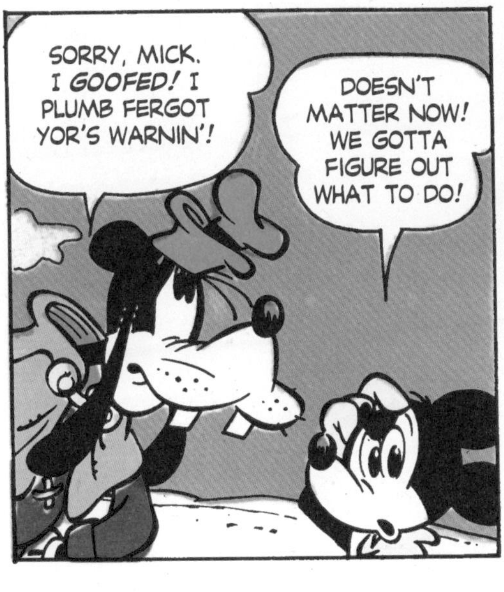
SORRY, MICK. I GOOFED! I PLUMB FERGOT YOR'S WARNIN'!
DOESN'T MATTER NOW! WE GOTTA FIGURE OUT WHAT TO DO!

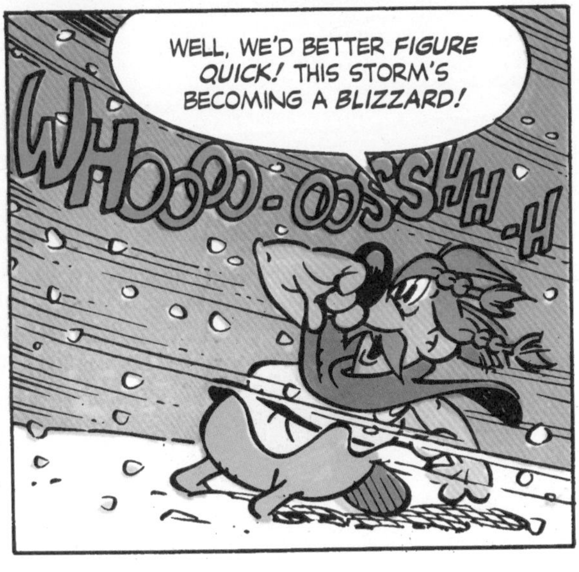
WELL, WE'D BETTER FIGURE QUICK! THIS STORM'S BECOMING A BLIZZARD!
WHOOOO-OOSSHH-H

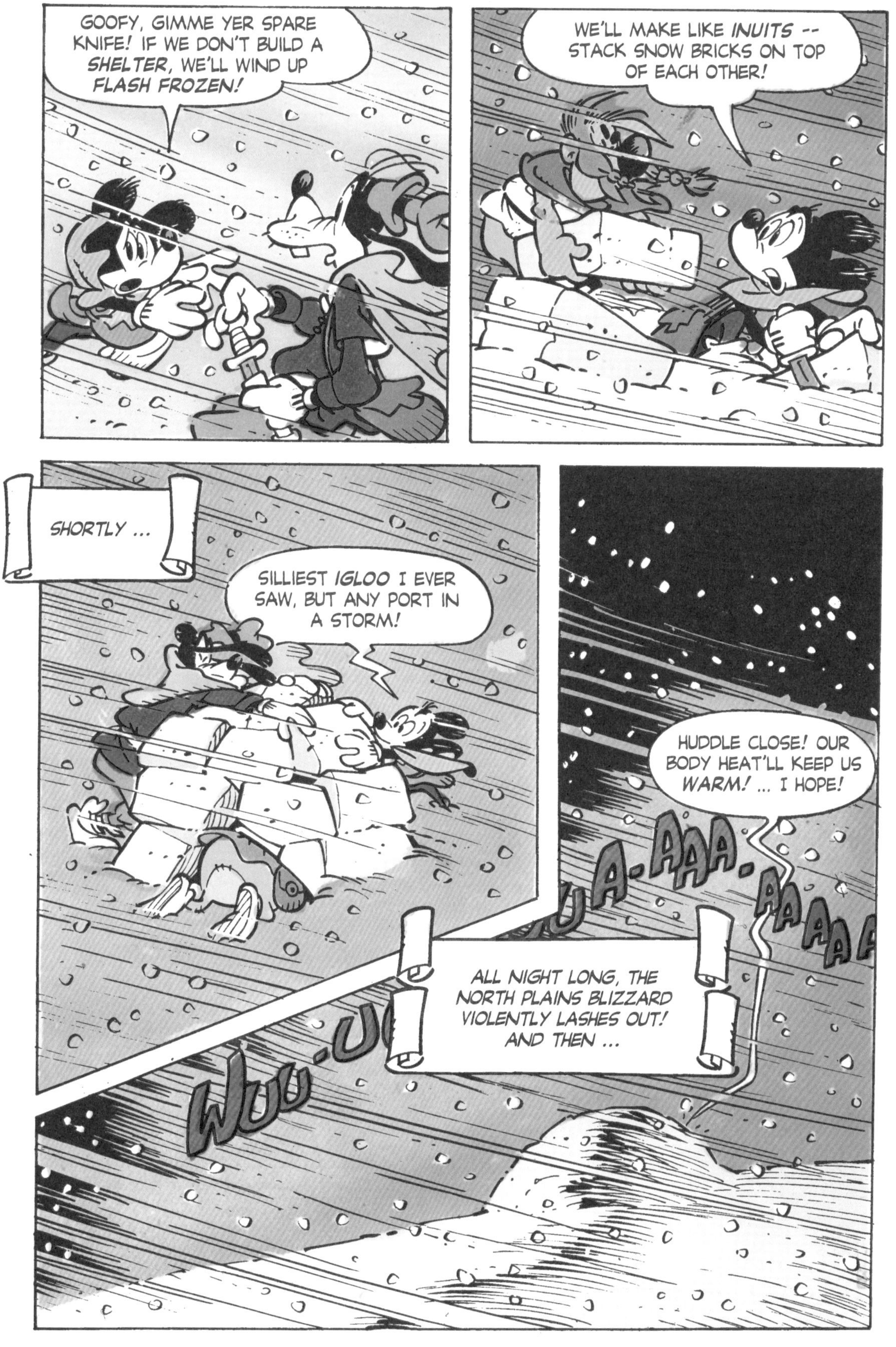
GOOFY, GIMME YER SPARE KNIFE! IF WE DON'T BUILD A SHELTER, WE'LL WIND UP FLASH FROZEN!
WE'LL MAKE LIKE INUITS -- STACK SNOW BRICKS ON TOP OF EACH OTHER!
SHORTLY ...
SILLIEST IGLOO I EVER SAW, BUT ANY PORT IN A STORM!
HUDDLE CLOSE! OUR BODY HEAT'LL KEEP US WARM! ... I HOPE!
WUU-UU A-AAA-AAAAA
ALL NIGHT LONG, THE NORTH PLAINS BLIZZARD VIOLENTLY LASHES OUT! AND THEN ...

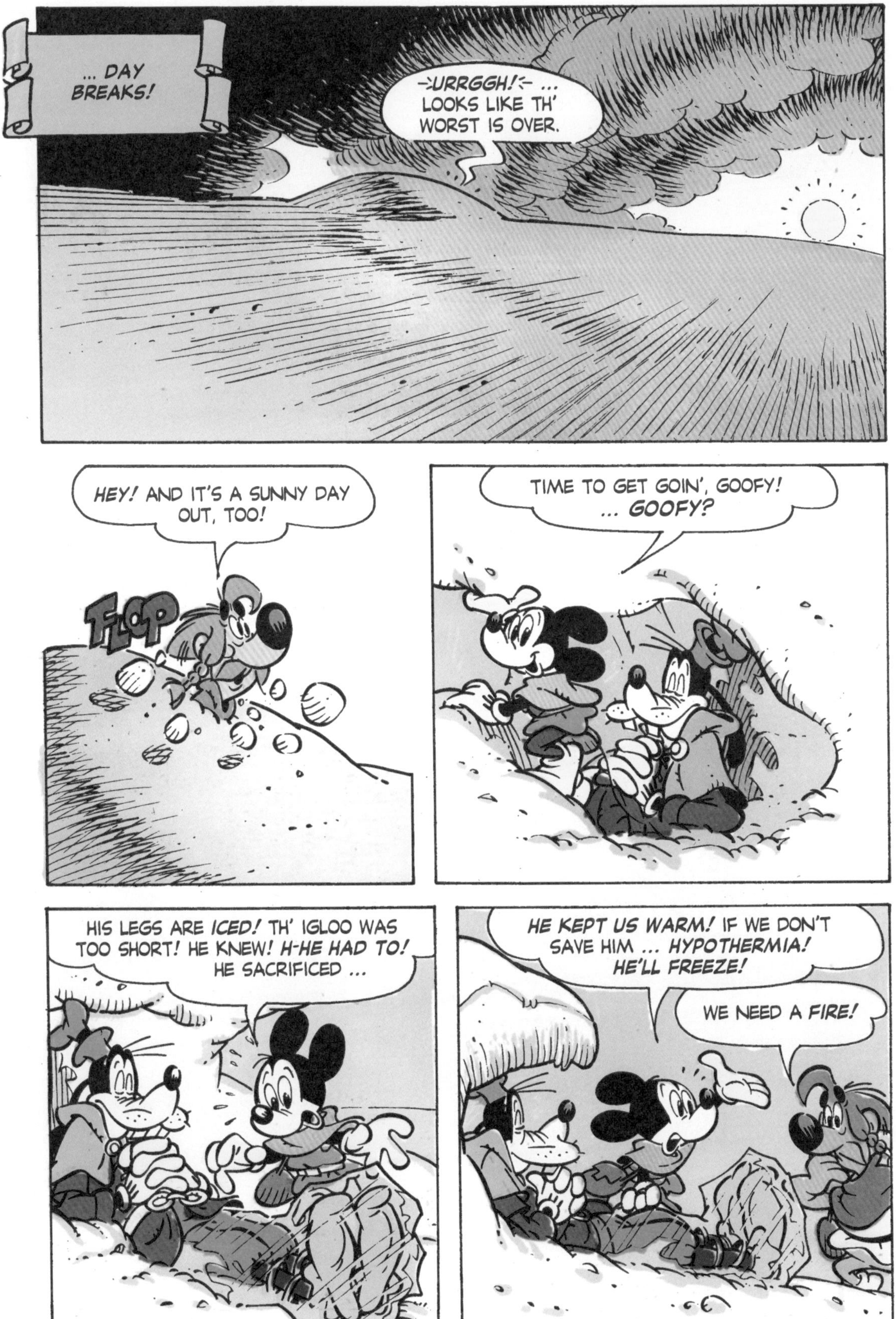
... DAY BREAKS!
URRGGH! ... LOOKS LIKE TH' WORST IS OVER.
HEY! AND IT'S A SUNNY DAY OUT, TOO!
FLOP
TIME TO GET GOIN', GOOFY! ... GOOFY?
HIS LEGS ARE ICED! TH' IGLOO WAS TOO SHORT! HE KNEW! H-HE HAD TO! HE SACRIFICED ...
HE KEPT US WARM! IF WE DON'T SAVE HIM ... HYPOTHERMIA! HE'LL FREEZE!
WE NEED A FIRE!

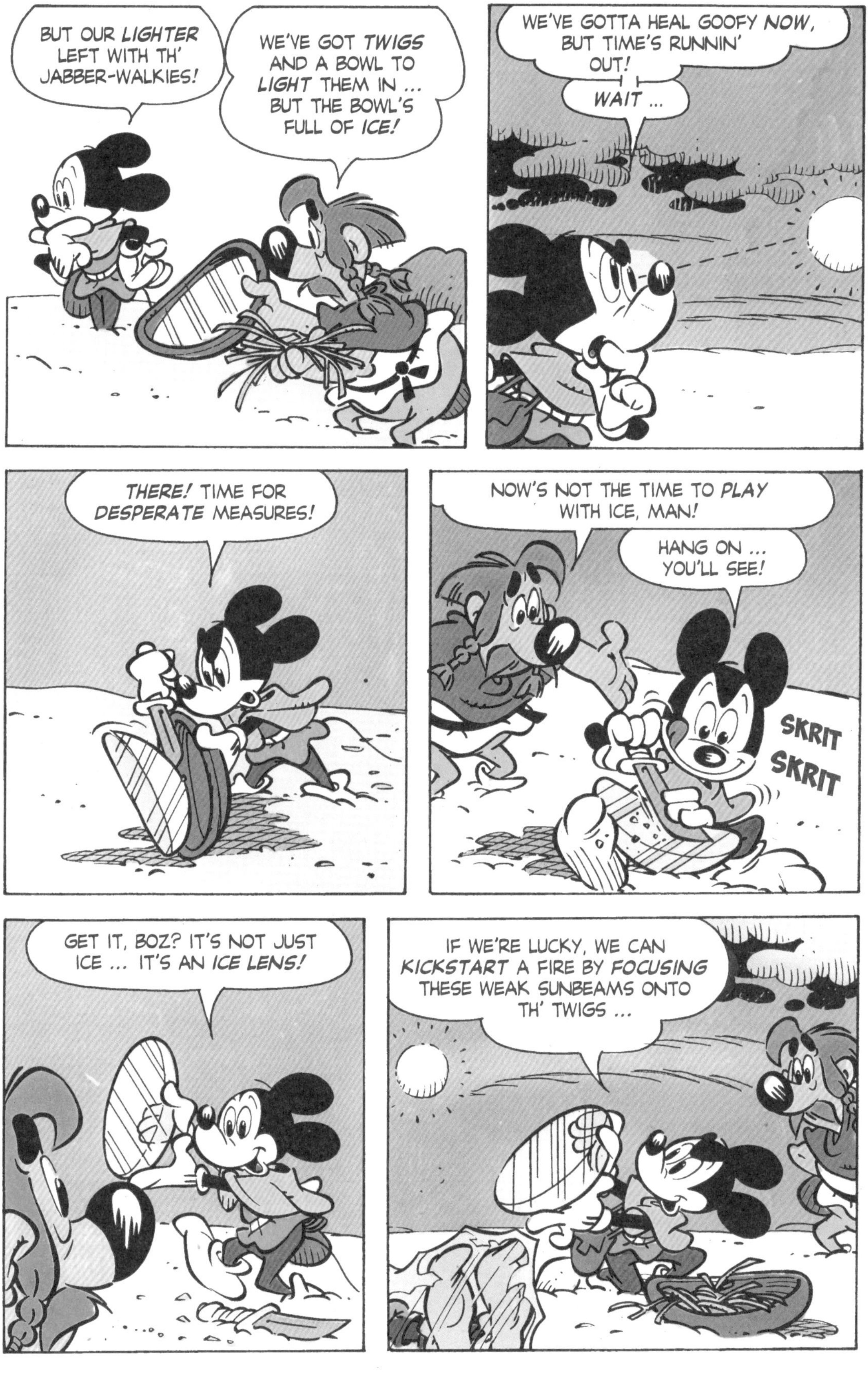
BUT OUR LIGHTER LEFT WITH TH' JABBER-WALKIES!
WE'VE GOT TWIGS AND A BOWL TO LIGHT THEM IN ... BUT THE BOWL'S FULL OF ICE!
WE'VE GOTTA HEAL GOOFY NOW, BUT TIME'S RUNNIN' OUT!
WAIT ...
THERE! TIME FOR DESPERATE MEASURES!
NOW'S NOT THE TIME TO PLAY WITH ICE, MAN!
HANG ON ... YOU'LL SEE!
SKRIT
SKRIT
GET IT, BOZ? IT'S NOT JUST ICE ... IT'S AN ICE LENS!
IF WE'RE LUCKY, WE CAN KICKSTART A FIRE BY FOCUSING THESE WEAK SUNBEAMS ONTO TH' TWIGS ...

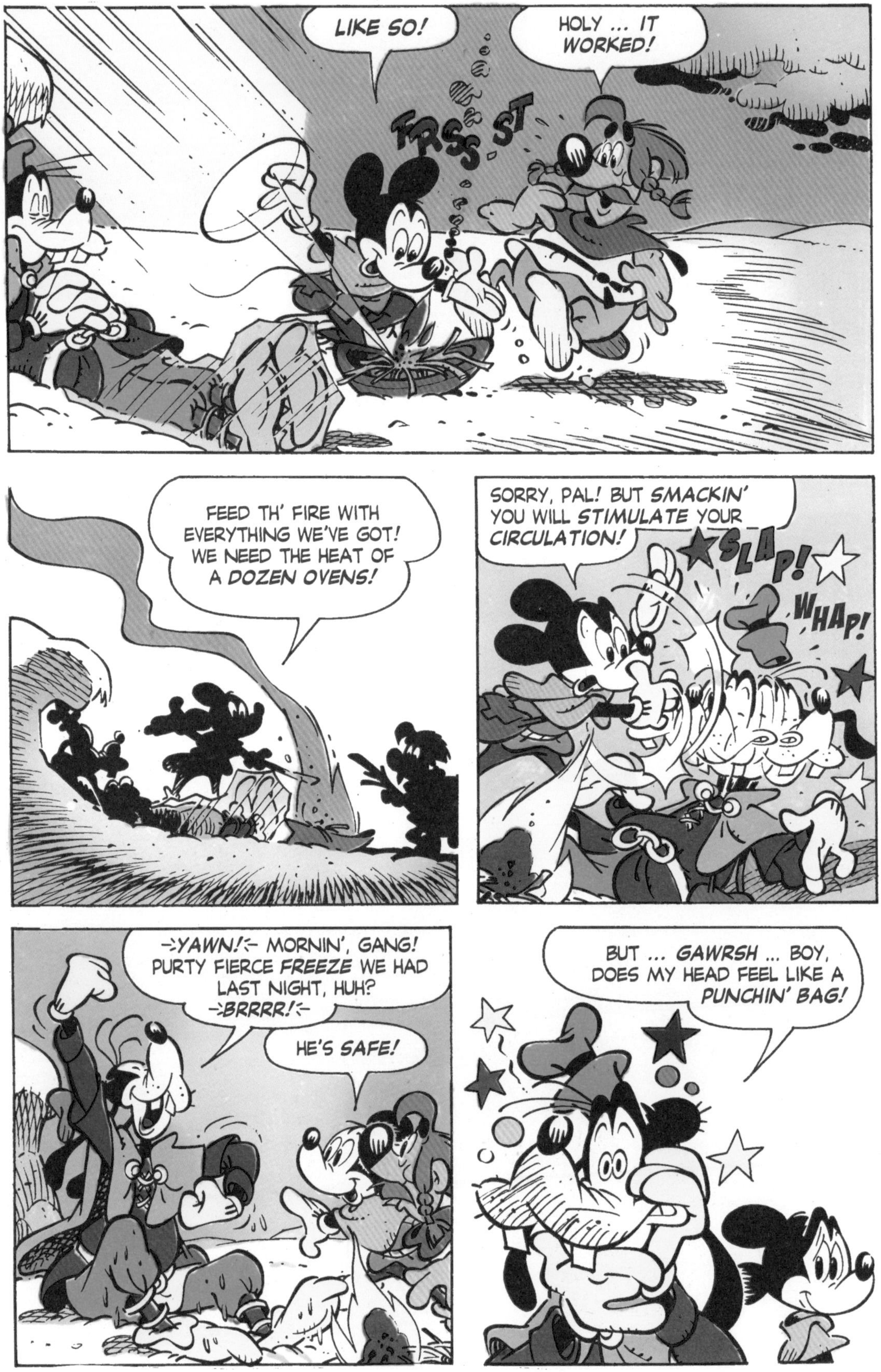
LIKE SO!
HOLY ... IT WORKED!
FRSSSST
FEED TH' FIRE WITH EVERYTHING WE'VE GOT! WE NEED THE HEAT OF A DOZEN OVENS!
SORRY, PAL! BUT SMACKIN' YOU WILL STIMULATE YOUR CIRCULATION!
SLAP!
WHAP!
-YAWN!- MORNIN', GANG! PURTY FIERCE FREEZE WE HAD LAST NIGHT, HUH? -BRRRR!-
HE'S SAFE!
BUT ... GAWRSH ... BOY, DOES MY HEAD FEEL LIKE A PUNCHIN' BAG!

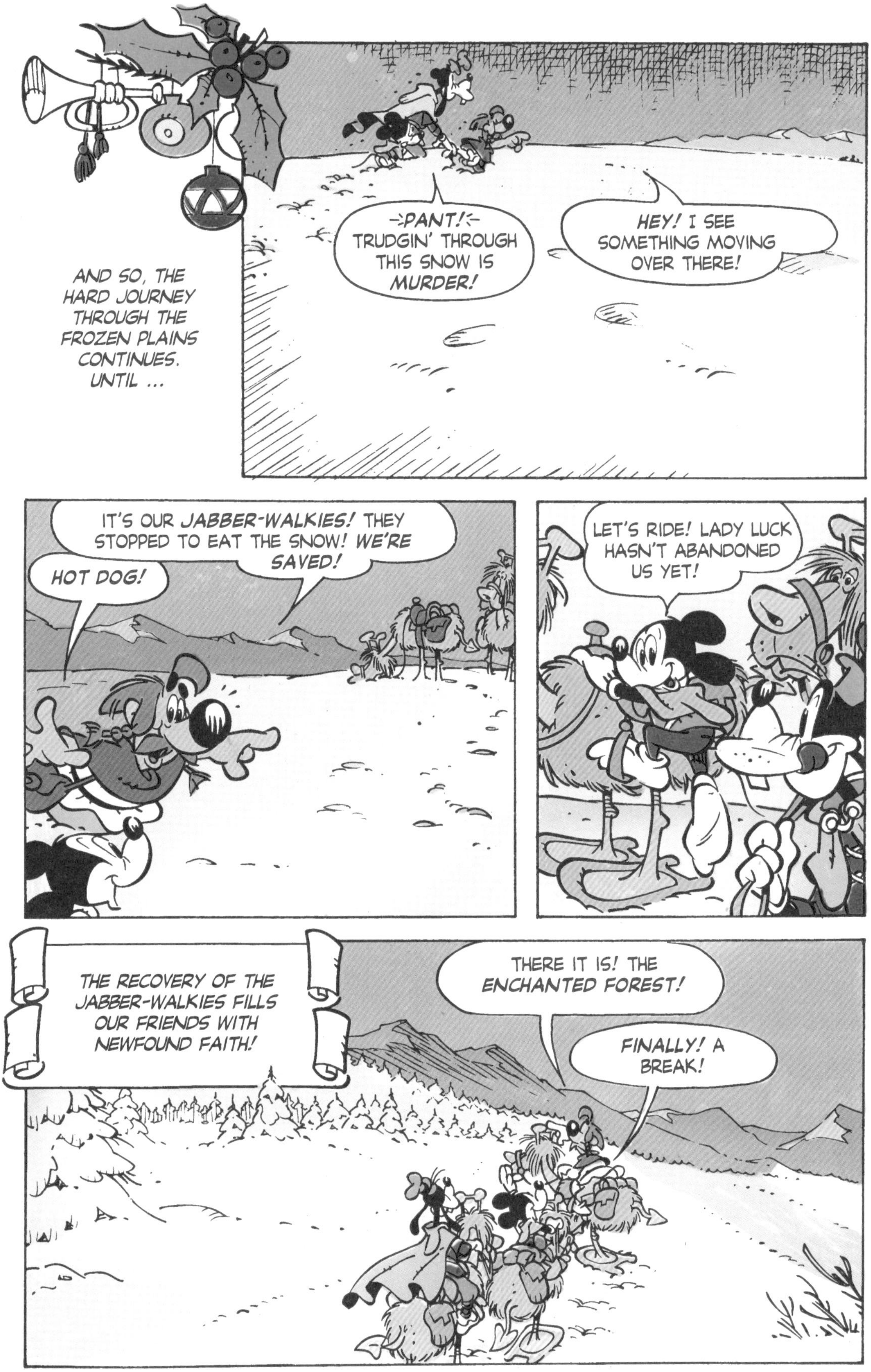
AND SO, THE HARD JOURNEY THROUGH THE FROZEN PLAINS CONTINUES. UNTIL ...
-PANT!- TRUDGIN' THROUGH THIS SNOW IS MURDER!
HEY! I SEE SOMETHING MOVING OVER THERE!
HOT DOG!
IT'S OUR JABBER-WALKIES! THEY STOPPED TO EAT THE SNOW! WE'RE SAVED!
LET'S RIDE! LADY LUCK HASN'T ABANDONED US YET!
THE RECOVERY OF THE JABBER-WALKIES FILLS OUR FRIENDS WITH NEWFOUND FAITH!
THERE IT IS! THE ENCHANTED FOREST!
FINALLY! A BREAK!

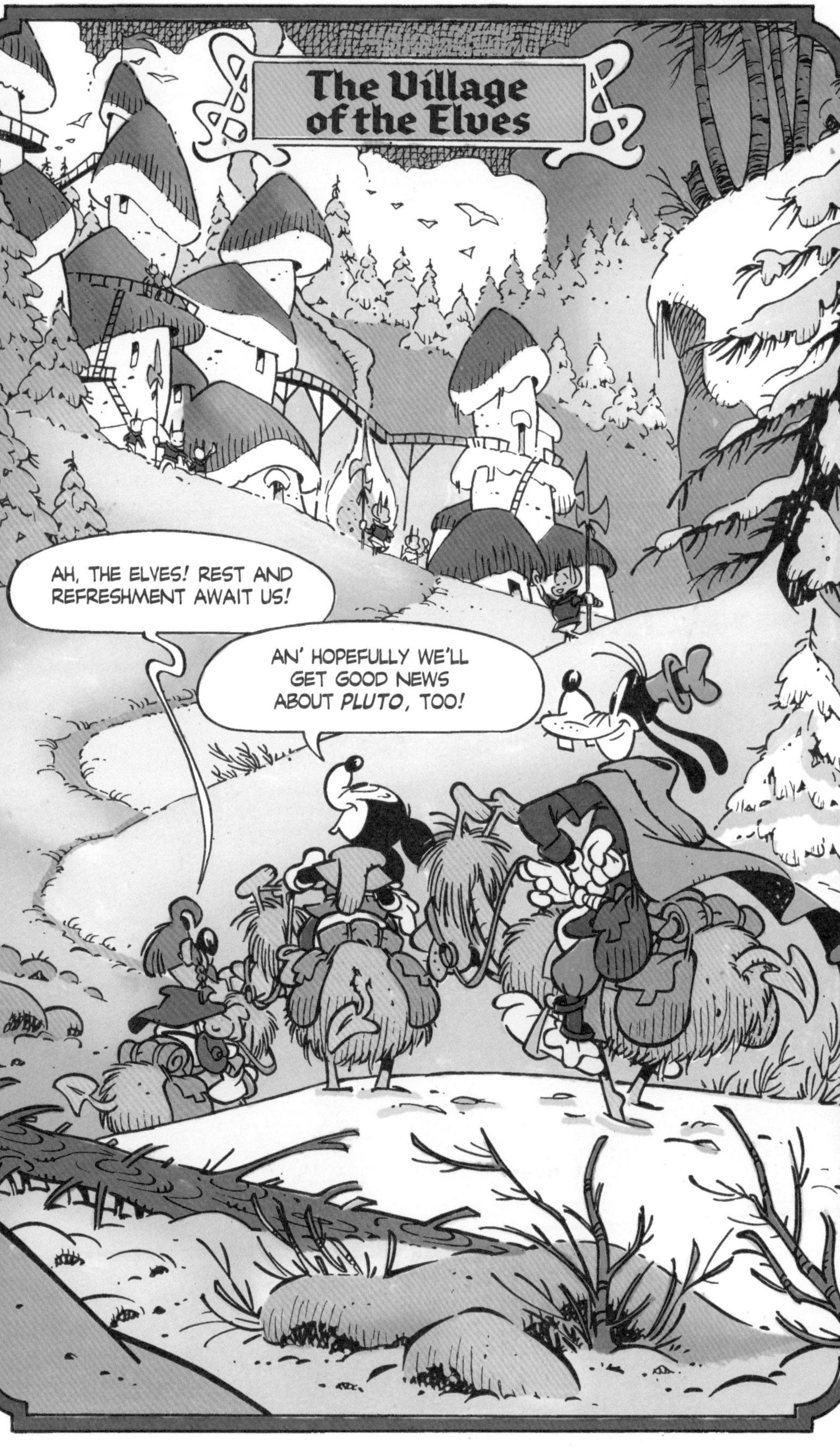
The Village of the Elves
AH, THE ELVES! REST AND REFRESHMENT AWAIT US!
AN' HOPEFULLY WE'LL GET GOOD NEWS ABOUT PLUTO, TOO!

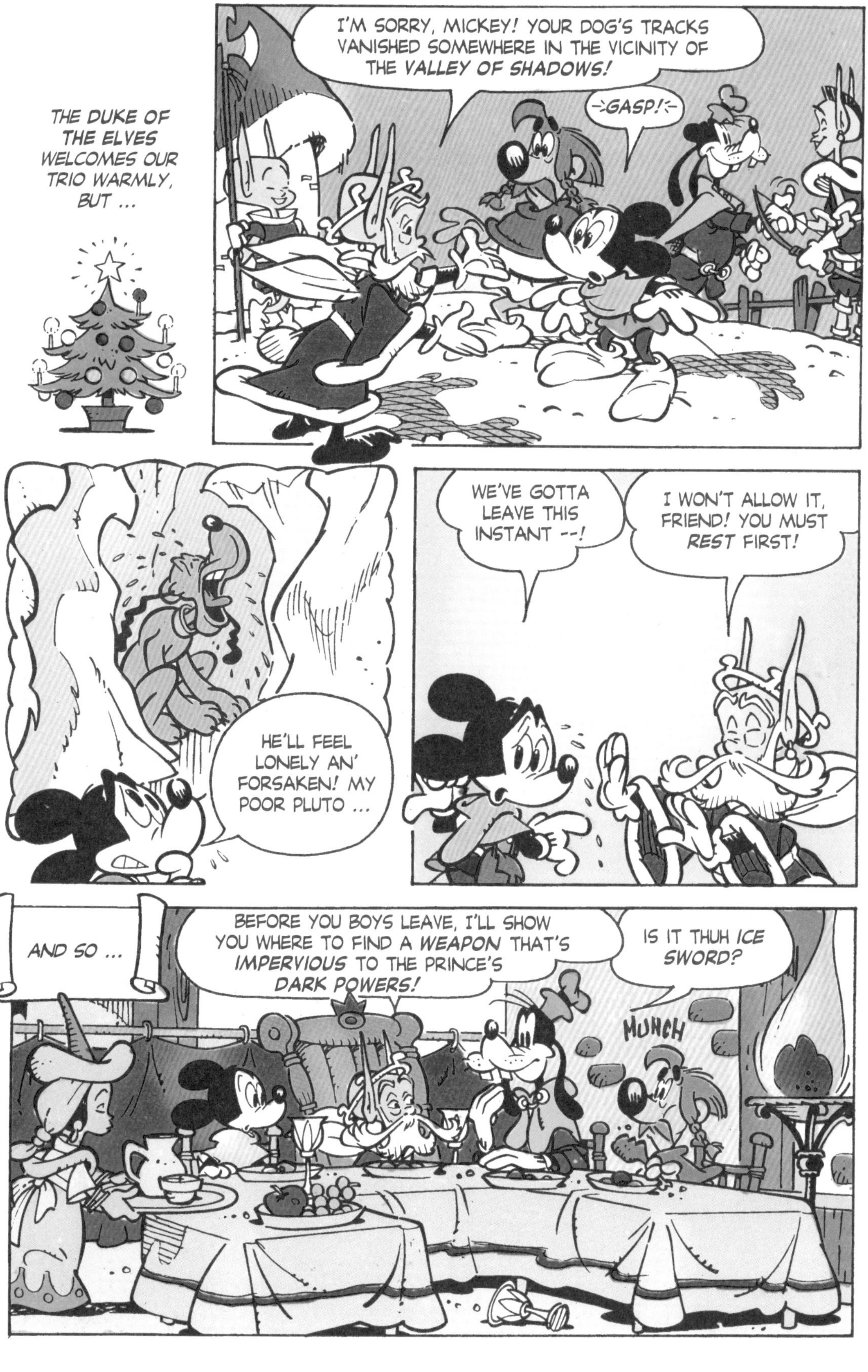
THE DUKE OF THE ELVES WELCOMES OUR TRIO WARMLY, BUT ...
I'M SORRY, MICKEY! YOUR DOG'S TRACKS VANISHED SOMEWHERE IN THE VICINITY OF THE VALLEY OF SHADOWS!
GASP!
HE'LL FEEL LONELY AN' FORSAKEN! MY POOR PLUTO ...
WE'VE GOTTA LEAVE THIS INSTANT --!
I WON'T ALLOW IT, FRIEND! YOU MUST REST FIRST!
AND SO ...
BEFORE YOU BOYS LEAVE, I'LL SHOW YOU WHERE TO FIND A WEAPON THAT'S IMPERVIOUS TO THE PRINCE'S DARK POWERS!
IS IT THUH ICE SWORD?
MUNCH

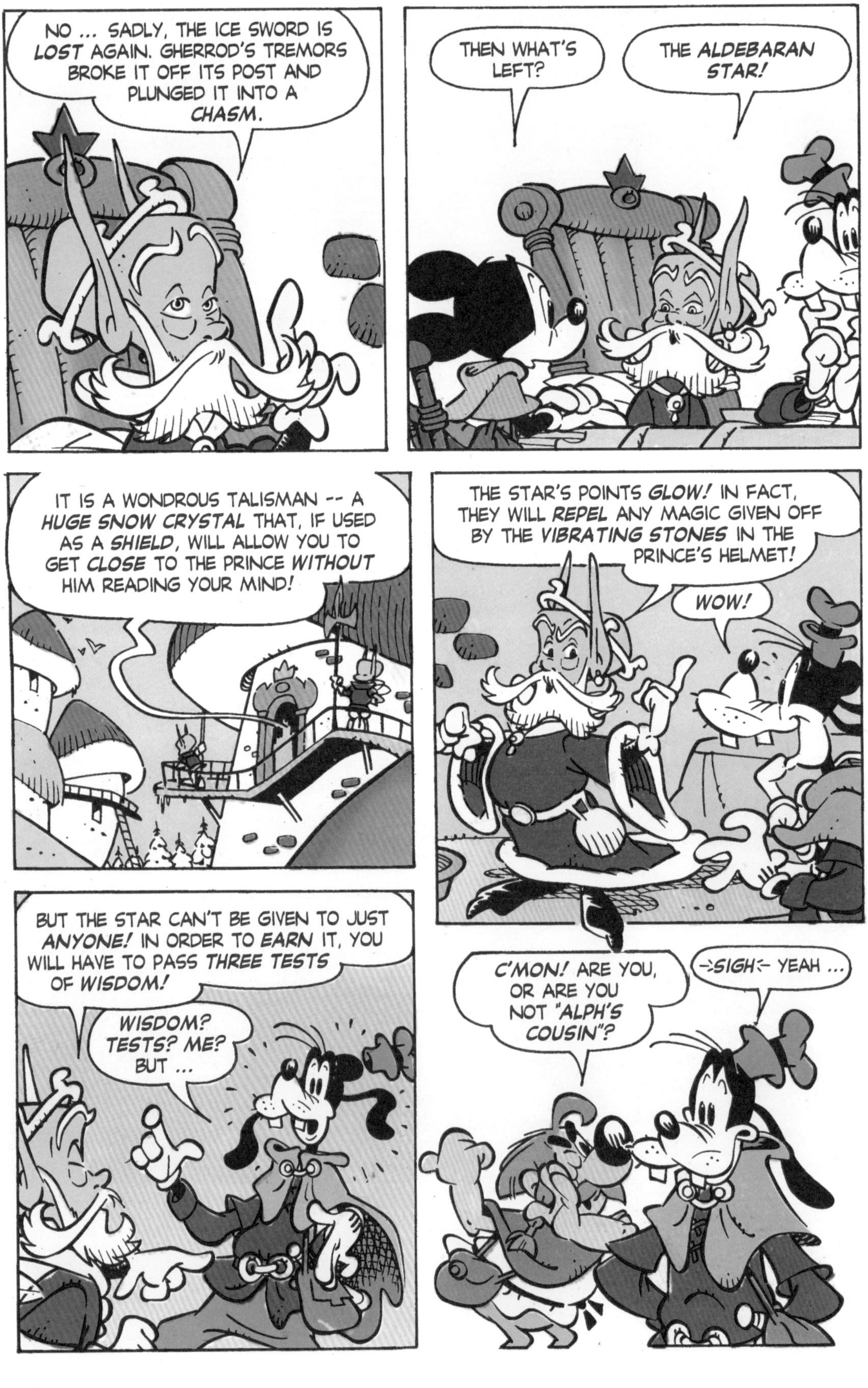
NO ... SADLY, THE ICE SWORD IS LOST AGAIN. GHERROD'S TREMORS BROKE IT OFF ITS POST AND PLUNGED IT INTO A CHASM.
THEN WHAT'S LEFT?
THE ALDEBARAN STAR!
IT IS A WONDROUS TALISMAN -- A HUGE SNOW CRYSTAL THAT, IF USED AS A SHIELD, WILL ALLOW YOU TO GET CLOSE TO THE PRINCE WITHOUT HIM READING YOUR MIND!
THE STAR'S POINTS GLOW! IN FACT, THEY WILL REPEL ANY MAGIC GIVEN OFF BY THE VIBRATING STONES IN THE PRINCE'S HELMET!
WOW!
BUT THE STAR CAN'T BE GIVEN TO JUST ANYONE! IN ORDER TO EARN IT, YOU WILL HAVE TO PASS THREE TESTS OF WISDOM!
WISDOM? TESTS? ME? BUT ...
C'MON! ARE YOU, OR ARE YOU NOT "ALPH'S COUSIN"?
-SIGH- YEAH ...

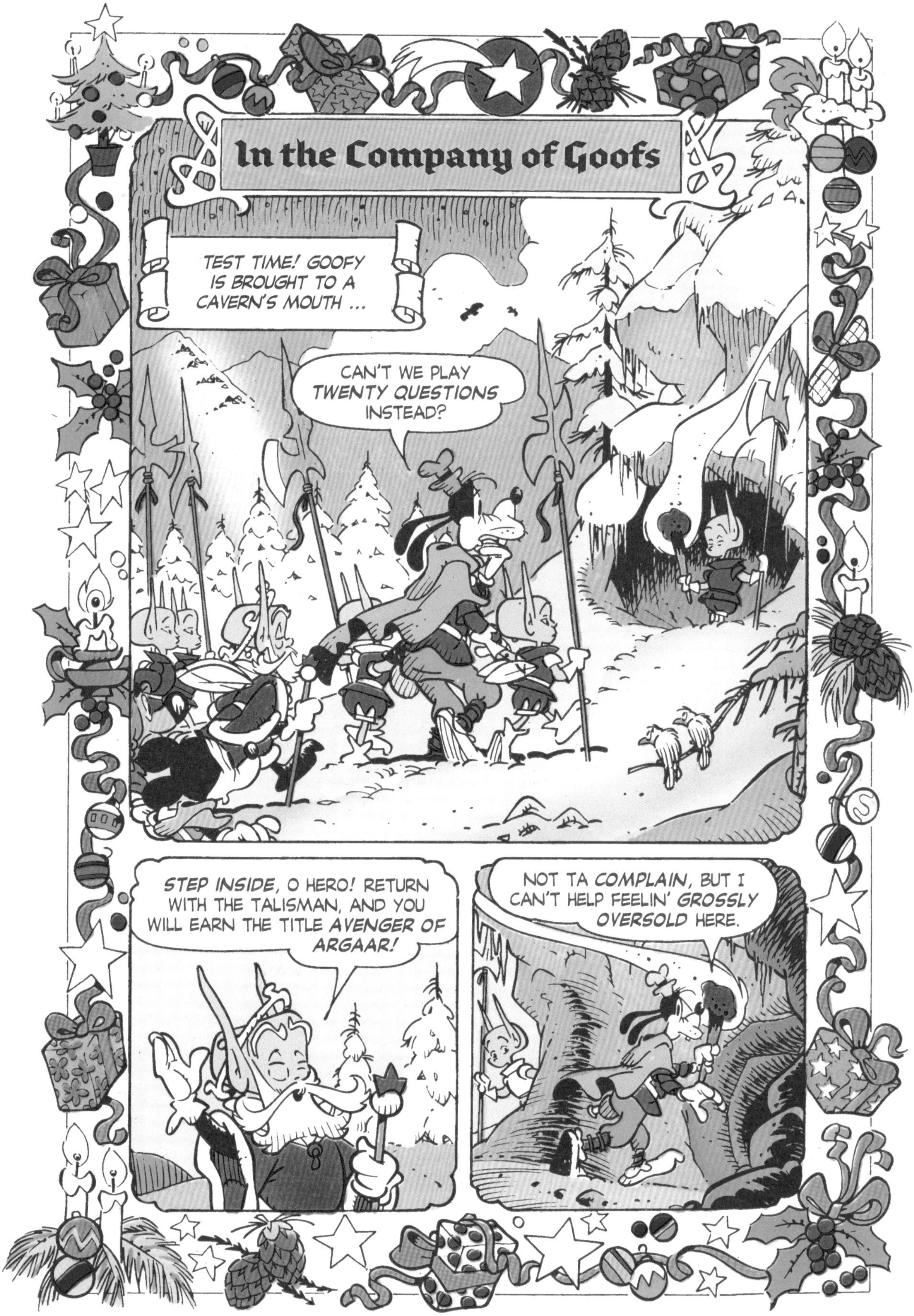
In the Company of Goofs
TEST TIME! GOOFY IS BROUGHT TO A CAVERN'S MOUTH ...
CAN'T WE PLAY TWENTY QUESTIONS INSTEAD?
STEP INSIDE, O HERO! RETURN WITH THE TALISMAN, AND YOU WILL EARN THE TITLE AVENGER OF ARGAAR!
NOT TA COMPLAIN, BUT I CAN'T HELP FEELIN' GROSSLY OVERSOLD HERE.

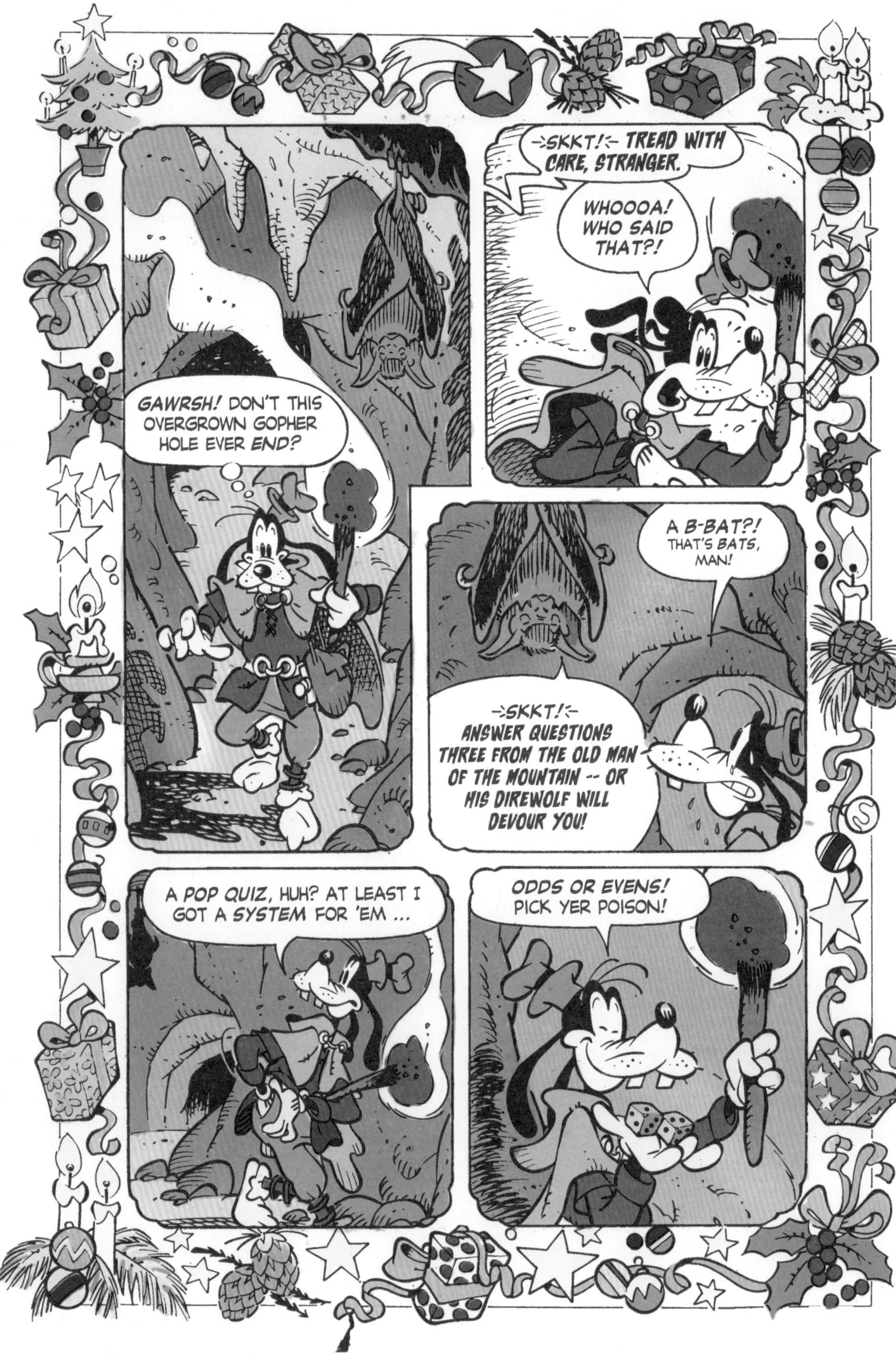

GAWRSH! DON'T THIS OVERGROWN GOPHER HOLE EVER END?
-SKKT!- TREAD WITH CARE, STRANGER.
WHOOOA! WHO SAID THAT?!
A B-BAT?! THAT'S BATS, MAN!
-SKKT!- ANSWER QUESTIONS THREE FROM THE OLD MAN OF THE MOUNTAIN -- OR HIS DIREWOLF WILL DEVOUR YOU!
A POP QUIZ, HUH? AT LEAST I GOT A SYSTEM FOR 'EM ...
ODDS OR EVENS! PICK YER POISON!

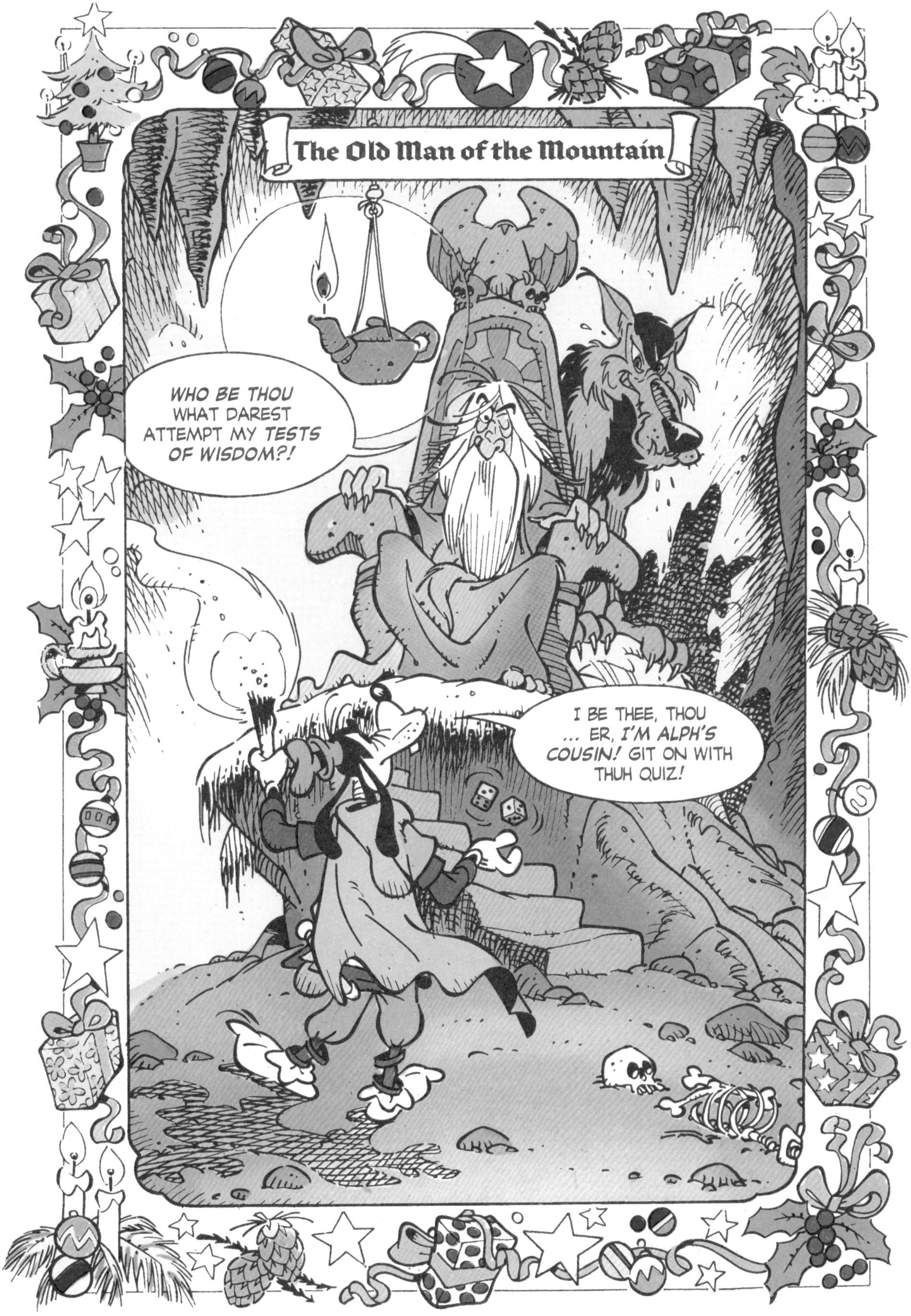
The Old Man of the Mountain
WHO BE THOU WHAT DAREST ATTEMPT MY TESTS OF WISDOM?!
I BE THEE, THOU ... ER, I'M ALPH'S COUSIN! GIT ON WITH THUH QUIZ!

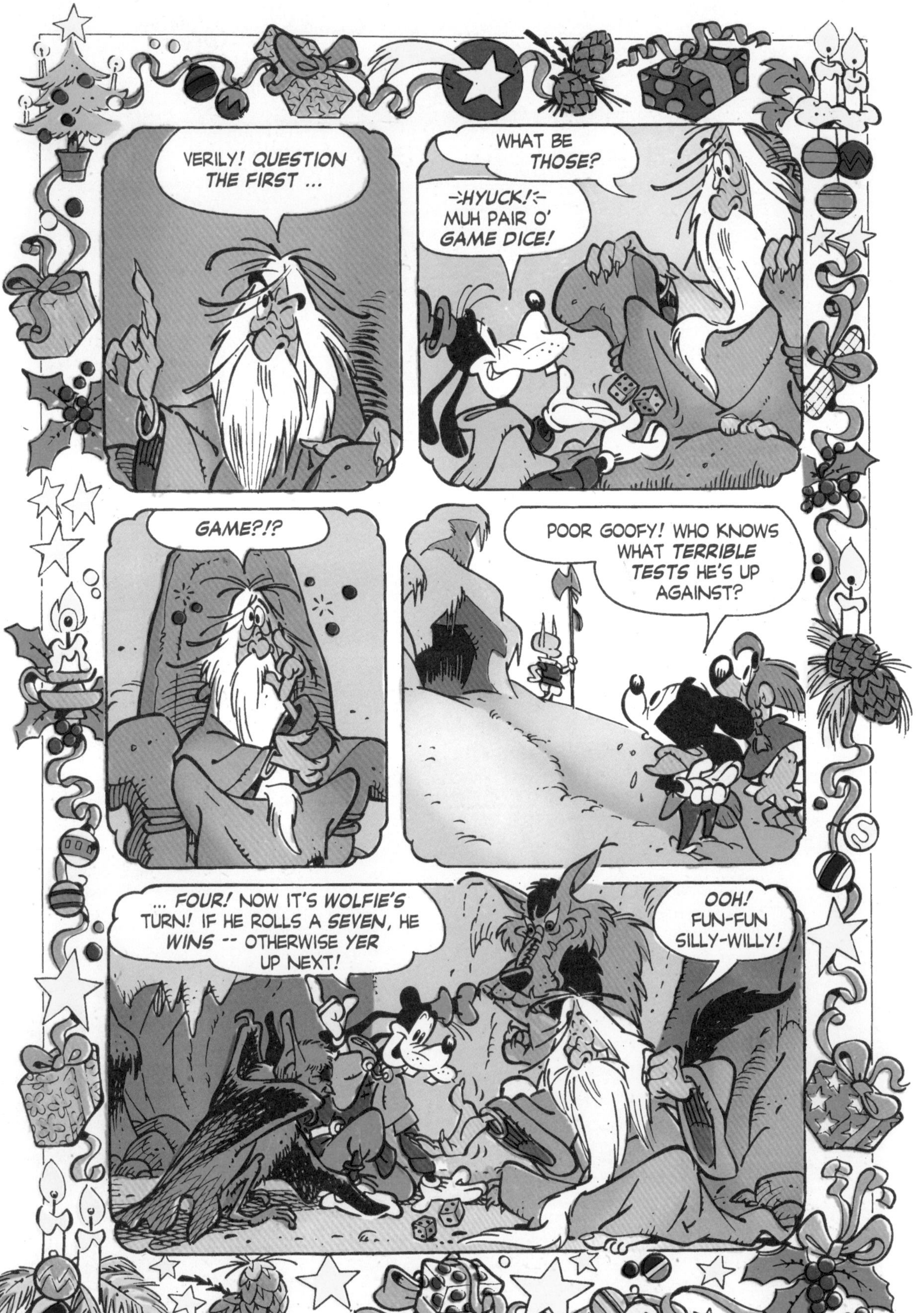
VERILY! QUESTION THE FIRST ...
WHAT BE THOSE?
-HYUCK!- MUH PAIR O' GAME DICE!
GAME?!?
POOR GOOFY! WHO KNOWS WHAT TERRIBLE TESTS HE'S UP AGAINST?
... FOUR! NOW IT'S WOLFIE'S TURN! IF HE ROLLS A SEVEN, HE WINS -- OTHERWISE YER UP NEXT!
OOH! FUN-FUN SILLY-WILLY!

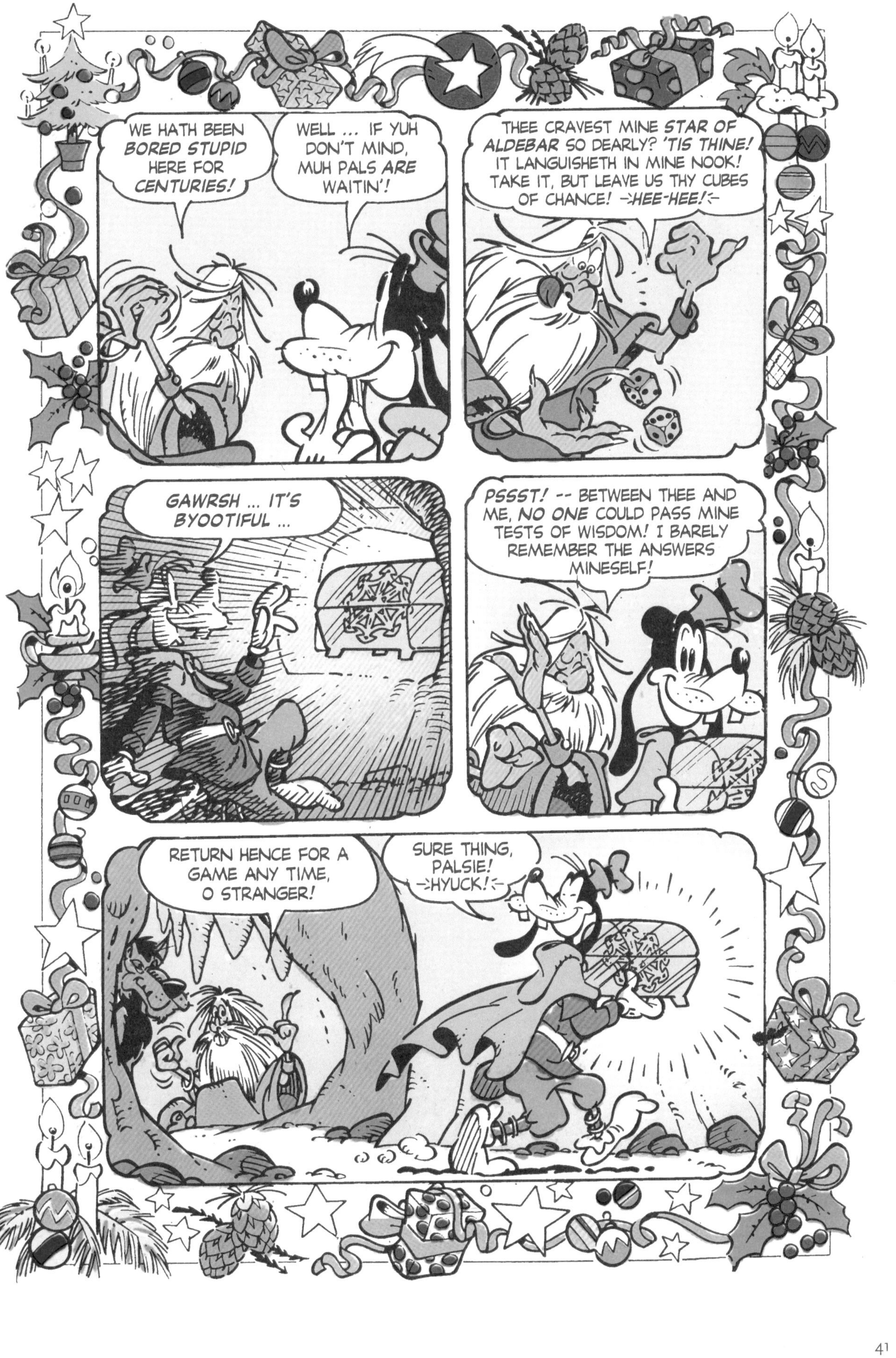
WE HATH BEEN BORED STUPID HERE FOR CENTURIES!
WELL ... IF YUH DON'T MIND, MUH PALS ARE WAITIN'!
THEE CRAVEST MINE STAR OF ALDEBAR SO DEARLY? 'TIS THINE! IT LANGUISHETH IN MINE NOOK! TAKE IT, BUT LEAVE US THY CUBES OF CHANCE! HEE-HEE!
GAWRSH ... IT'S BYOOTIFUL ...
PSSST! -- BETWEEN THEE AND ME, NO ONE COULD PASS MINE TESTS OF WISDOM! I BARELY REMEMBER THE ANSWERS MINESELF!
RETURN HENCE FOR A GAME ANY TIME, O STRANGER!
SURE THING, PALSIE! HYUCK!

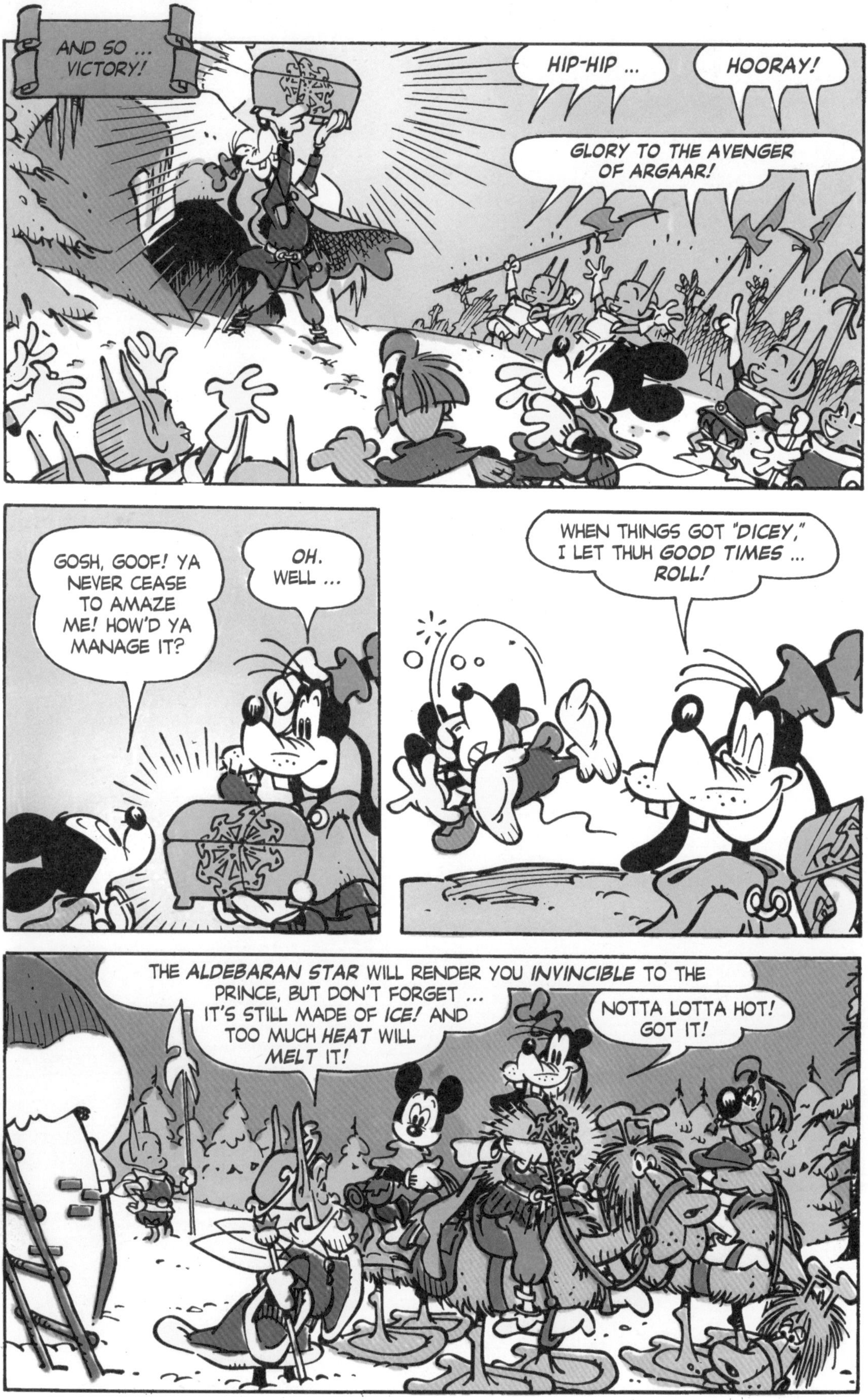
AND SO ... VICTORY!
HIP-HIP ...
HOORAY!
GLORY TO THE AVENGER OF ARGAAR!
GOSH, GOOF! YA NEVER CEASE TO AMAZE ME! HOW'D YA MANAGE IT?
OH. WELL ...
WHEN THINGS GOT "DICEY," I LET THUH GOOD TIMES ... ROLL!
THE ALDEBARAN STAR WILL RENDER YOU INVINCIBLE TO THE PRINCE, BUT DON'T FORGET ... IT'S STILL MADE OF ICE! AND TOO MUCH HEAT WILL MELT IT!
NOTTA LOTTA HOT! GOT IT!

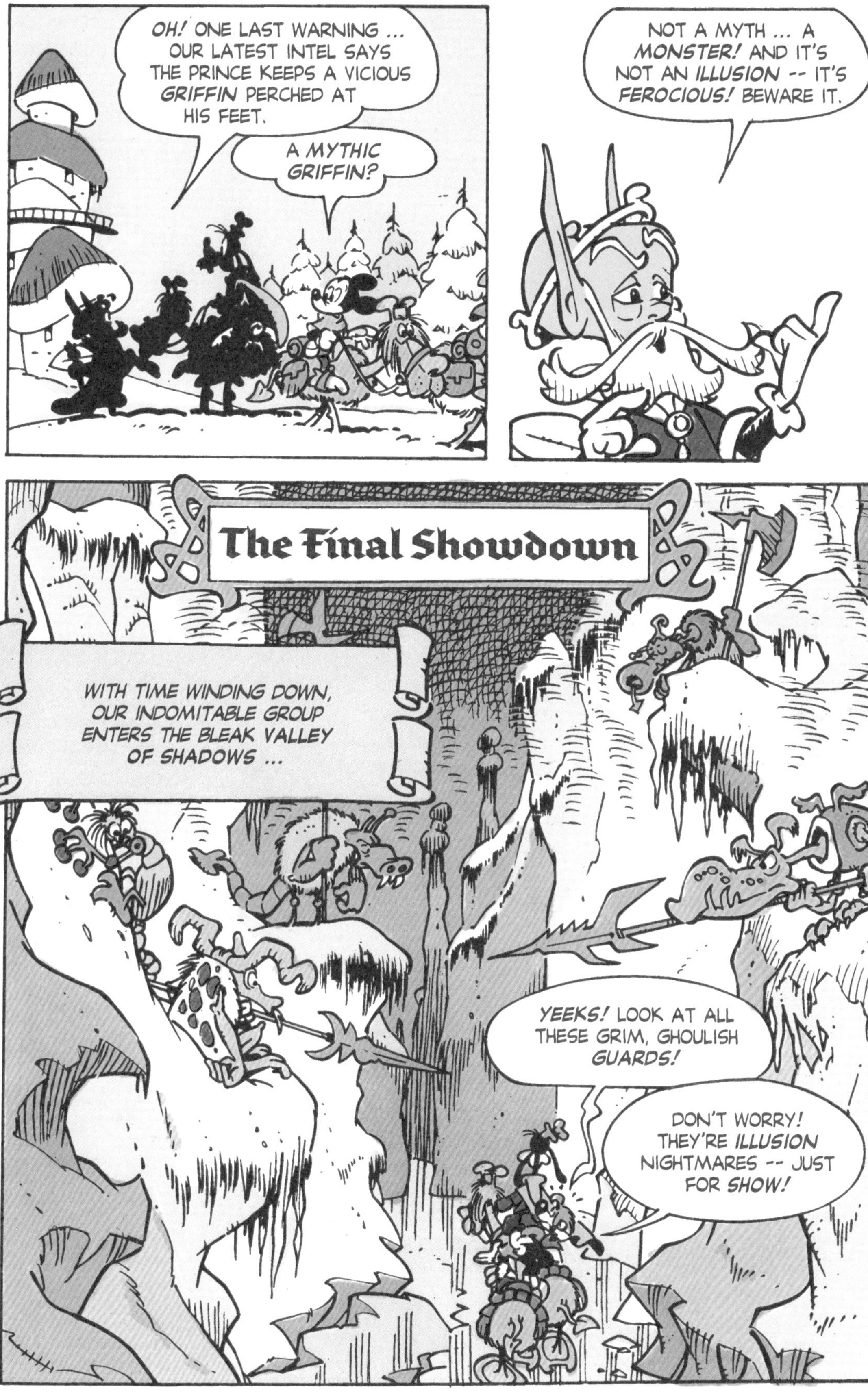

OH! ONE LAST WARNING ... OUR LATEST INTEL SAYS THE PRINCE KEEPS A VICIOUS GRIFFIN PERCHED AT HIS FEET.
A MYTHIC GRIFFIN?
NOT A MYTH ... A MONSTER! AND IT'S NOT AN ILLUSION -- IT'S FEROCIOUS! BEWARE IT.
The Final Showdown
WITH TIME WINDING DOWN, OUR INDOMITABLE GROUP ENTERS THE BLEAK VALLEY OF SHADOWS ...
YEEKS! LOOK AT ALL THESE GRIM, GHOULISH GUARDS!
DON'T WORRY! THEY'RE ILLUSION NIGHTMARES -- JUST FOR SHOW!

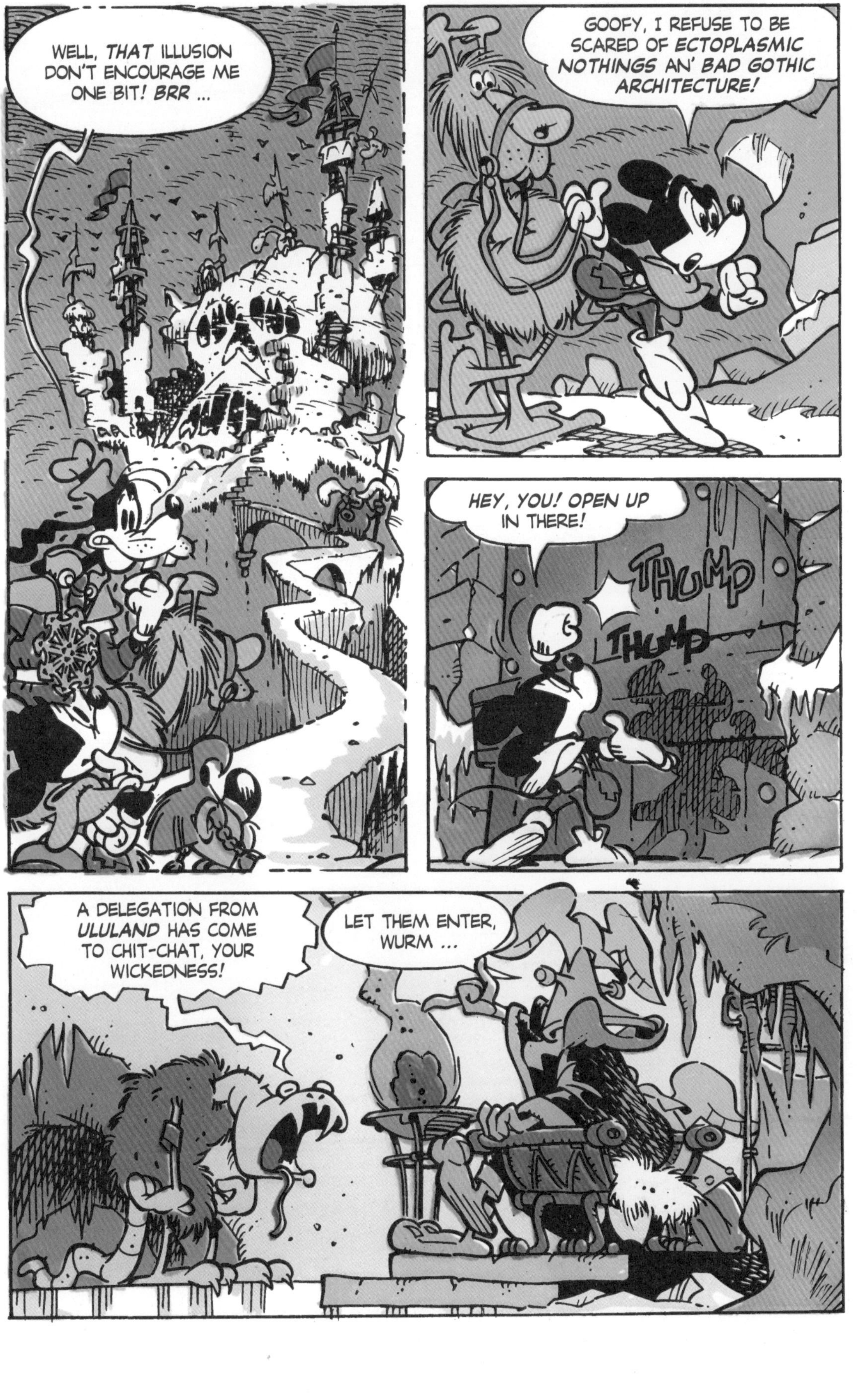
WELL, THAT ILLUSION DON'T ENCOURAGE ME ONE BIT! BRR ...
GOOFY, I REFUSE TO BE SCARED OF ECTOPLASMIC NOTHINGS AN' BAD GOTHIC ARCHITECTURE!
HEY, YOU! OPEN UP IN THERE!
THUMP
THUMP
A DELEGATION FROM ULULAND HAS COME TO CHIT-CHAT, YOUR WICKEDNESS!
LET THEM ENTER, WURM ...

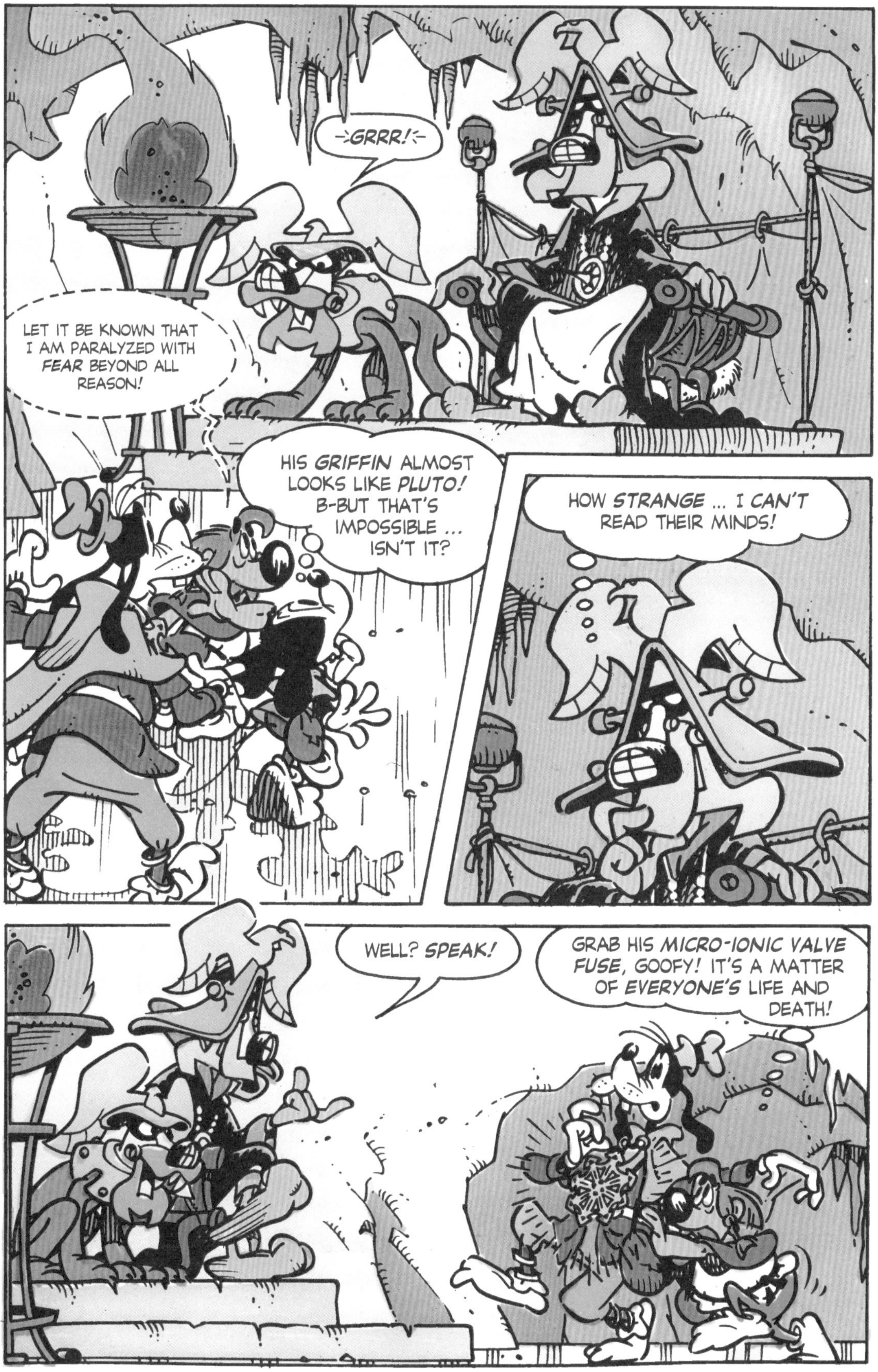

GRRR!
LET IT BE KNOWN THAT I AM PARALYZED WITH FEAR BEYOND ALL REASON!
HIS GRIFFIN ALMOST LOOKS LIKE PLUTO! B-BUT THAT'S IMPOSSIBLE ... ISN'T IT?
HOW STRANGE ... I CAN'T READ THEIR MINDS!
WELL? SPEAK!
GRAB HIS MICRO-IONIC VALVE FUSE, GOOFY! IT'S A MATTER OF EVERYONE'S LIFE AND DEATH!

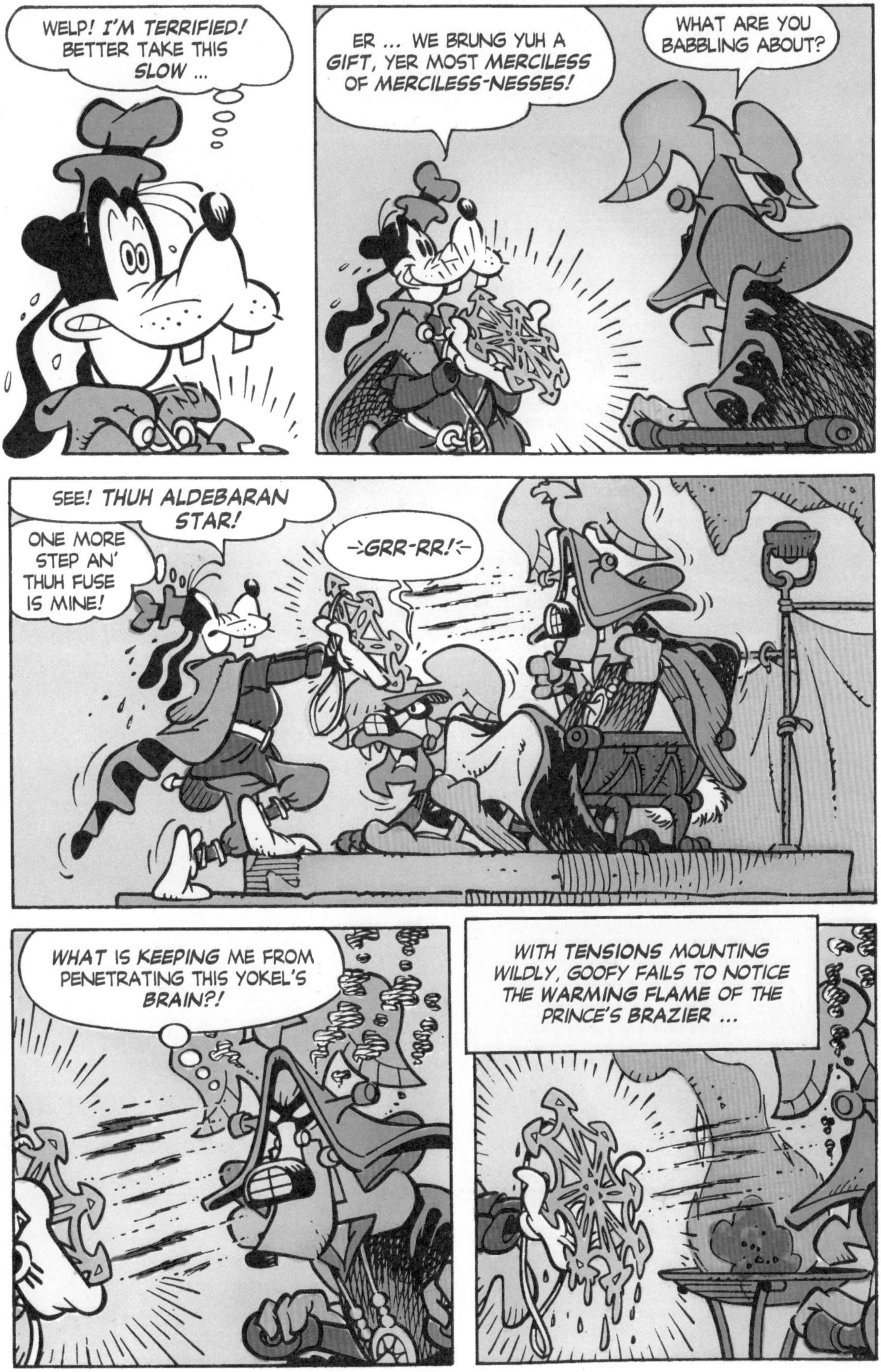

WELP! I'M TERRIFIED! BETTER TAKE THIS SLOW ...
ER ... WE BRUNG YUH A GIFT, YER MOST MERCILESS OF MERCILESS-NESSES!
WHAT ARE YOU BABBLING ABOUT?
SEE! THUH ALDEBARAN STAR!
ONE MORE STEP AN' THUH FUSE IS MINE!
GRR-RR!
WHAT IS KEEPING ME FROM PENETRATING THIS YOKEL'S BRAIN?!
WITH TENSIONS MOUNTING WILDLY, GOOFY FAILS TO NOTICE THE WARMING FLAME OF THE PRINCE'S BRAZIER ...

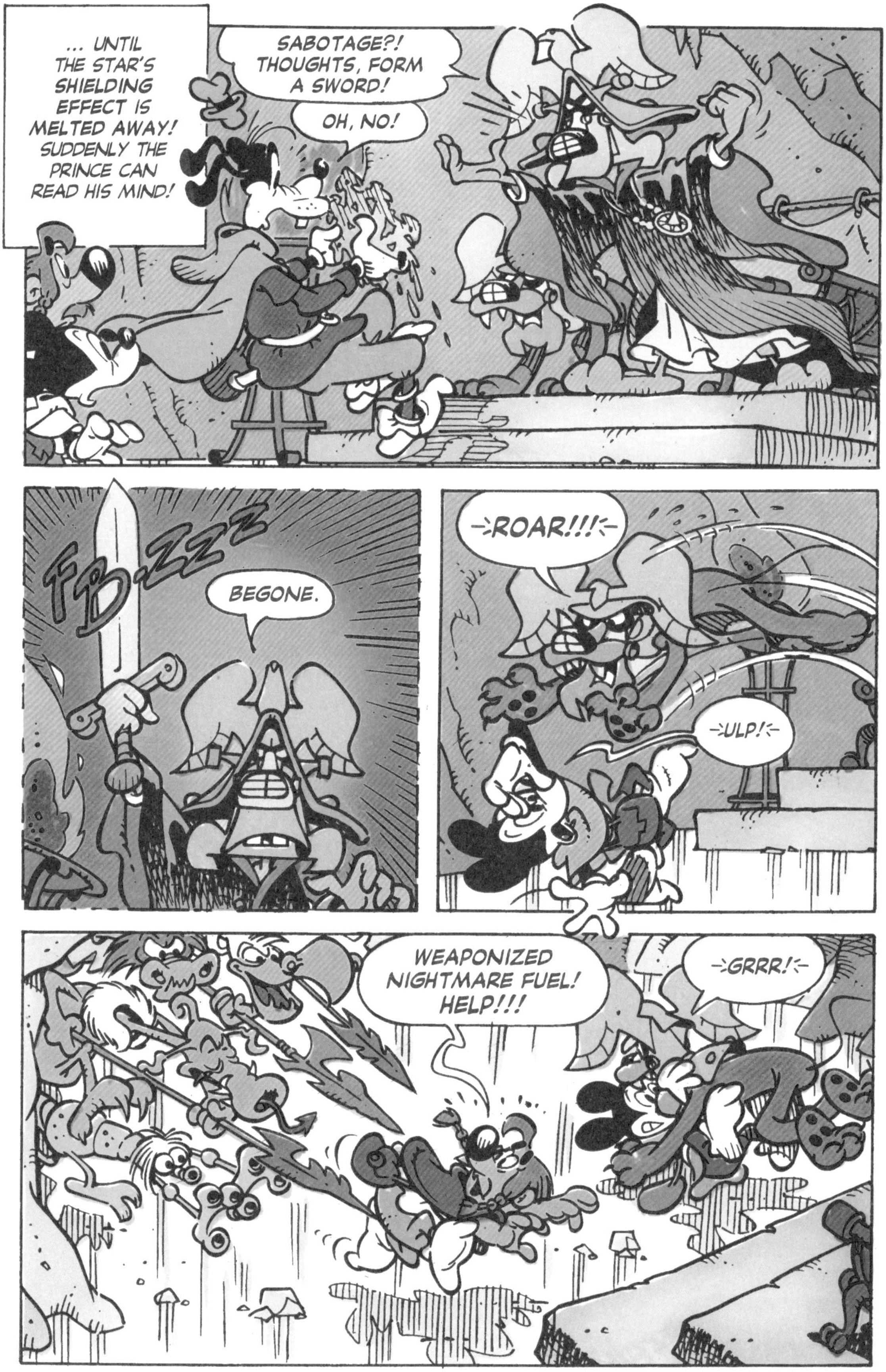
... UNTIL THE STAR'S SHIELDING EFFECT IS MELTED AWAY! SUDDENLY THE PRINCE CAN READ HIS MIND!
SABOTAGE?! THOUGHTS, FORM A SWORD!
OH, NO!
FBZZZ
BEGONE.
ROAR!!!
ULP!
WEAPONIZED NIGHTMARE FUEL! HELP!!!
GRRR!

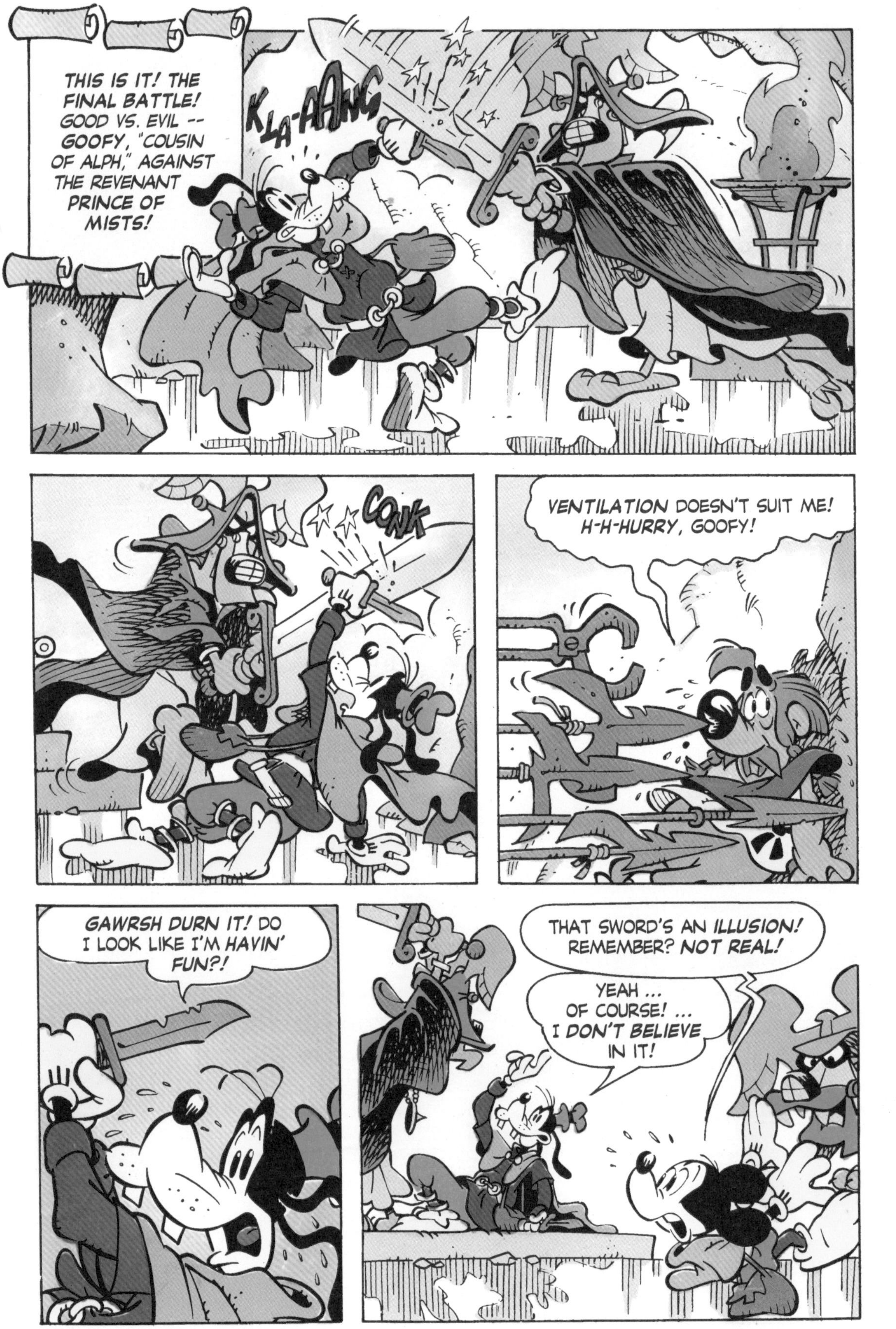
THIS IS IT! THE FINAL BATTLE! GOOD VS. EVIL -- GOOFY, "COUSIN OF ALPH," AGAINST THE REVENANT PRINCE OF MISTS!
KLA-AANG
CONK
VENTILATION DOESN'T SUIT ME! H-H-HURRY, GOOFY!
GAWRSH DURN IT! DO I LOOK LIKE I'M HAVIN' FUN?!
THAT SWORD'S AN ILLUSION! REMEMBER? NOT REAL!
YEAH ... OF COURSE! ... I DON'T BELIEVE IN IT!

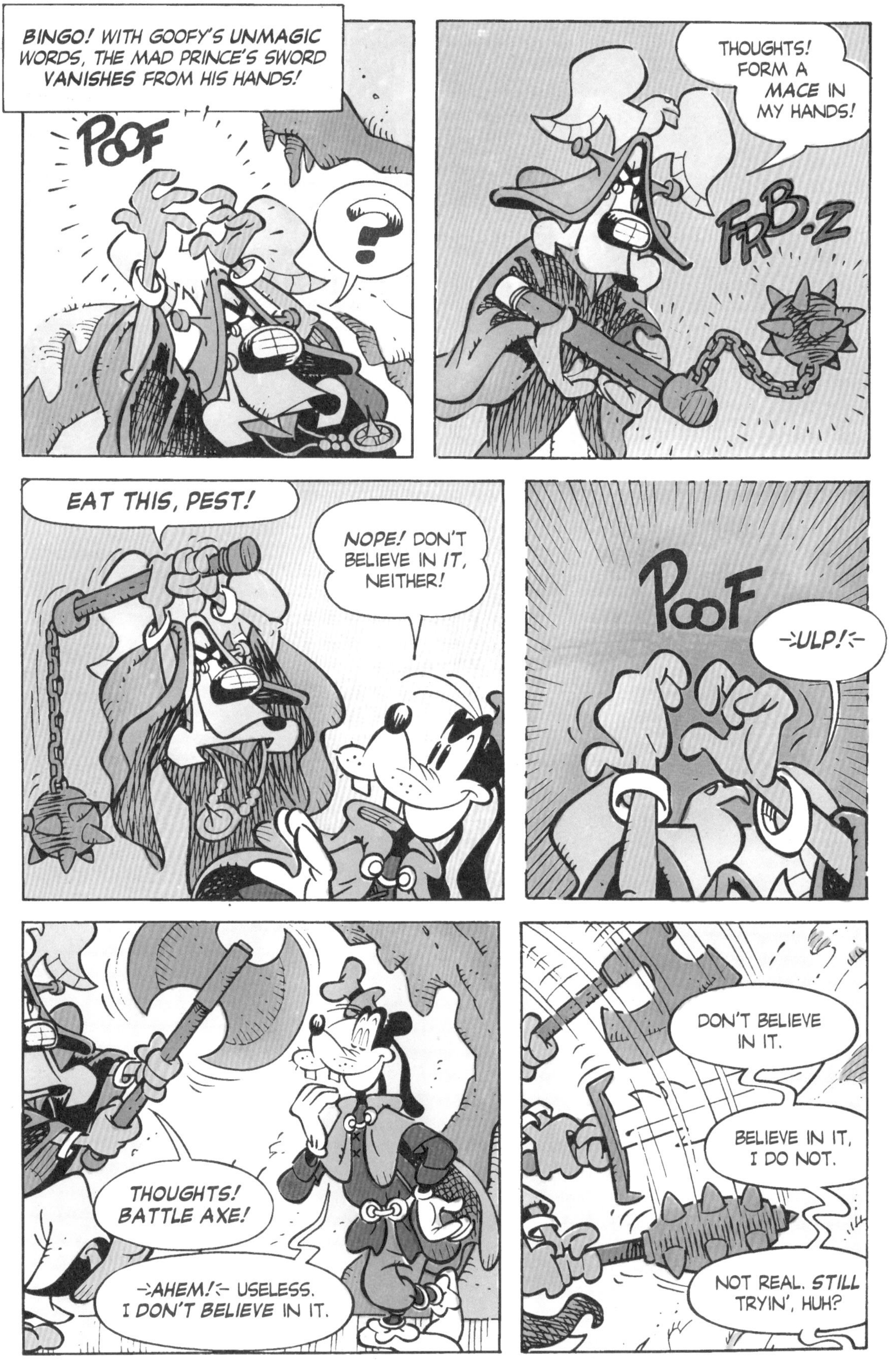
BINGO! WITH GOOFY'S UNMAGIC WORDS, THE MAD PRINCE'S SWORD VANISHES FROM HIS HANDS!
POOF
?
THOUGHTS! FORM A MACE IN MY HANDS!
FRB-Z
EAT THIS, PEST!
NOPE! DON'T BELIEVE IN IT, NEITHER!
POOF
ULP!
THOUGHTS! BATTLE AXE!
AHEM! USELESS. I DON'T BELIEVE IN IT.
DON'T BELIEVE IN IT.
BELIEVE IN IT, I DO NOT.
NOT REAL. STILL TRYIN', HUH?

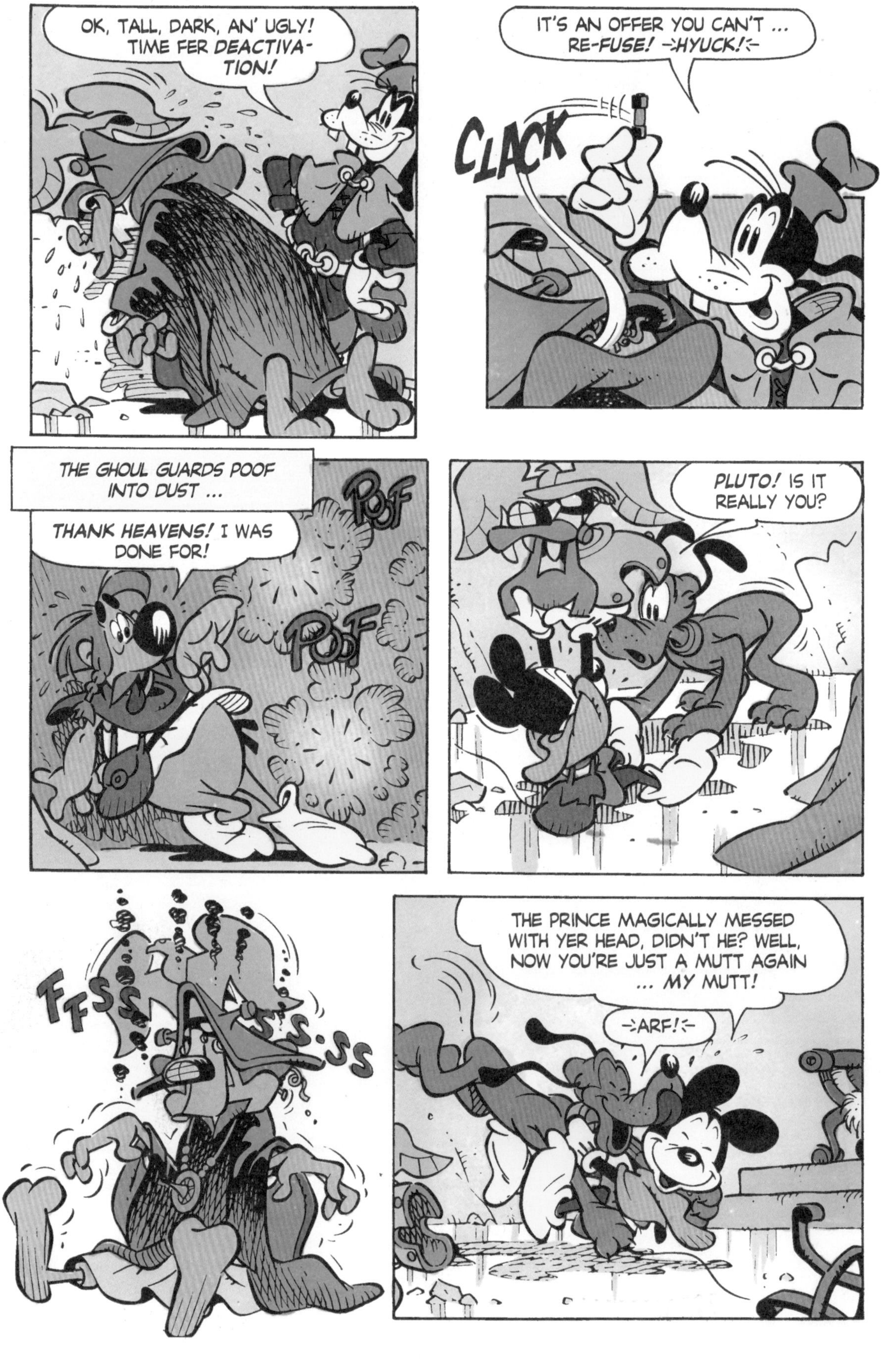
OK, TALL, DARK, AN' UGLY! TIME FER DEACTIVA-TION!
IT'S AN OFFER YOU CAN'T ... RE-FUSE! -HYUCK!-
CLACK
THE GHOUL GUARDS POOF INTO DUST ...
THANK HEAVENS! I WAS DONE FOR!
POOF
POOF
PLUTO! IS IT REALLY YOU?
FFSSS SSS
THE PRINCE MAGICALLY MESSED WITH YER HEAD, DIDN'T HE? WELL, NOW YOU'RE JUST A MUTT AGAIN ... MY MUTT!
-ARF!-

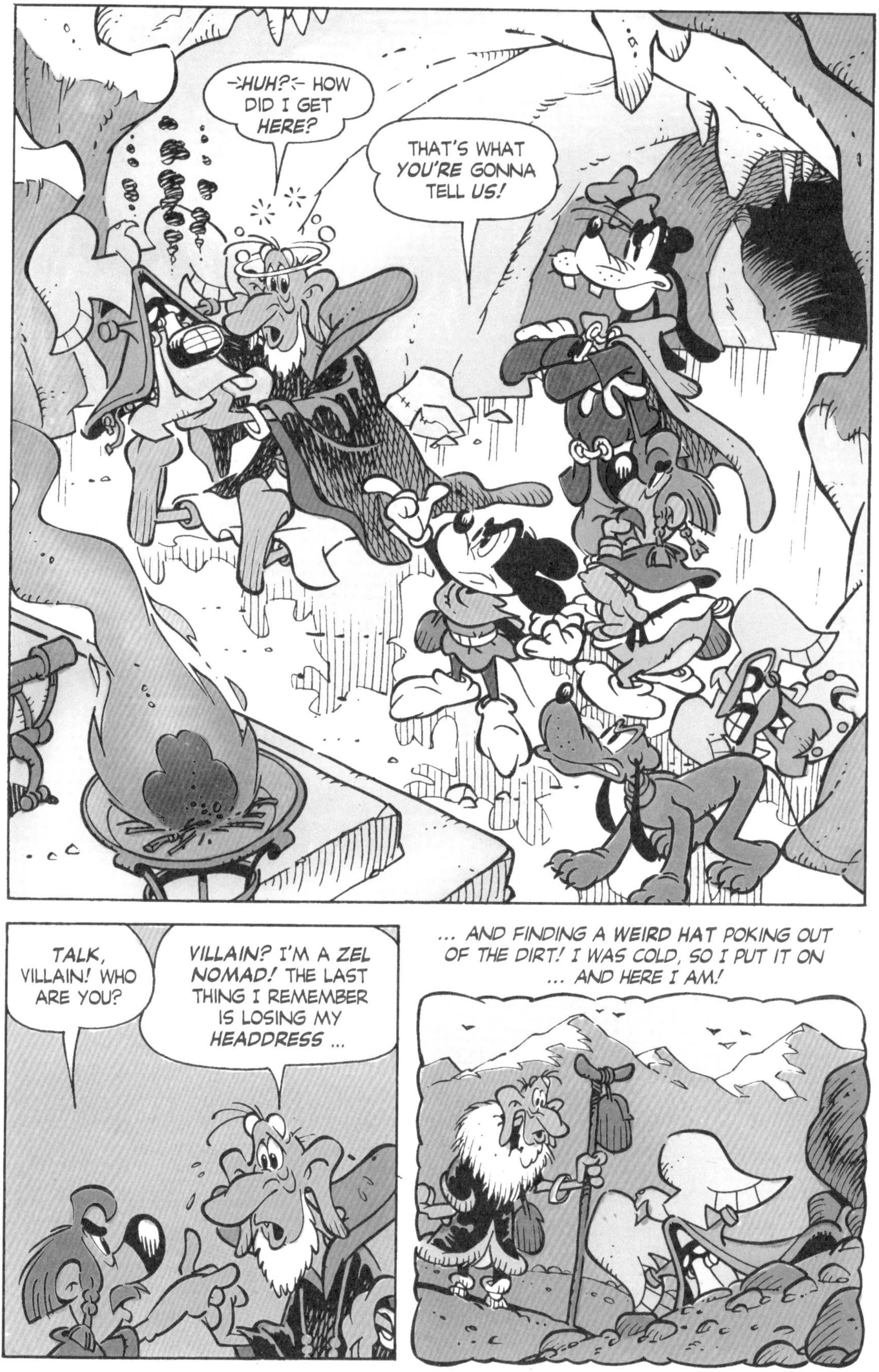
HUH? HOW DID I GET HERE?
THAT'S WHAT YOU'RE GONNA TELL US!
TALK, VILLAIN! WHO ARE YOU?
VILLAIN? I'M A ZEL NOMAD! THE LAST THING I REMEMBER IS LOSING MY HEADDRESS ...
... AND FINDING A WEIRD HAT POKING OUT OF THE DIRT! I WAS COLD, SO I PUT IT ON ... AND HERE I AM!

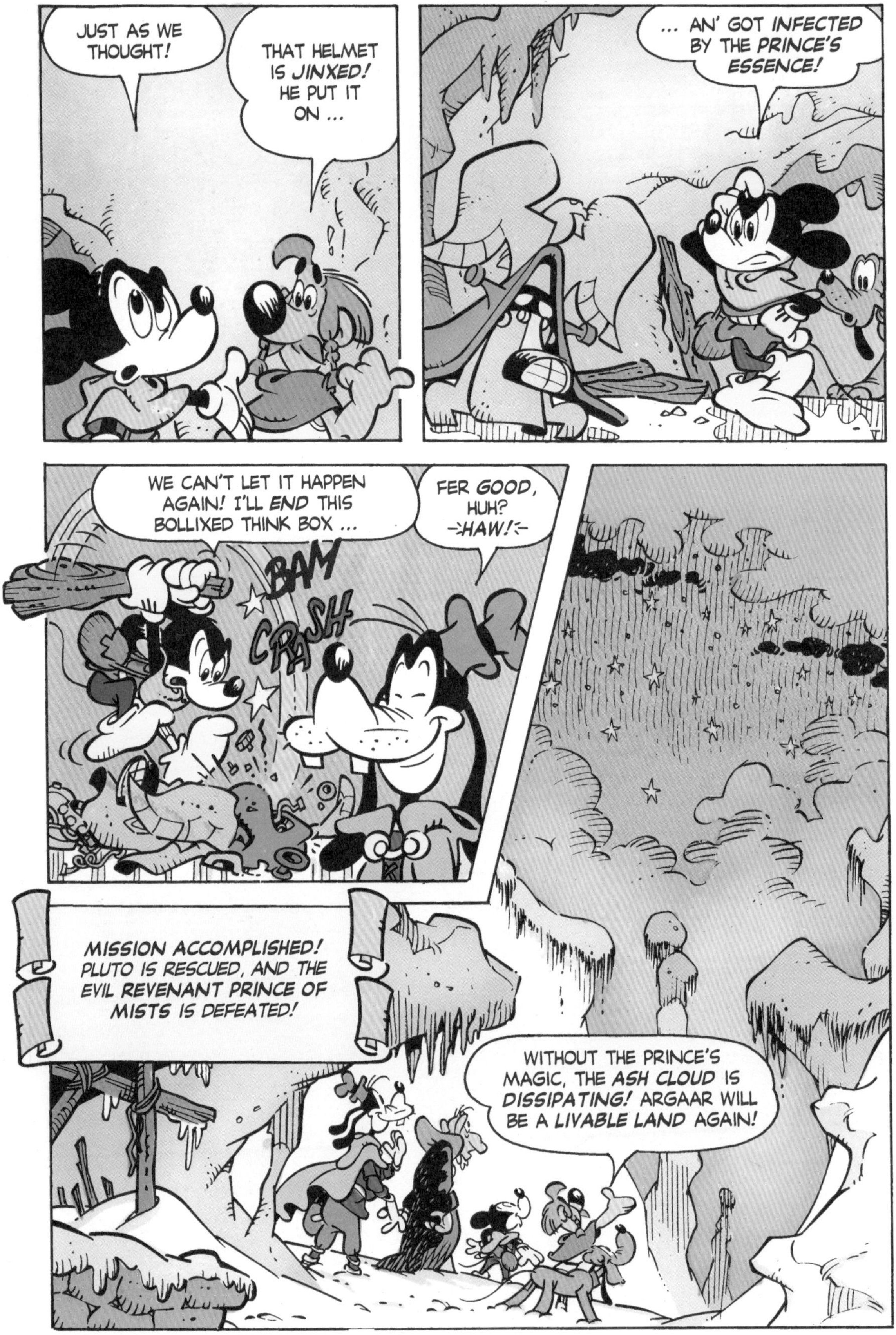
JUST AS WE THOUGHT!
THAT HELMET IS JINXED! HE PUT IT ON ...
... AN' GOT INFECTED BY THE PRINCE'S ESSENCE!
WE CAN'T LET IT HAPPEN AGAIN! I'LL END THIS BOLLIXED THINK BOX ...
FER GOOD, HUH? HAW!
BAM
CRASH
MISSION ACCOMPLISHED! PLUTO IS RESCUED, AND THE EVIL REVENANT PRINCE OF MISTS IS DEFEATED!
WITHOUT THE PRINCE'S MAGIC, THE ASH CLOUD IS DISSIPATING! ARGAAR WILL BE A LIVABLE LAND AGAIN!

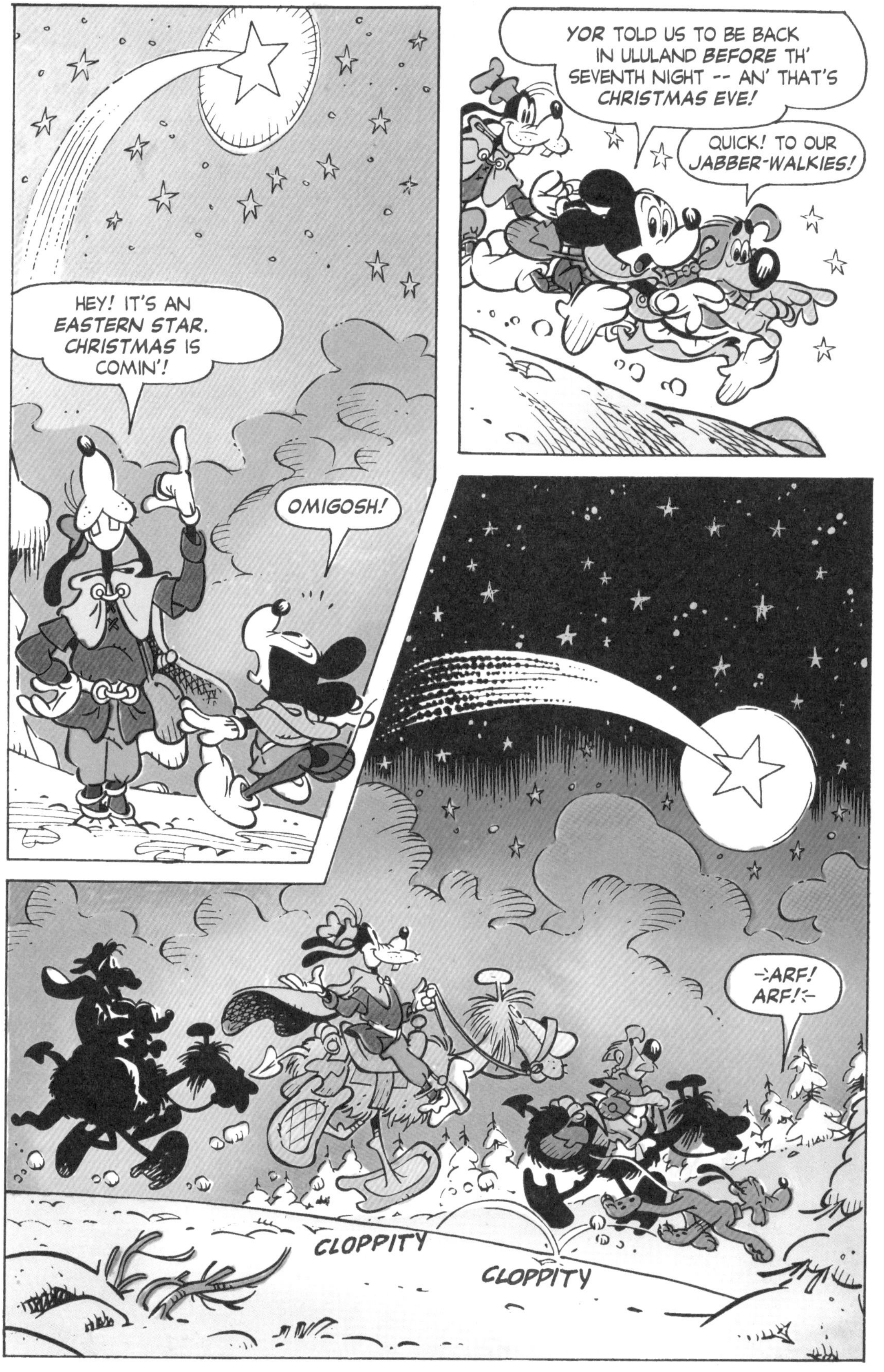
HEY! IT'S AN EASTERN STAR. CHRISTMAS IS COMIN'!
OMIGOSH!
YOR TOLD US TO BE BACK IN ULULAND BEFORE TH' SEVENTH NIGHT -- AN' THAT'S CHRISTMAS EVE!
QUICK! TO OUR JABBER-WALKIES!
ARF! ARF!
CLOPPITY
CLOPPITY

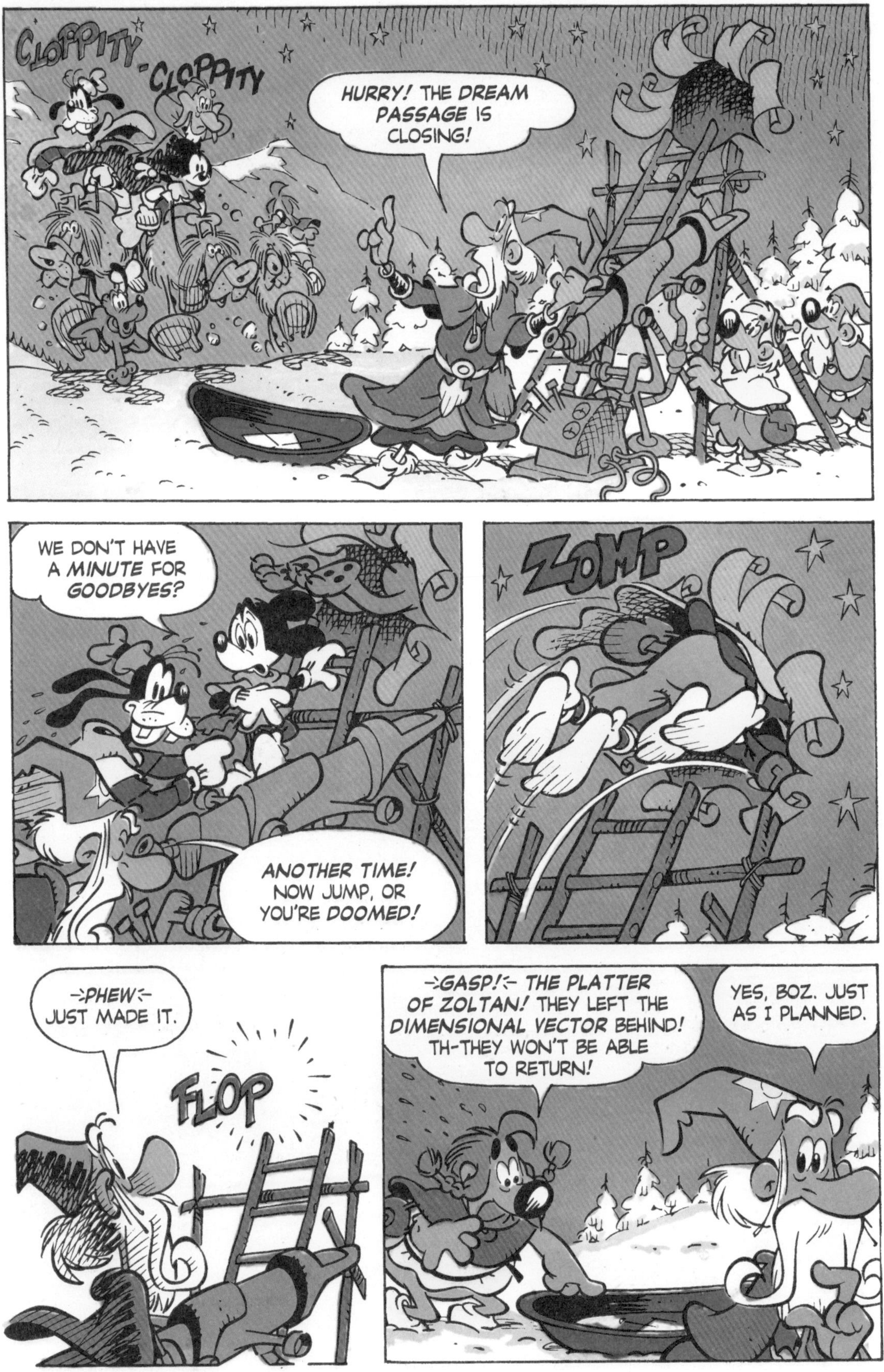
CLOPPITY-CLOPPITY
HURRY! THE DREAM PASSAGE IS CLOSING!
WE DON'T HAVE A MINUTE FOR GOODBYES?
ANOTHER TIME! NOW JUMP, OR YOU'RE DOOMED!
ZOMP
-PHEW- JUST MADE IT.
FLOP
-GASP!- THE PLATTER OF ZOLTAN! THEY LEFT THE DIMENSIONAL VECTOR BEHIND! TH-THEY WON'T BE ABLE TO RETURN!
YES, BOZ. JUST AS I PLANNED.

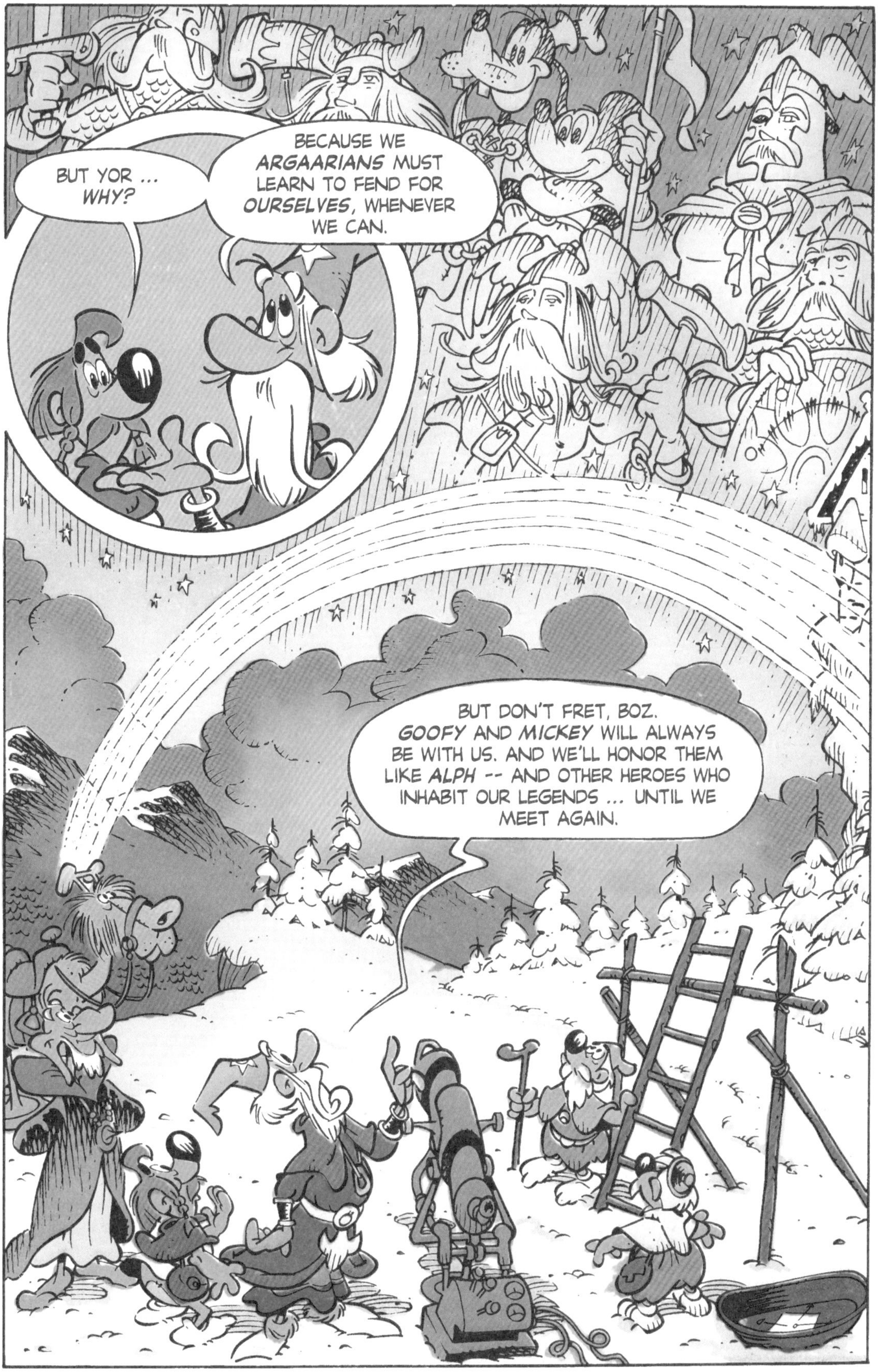
BUT YOR ... WHY?
BECAUSE WE ARGAARIANS MUST LEARN TO FEND FOR OURSELVES, WHENEVER WE CAN.
BUT DON'T FRET, BOZ. GOOFY AND MICKEY WILL ALWAYS BE WITH US. AND WE'LL HONOR THEM LIKE ALPH -- AND OTHER HEROES WHO INHABIT OUR LEGENDS ... UNTIL WE MEET AGAIN.

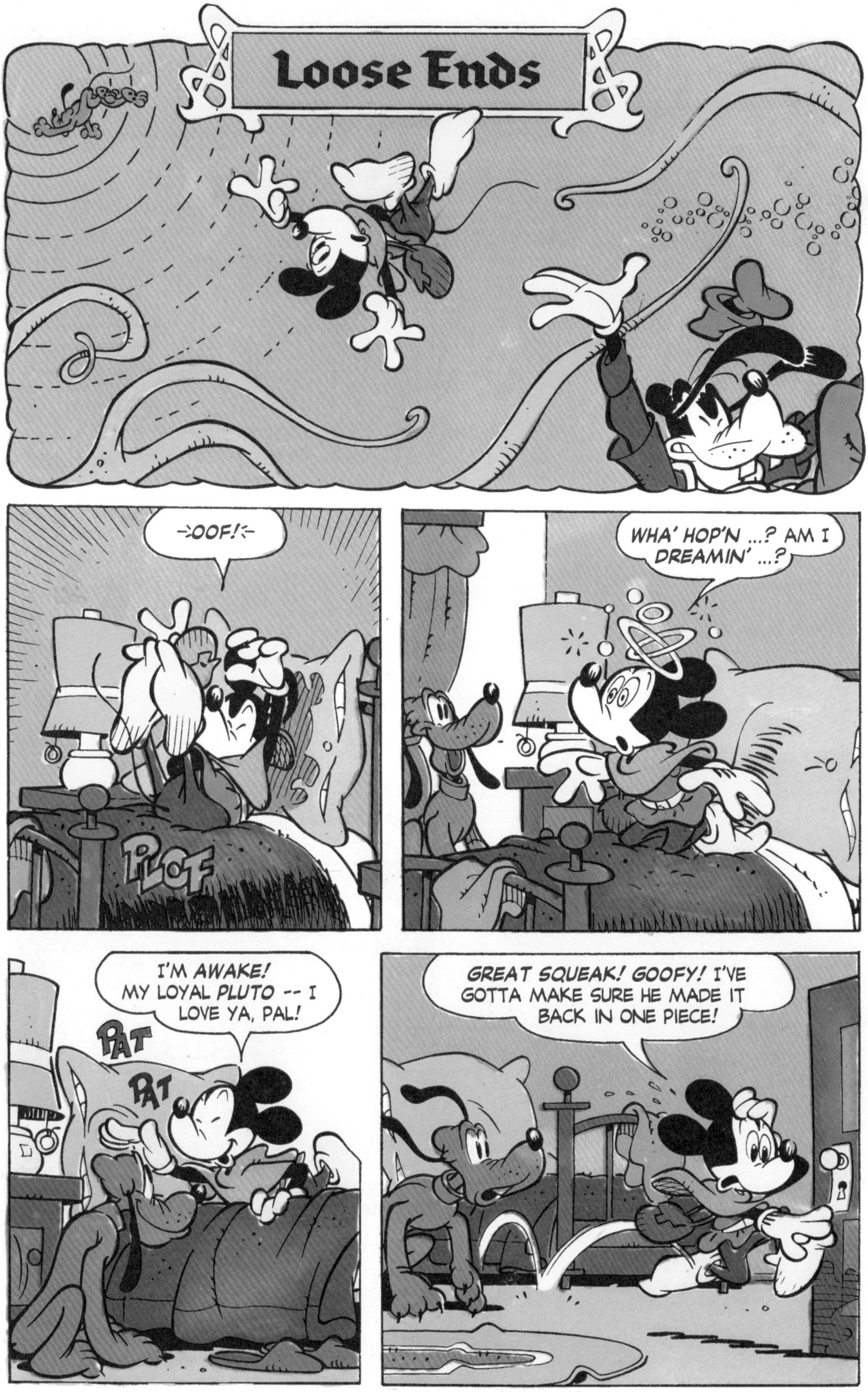
Loose Ends
-OOF!-
PLOF
WHA' HOP'N ...? AM I DREAMIN' ...?
I'M AWAKE! MY LOYAL PLUTO -- I LOVE YA, PAL!
PAT
PAT
GREAT SQUEAK! GOOFY! I'VE GOTTA MAKE SURE HE MADE IT BACK IN ONE PIECE!

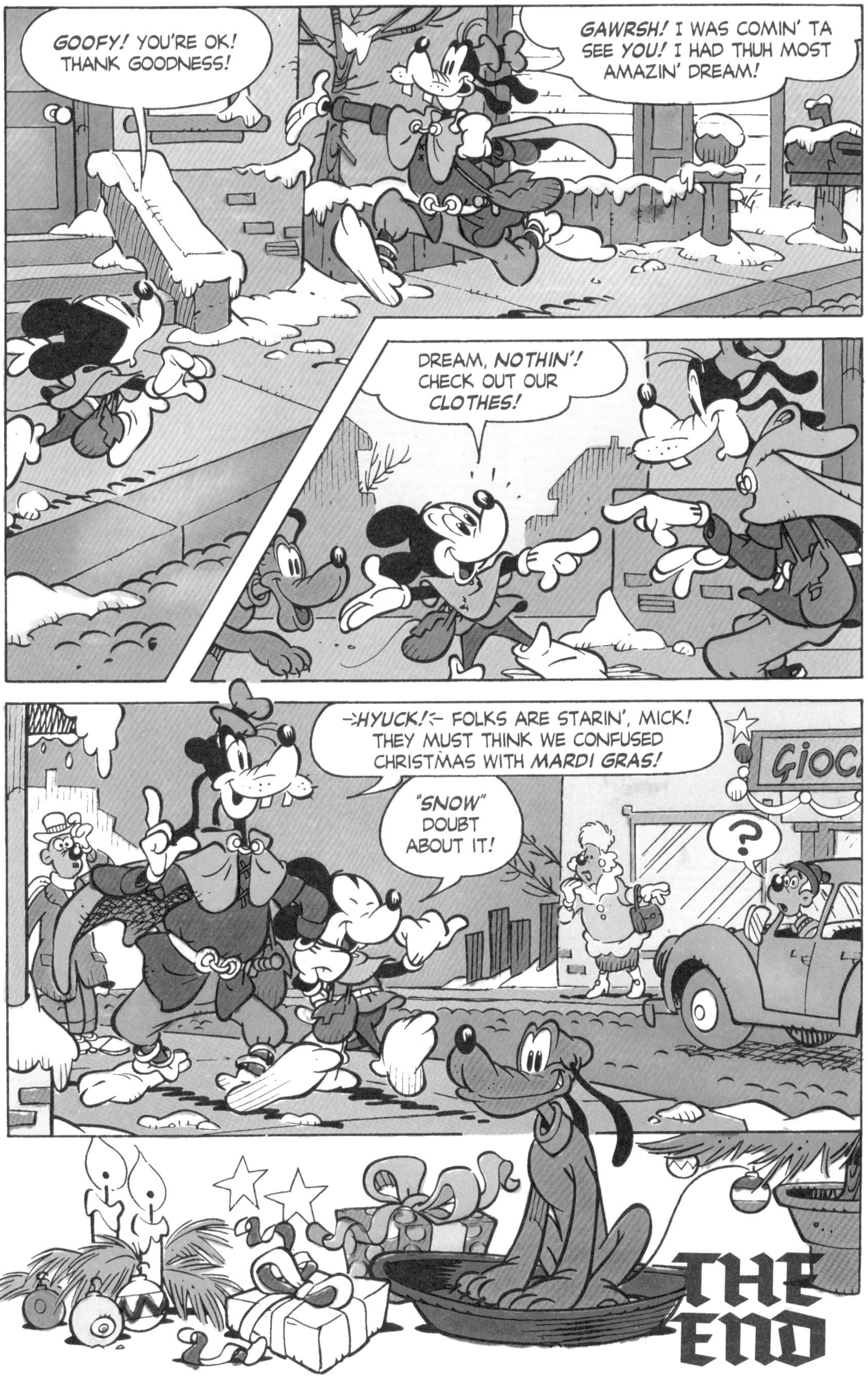
GOOFY! YOU'RE OK! THANK GOODNESS!
GAWRSH! I WAS COMIN' TA SEE YOU! I HAD THUH MOST AMAZIN' DREAM!
DREAM, NOTHIN'! CHECK OUT OUR CLOTHES!
—HYUCK!— FOLKS ARE STARIN', MICK! THEY MUST THINK WE CONFUSED CHRISTMAS WITH MARDI GRAS!
"SNOW" DOUBT ABOUT IT!
?
THE END

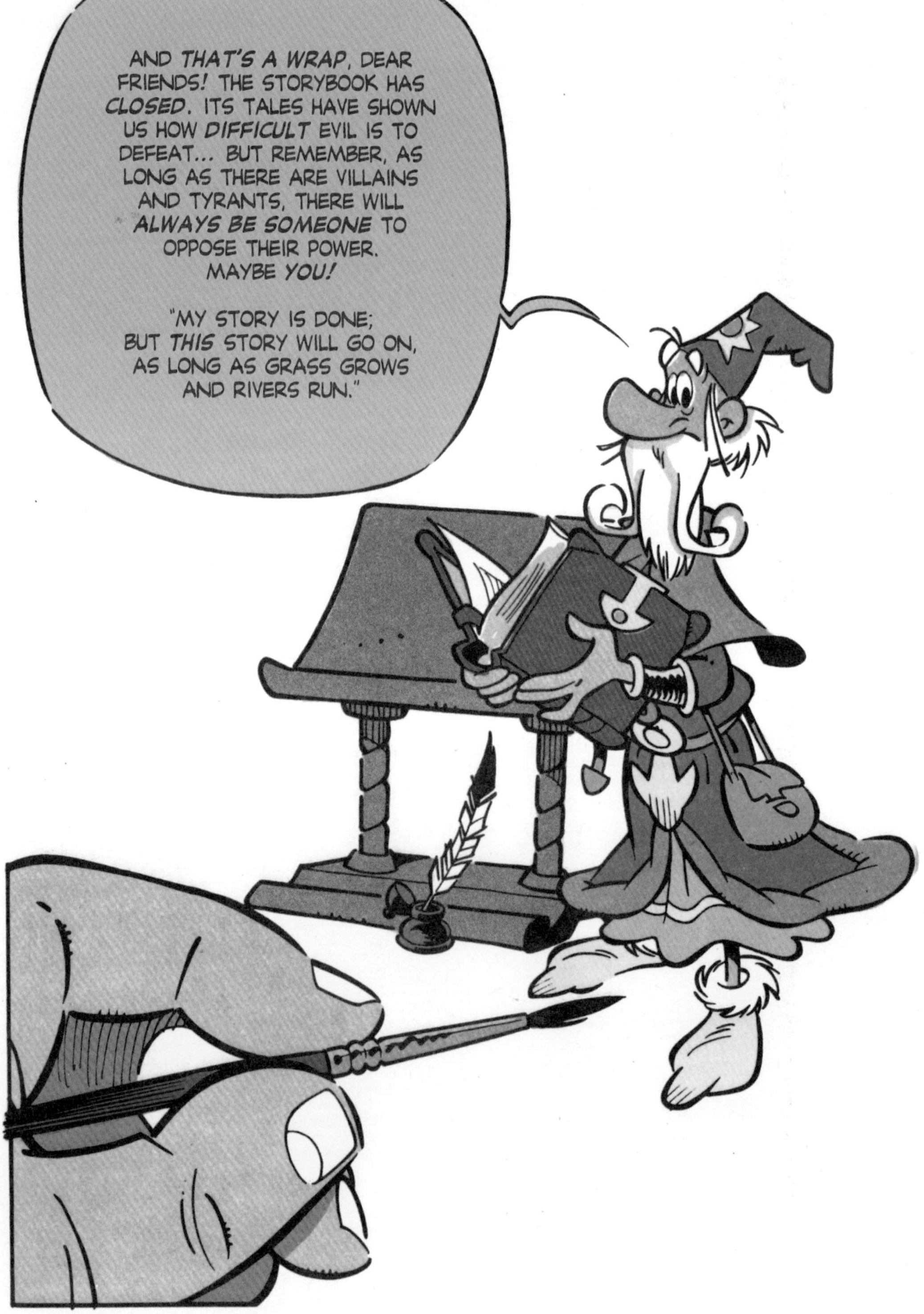
AND THAT'S A WRAP, DEAR FRIENDS! THE STORYBOOK HAS CLOSED. ITS TALES HAVE SHOWN US HOW DIFFICULT EVIL IS TO DEFEAT... BUT REMEMBER, AS LONG AS THERE ARE VILLAINS AND TYRANTS, THERE WILL ALWAYS BE SOMEONE TO OPPOSE THEIR POWER. MAYBE YOU!
"MY STORY IS DONE; BUT THIS STORY WILL GO ON, AS LONG AS GRASS GROWS AND RIVERS RUN."

Massimo De Vita's first three "Ice Sword Saga" stories were anthologized as a trilogy in 1989. For that book, De Vita drew this special concluding panel to follow "The Prince of Mists Strikes Back." Notably, the hand-of-the-artist motif would play an important role in De Vita's eventual fourth "Ice Sword" story — which begins on the next page!

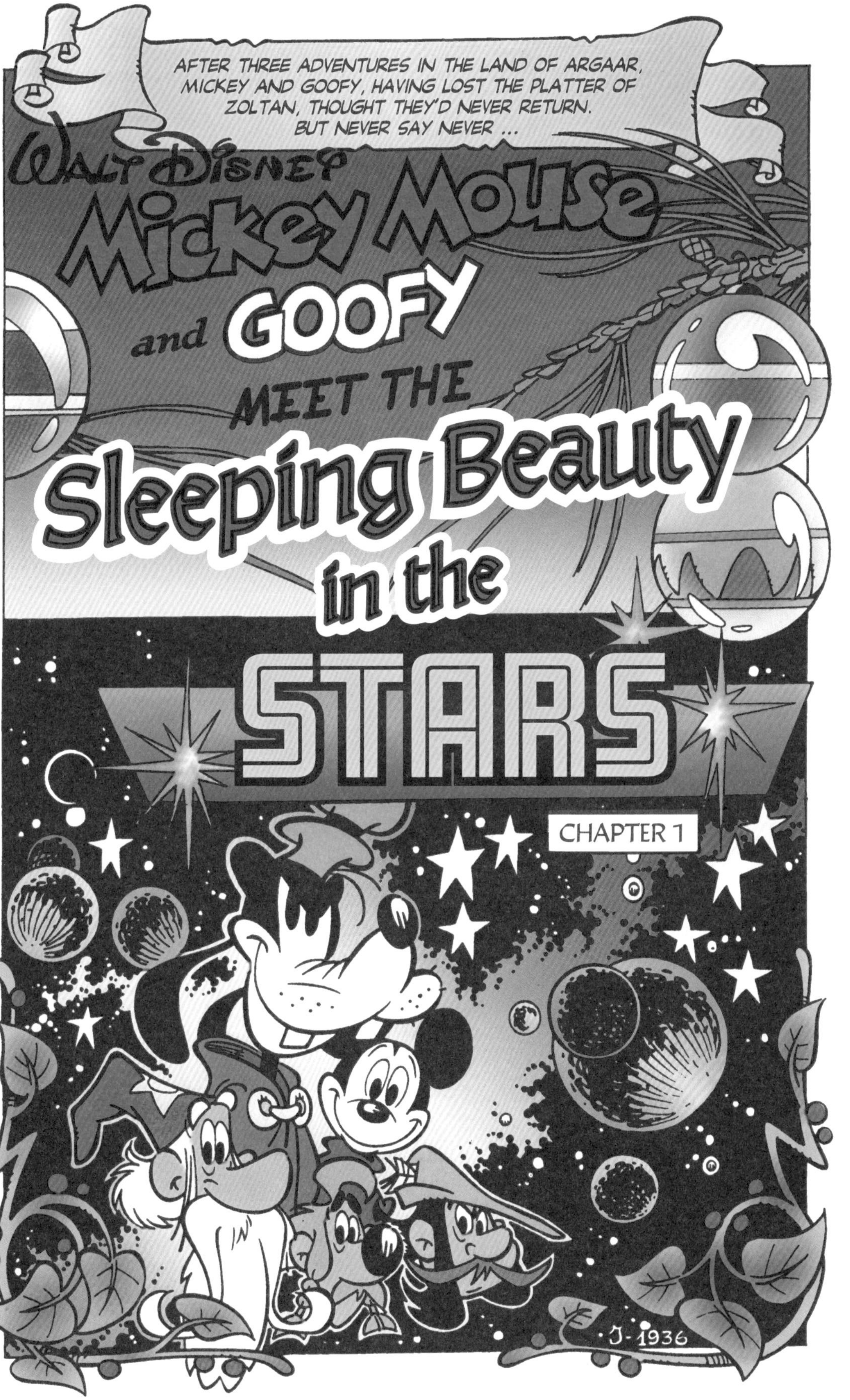
AFTER THREE ADVENTURES IN THE LAND OF ARGAAR, MICKEY AND GOOFY, HAVING LOST THE PLATTER OF ZOLTAN, THOUGHT THEY'D NEVER RETURN. BUT NEVER SAY NEVER ...
WALT DISNEY
Mickey Mouse
and GOOFY
MEET THE
Sleeping Beauty in the STARS
CHAPTER 1
J-1936

STORY AND ART BY MASSIMO DE VITA • TRANSLATION AND DIALOGUE BY JOE TORCIVIA • LETTERING BY PAUL BARESH AND CHRISTINA HWANG • COLORING BY DISNEY ITALIA • EDITING BY DAVID GERSTEIN AND J. MICHAEL CATRON

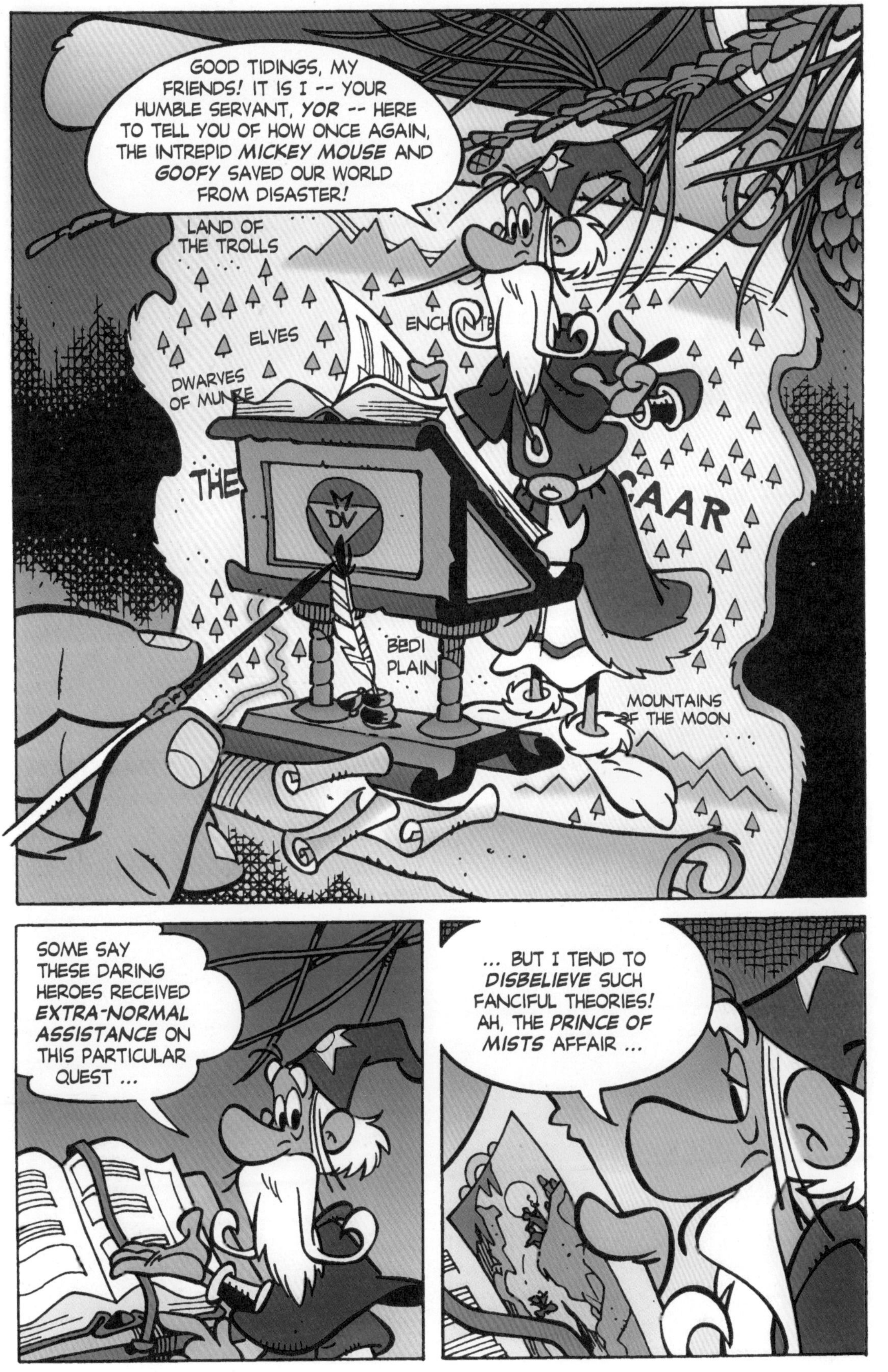
GOOD TIDINGS, MY FRIENDS! IT IS I -- YOUR HUMBLE SERVANT, YOR -- HERE TO TELL YOU OF HOW ONCE AGAIN, THE INTREPID MICKEY MOUSE AND GOOFY SAVED OUR WORLD FROM DISASTER!
LAND OF THE TROLLS
ELVES
DWARVES
BEDI PLAIN
MOUNTAINS OF THE MOON
SOME SAY THESE DARING HEROES RECEIVED EXTRA-NORMAL ASSISTANCE ON THIS PARTICULAR QUEST ...
... BUT I TEND TO DISBELIEVE SUCH FANCIFUL THEORIES! AH, THE PRINCE OF MISTS AFFAIR ...

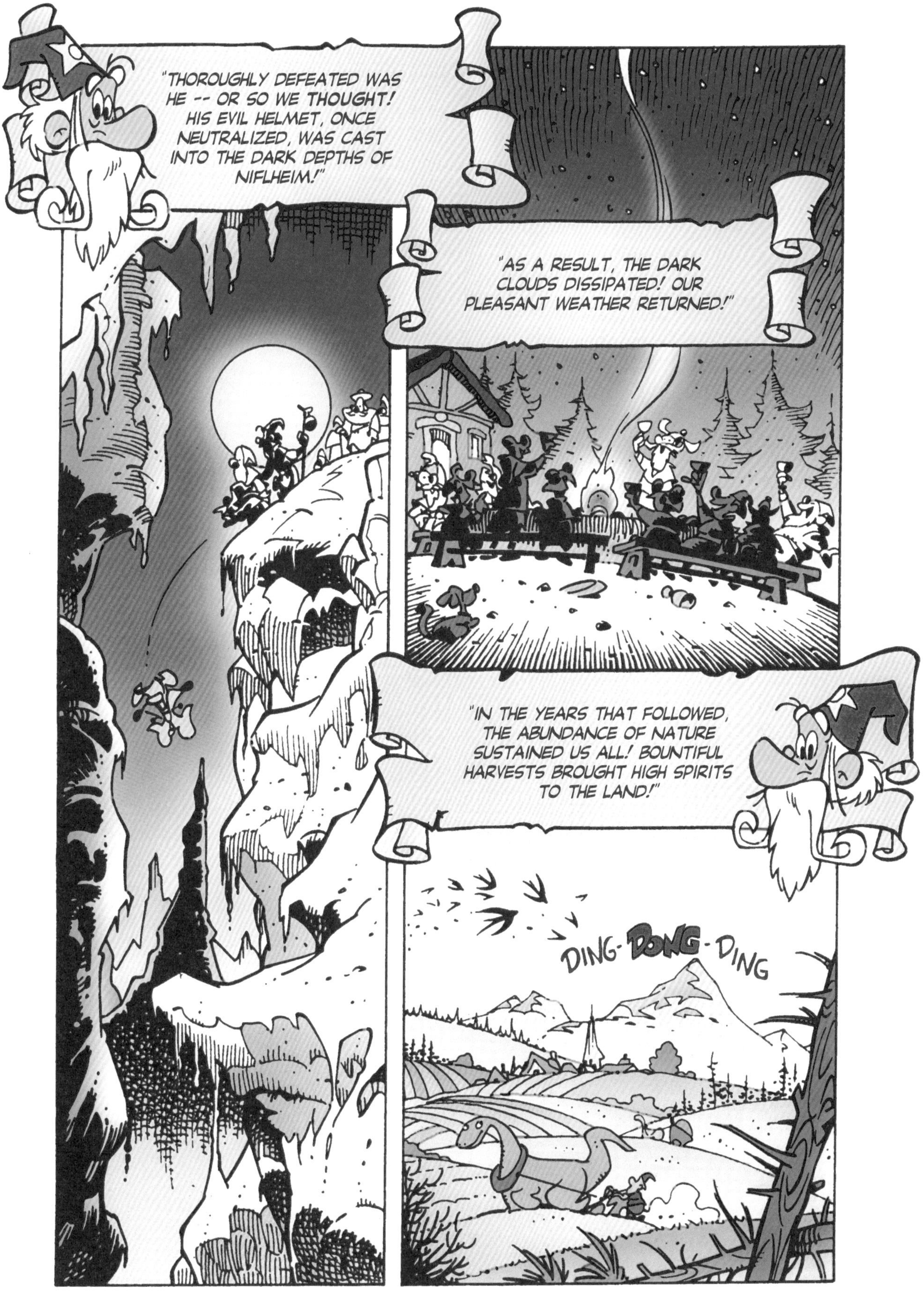
"THOROUGHLY DEFEATED WAS HE -- OR SO WE THOUGHT! HIS EVIL HELMET, ONCE NEUTRALIZED, WAS CAST INTO THE DARK DEPTHS OF NIFLHEIM!"
"AS A RESULT, THE DARK CLOUDS DISSIPATED! OUR PLEASANT WEATHER RETURNED!"
"IN THE YEARS THAT FOLLOWED, THE ABUNDANCE OF NATURE SUSTAINED US ALL! BOUNTIFUL HARVESTS BROUGHT HIGH SPIRITS TO THE LAND!"
DING-DONG-DING

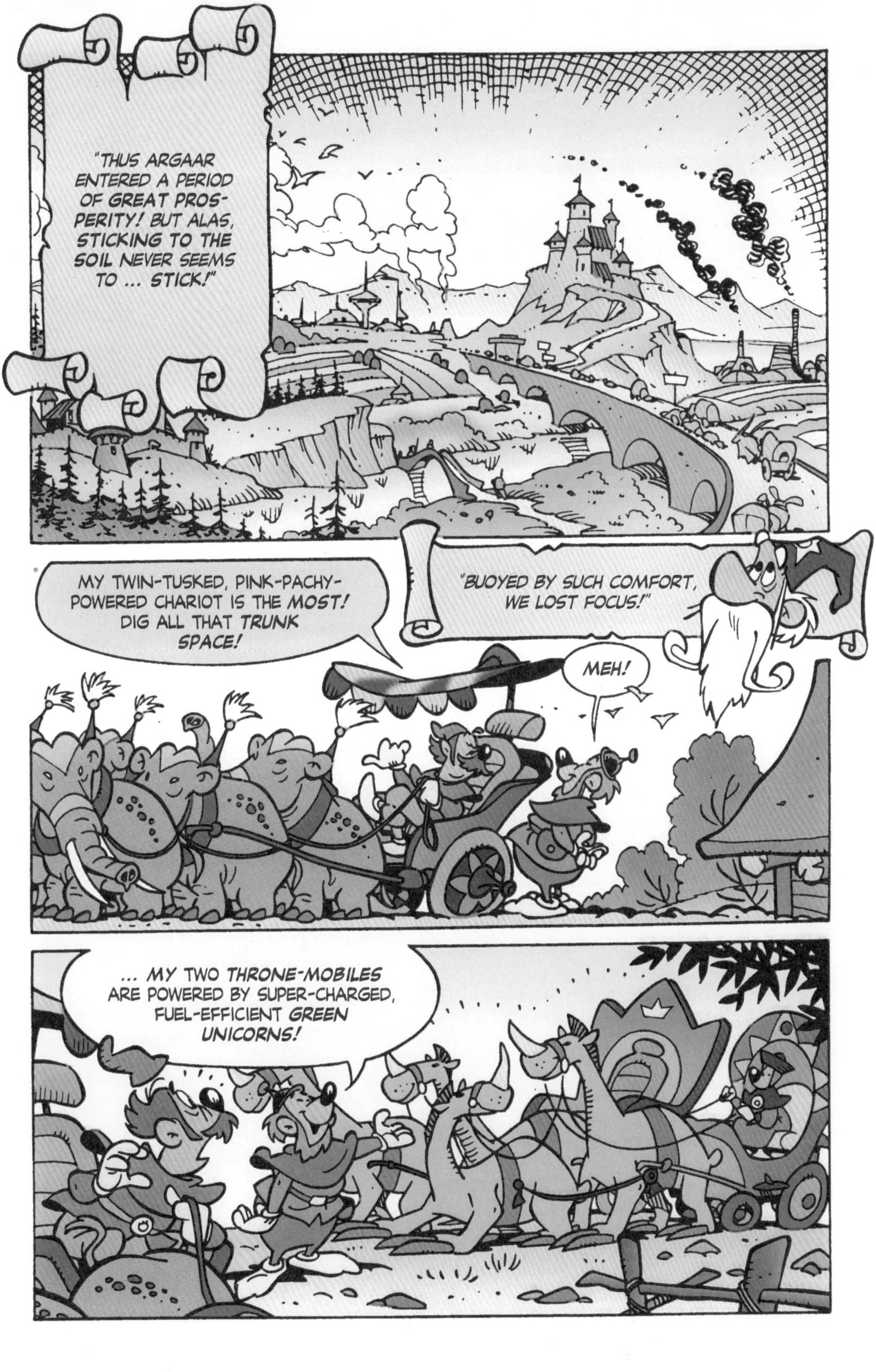
"THUS ARGAAR ENTERED A PERIOD OF GREAT PROSPERITY! BUT ALAS, STICKING TO THE SOIL NEVER SEEMS TO ... STICK!"
MY TWIN-TUSKED, PINK-PACHY-POWERED CHARIOT IS THE MOST! DIG ALL THAT TRUNK SPACE!
"BUOYED BY SUCH COMFORT, WE LOST FOCUS!"
MEH!
... MY TWO THRONE-MOBILES ARE POWERED BY SUPER-CHARGED, FUEL-EFFICIENT GREEN UNICORNS!

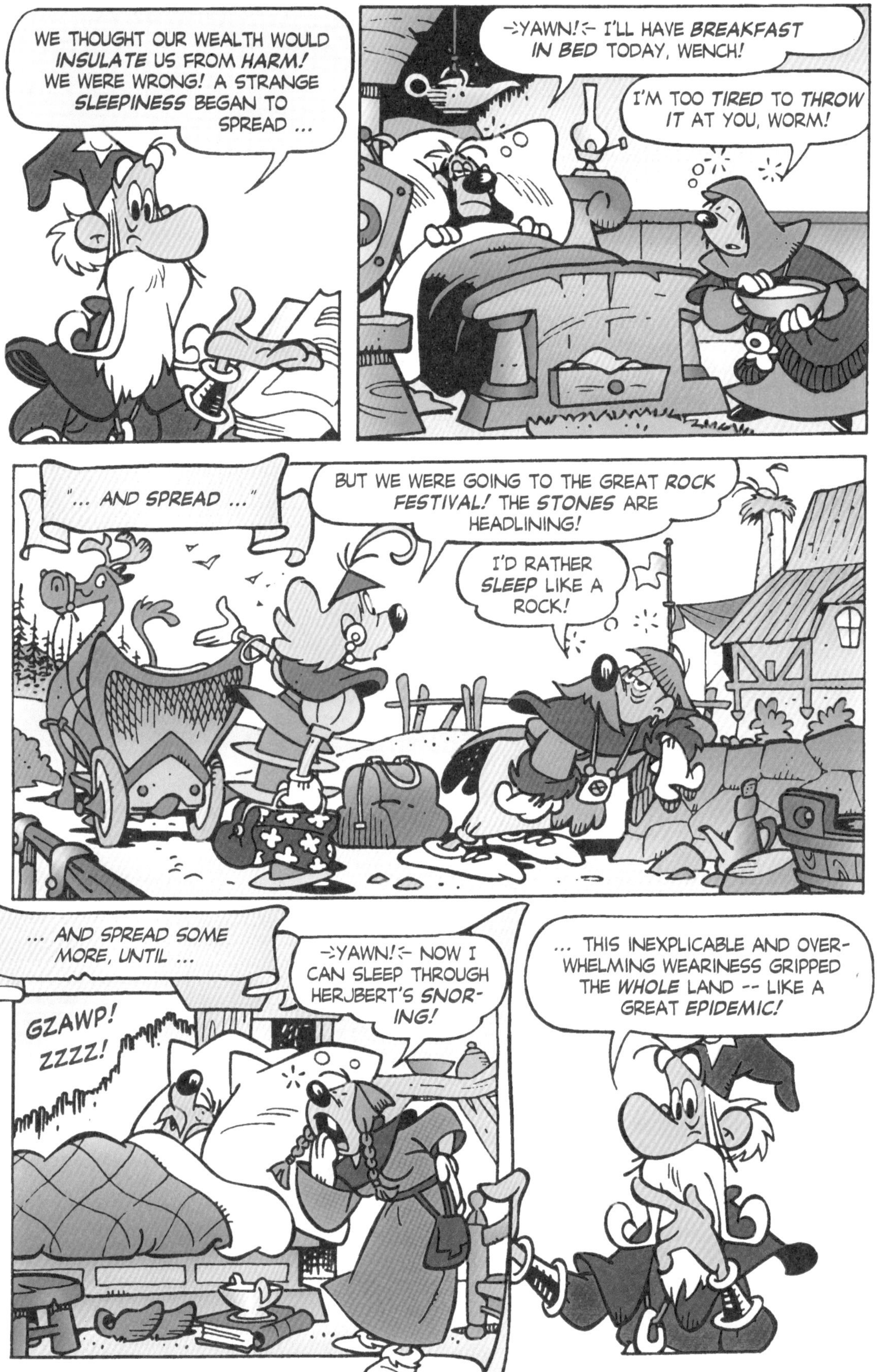
WE THOUGHT OUR WEALTH WOULD INSULATE US FROM HARM! WE WERE WRONG! A STRANGE SLEEPINESS BEGAN TO SPREAD ...
–YAWN!– I'LL HAVE BREAKFAST IN BED TODAY, WENCH!
I'M TOO TIRED TO THROW IT AT YOU, WORM!
"... AND SPREAD ..."
BUT WE WERE GOING TO THE GREAT ROCK FESTIVAL! THE STONES ARE HEADLINING!
I'D RATHER SLEEP LIKE A ROCK!
... AND SPREAD SOME MORE, UNTIL ...
GZAWP! ZZZZ!
–YAWN!– NOW I CAN SLEEP THROUGH HERJBERT'S SNORING!
... THIS INEXPLICABLE AND OVERWHELMING WEARINESS GRIPPED THE WHOLE LAND -- LIKE A GREAT EPIDEMIC!

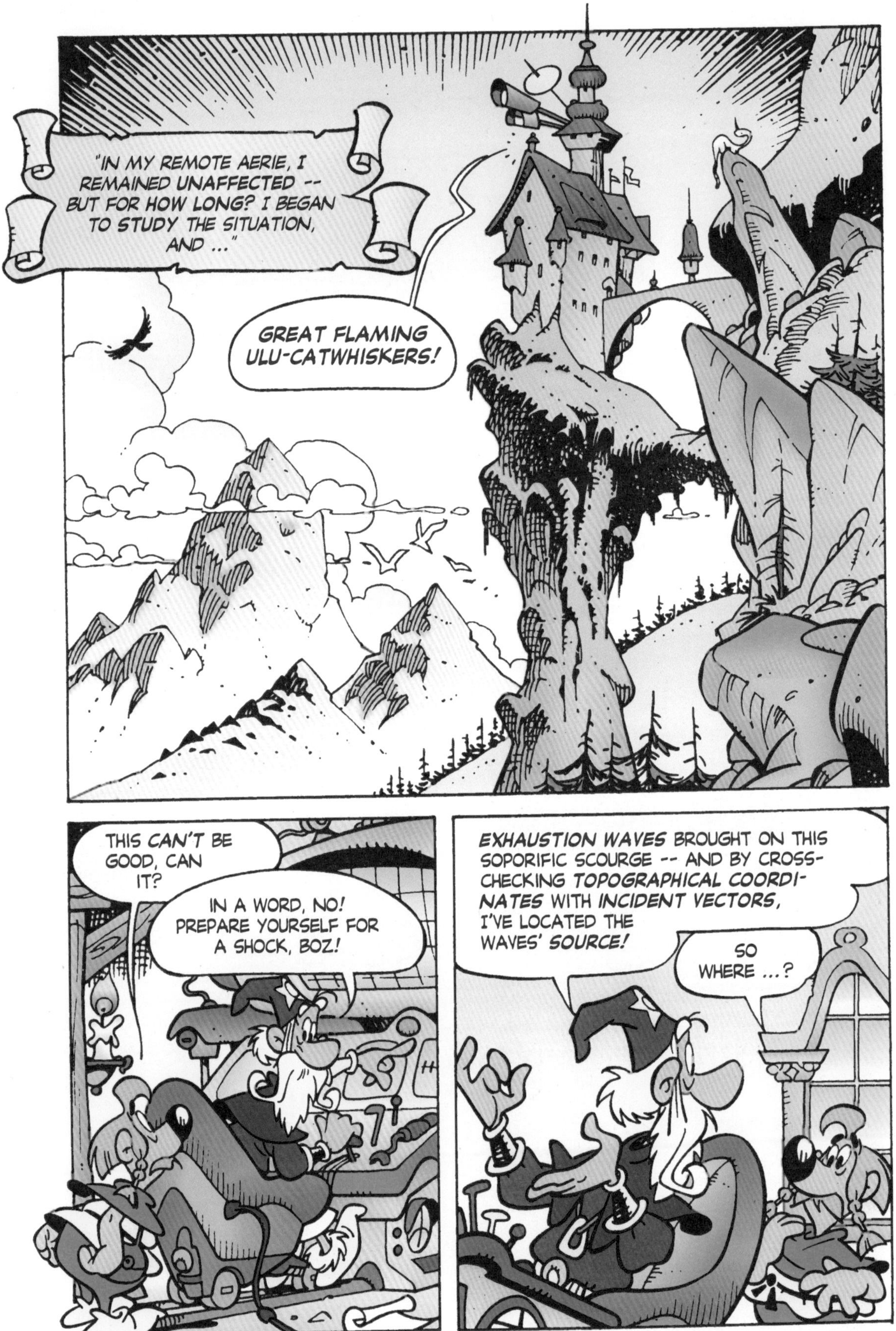
"IN MY REMOTE AERIE, I REMAINED UNAFFECTED -- BUT FOR HOW LONG? I BEGAN TO STUDY THE SITUATION, AND ..."
GREAT FLAMING ULU-CATWHISKERS!
THIS CAN'T BE GOOD, CAN IT?
IN A WORD, NO! PREPARE YOURSELF FOR A SHOCK, BOZ!
EXHAUSTION WAVES BROUGHT ON THIS SOPORIFIC SCOURGE -- AND BY CROSS-CHECKING TOPOGRAPHICAL COORDINATES WITH INCIDENT VECTORS, I'VE LOCATED THE WAVES' SOURCE!
SO WHERE ...?

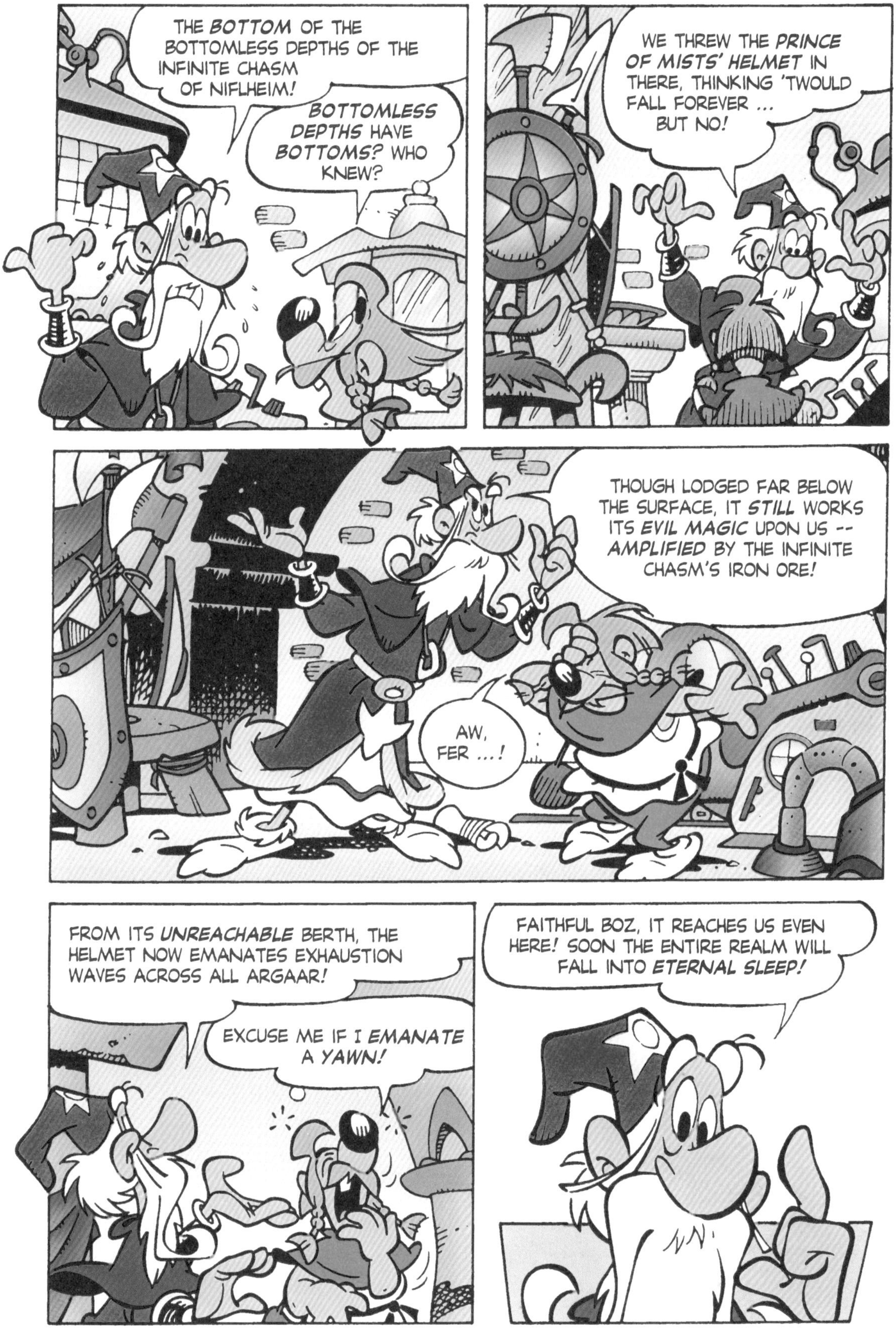

THE *BOTTOM* OF THE BOTTOMLESS DEPTHS OF THE INFINITE CHASM OF NIFLHEIM!
BOTTOMLESS DEPTHS HAVE *BOTTOMS?* WHO KNEW?
WE THREW THE *PRINCE OF MISTS' HELMET* IN THERE, THINKING 'TWOULD FALL FOREVER ... BUT NO!
THOUGH LODGED FAR BELOW THE SURFACE, IT *STILL* WORKS ITS *EVIL MAGIC* UPON US -- *AMPLIFIED* BY THE INFINITE CHASM'S IRON ORE!
AW, FER ...!
FROM ITS *UNREACHABLE* BERTH, THE HELMET NOW EMANATES EXHAUSTION WAVES ACROSS ALL ARGAAR!
EXCUSE ME IF I *EMANATE* A *YAWN!*
FAITHFUL BOZ, IT REACHES US EVEN HERE! SOON THE ENTIRE REALM WILL FALL INTO *ETERNAL SLEEP!*

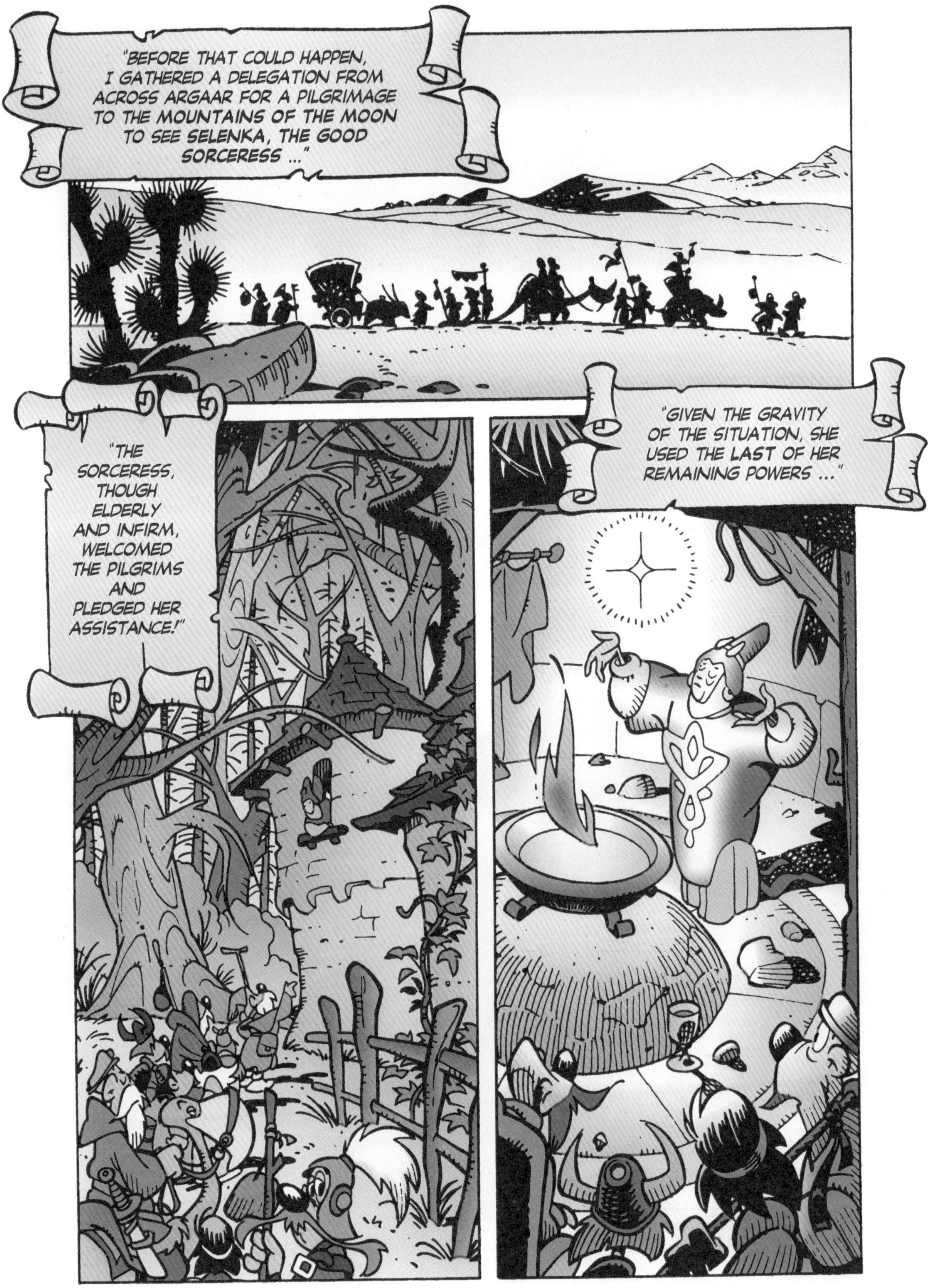
"BEFORE THAT COULD HAPPEN, I GATHERED A DELEGATION FROM ACROSS ARGAAR FOR A PILGRIMAGE TO THE MOUNTAINS OF THE MOON TO SEE SELENKA, THE GOOD SORCERESS ..."
"THE SORCERESS, THOUGH ELDERLY AND INFIRM, WELCOMED THE PILGRIMS AND PLEDGED HER ASSISTANCE!"
"GIVEN THE GRAVITY OF THE SITUATION, SHE USED THE LAST OF HER REMAINING POWERS ..."

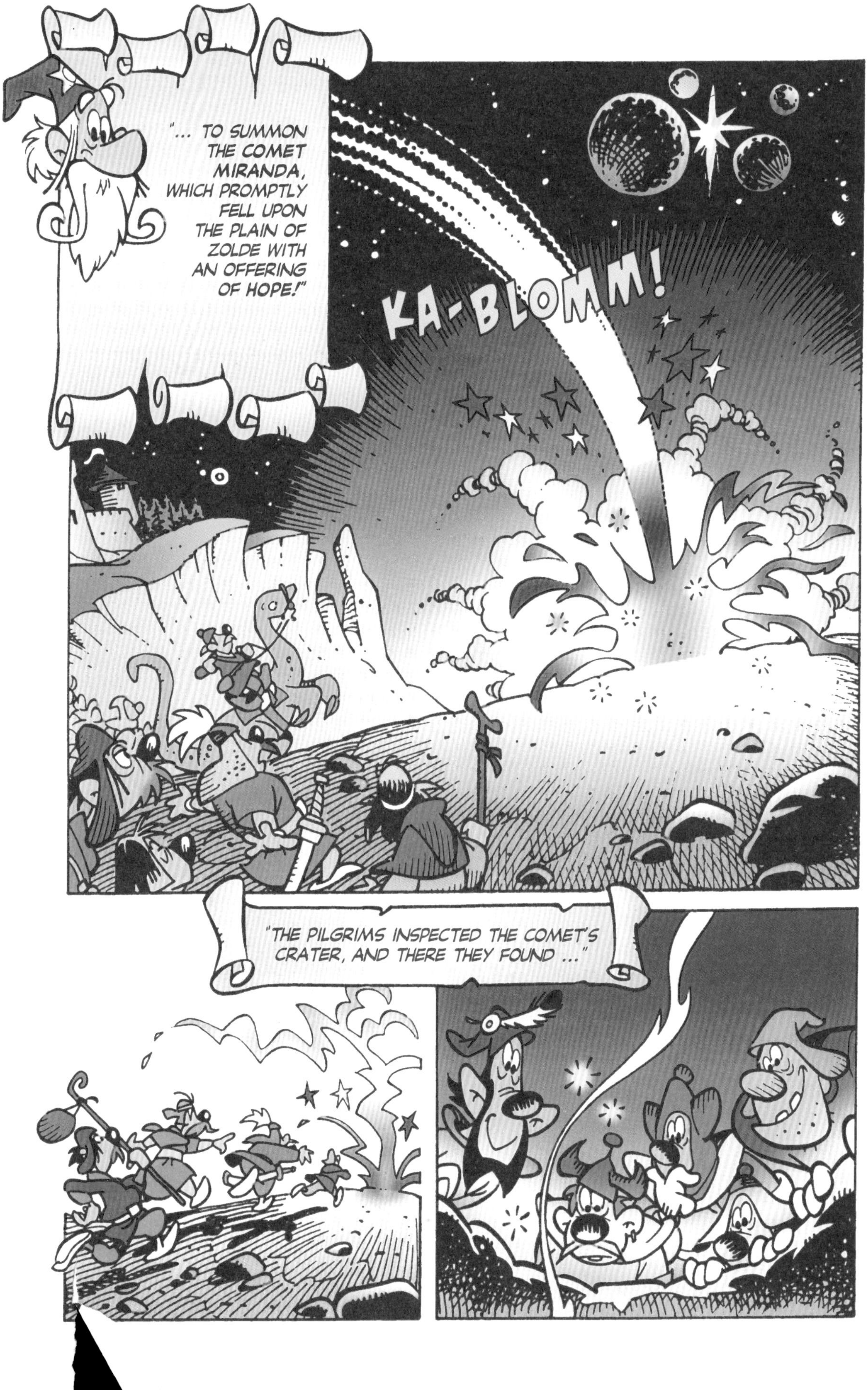
"... TO SUMMON THE COMET MIRANDA, WHICH PROMPTLY FELL UPON THE PLAIN OF ZOLDE WITH AN OFFERING OF HOPE!"
KA-BLOMM!
"THE PILGRIMS INSPECTED THE COMET'S CRATER, AND THERE THEY FOUND ..."

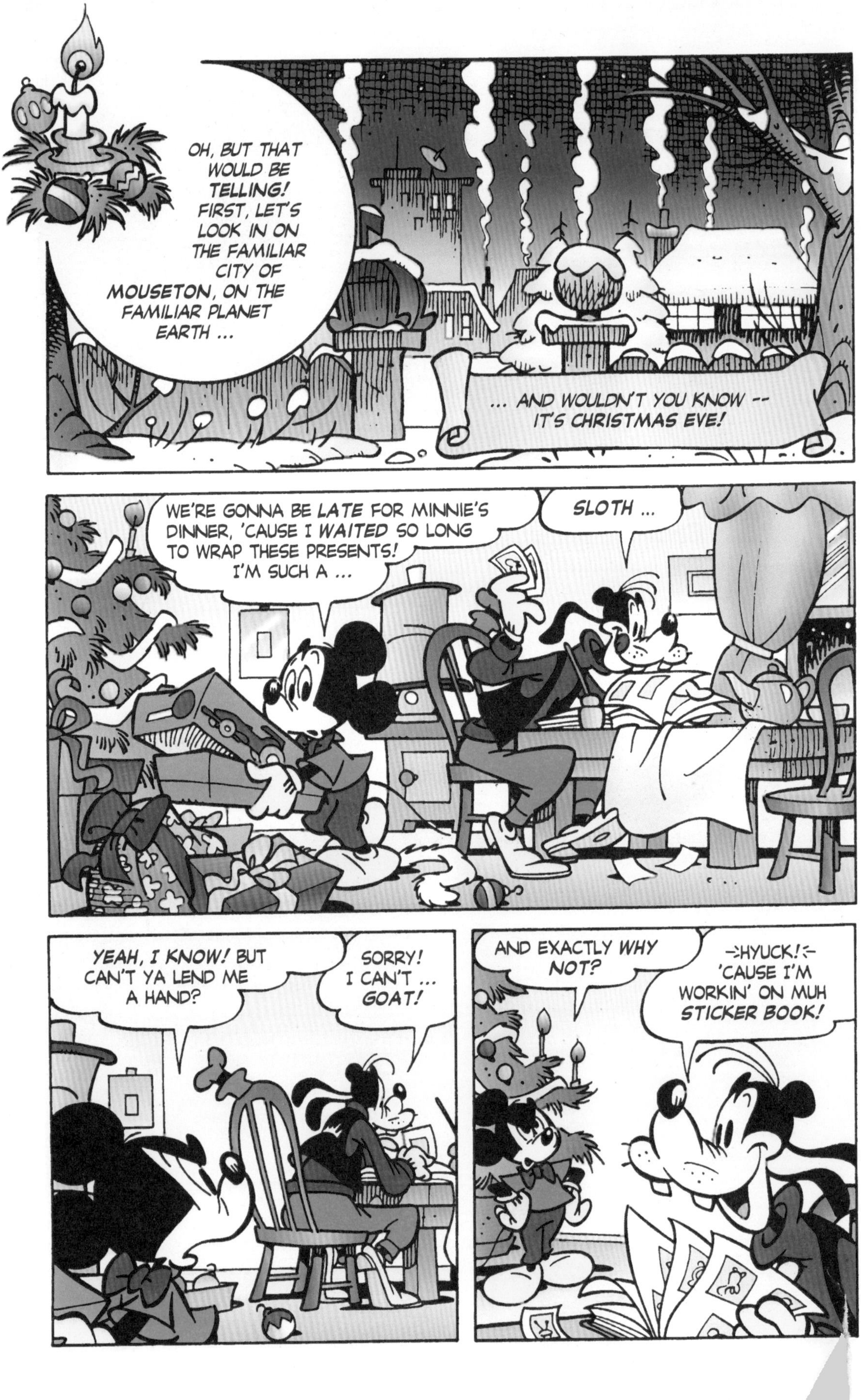
OH, BUT THAT WOULD BE TELLING! FIRST, LET'S LOOK IN ON THE FAMILIAR CITY OF MOUSETON, ON THE FAMILIAR PLANET EARTH ...
... AND WOULDN'T YOU KNOW -- IT'S CHRISTMAS EVE!
WE'RE GONNA BE LATE FOR MINNIE'S DINNER, 'CAUSE I WAITED SO LONG TO WRAP THESE PRESENTS! I'M SUCH A ...
SLOTH ...
YEAH, I KNOW! BUT CAN'T YA LEND ME A HAND?
SORRY! I CAN'T ... GOAT!
AND EXACTLY WHY NOT?
HYUCK! 'CAUSE I'M WORKIN' ON MUH STICKER BOOK!

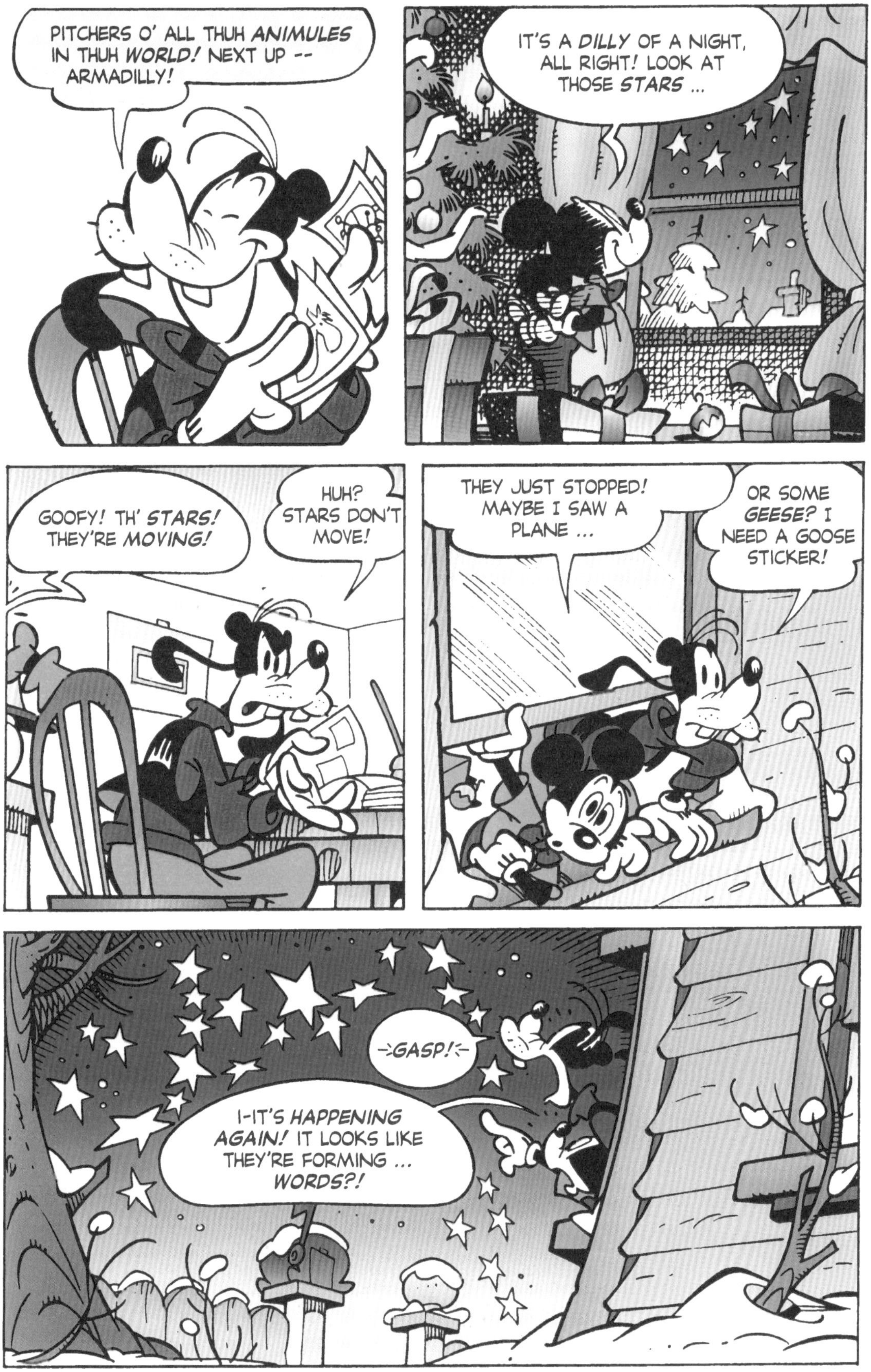
PITCHERS O' ALL THUH ANIMULES IN THUH WORLD! NEXT UP -- ARMADILLY!
IT'S A DILLY OF A NIGHT, ALL RIGHT! LOOK AT THOSE STARS ...
GOOFY! TH' STARS! THEY'RE MOVING!
HUH? STARS DON'T MOVE!
THEY JUST STOPPED! MAYBE I SAW A PLANE ...
OR SOME GEESE? I NEED A GOOSE STICKER!
-GASP!-
I-IT'S HAPPENING AGAIN! IT LOOKS LIKE THEY'RE FORMING ... WORDS?!

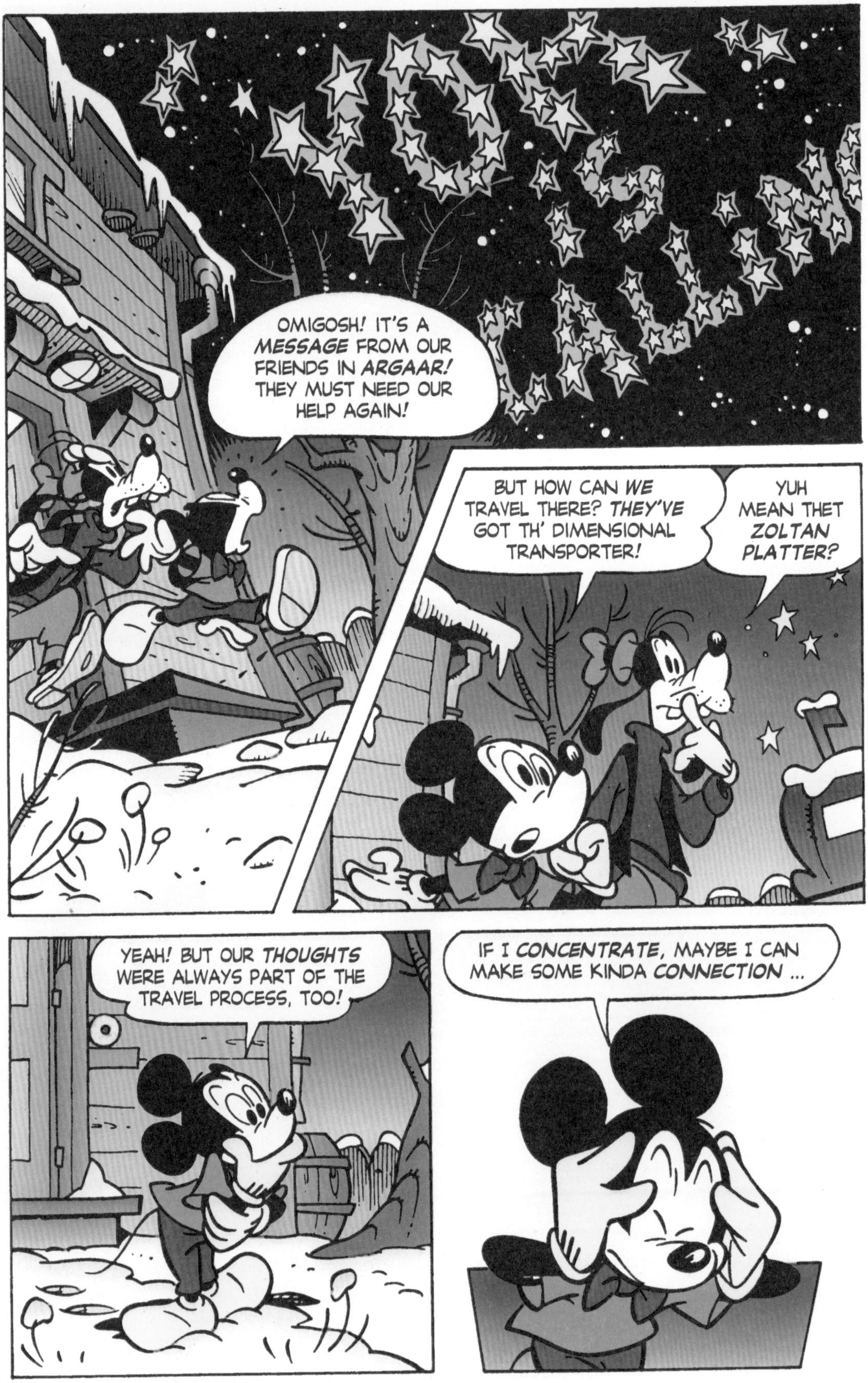
OMIGOSH! IT'S A MESSAGE FROM OUR FRIENDS IN ARGAAR! THEY MUST NEED OUR HELP AGAIN!
BUT HOW CAN WE TRAVEL THERE? THEY'VE GOT TH' DIMENSIONAL TRANSPORTER!
YUH MEAN THET ZOLTAN PLATTER?
YEAH! BUT OUR THOUGHTS WERE ALWAYS PART OF THE TRAVEL PROCESS, TOO!
IF I CONCENTRATE, MAYBE I CAN MAKE SOME KINDA CONNECTION ...

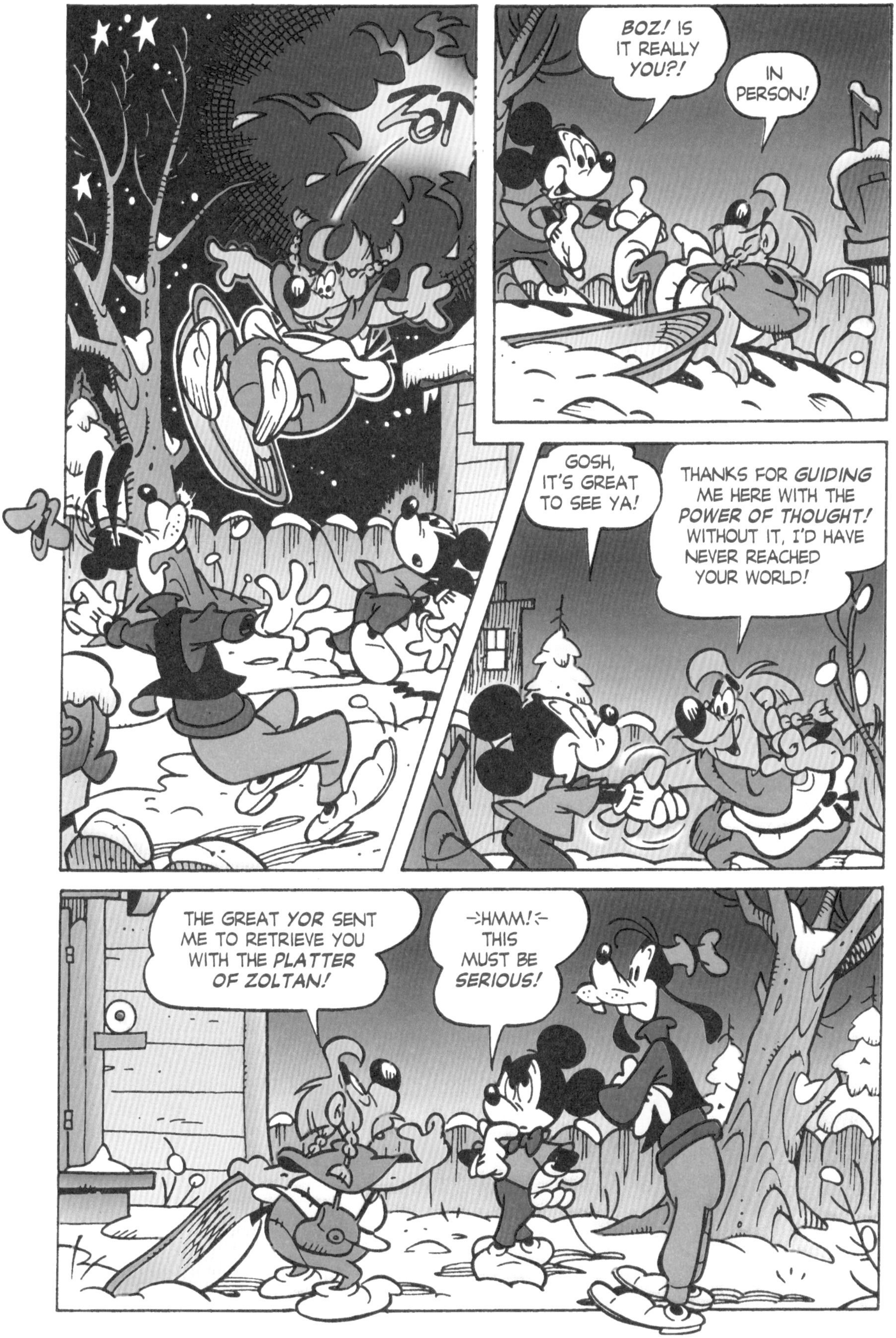
ZOT
BOZ! IS IT REALLY YOU?!
IN PERSON!
GOSH, IT'S GREAT TO SEE YA!
THANKS FOR GUIDING ME HERE WITH THE POWER OF THOUGHT! WITHOUT IT, I'D HAVE NEVER REACHED YOUR WORLD!
THE GREAT YOR SENT ME TO RETRIEVE YOU WITH THE PLATTER OF ZOLTAN!
HMM! THIS MUST BE SERIOUS!

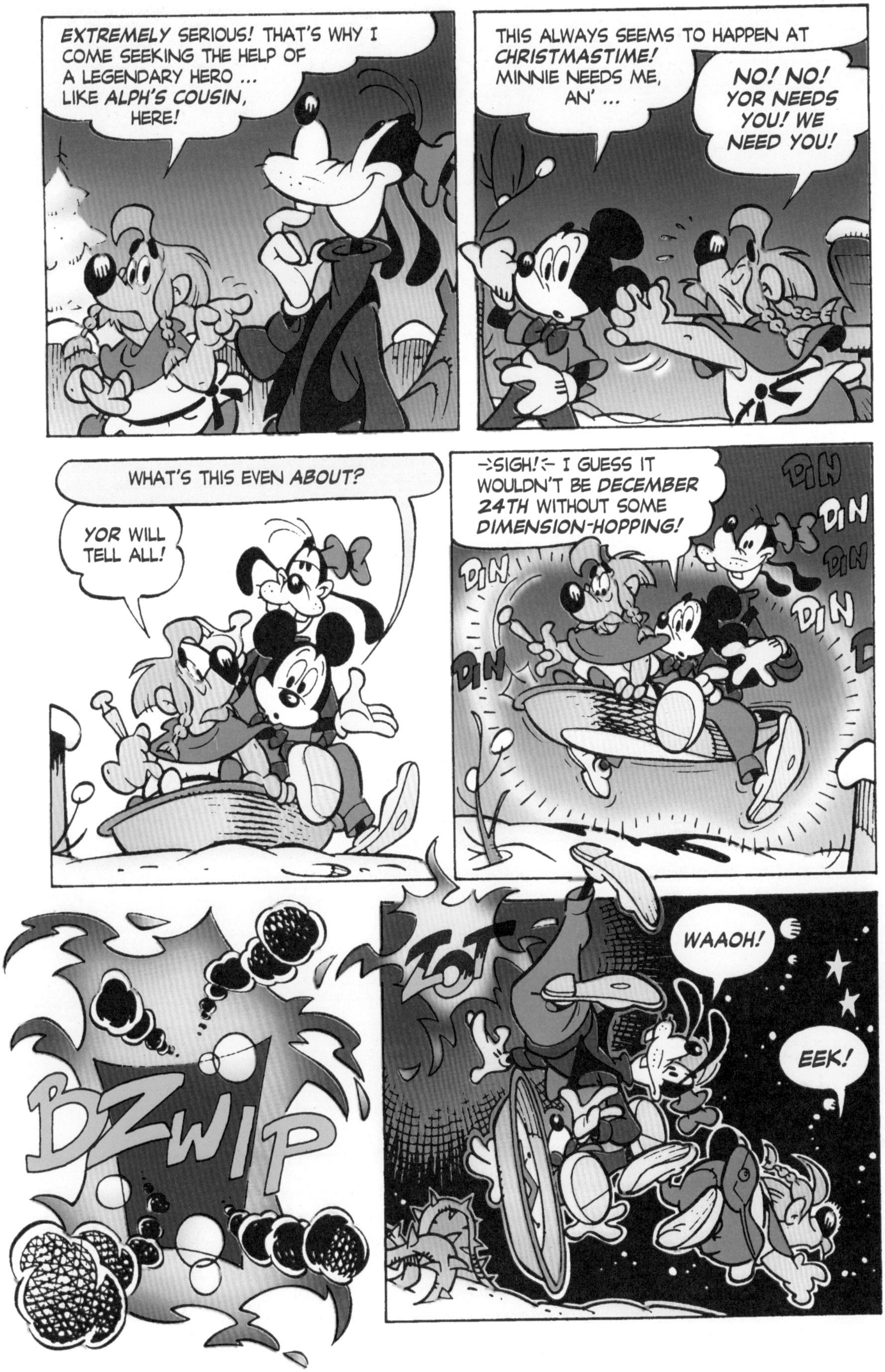
EXTREMELY SERIOUS! THAT'S WHY I COME SEEKING THE HELP OF A LEGENDARY HERO ... LIKE ALPH'S COUSIN, HERE!
THIS ALWAYS SEEMS TO HAPPEN AT CHRISTMASTIME! MINNIE NEEDS ME, AN' ...
NO! NO! YOR NEEDS YOU! WE NEED YOU!
WHAT'S THIS EVEN ABOUT?
YOR WILL TELL ALL!
SIGH! I GUESS IT WOULDN'T BE DECEMBER 24TH WITHOUT SOME DIMENSION-HOPPING!
DIN DIN DIN DIN DIN DIN
BZWIP
ZOT
WAAOH!
EEK!

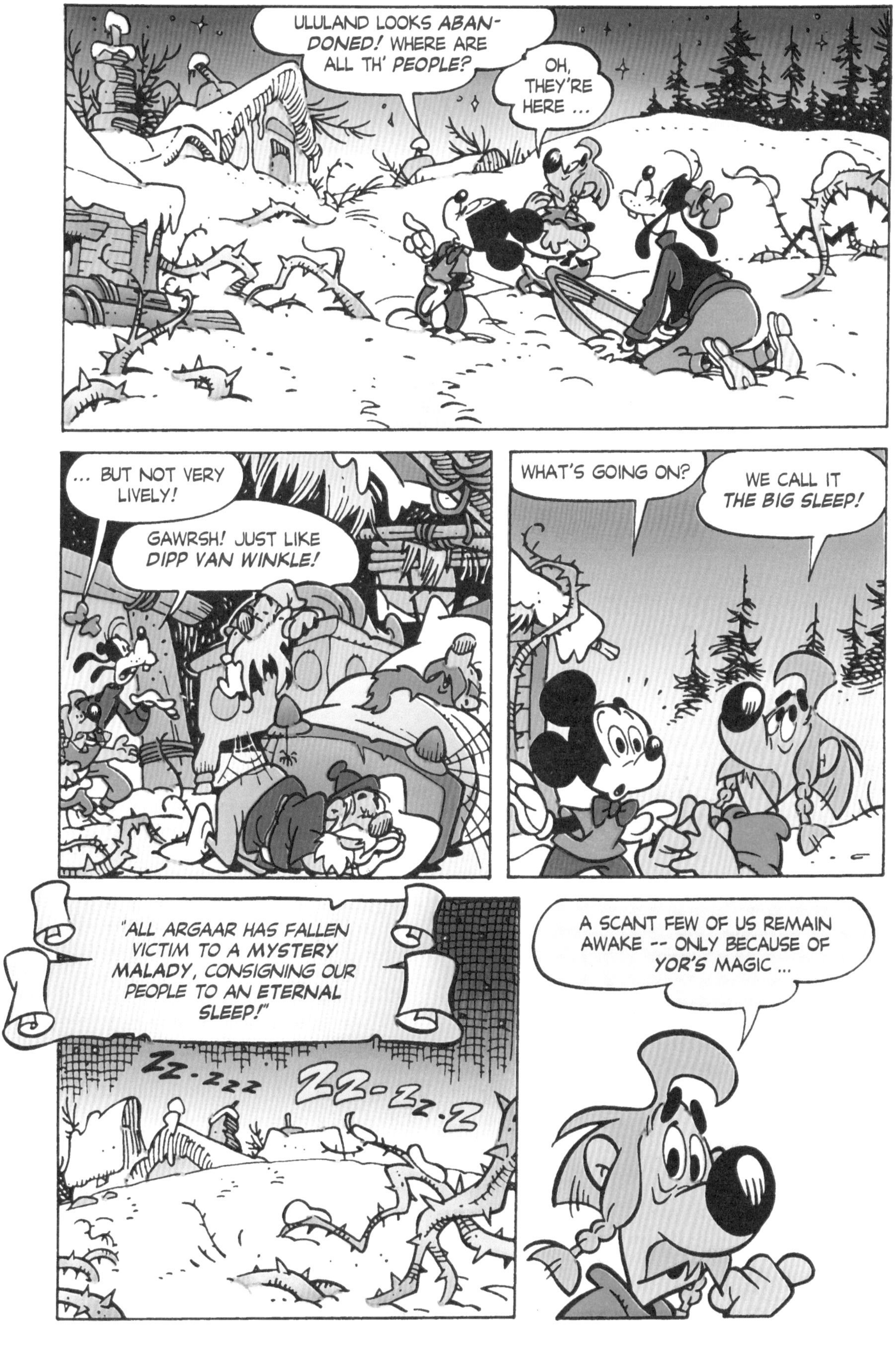

ULULAND LOOKS ABAN-DONED! WHERE ARE ALL TH' PEOPLE?
OH, THEY'RE HERE ...
... BUT NOT VERY LIVELY!
GAWRSH! JUST LIKE DIPP VAN WINKLE!
WHAT'S GOING ON?
WE CALL IT THE BIG SLEEP!
"ALL ARGAAR HAS FALLEN VICTIM TO A MYSTERY MALADY, CONSIGNING OUR PEOPLE TO AN ETERNAL SLEEP!"
ZZ-ZZZ
ZZ-ZZ-Z
A SCANT FEW OF US REMAIN AWAKE -- ONLY BECAUSE OF YOR'S MAGIC ...

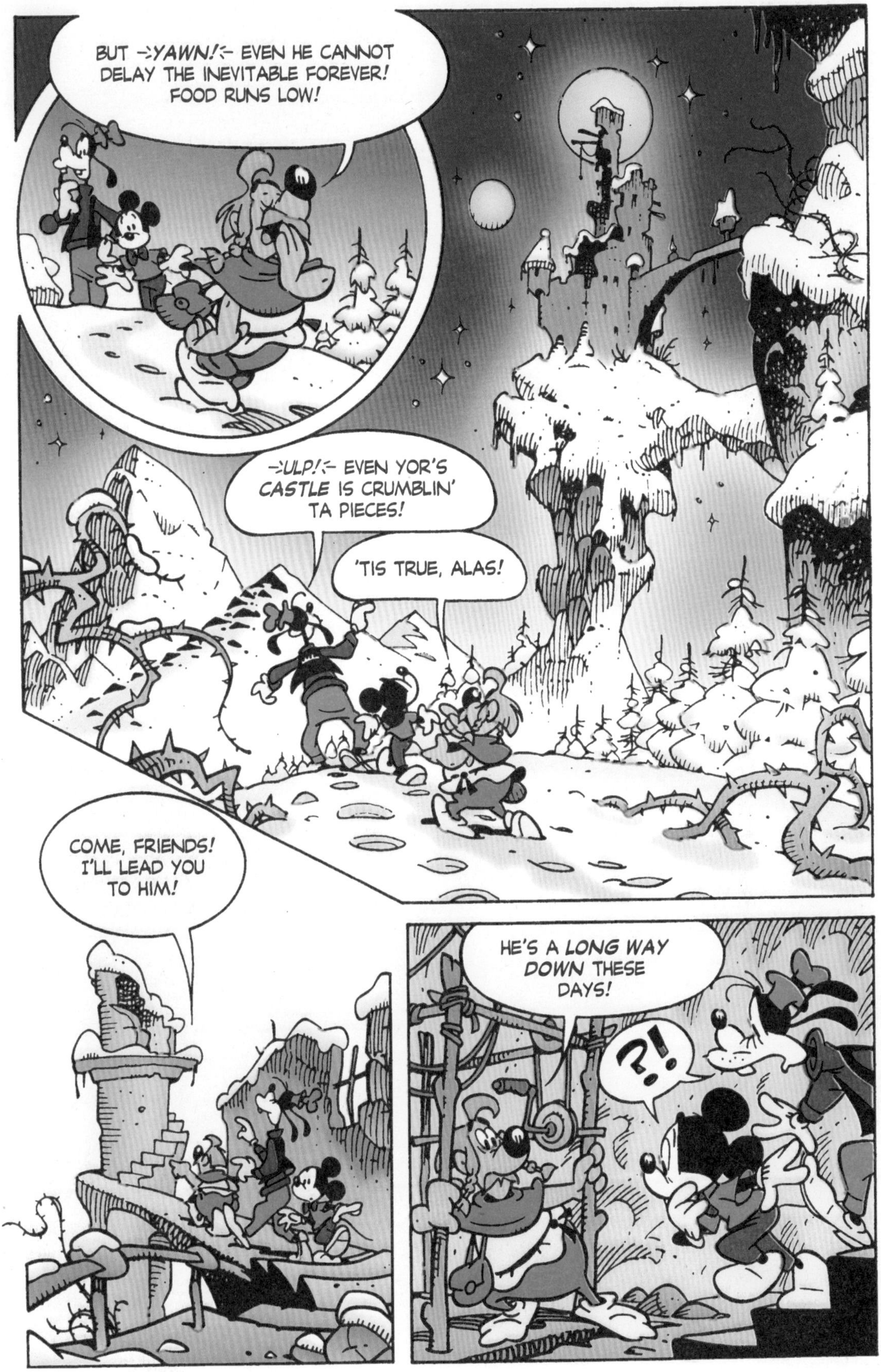
BUT ⇥YAWN!⇤ EVEN HE CANNOT DELAY THE INEVITABLE FOREVER! FOOD RUNS LOW!
⇥ULP!⇤ EVEN YOR'S CASTLE IS CRUMBLIN' TA PIECES!
'TIS TRUE, ALAS!
COME, FRIENDS! I'LL LEAD YOU TO HIM!
HE'S A LONG WAY DOWN THESE DAYS!
?!

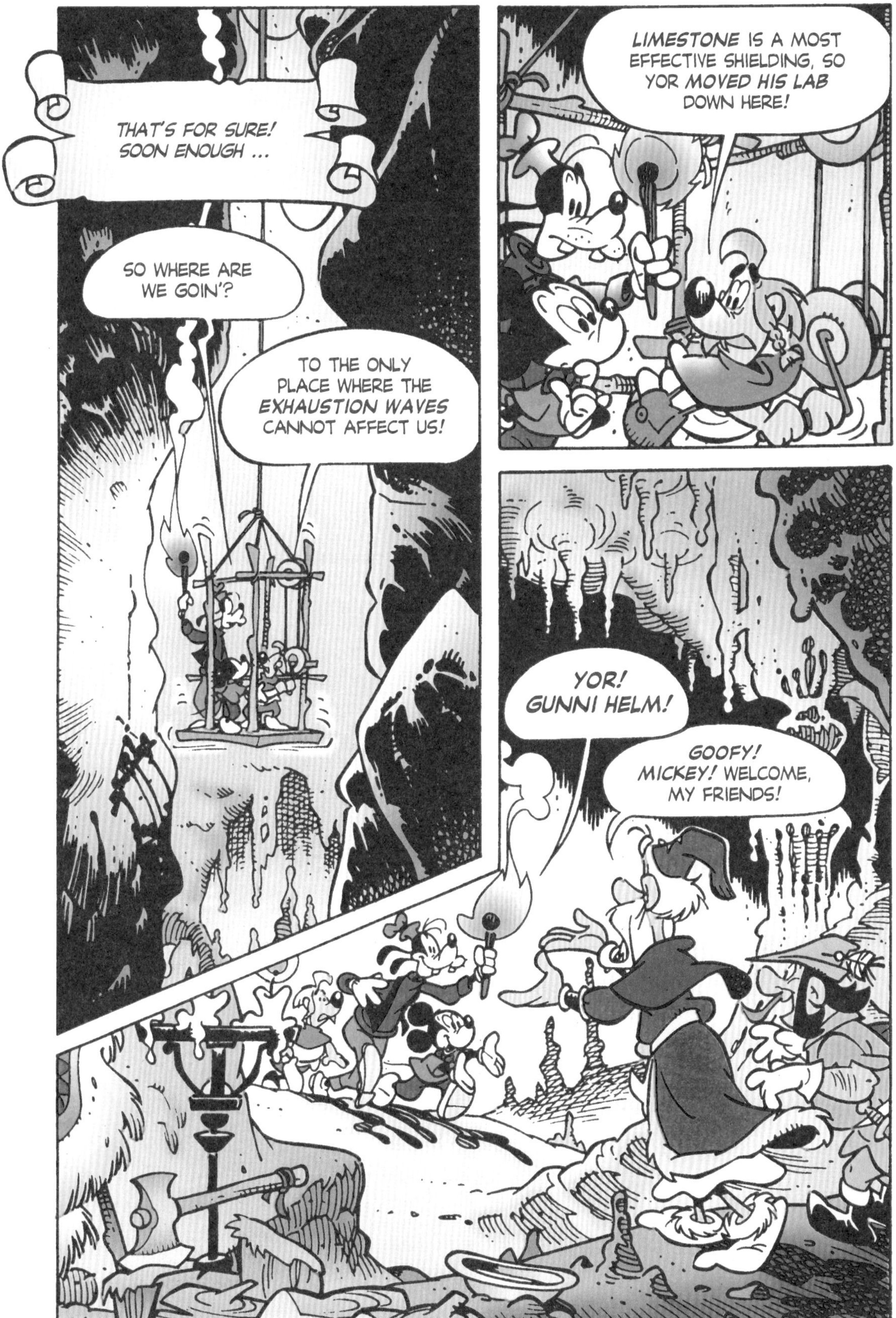
THAT'S FOR SURE! SOON ENOUGH ...
SO WHERE ARE WE GOIN'?
TO THE ONLY PLACE WHERE THE EXHAUSTION WAVES CANNOT AFFECT US!
LIMESTONE IS A MOST EFFECTIVE SHIELDING, SO YOR MOVED HIS LAB DOWN HERE!
YOR! GUNNI HELM!
GOOFY! MICKEY! WELCOME, MY FRIENDS!

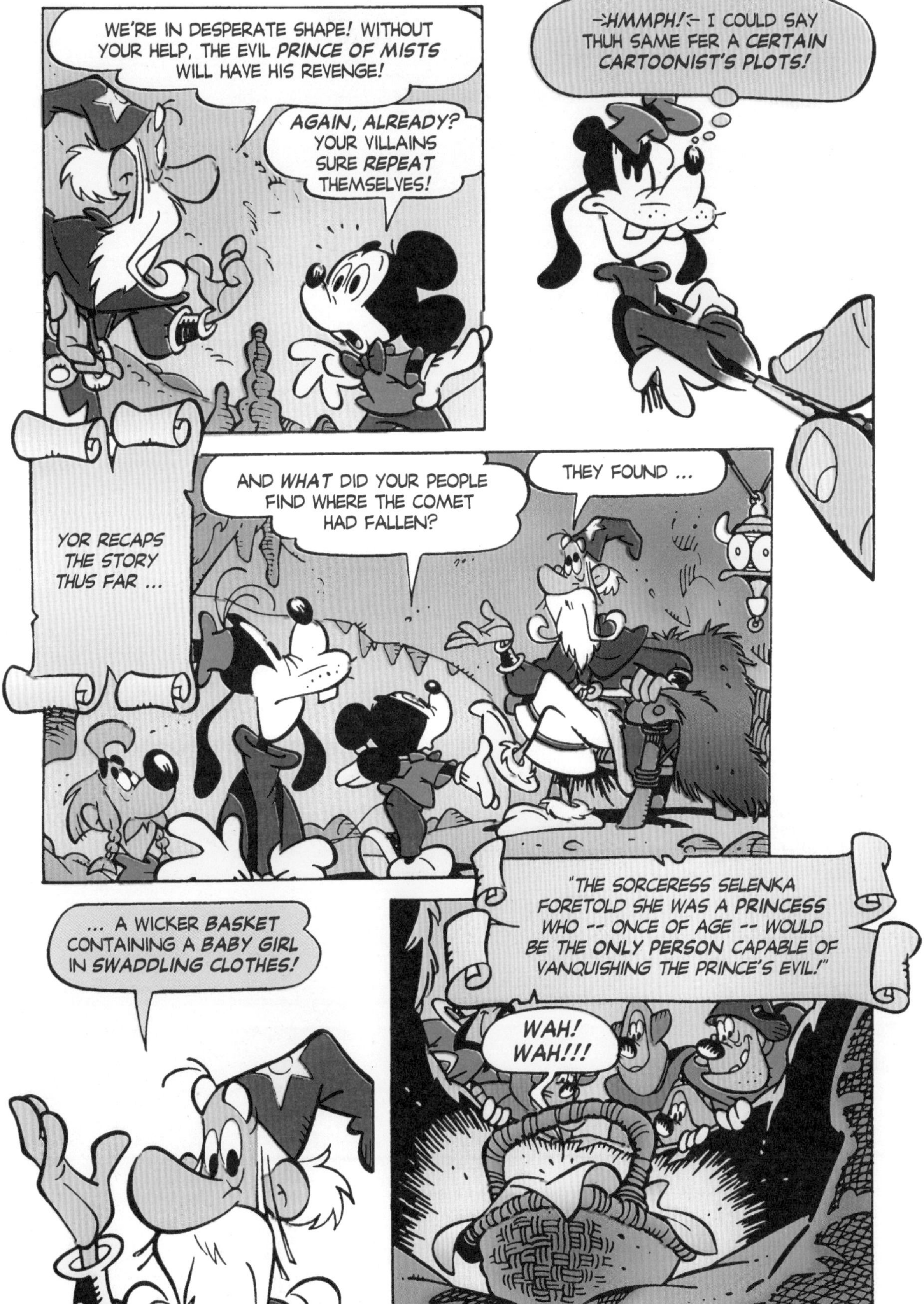
WE'RE IN DESPERATE SHAPE! WITHOUT YOUR HELP, THE EVIL PRINCE OF MISTS WILL HAVE HIS REVENGE!
AGAIN, ALREADY? YOUR VILLAINS SURE REPEAT THEMSELVES!
-HMMPH!- I COULD SAY THUH SAME FER A CERTAIN CARTOONIST'S PLOTS!
YOR RECAPS THE STORY THUS FAR ...
AND WHAT DID YOUR PEOPLE FIND WHERE THE COMET HAD FALLEN?
THEY FOUND ...
... A WICKER BASKET CONTAINING A BABY GIRL IN SWADDLING CLOTHES!
"THE SORCERESS SELENKA FORETOLD SHE WAS A PRINCESS WHO -- ONCE OF AGE -- WOULD BE THE ONLY PERSON CAPABLE OF VANQUISHING THE PRINCE'S EVIL!"
WAH! WAH!!!

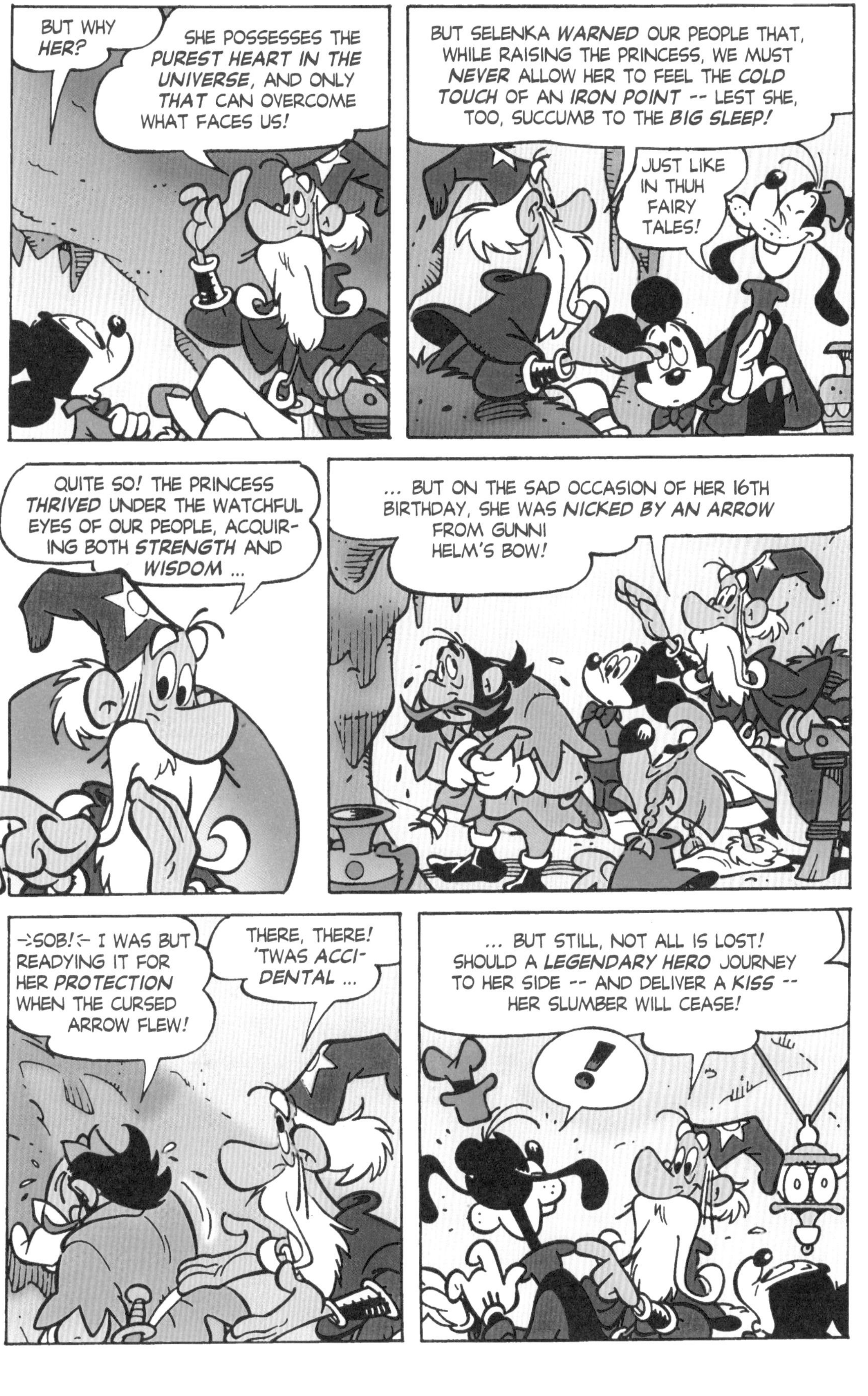
BUT WHY HER?
SHE POSSESSES THE PUREST HEART IN THE UNIVERSE, AND ONLY THAT CAN OVERCOME WHAT FACES US!
BUT SELENKA WARNED OUR PEOPLE THAT, WHILE RAISING THE PRINCESS, WE MUST NEVER ALLOW HER TO FEEL THE COLD TOUCH OF AN IRON POINT -- LEST SHE, TOO, SUCCUMB TO THE BIG SLEEP!
JUST LIKE IN THUH FAIRY TALES!
QUITE SO! THE PRINCESS THRIVED UNDER THE WATCHFUL EYES OF OUR PEOPLE, ACQUIRING BOTH STRENGTH AND WISDOM ...
... BUT ON THE SAD OCCASION OF HER 16TH BIRTHDAY, SHE WAS NICKED BY AN ARROW FROM GUNNI HELM'S BOW!
-SOB!- I WAS BUT READYING IT FOR HER PROTECTION WHEN THE CURSED ARROW FLEW!
THERE, THERE! 'TWAS ACCIDENTAL ...
... BUT STILL, NOT ALL IS LOST! SHOULD A LEGENDARY HERO JOURNEY TO HER SIDE -- AND DELIVER A KISS -- HER SLUMBER WILL CEASE!
!

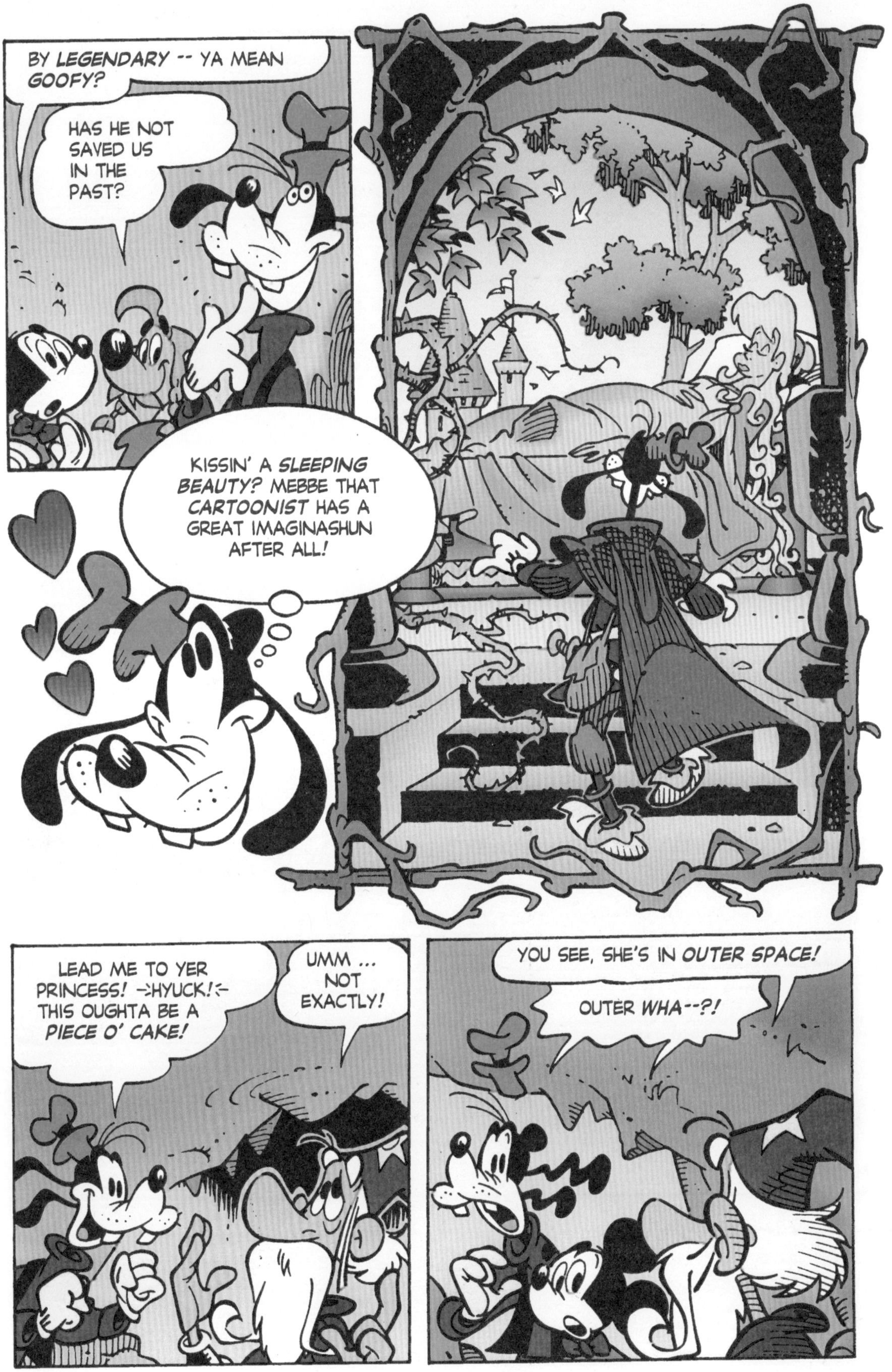
BY LEGENDARY -- YA MEAN GOOFY?
HAS HE NOT SAVED US IN THE PAST?
KISSIN' A SLEEPING BEAUTY? MEBBE THAT CARTOONIST HAS A GREAT IMAGINASHUN AFTER ALL!
LEAD ME TO YER PRINCESS! HYUCK! THIS OUGHTA BE A PIECE O' CAKE!
UMM ... NOT EXACTLY!
YOU SEE, SHE'S IN OUTER SPACE!
OUTER WHA--?!

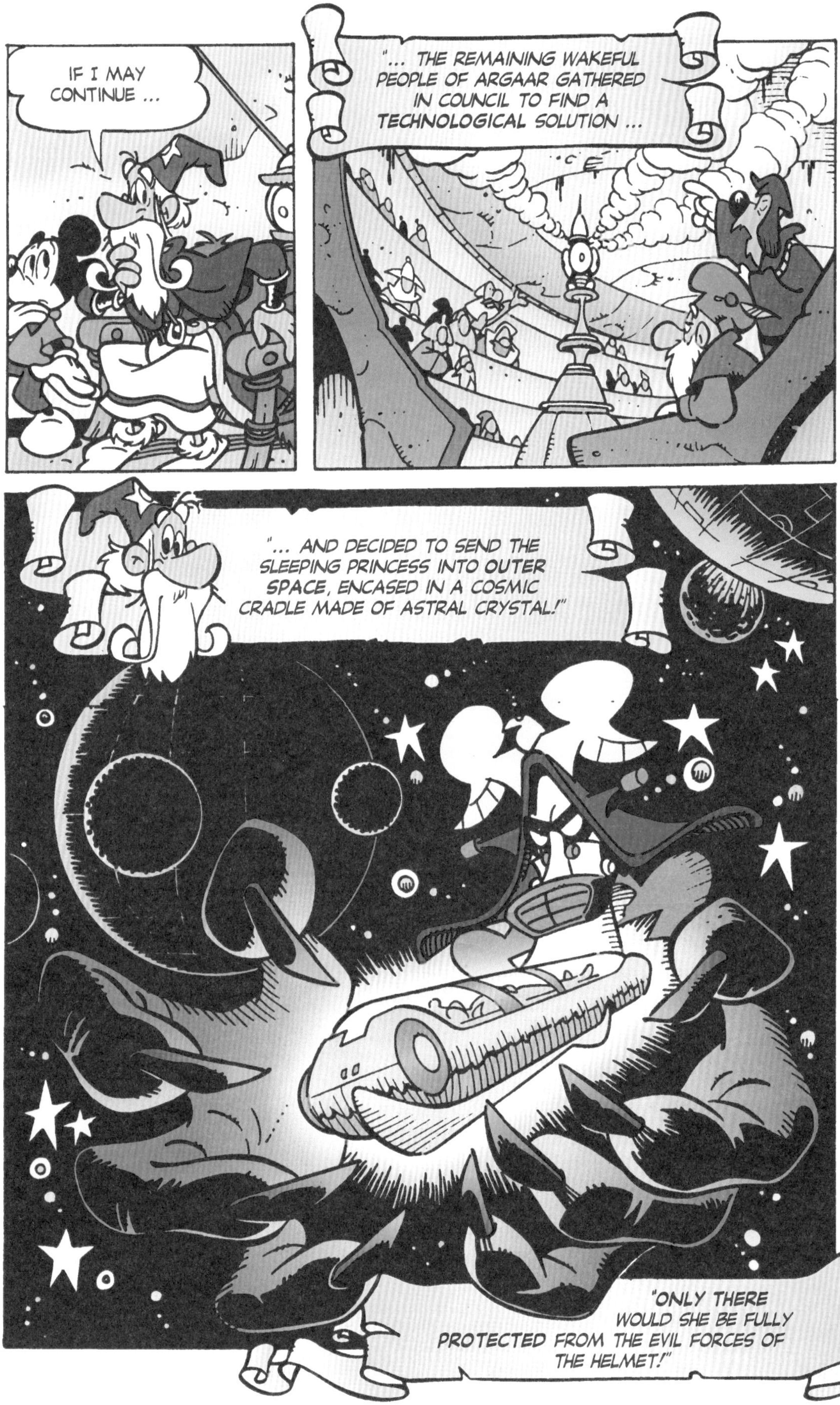
IF I MAY CONTINUE ...
"... THE REMAINING WAKEFUL PEOPLE OF ARGAAR GATHERED IN COUNCIL TO FIND A TECHNOLOGICAL SOLUTION ...
"... AND DECIDED TO SEND THE SLEEPING PRINCESS INTO OUTER SPACE, ENCASED IN A COSMIC CRADLE MADE OF ASTRAL CRYSTAL!"
"ONLY THERE WOULD SHE BE FULLY PROTECTED FROM THE EVIL FORCES OF THE HELMET!"

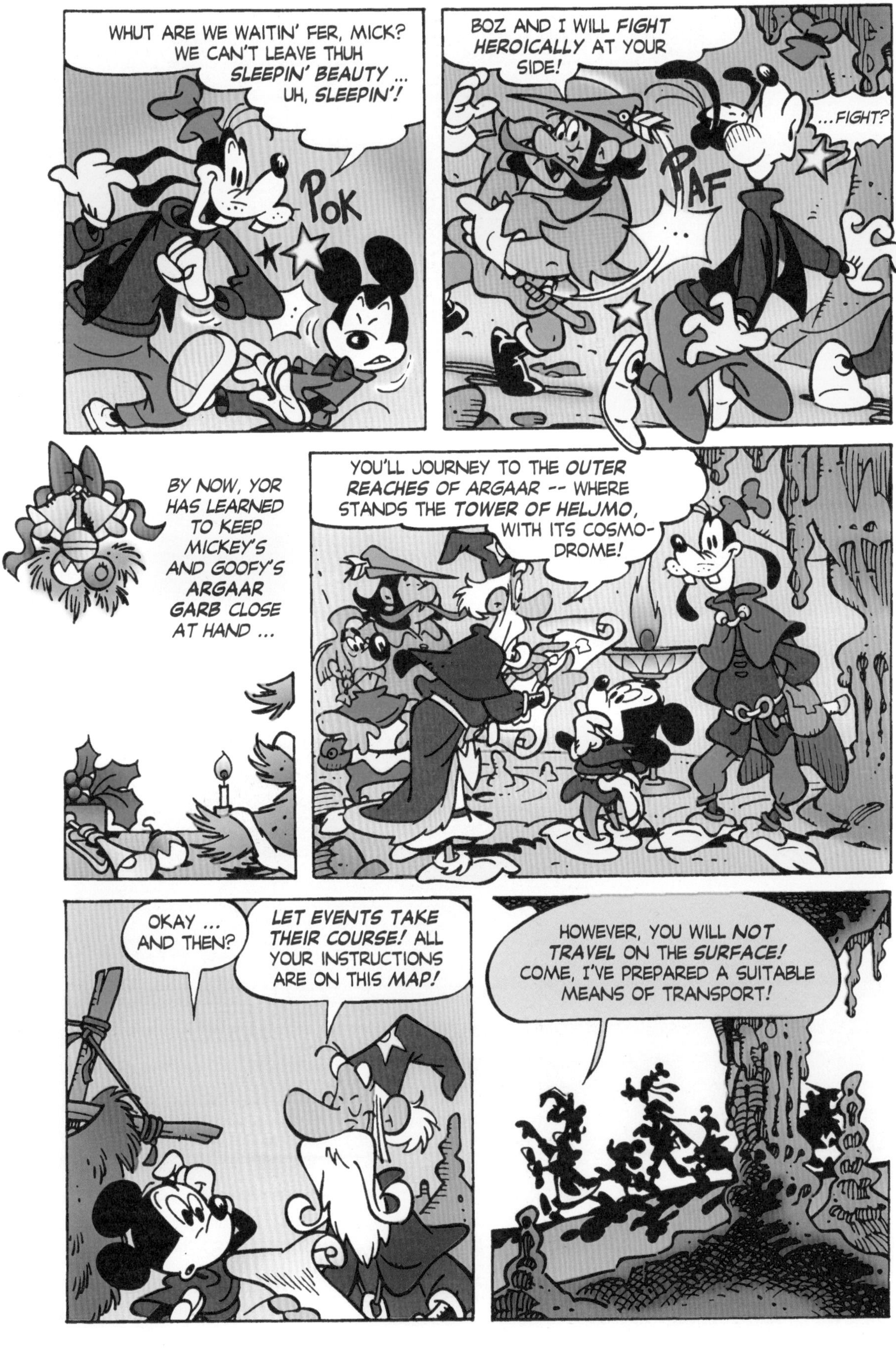
WHUT ARE WE WAITIN' FER, MICK? WE CAN'T LEAVE THUH SLEEPIN' BEAUTY ... UH, SLEEPIN'!
POK
BOZ AND I WILL FIGHT HEROICALLY AT YOUR SIDE!
PAF
...FIGHT?
BY NOW, YOR HAS LEARNED TO KEEP MICKEY'S AND GOOFY'S ARGAAR GARB CLOSE AT HAND ...
YOU'LL JOURNEY TO THE OUTER REACHES OF ARGAAR -- WHERE STANDS THE TOWER OF HELJMO, WITH ITS COSMO-DROME!
OKAY ... AND THEN?
LET EVENTS TAKE THEIR COURSE! ALL YOUR INSTRUCTIONS ARE ON THIS MAP!
HOWEVER, YOU WILL NOT TRAVEL ON THE SURFACE! COME, I'VE PREPARED A SUITABLE MEANS OF TRANSPORT!

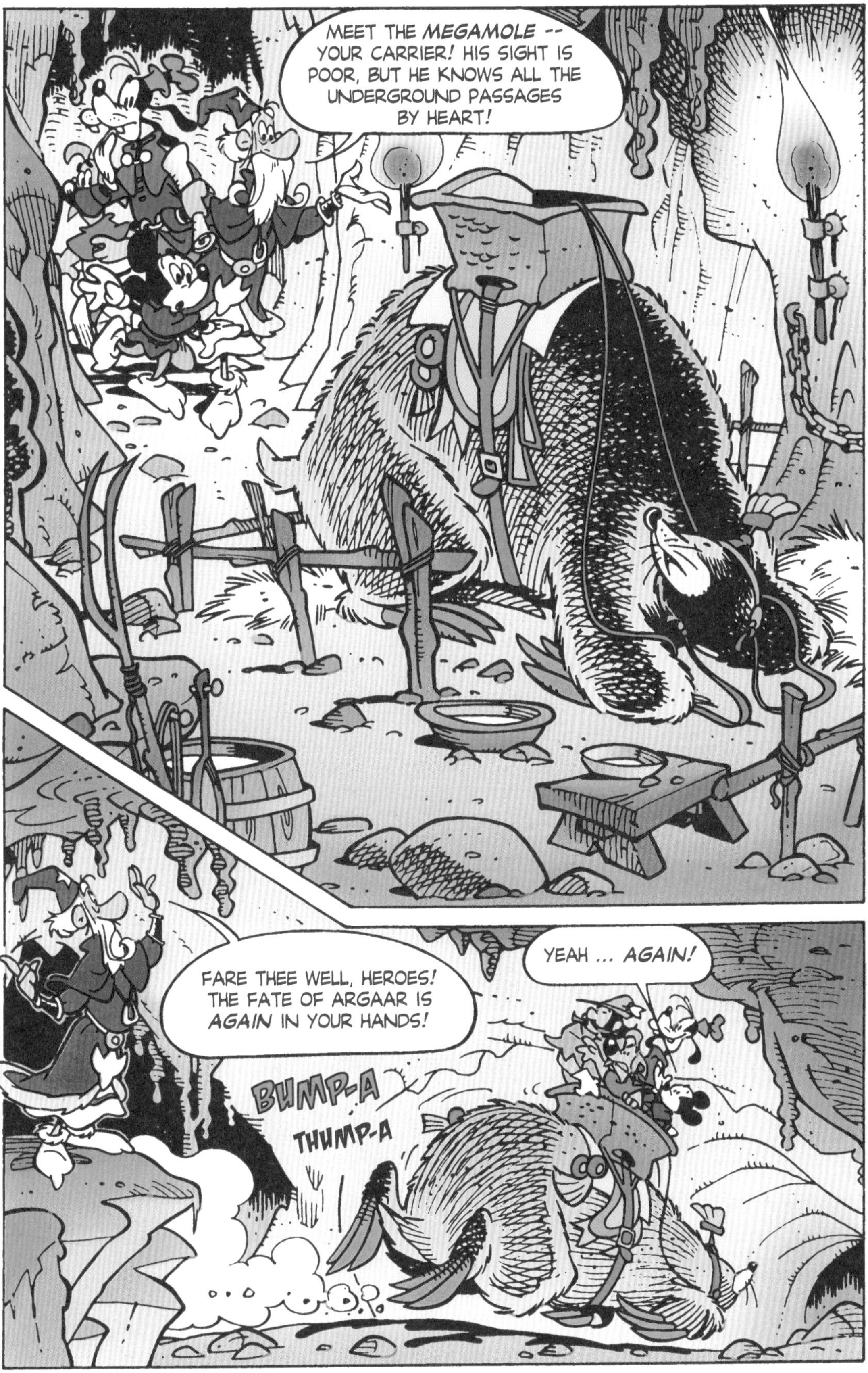

MEET THE MEGAMOLE -- YOUR CARRIER! HIS SIGHT IS POOR, BUT HE KNOWS ALL THE UNDERGROUND PASSAGES BY HEART!
FARE THEE WELL, HEROES! THE FATE OF ARGAAR IS AGAIN IN YOUR HANDS!
YEAH ... AGAIN!
BUMP-A
THUMP-A

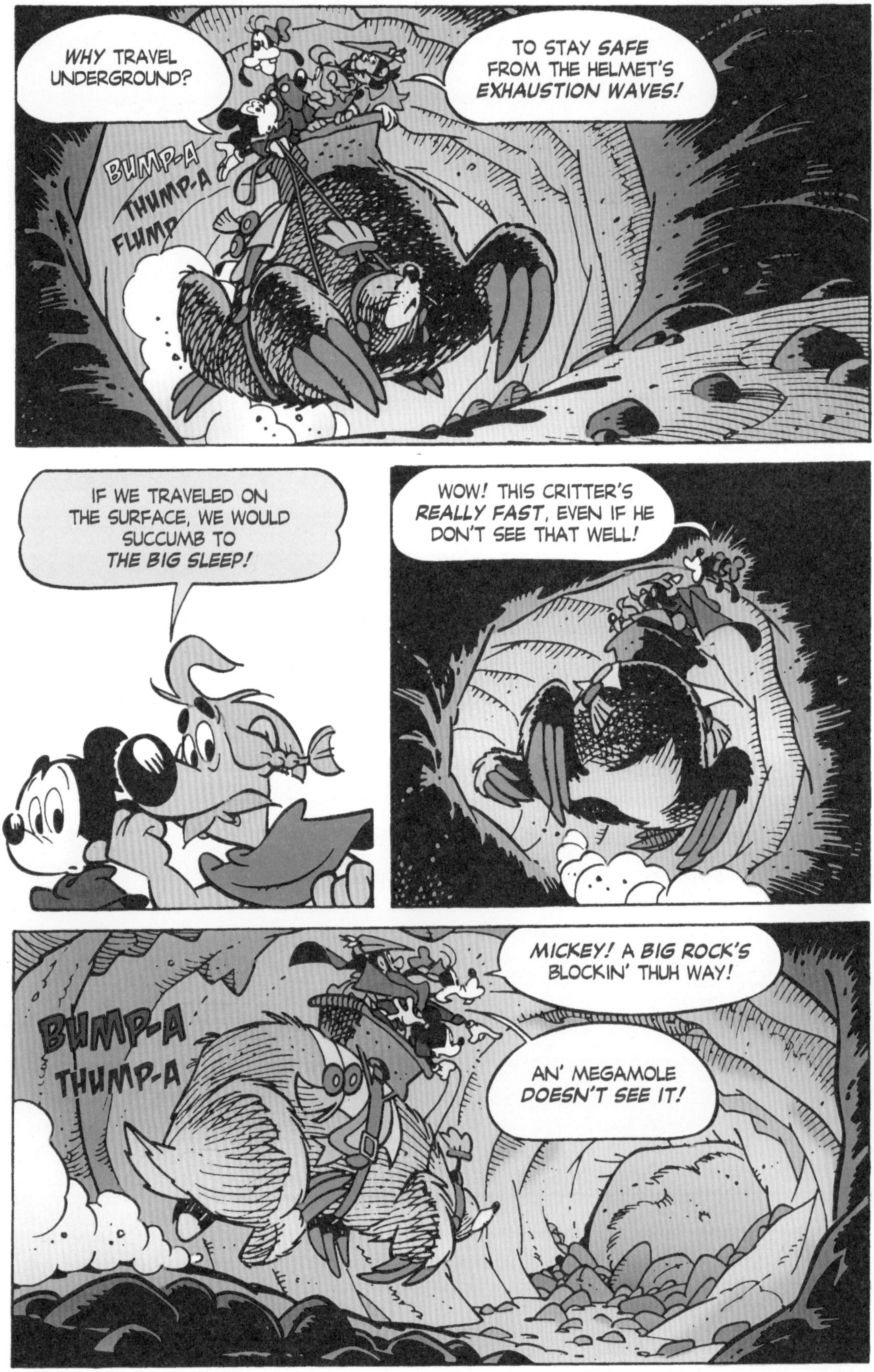
WHY TRAVEL UNDERGROUND?
TO STAY *SAFE* FROM THE HELMET'S *EXHAUSTION WAVES!*
BUMP-A
THUMP-A
FLUMP
IF WE TRAVELED ON THE SURFACE, WE WOULD SUCCUMB TO *THE BIG SLEEP!*
WOW! THIS CRITTER'S *REALLY FAST*, EVEN IF HE DON'T SEE THAT WELL!
MICKEY! A *BIG ROCK'S* BLOCKIN' THUH WAY!
BUMP-A
THUMP-A
AN' MEGAMOLE *DOESN'T SEE IT!*

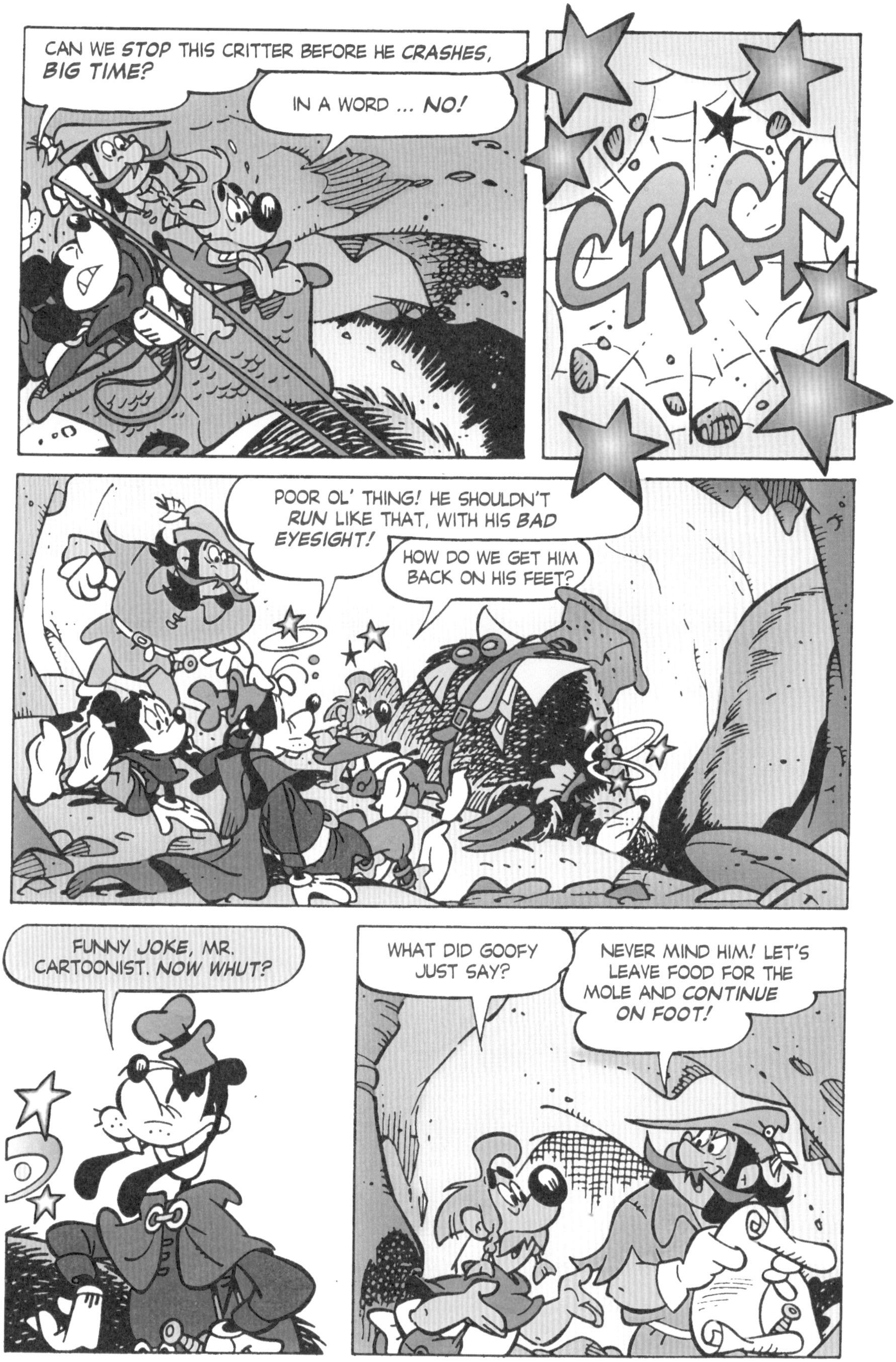

CAN WE STOP THIS CRITTER BEFORE HE CRASHES, BIG TIME?
IN A WORD ... NO!
CRACK
POOR OL' THING! HE SHOULDN'T RUN LIKE THAT, WITH HIS BAD EYESIGHT!
HOW DO WE GET HIM BACK ON HIS FEET?
FUNNY JOKE, MR. CARTOONIST. NOW WHUT?
WHAT DID GOOFY JUST SAY?
NEVER MIND HIM! LET'S LEAVE FOOD FOR THE MOLE AND CONTINUE ON FOOT!

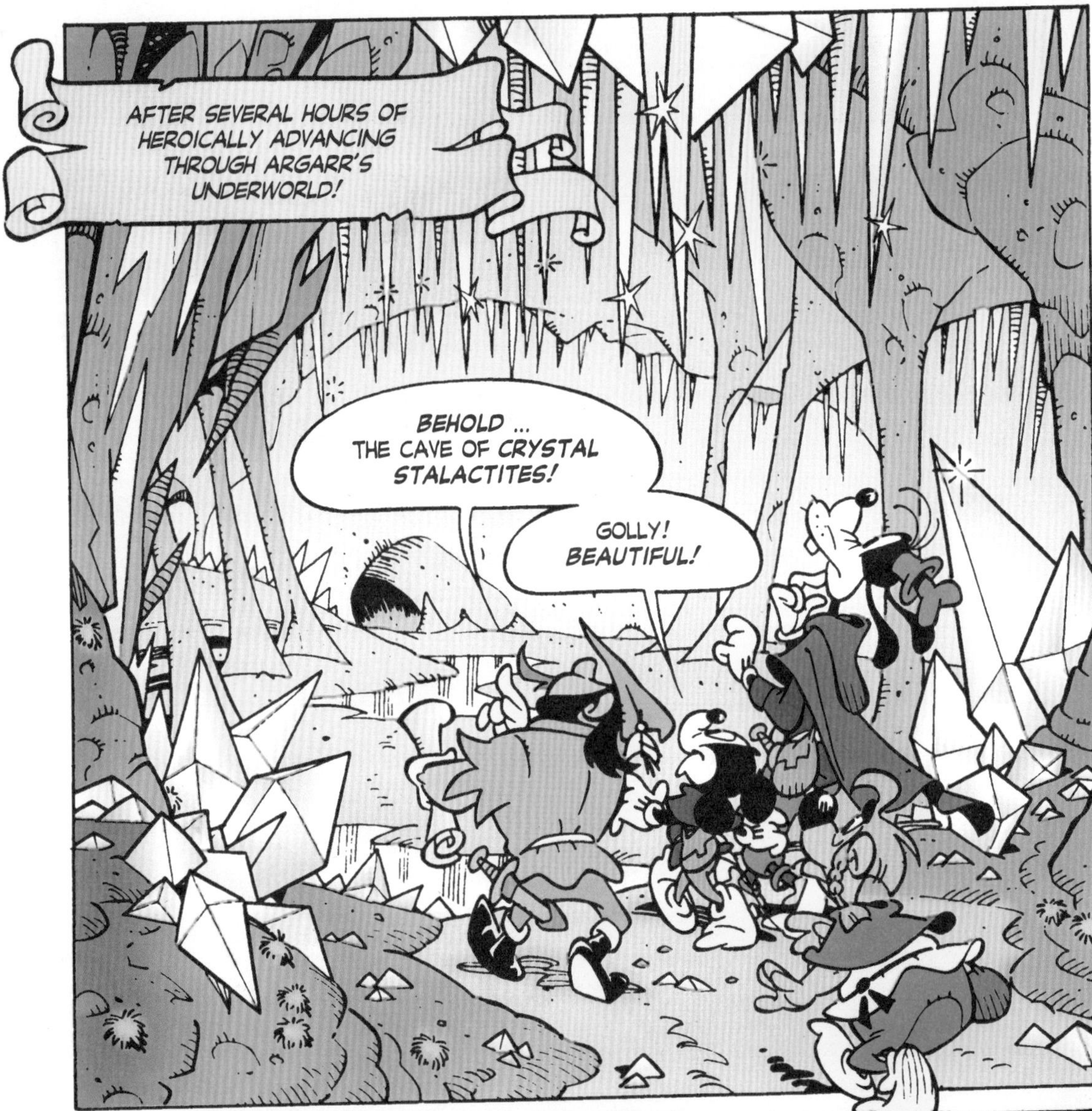
AFTER SEVERAL HOURS OF HEROICALLY ADVANCING THROUGH ARGARR'S UNDERWORLD!
BEHOLD ... THE CAVE OF CRYSTAL STALACTITES!
GOLLY! BEAUTIFUL!

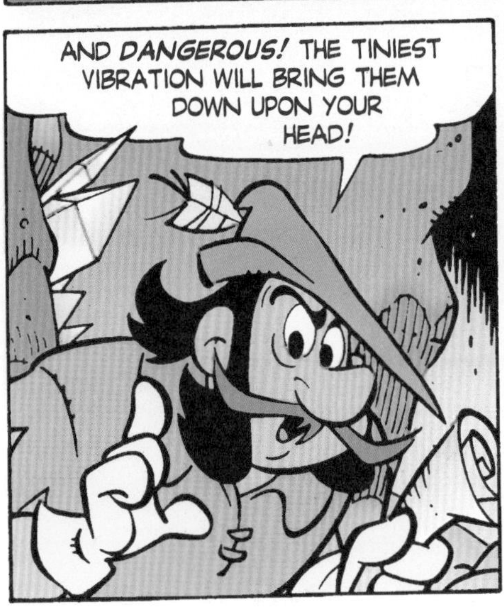
AND DANGEROUS! THE TINIEST VIBRATION WILL BRING THEM DOWN UPON YOUR HEAD!

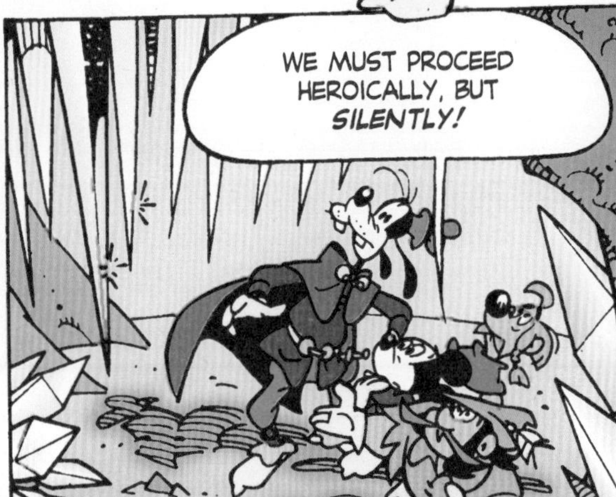
WE MUST PROCEED HEROICALLY, BUT SILENTLY!

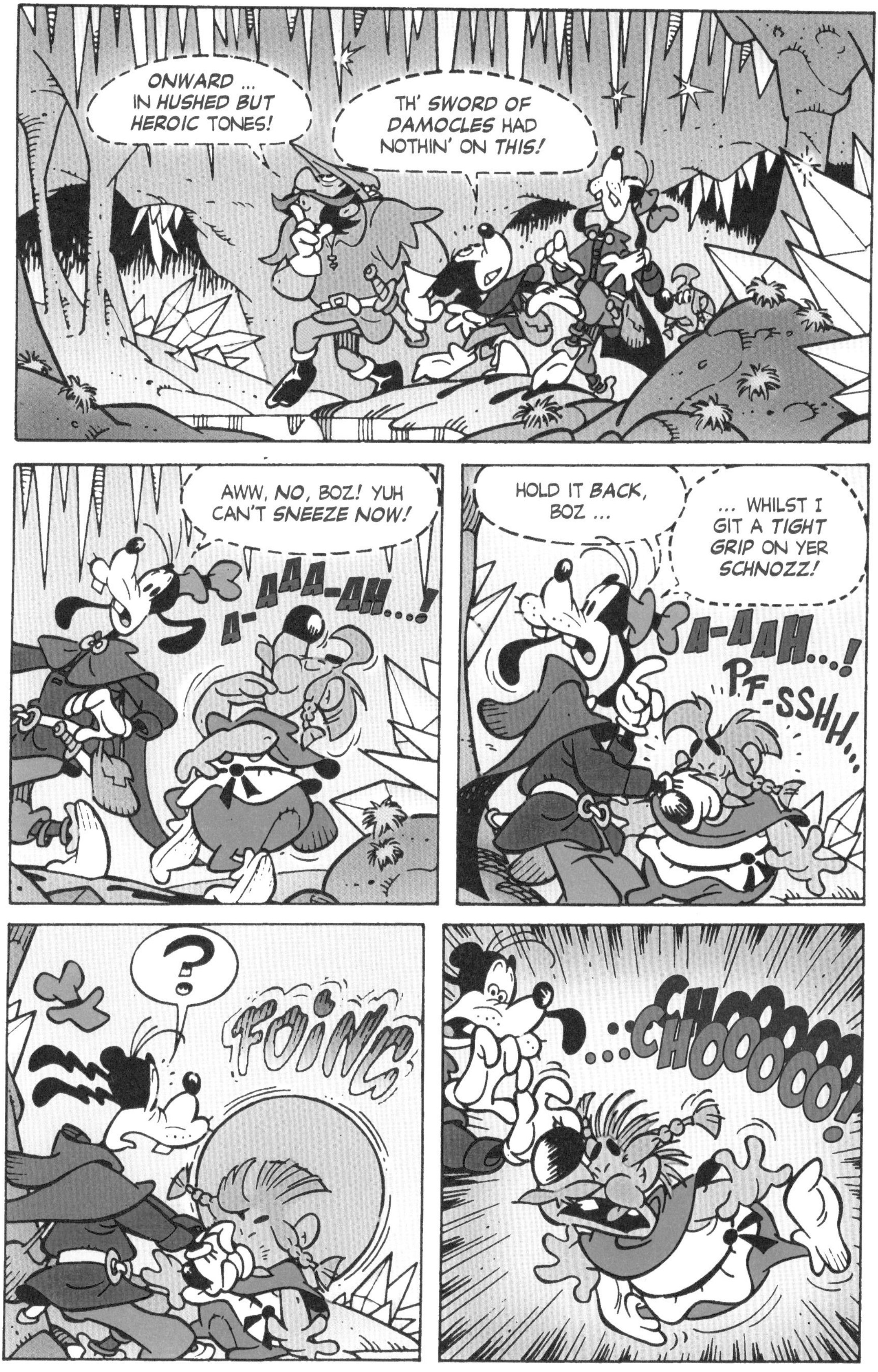
ONWARD ... IN HUSHED BUT HEROIC TONES!
TH' SWORD OF DAMOCLES HAD NOTHIN' ON THIS!
AWW, NO, BOZ! YUH CAN'T SNEEZE NOW!
A-AAA-AH...!
HOLD IT BACK, BOZ ...
... WHILST I GIT A TIGHT GRIP ON YER SCHNOZZ!
A-AAH...!
P.F-SSHH...
?
FOING
...CHOOOOOO
CHOOOOOO!

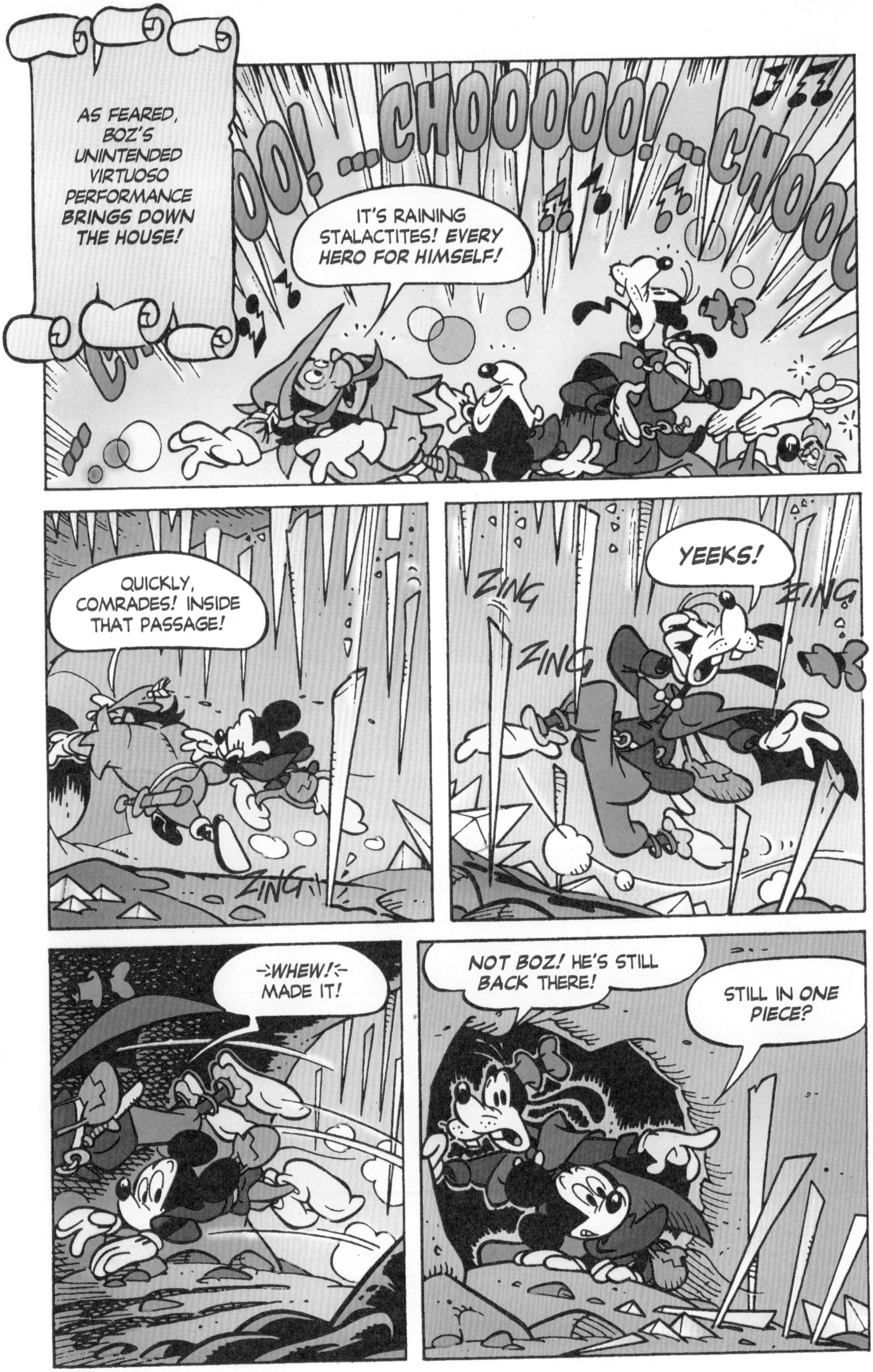

AS FEARED, BOZ'S UNINTENDED VIRTUOSO PERFORMANCE BRINGS DOWN THE HOUSE!
OO! ...CHOOOOOO! ...CHOO
IT'S RAINING STALACTITES! EVERY HERO FOR HIMSELF!
QUICKLY, COMRADES! INSIDE THAT PASSAGE!
ZING
YEEKS!
ZING
ZING
ZING
WHEW! MADE IT!
NOT BOZ! HE'S STILL BACK THERE!
STILL IN ONE PIECE?

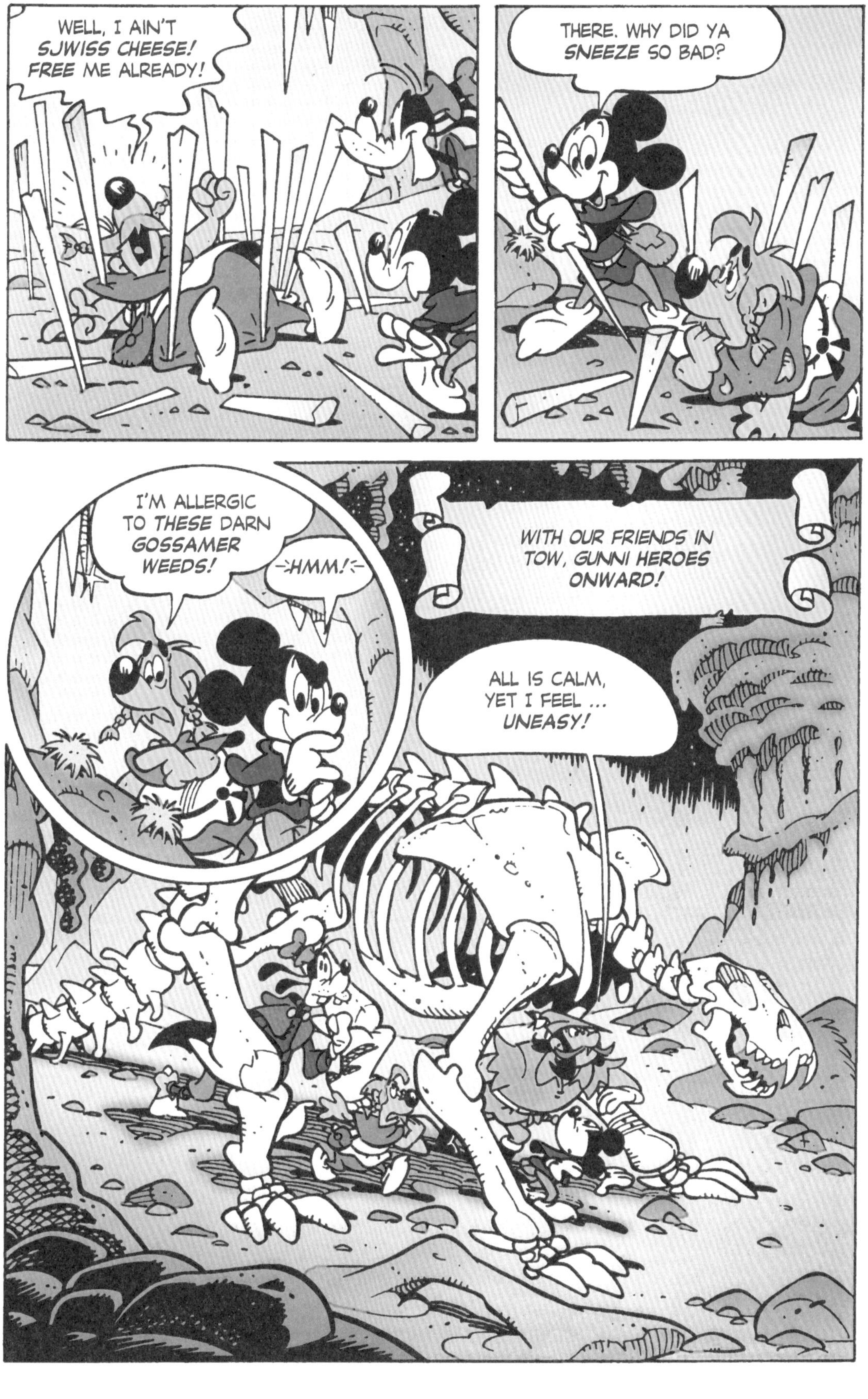

WELL, I AIN'T SJWISS CHEESE! FREE ME ALREADY!
THERE. WHY DID YA SNEEZE SO BAD?
I'M ALLERGIC TO THESE DARN GOSSAMER WEEDS!
HMM!
WITH OUR FRIENDS IN TOW, GUNNI HEROES ONWARD!
ALL IS CALM, YET I FEEL ... UNEASY!

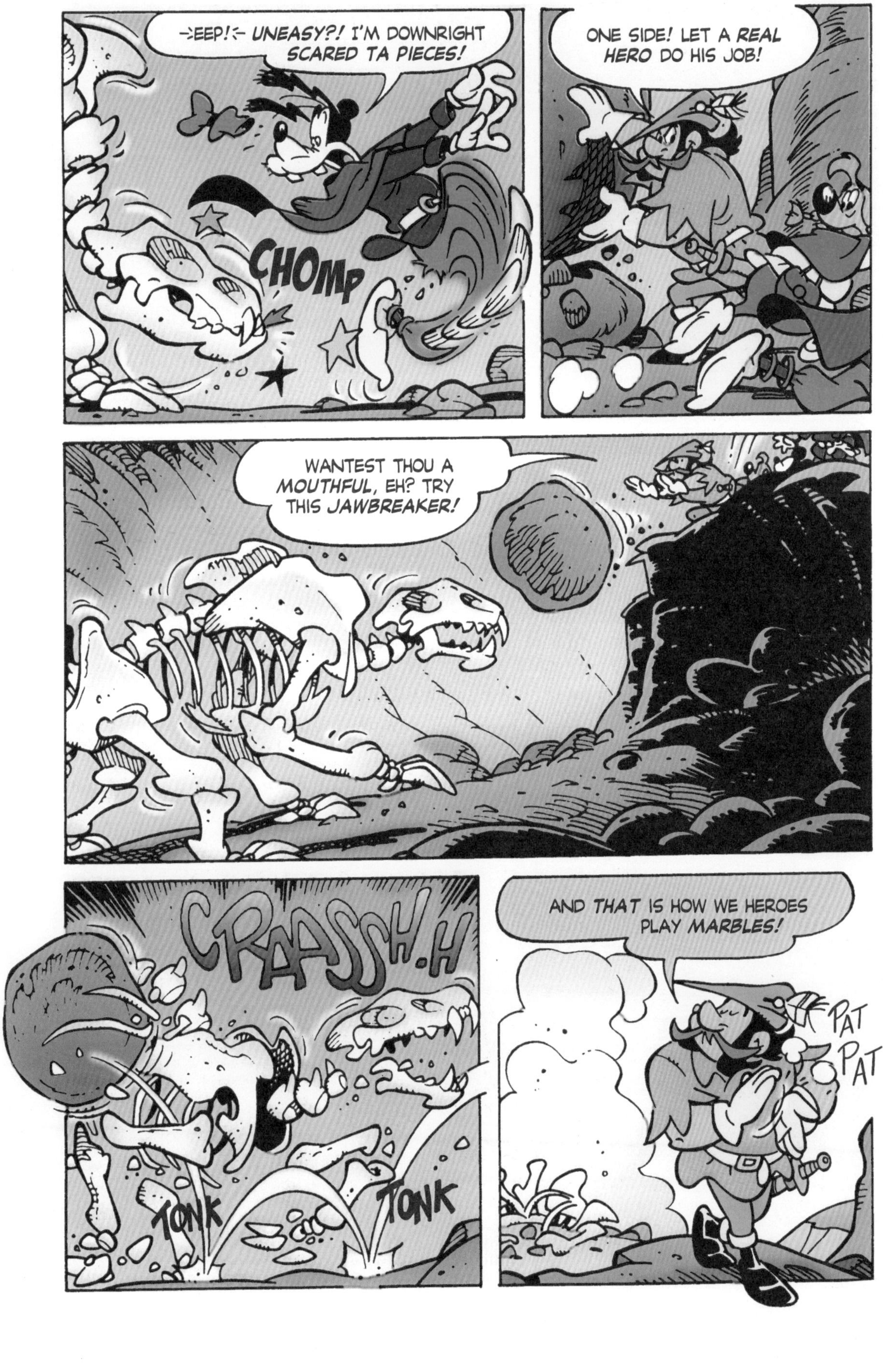
–EEP!– UNEASY?! I'M DOWNRIGHT SCARED TA PIECES!
CHOMP
ONE SIDE! LET A REAL HERO DO HIS JOB!
WANTEST THOU A MOUTHFUL, EH? TRY THIS JAWBREAKER!
CRAASSH.H
TONK
TONK
AND THAT IS HOW WE HEROES PLAY MARBLES!
PAT
PAT

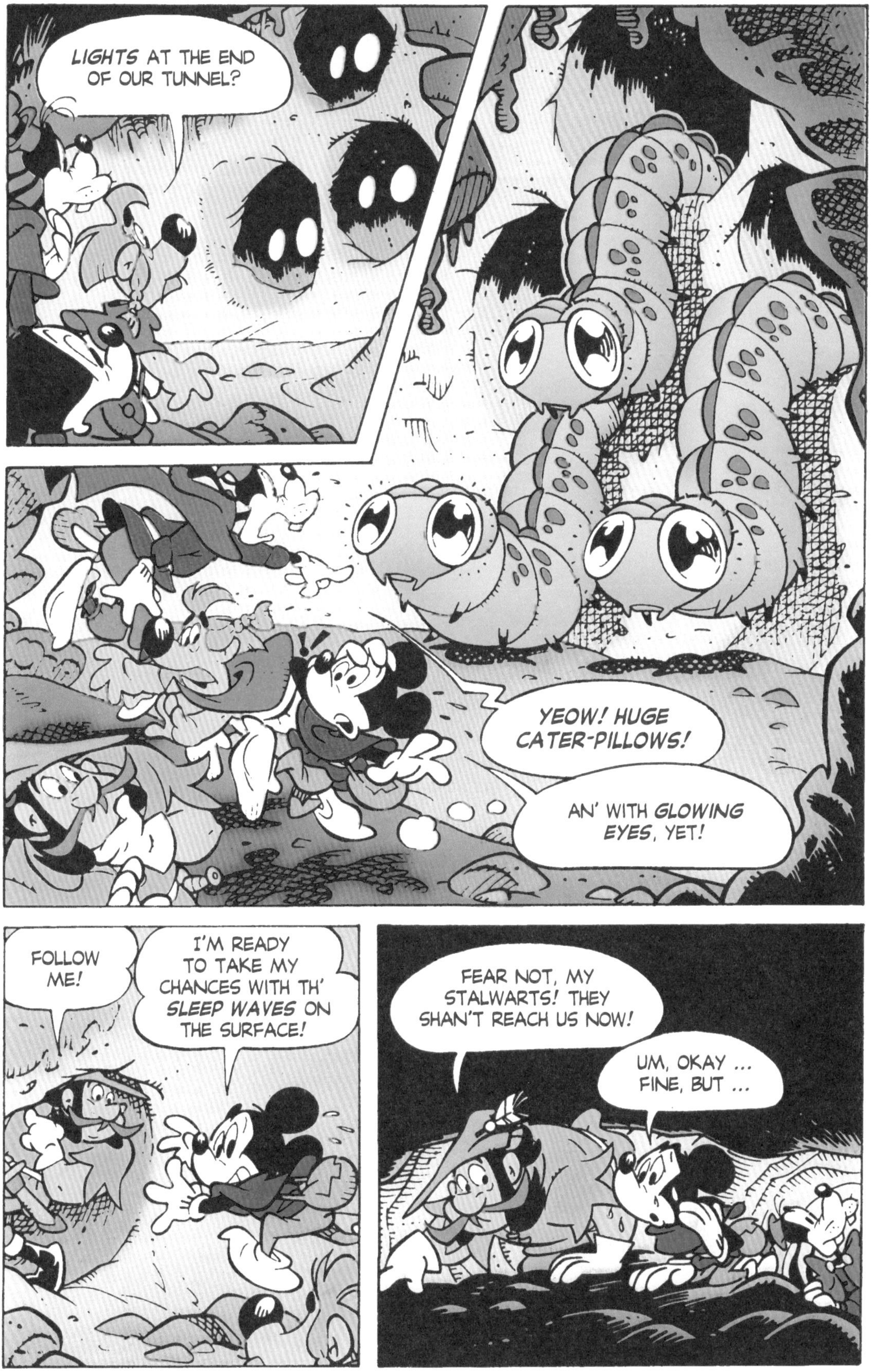
LIGHTS AT THE END OF OUR TUNNEL?
YEOW! HUGE CATER-PILLOWS!
AN' WITH GLOWING EYES, YET!
FOLLOW ME!
I'M READY TO TAKE MY CHANCES WITH TH' SLEEP WAVES ON THE SURFACE!
FEAR NOT, MY STALWARTS! THEY SHAN'T REACH US NOW!
UM, OKAY ... FINE, BUT ...

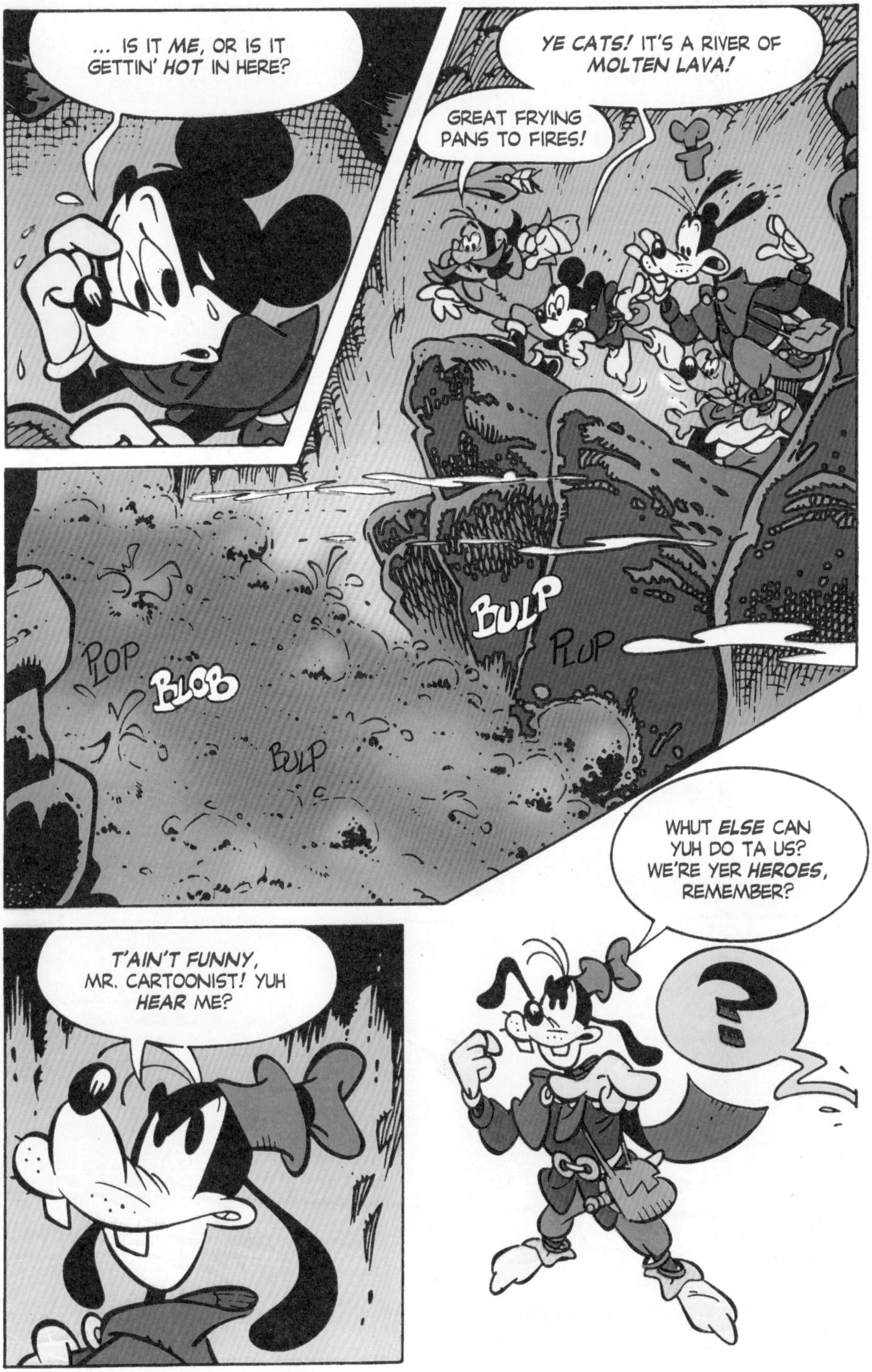
... IS IT *ME*, OR IS IT GETTIN' *HOT* IN HERE?
YE CATS! IT'S A RIVER OF *MOLTEN LAVA!*
GREAT FRYING PANS TO FIRES!
BULP
PLUP
PLOP
BLOB
BULP
T'AIN'T FUNNY, MR. CARTOONIST! YUH *HEAR* ME?
WHUT *ELSE* CAN YUH DO TA US? WE'RE YER *HEROES*, REMEMBER?
?

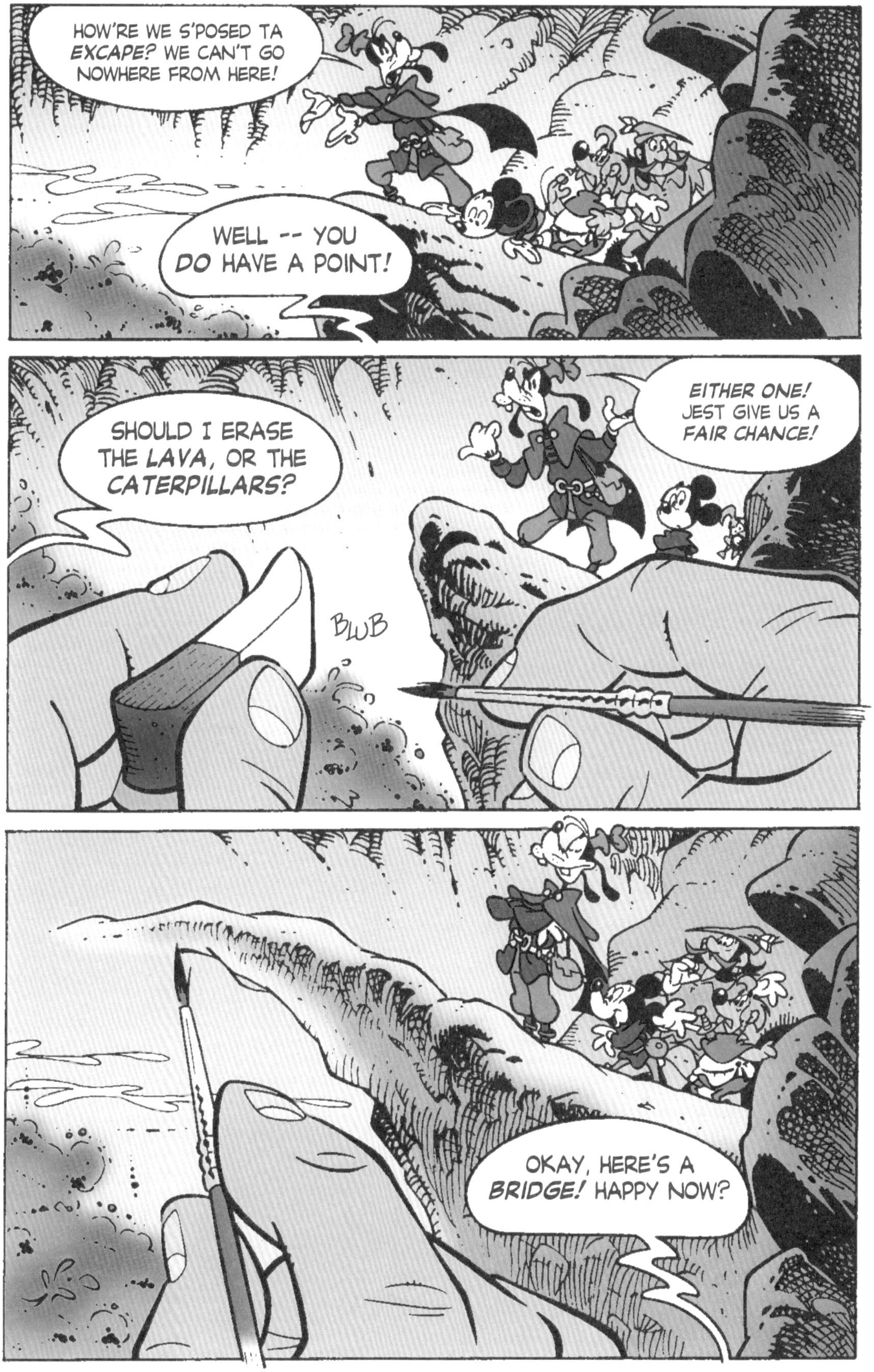
HOW'RE WE S'POSED TA EXCAPE? WE CAN'T GO NOWHERE FROM HERE!
WELL -- YOU DO HAVE A POINT!
SHOULD I ERASE THE LAVA, OR THE CATERPILLARS?
EITHER ONE! JEST GIVE US A FAIR CHANCE!
BLUB
OKAY, HERE'S A BRIDGE! HAPPY NOW?

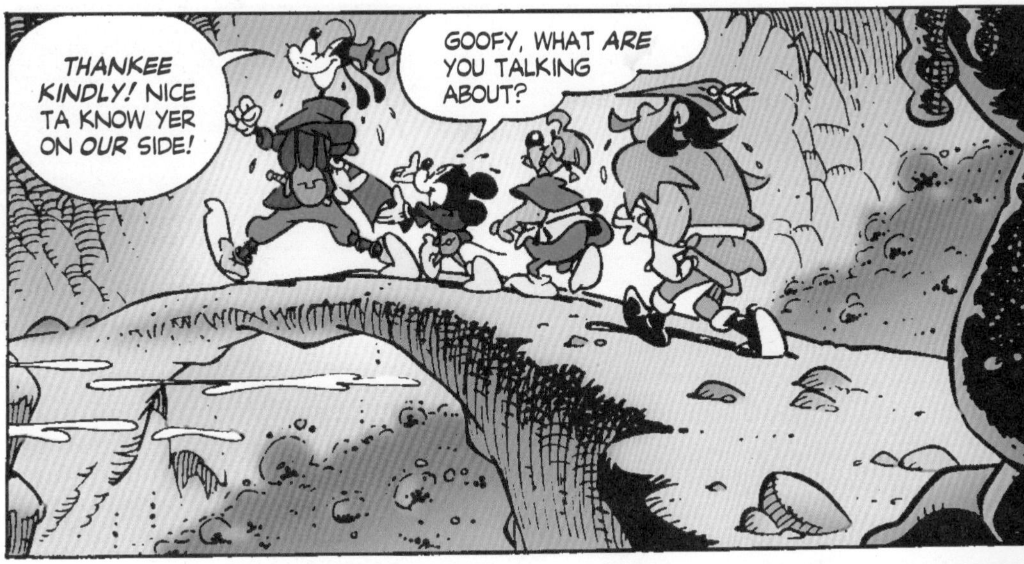
THANKEE KINDLY! NICE TA KNOW YER ON OUR SIDE!
GOOFY, WHAT ARE YOU TALKING ABOUT?

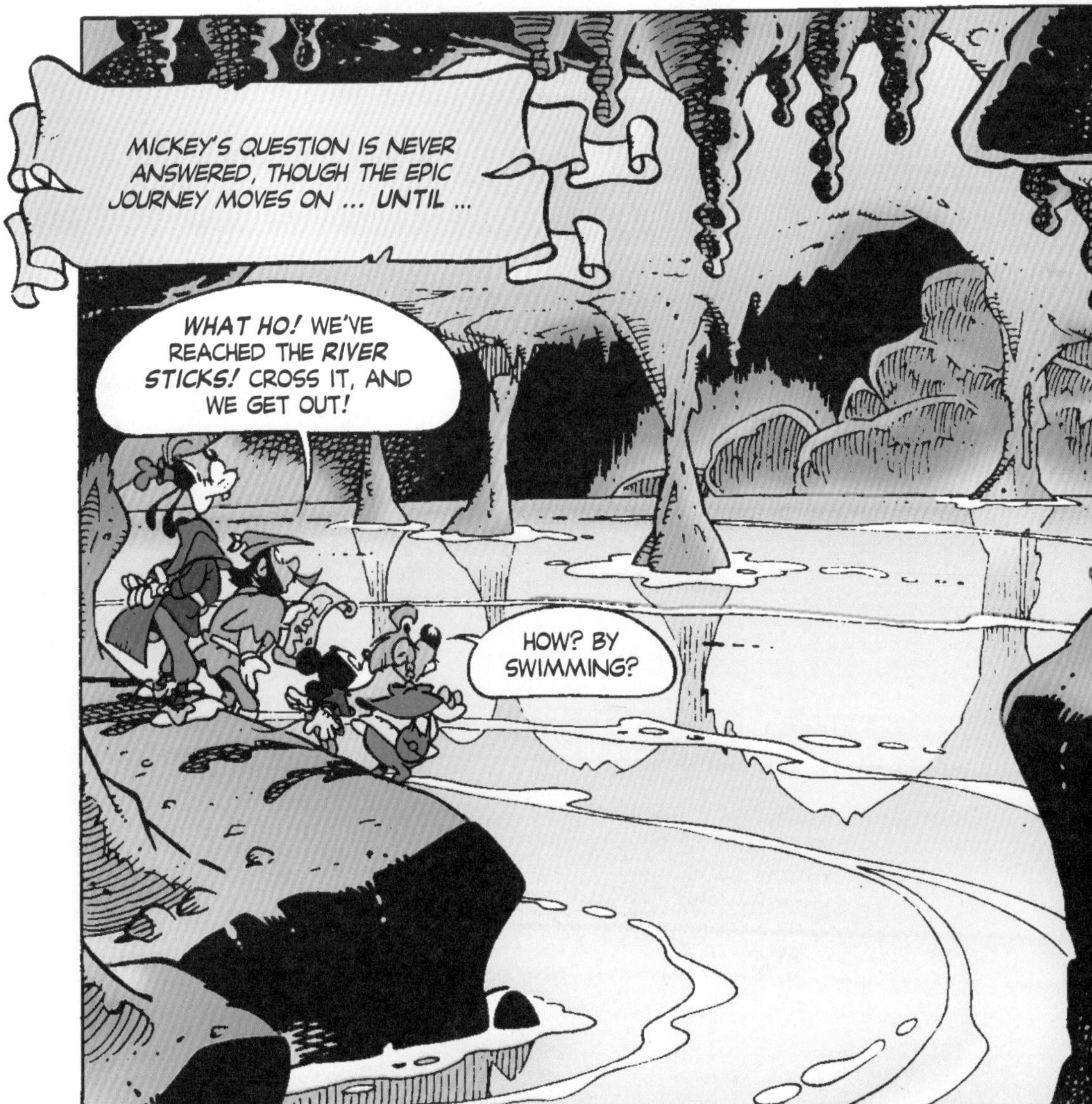
MICKEY'S QUESTION IS NEVER ANSWERED, THOUGH THE EPIC JOURNEY MOVES ON ... UNTIL ...
WHAT HO! WE'VE REACHED THE RIVER STICKS! CROSS IT, AND WE GET OUT!
HOW? BY SWIMMING?

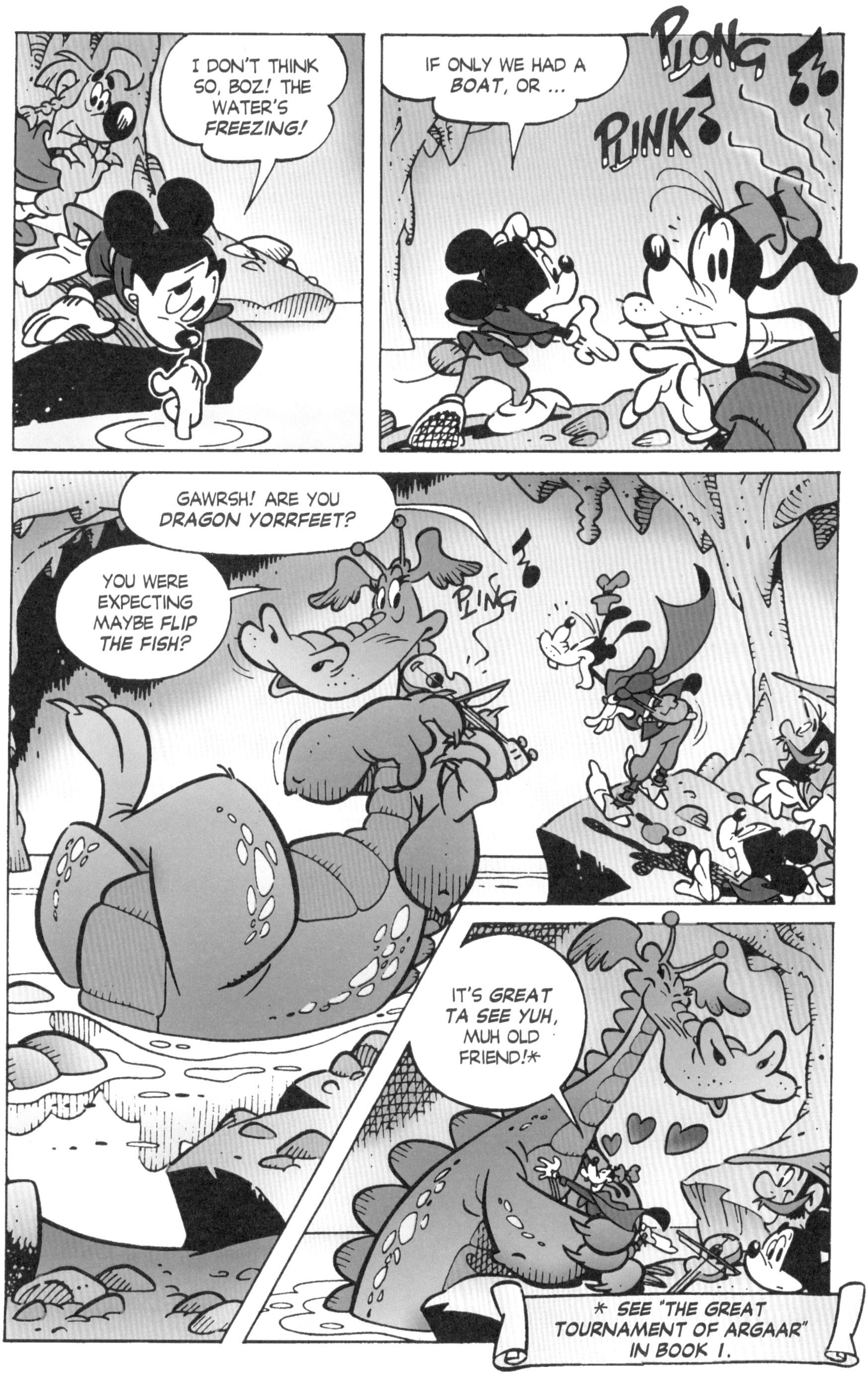
I DON'T THINK SO, BOZ! THE WATER'S FREEZING!
IF ONLY WE HAD A BOAT, OR ...
PLONG
PLINK
GAWRSH! ARE YOU DRAGON YORRFEET?
YOU WERE EXPECTING MAYBE FLIP THE FISH?
PLING
IT'S GREAT TA SEE YUH, MUH OLD FRIEND!*
* SEE "THE GREAT TOURNAMENT OF ARGAAR" IN BOOK I.

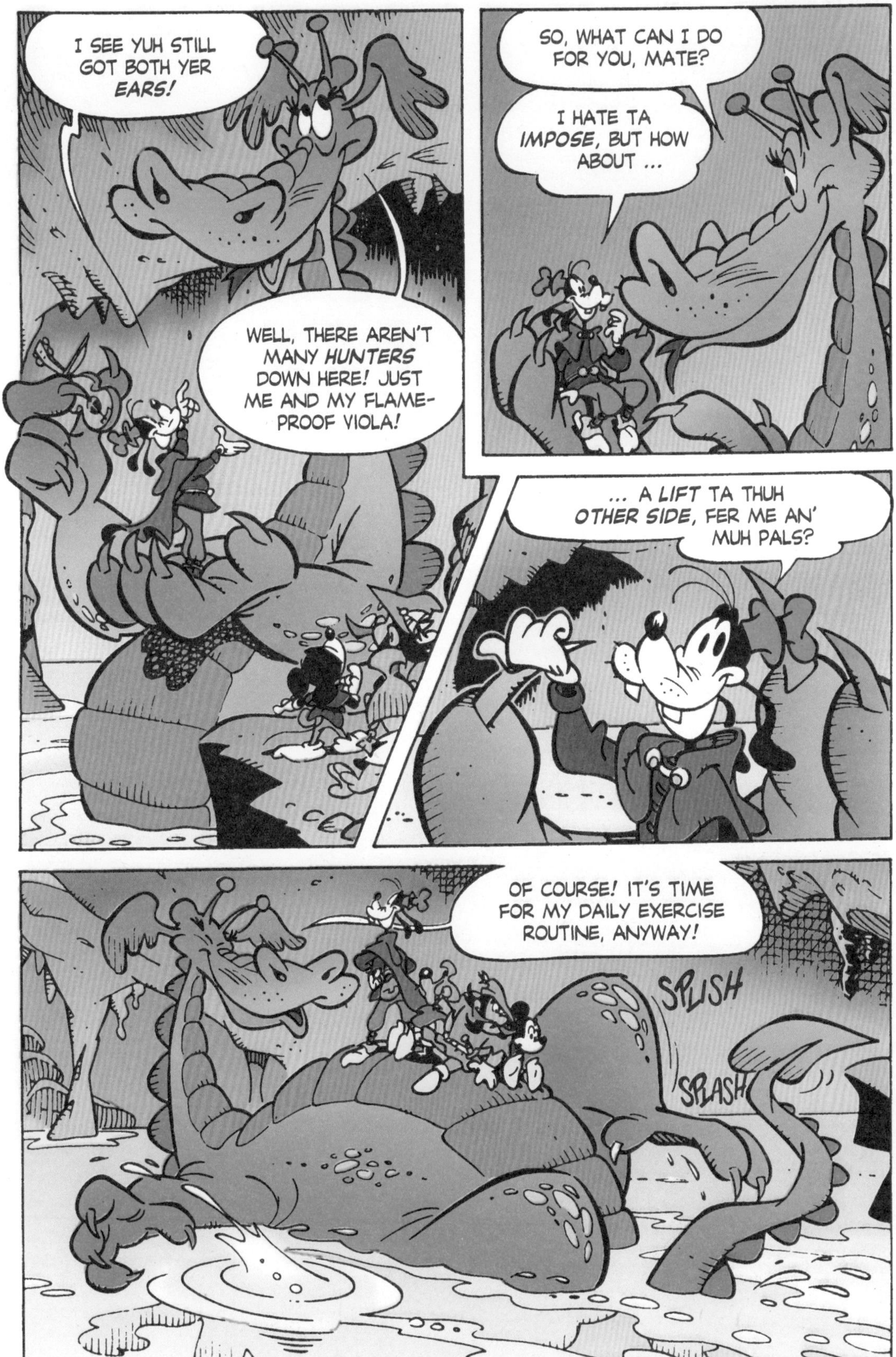
I SEE YUH STILL GOT BOTH YER EARS!
WELL, THERE AREN'T MANY HUNTERS DOWN HERE! JUST ME AND MY FLAME-PROOF VIOLA!
SO, WHAT CAN I DO FOR YOU, MATE?
I HATE TA IMPOSE, BUT HOW ABOUT ...
... A LIFT TA THUH OTHER SIDE, FER ME AN' MUH PALS?
OF COURSE! IT'S TIME FOR MY DAILY EXERCISE ROUTINE, ANYWAY!
SPLISH
SPLASH

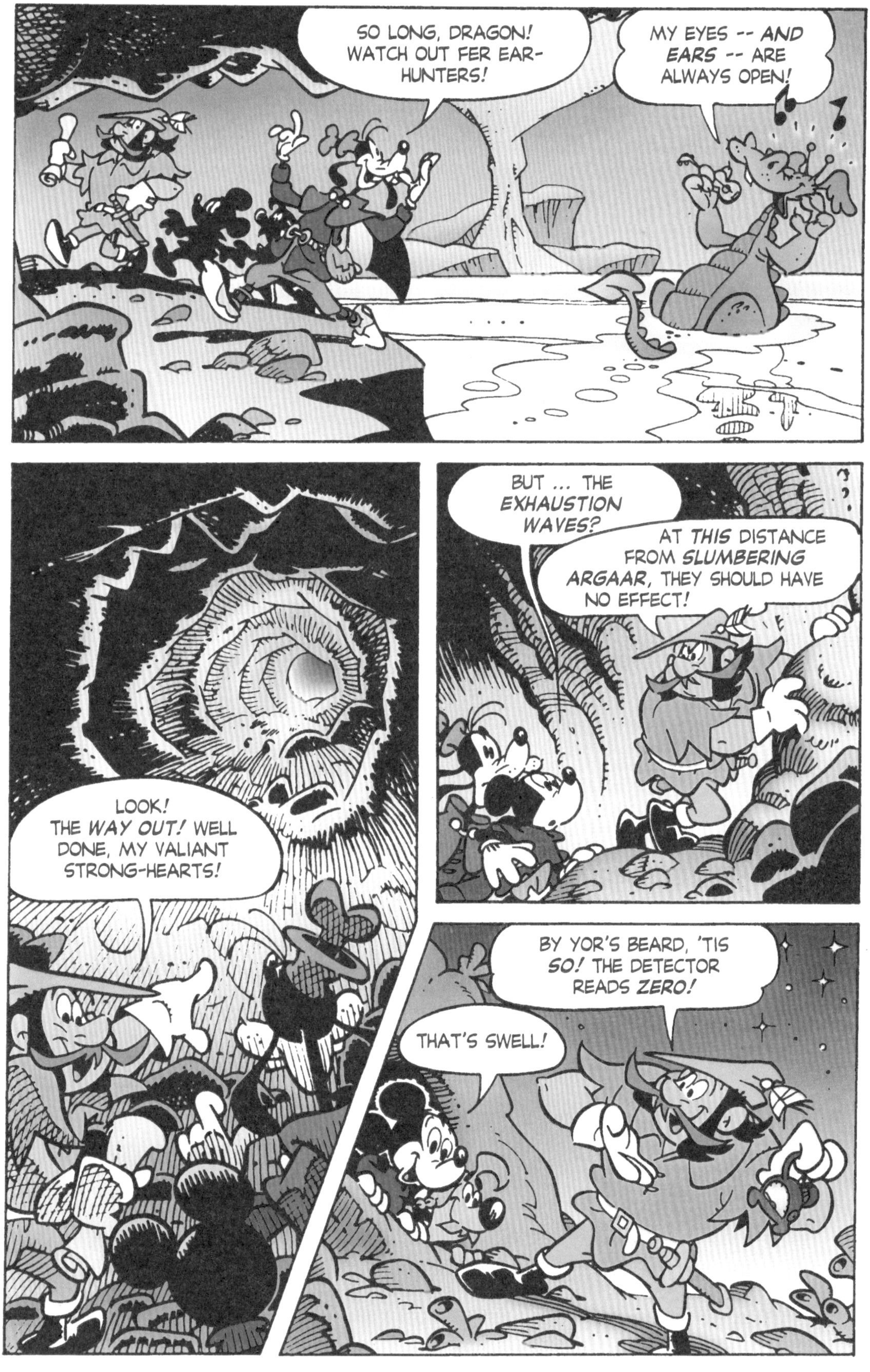
SO LONG, DRAGON! WATCH OUT FER EAR-HUNTERS!
MY EYES -- AND EARS -- ARE ALWAYS OPEN!
LOOK! THE WAY OUT! WELL DONE, MY VALIANT STRONG-HEARTS!
BUT ... THE EXHAUSTION WAVES?
AT THIS DISTANCE FROM SLUMBERING ARGAAR, THEY SHOULD HAVE NO EFFECT!
BY YOR'S BEARD, 'TIS SO! THE DETECTOR READS ZERO!
THAT'S SWELL!

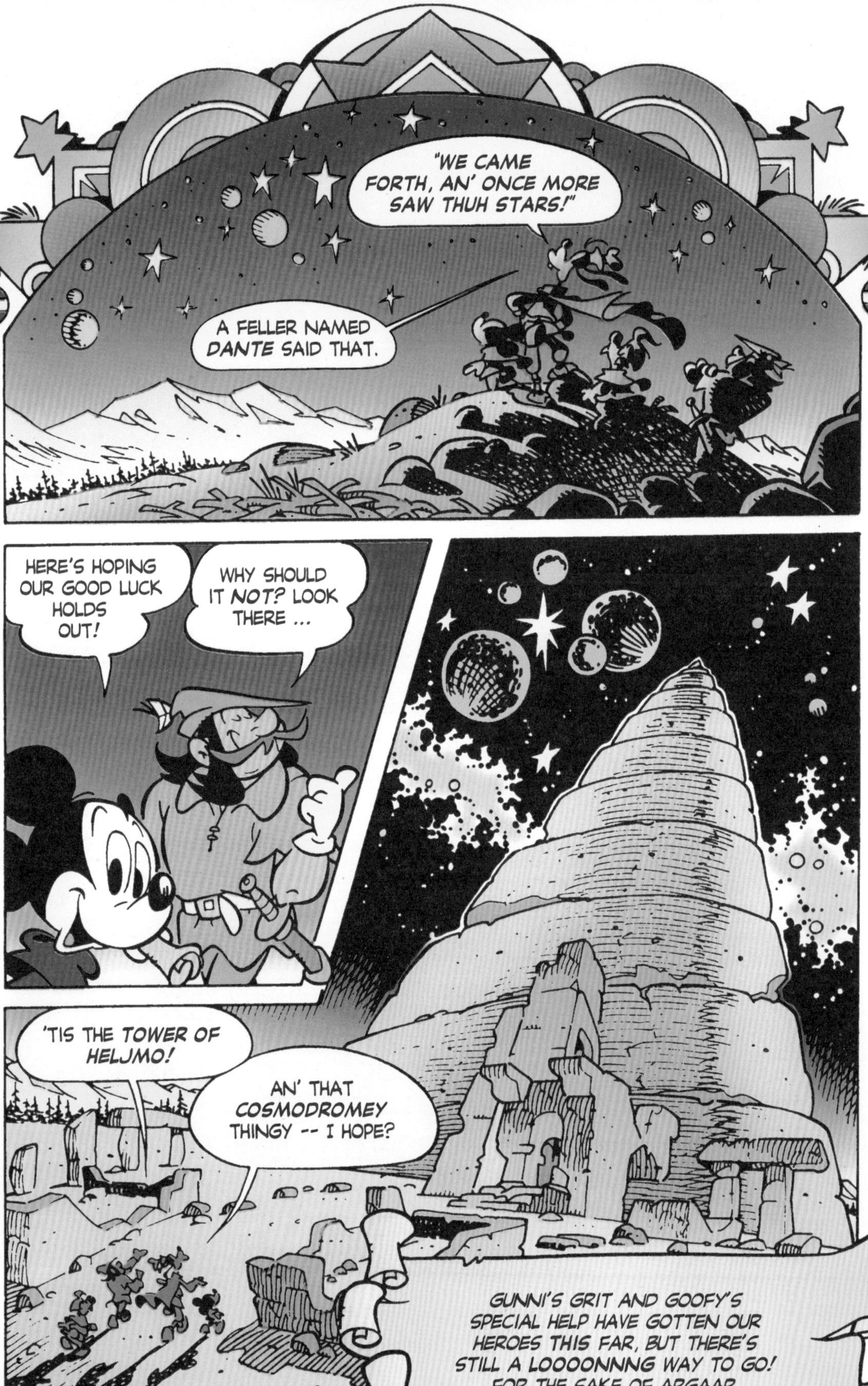
"WE CAME FORTH, AN' ONCE MORE SAW THUH STARS!"
A FELLER NAMED DANTE SAID THAT.
HERE'S HOPING OUR GOOD LUCK HOLDS OUT!
WHY SHOULD IT NOT? LOOK THERE ...
'TIS THE TOWER OF HELJMO!
AN' THAT COSMODROMEY THINGY -- I HOPE?
GUNNI'S GRIT AND GOOFY'S SPECIAL HELP HAVE GOTTEN OUR HEROES THIS FAR, BUT THERE'S STILL A LOOOONNNG WAY TO GO! FOR THE SAKE OF ARGAAR, PLEASE READ ON!

END OF CHAPTER ONE!

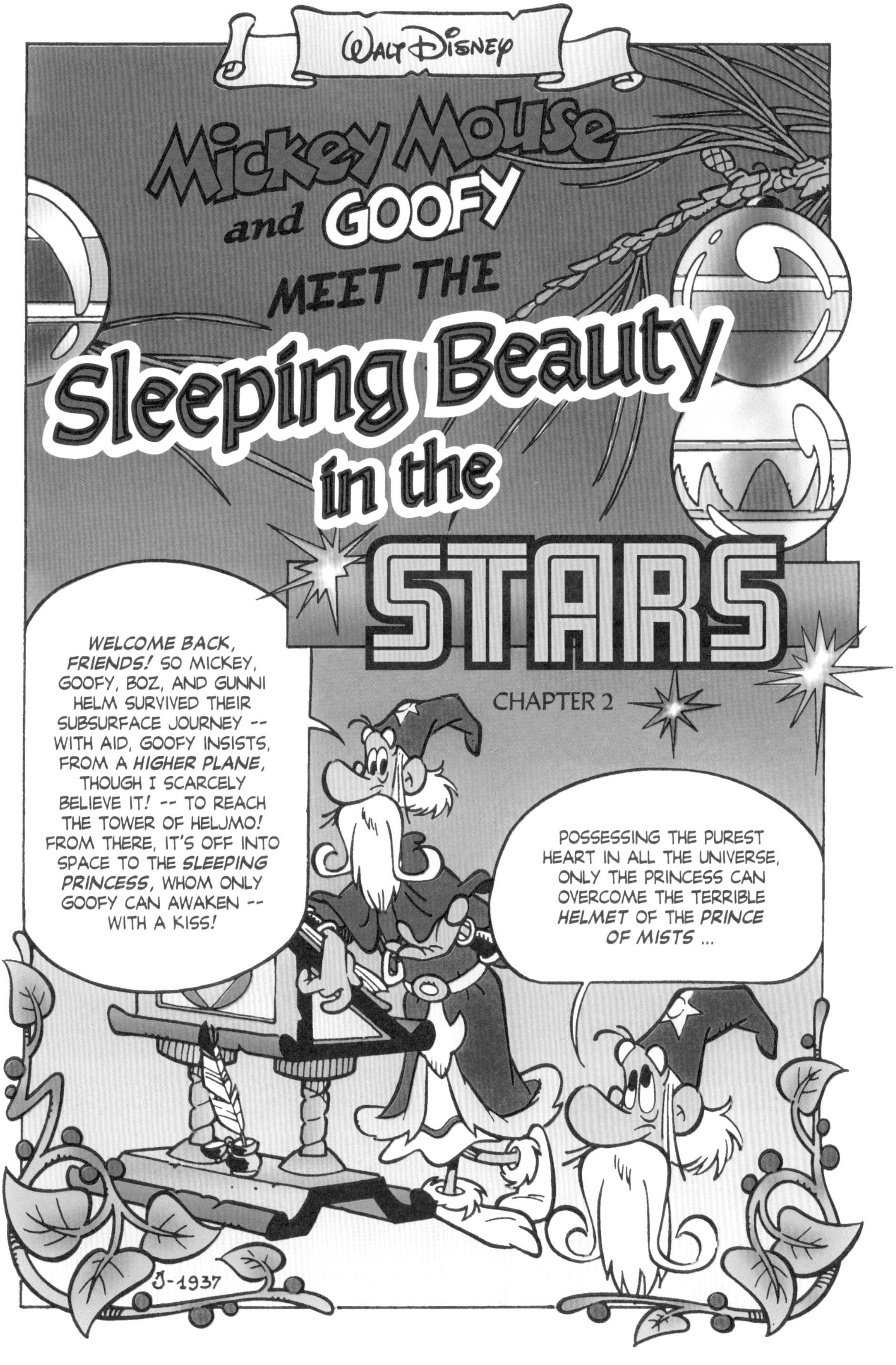
WALT DISNEY
Mickey Mouse and GOOFY MEET THE Sleeping Beauty in the STARS
CHAPTER 2
WELCOME BACK, FRIENDS! SO MICKEY, GOOFY, BOZ, AND GUNNI HELM SURVIVED THEIR SUBSURFACE JOURNEY -- WITH AID, GOOFY INSISTS, FROM A HIGHER PLANE, THOUGH I SCARCELY BELIEVE IT! -- TO REACH THE TOWER OF HELJMO! FROM THERE, IT'S OFF INTO SPACE TO THE SLEEPING PRINCESS, WHOM ONLY GOOFY CAN AWAKEN -- WITH A KISS!
POSSESSING THE PUREST HEART IN ALL THE UNIVERSE, ONLY THE PRINCESS CAN OVERCOME THE TERRIBLE HELMET OF THE PRINCE OF MISTS ...
J-1937

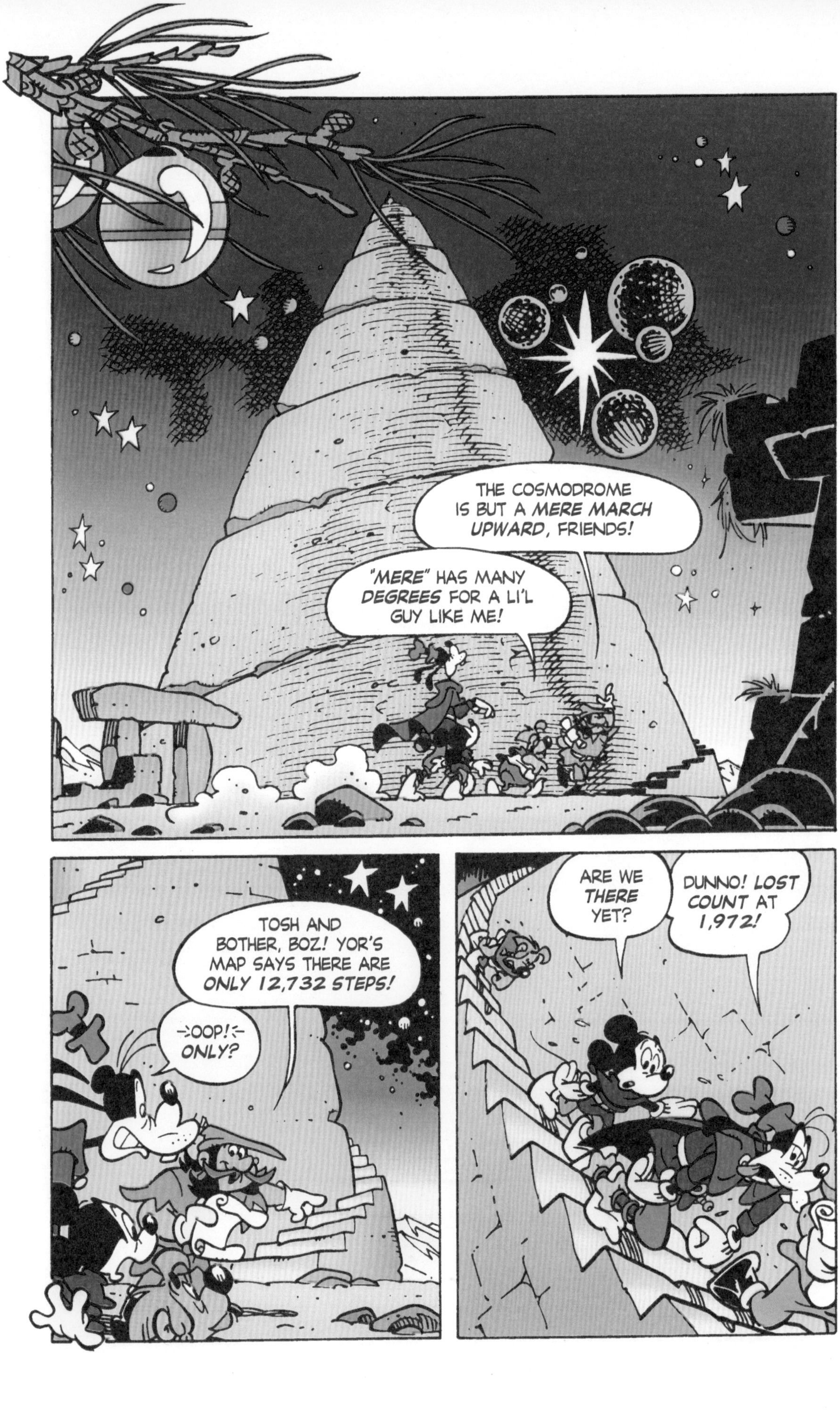
THE COSMODROME IS BUT A MERE MARCH UPWARD, FRIENDS!
"MERE" HAS MANY DEGREES FOR A LI'L GUY LIKE ME!
TOSH AND BOTHER, BOZ! YOR'S MAP SAYS THERE ARE ONLY 12,732 STEPS!
OOP! ONLY?
ARE WE THERE YET?
DUNNO! LOST COUNT AT 1,972!

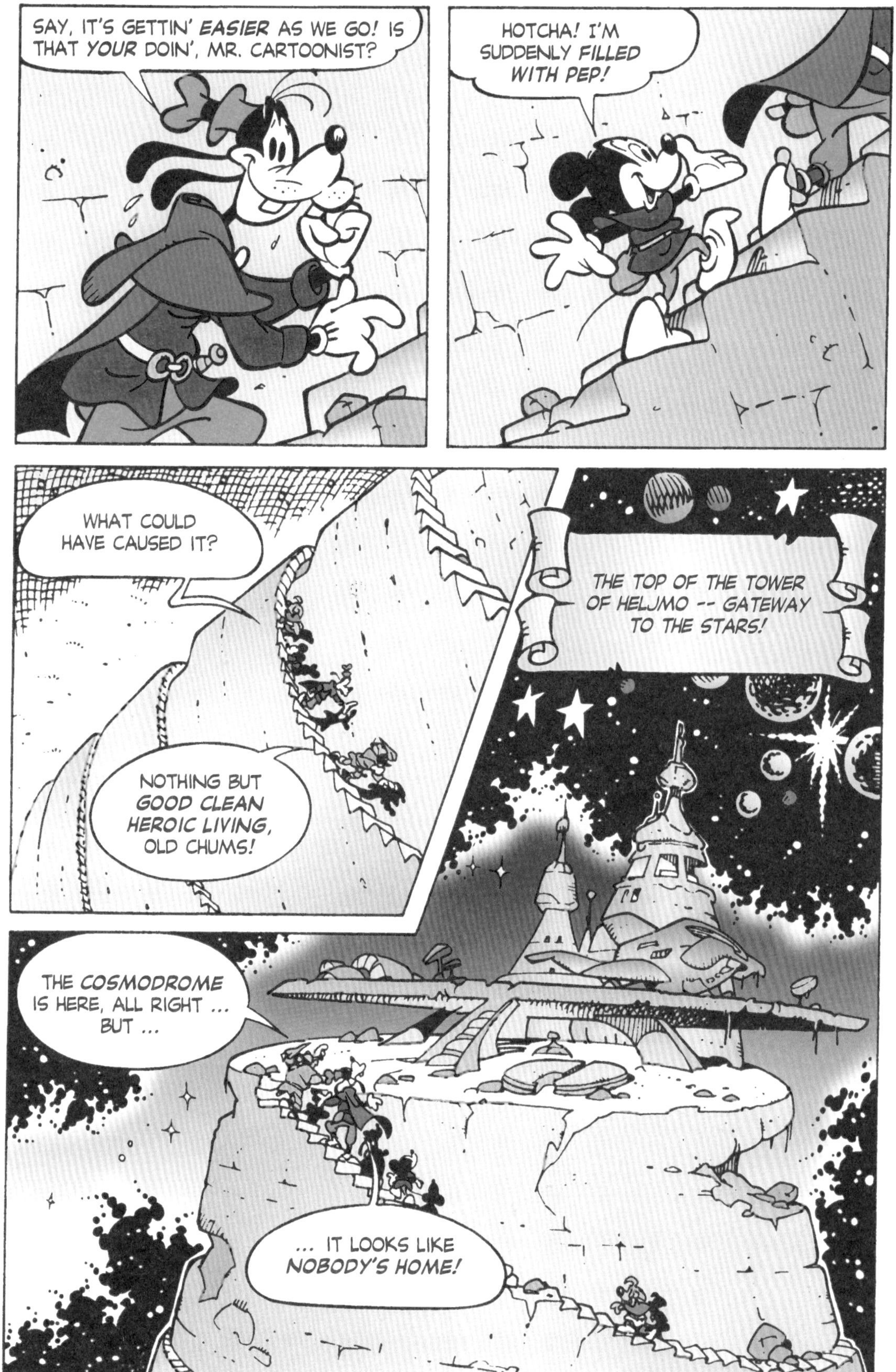
SAY, IT'S GETTIN' EASIER AS WE GO! IS THAT YOUR DOIN', MR. CARTOONIST?
HOTCHA! I'M SUDDENLY FILLED WITH PEP!
WHAT COULD HAVE CAUSED IT?
NOTHING BUT GOOD CLEAN HEROIC LIVING, OLD CHUMS!
THE TOP OF THE TOWER OF HELJMO -- GATEWAY TO THE STARS!
THE COSMODROME IS HERE, ALL RIGHT ... BUT ...
... IT LOOKS LIKE NOBODY'S HOME!

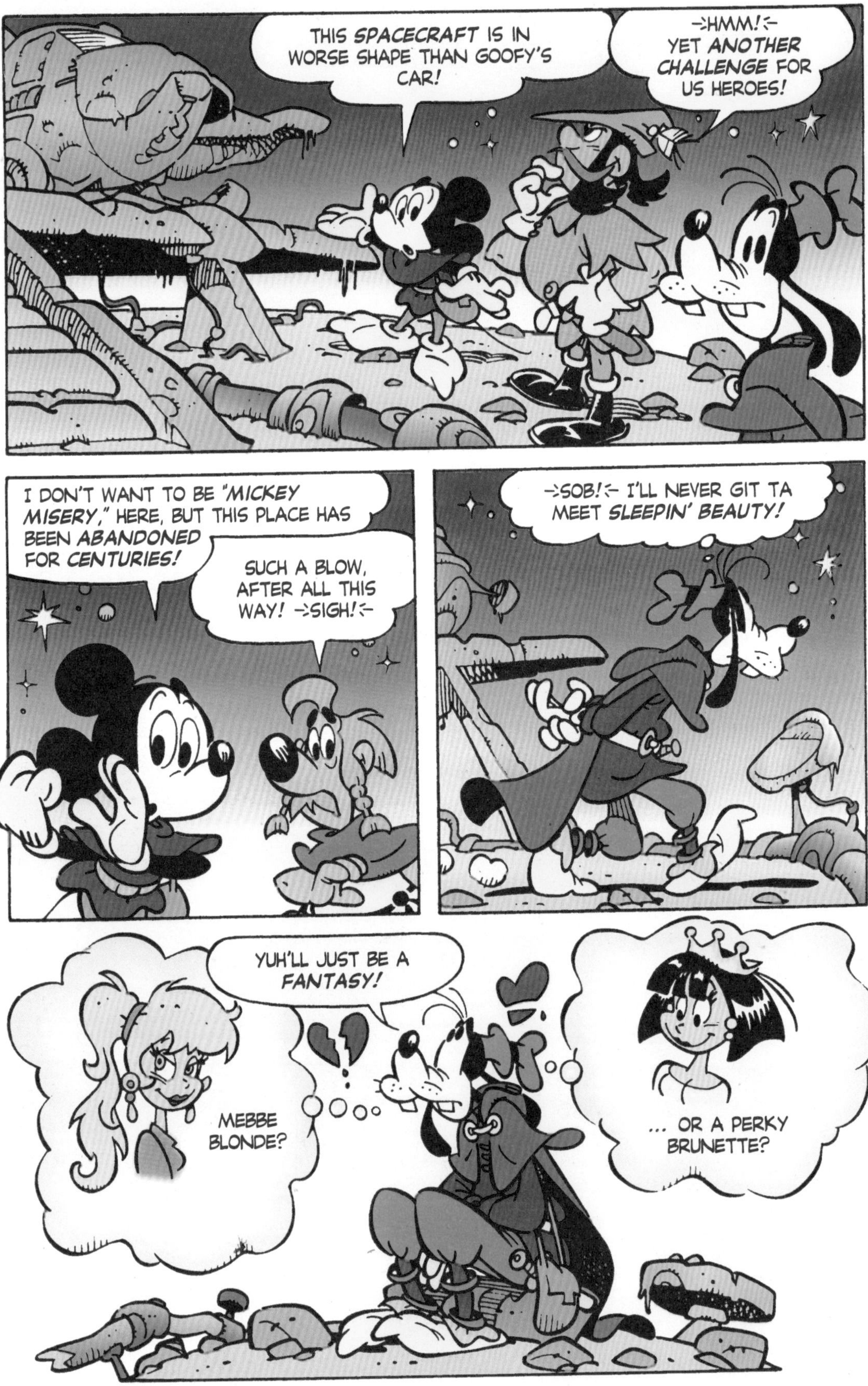
THIS SPACECRAFT IS IN WORSE SHAPE THAN GOOFY'S CAR!
-HMM!- YET ANOTHER CHALLENGE FOR US HEROES!
I DON'T WANT TO BE "MICKEY MISERY," HERE, BUT THIS PLACE HAS BEEN ABANDONED FOR CENTURIES!
SUCH A BLOW, AFTER ALL THIS WAY! -SIGH!-
-SOB!- I'LL NEVER GIT TA MEET SLEEPIN' BEAUTY!
YUH'LL JUST BE A FANTASY!
MEBBE BLONDE?
... OR A PERKY BRUNETTE?

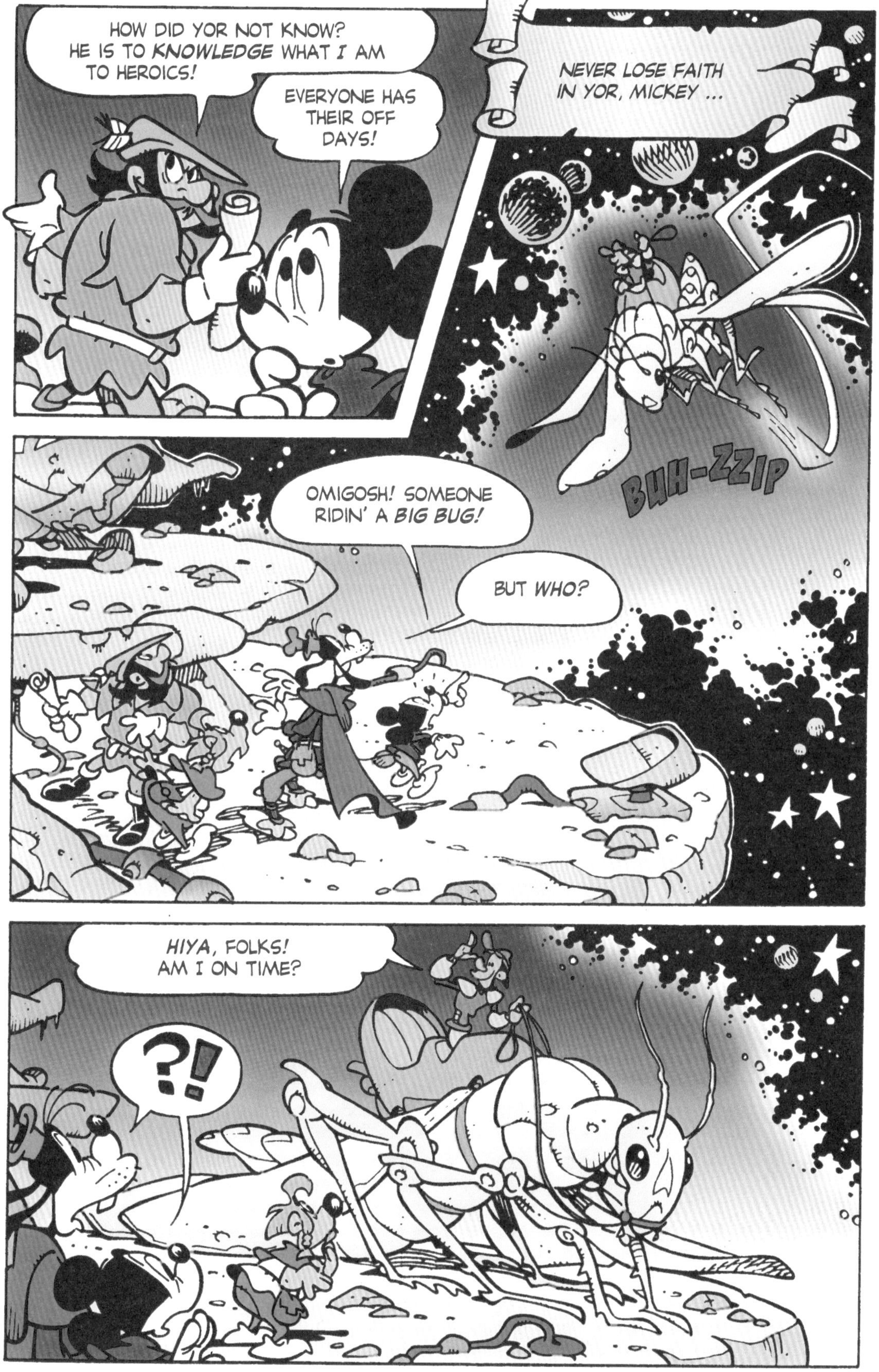
HOW DID YOR NOT KNOW? HE IS TO KNOWLEDGE WHAT I AM TO HEROICS!
EVERYONE HAS THEIR OFF DAYS!
NEVER LOSE FAITH IN YOR, MICKEY ...
BUH-ZZIP
OMIGOSH! SOMEONE RIDIN' A BIG BUG!
BUT WHO?
HIYA, FOLKS! AM I ON TIME?
?!

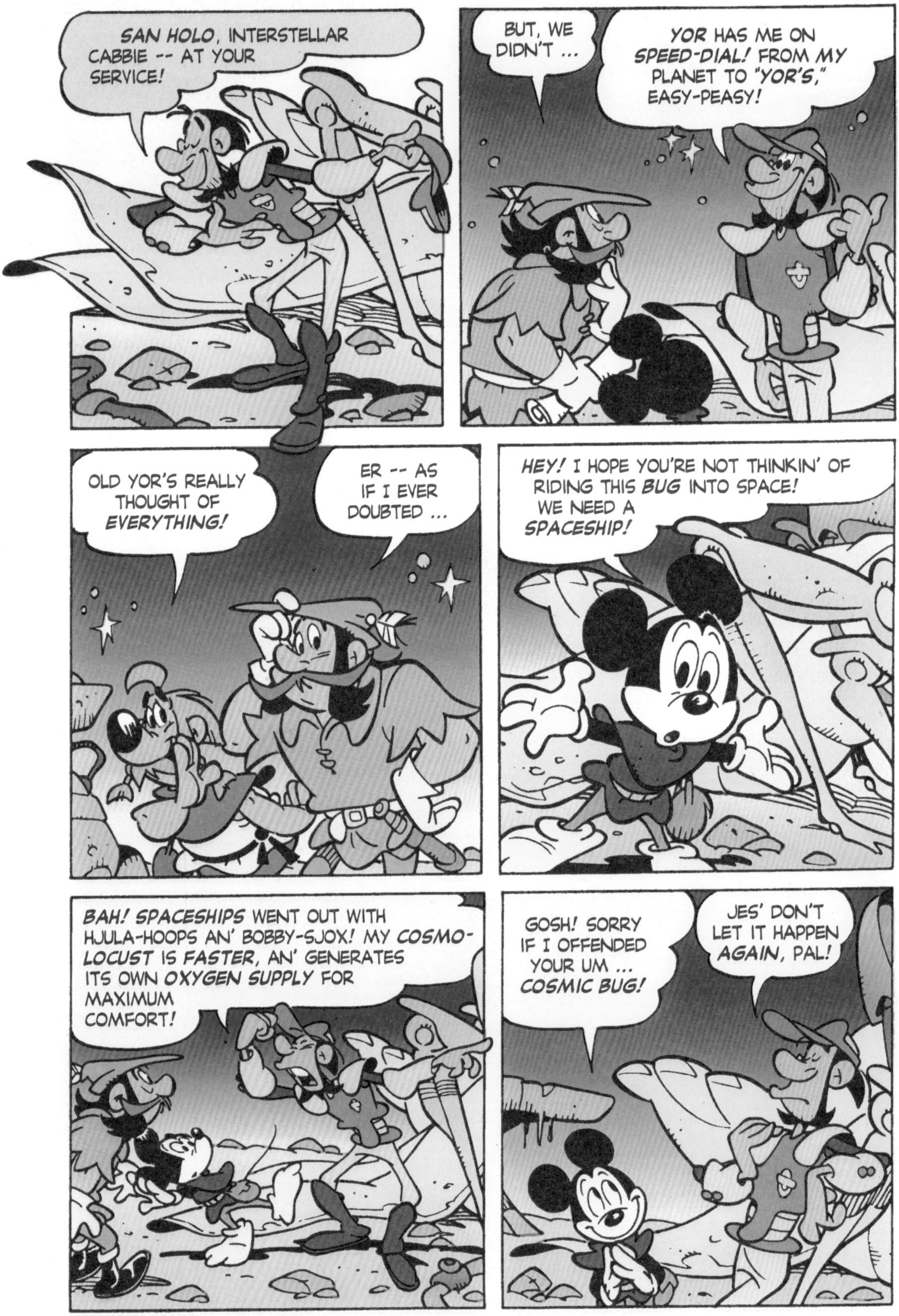
SAN HOLO, INTERSTELLAR CABBIE -- AT YOUR SERVICE!
BUT, WE DIDN'T ...
YOR HAS ME ON SPEED-DIAL! FROM MY PLANET TO "YOR'S," EASY-PEASY!
OLD YOR'S REALLY THOUGHT OF EVERYTHING!
ER -- AS IF I EVER DOUBTED ...
HEY! I HOPE YOU'RE NOT THINKIN' OF RIDING THIS BUG INTO SPACE! WE NEED A SPACESHIP!
BAH! SPACESHIPS WENT OUT WITH HJULA-HOOPS AN' BOBBY-SJOX! MY COSMO-LOCUST IS FASTER, AN' GENERATES ITS OWN OXYGEN SUPPLY FOR MAXIMUM COMFORT!
GOSH! SORRY IF I OFFENDED YOUR UM ... COSMIC BUG!
JES' DON'T LET IT HAPPEN AGAIN, PAL!

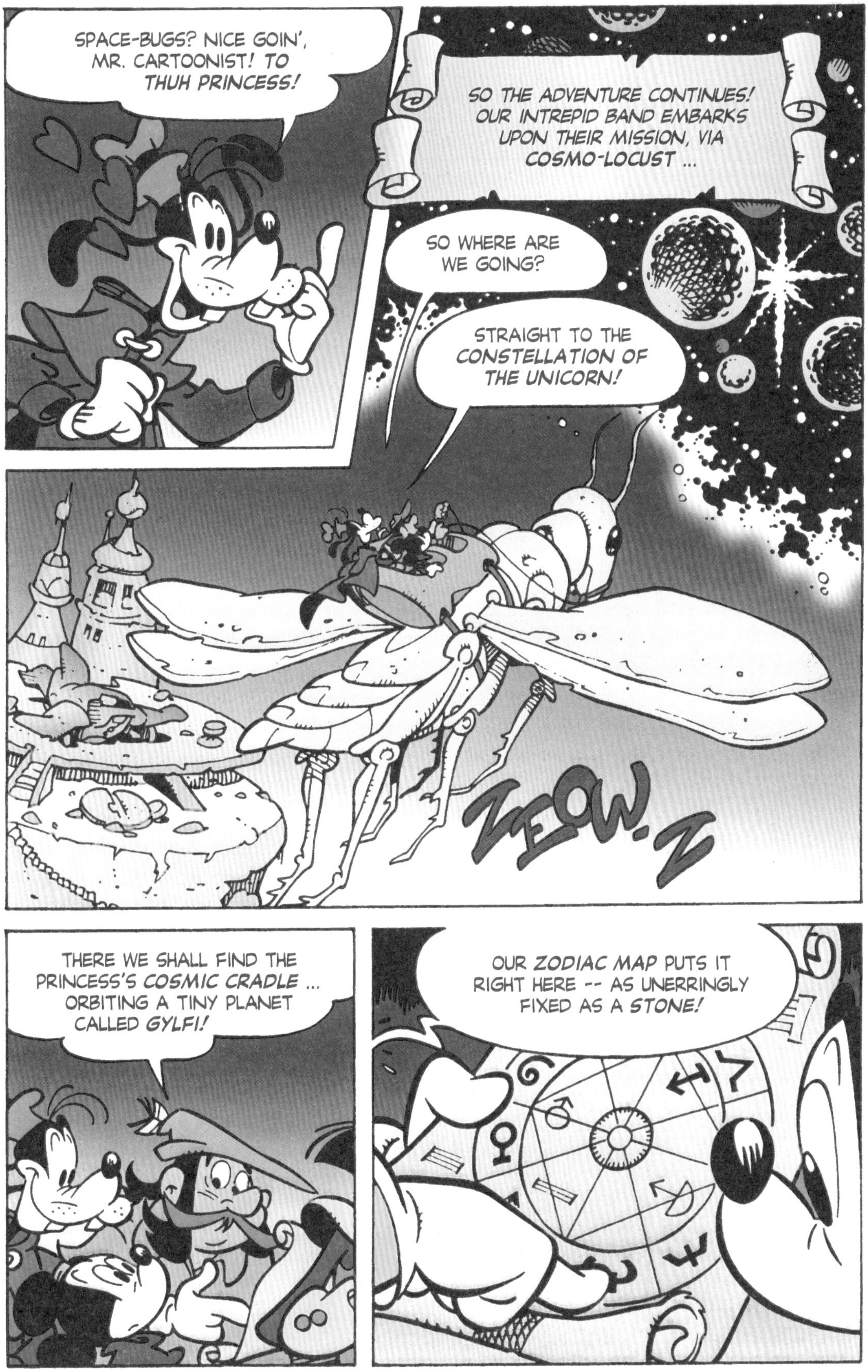
SPACE-BUGS? NICE GOIN', MR. CARTOONIST! TO THUH PRINCESS!
SO THE ADVENTURE CONTINUES! OUR INTREPID BAND EMBARKS UPON THEIR MISSION, VIA COSMO-LOCUST ...
SO WHERE ARE WE GOING?
STRAIGHT TO THE CONSTELLATION OF THE UNICORN!
ZEOW-Z
THERE WE SHALL FIND THE PRINCESS'S COSMIC CRADLE ... ORBITING A TINY PLANET CALLED GYLFI!
OUR ZODIAC MAP PUTS IT RIGHT HERE -- AS UNERRINGLY FIXED AS A STONE!

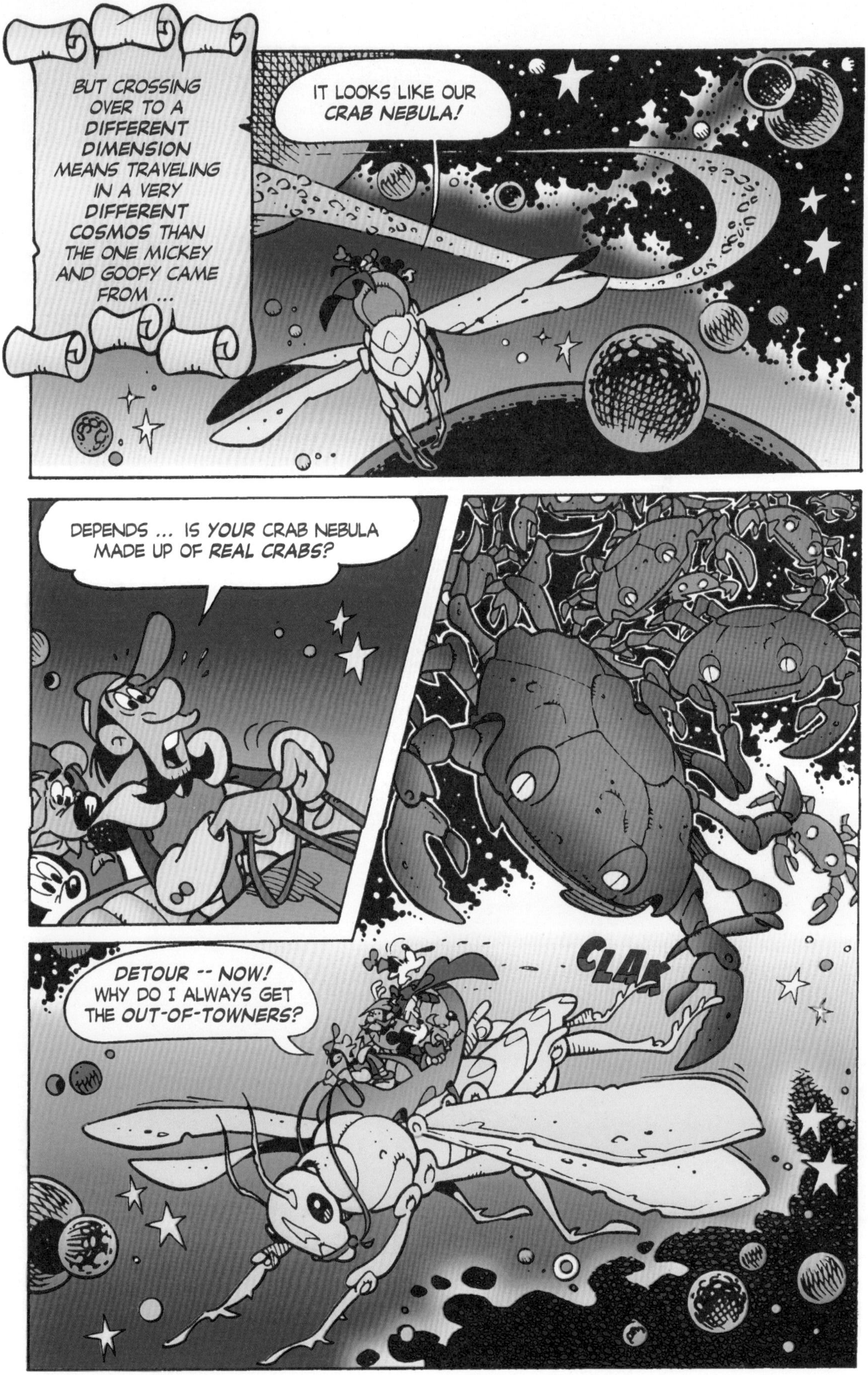
BUT CROSSING OVER TO A DIFFERENT DIMENSION MEANS TRAVELING IN A VERY DIFFERENT COSMOS THAN THE ONE MICKEY AND GOOFY CAME FROM ...
IT LOOKS LIKE OUR CRAB NEBULA!
DEPENDS ... IS YOUR CRAB NEBULA MADE UP OF REAL CRABS?
CLAK
DETOUR -- NOW! WHY DO I ALWAYS GET THE OUT-OF-TOWNERS?

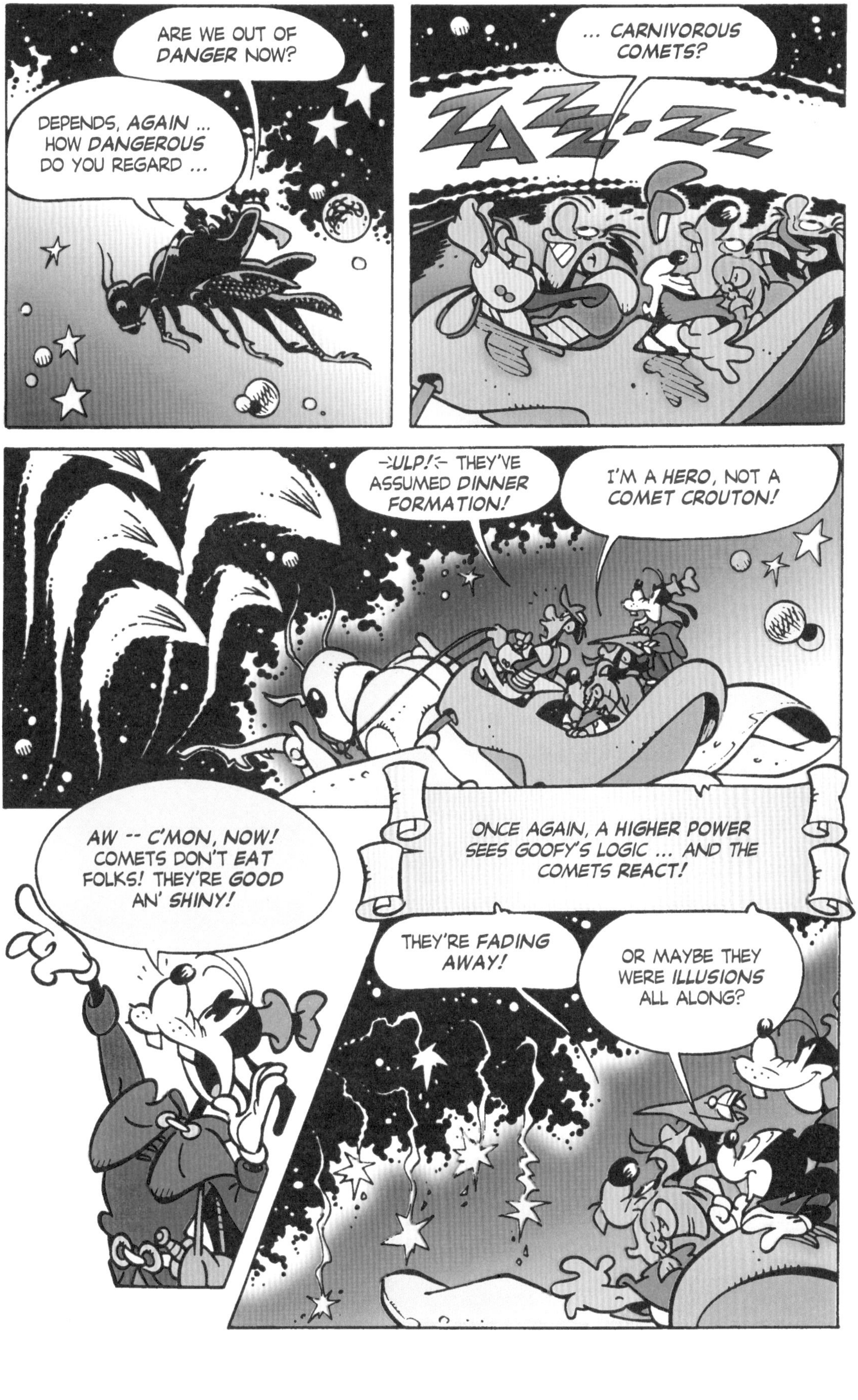
ARE WE OUT OF DANGER NOW?
DEPENDS, AGAIN ... HOW DANGEROUS DO YOU REGARD ...
... CARNIVOROUS COMETS?
ZAZZ-ZZZ
-ULP!- THEY'VE ASSUMED DINNER FORMATION!
I'M A HERO, NOT A COMET CROUTON!
AW -- C'MON, NOW! COMETS DON'T EAT FOLKS! THEY'RE GOOD AN' SHINY!
ONCE AGAIN, A HIGHER POWER SEES GOOFY'S LOGIC ... AND THE COMETS REACT!
THEY'RE FADING AWAY!
OR MAYBE THEY WERE ILLUSIONS ALL ALONG?

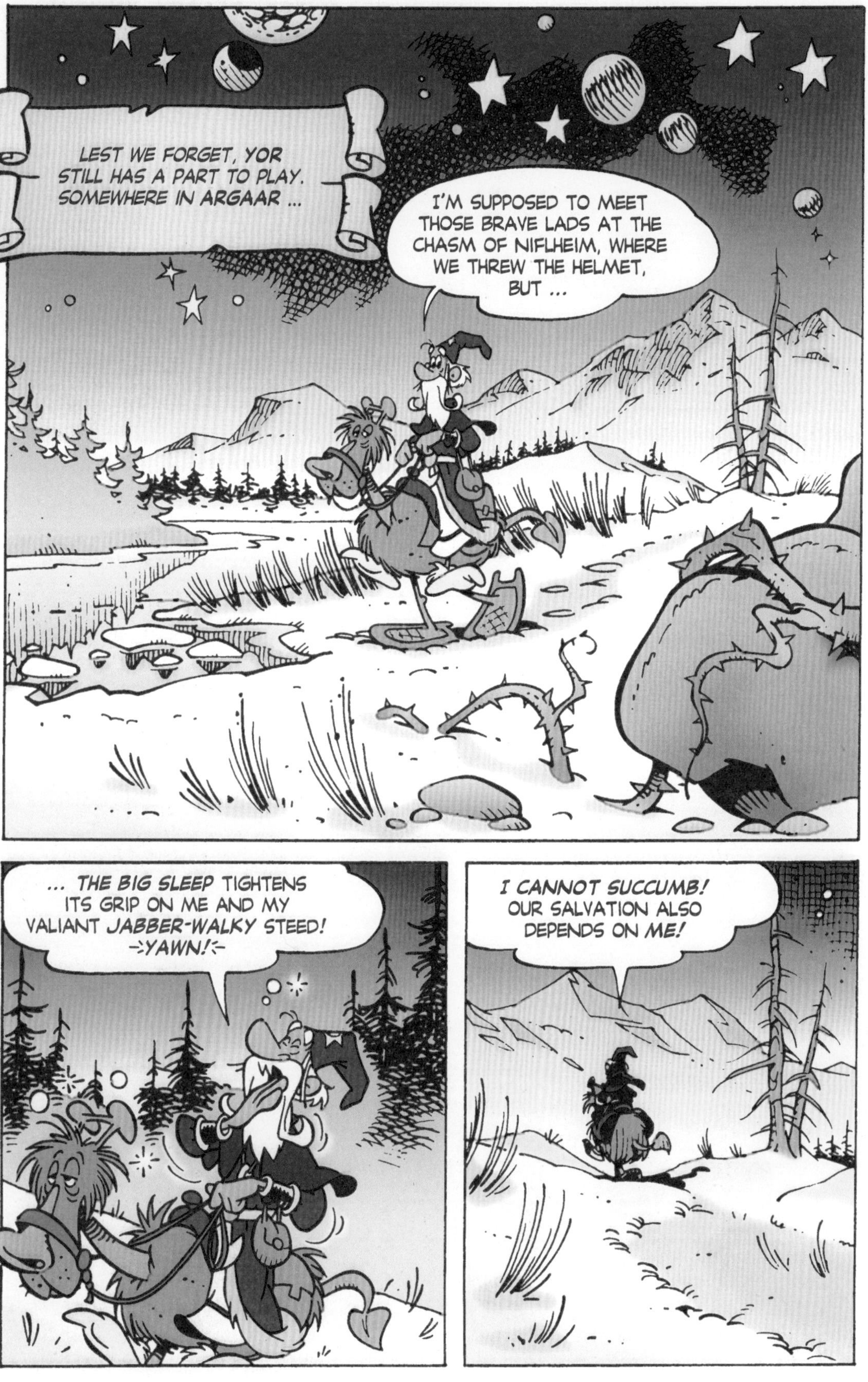
LEST WE FORGET, YOR STILL HAS A PART TO PLAY. SOMEWHERE IN ARGAAR ...
I'M SUPPOSED TO MEET THOSE BRAVE LADS AT THE CHASM OF NIFLHEIM, WHERE WE THREW THE HELMET, BUT ...
... THE BIG SLEEP TIGHTENS ITS GRIP ON ME AND MY VALIANT JABBER-WALKY STEED! -YAWN!-
I CANNOT SUCCUMB! OUR SALVATION ALSO DEPENDS ON ME!

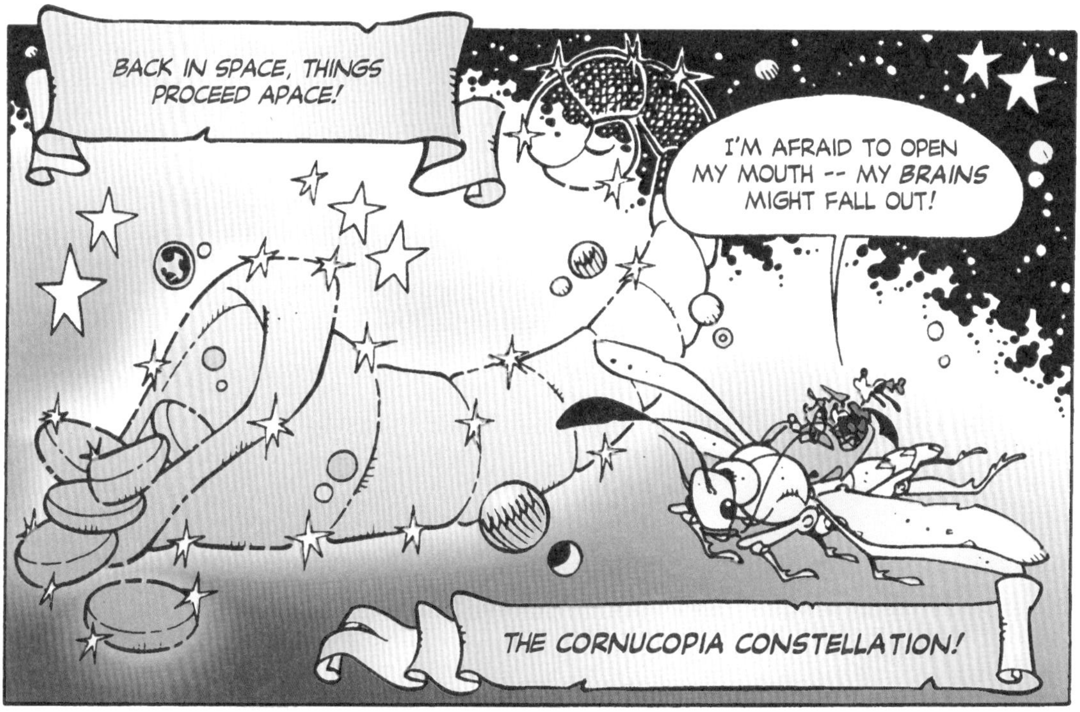
BACK IN SPACE, THINGS PROCEED APACE!
I'M AFRAID TO OPEN MY MOUTH -- MY *BRAINS* MIGHT FALL OUT!
THE CORNUCOPIA CONSTELLATION!

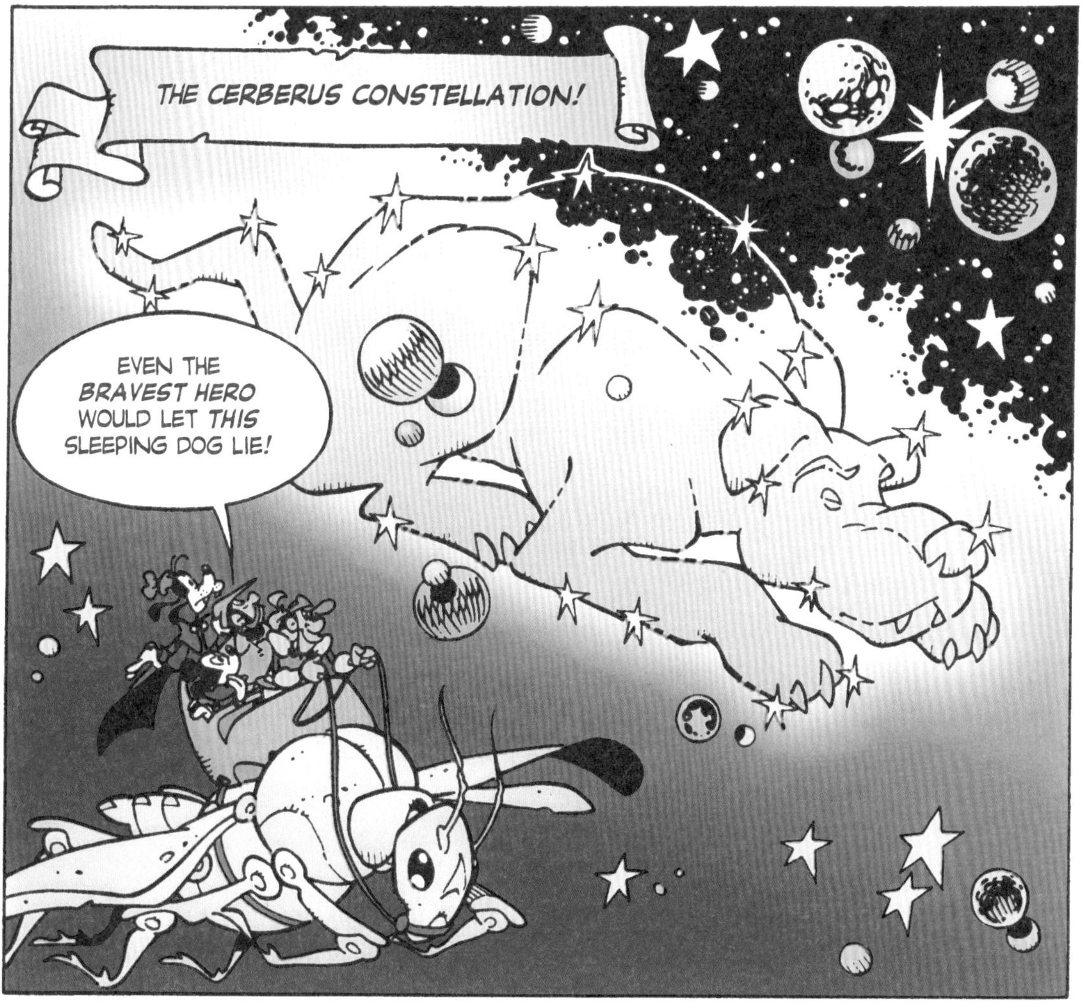
THE CERBERUS CONSTELLATION!
EVEN THE *BRAVEST HERO* WOULD LET *THIS* SLEEPING DOG LIE!

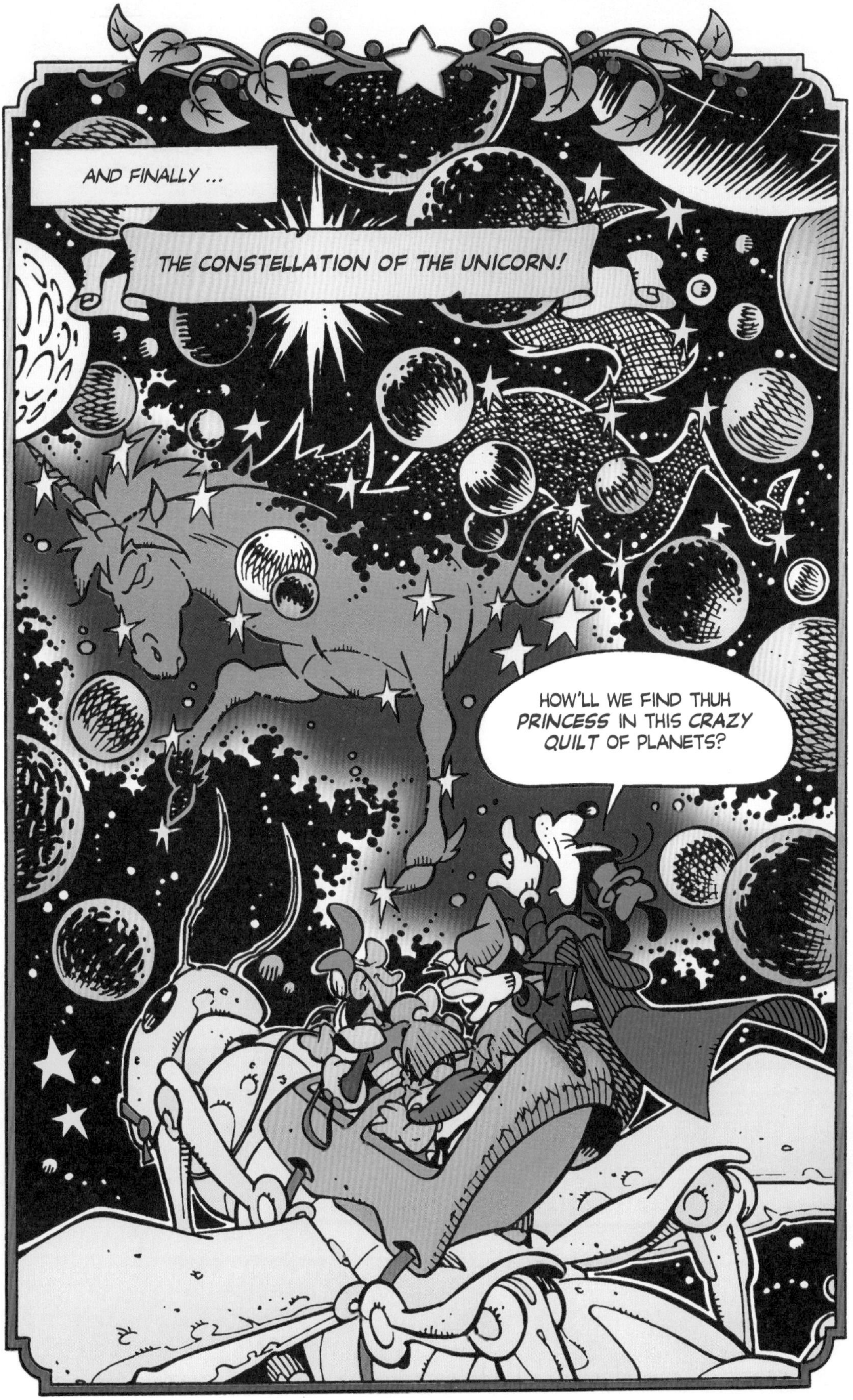
AND FINALLY ...
THE CONSTELLATION OF THE UNICORN!
HOW'LL WE FIND THUH PRINCESS IN THIS CRAZY QUILT OF PLANETS?

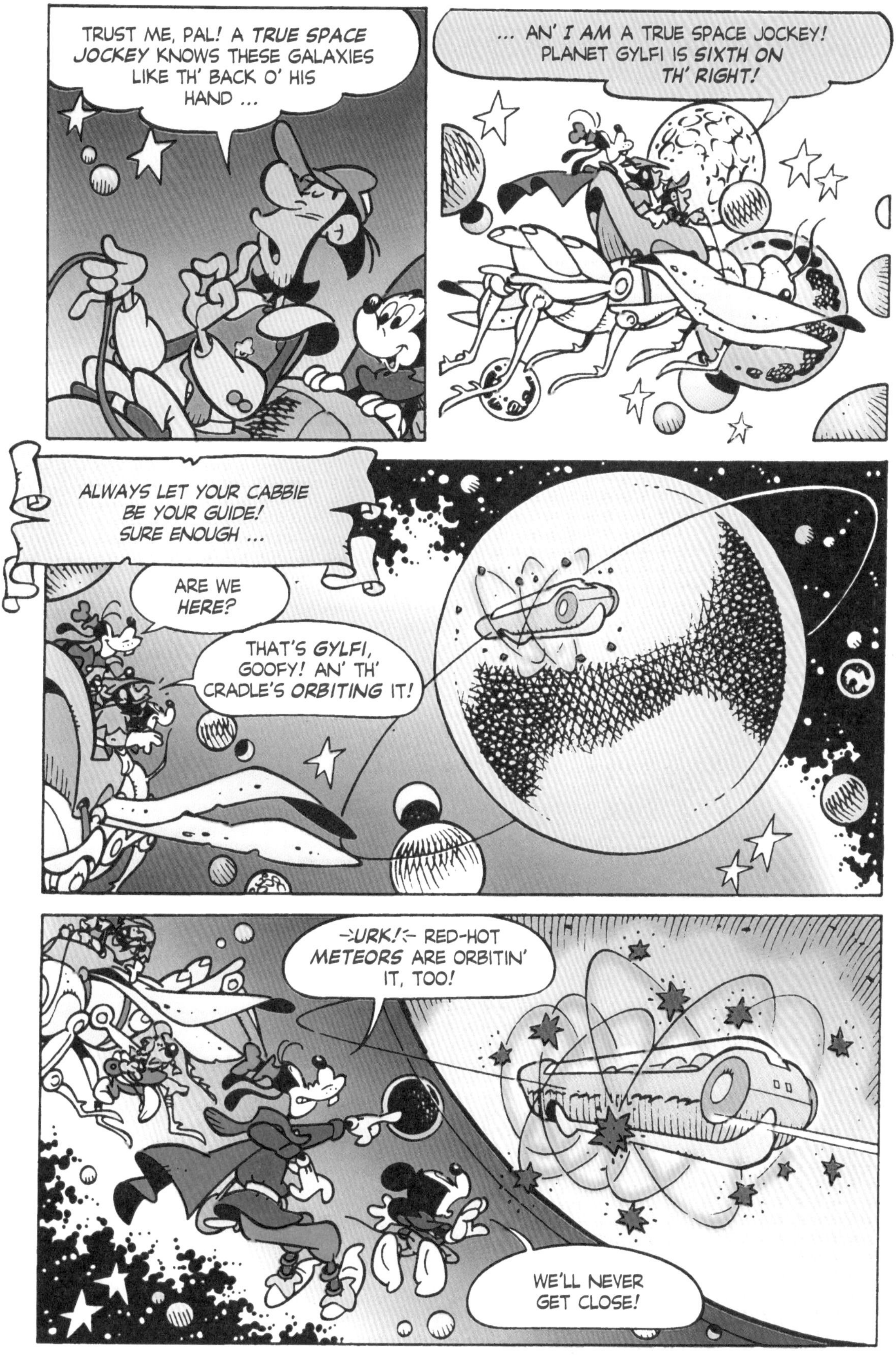
TRUST ME, PAL! A TRUE SPACE JOCKEY KNOWS THESE GALAXIES LIKE TH' BACK O' HIS HAND ...
... AN' I AM A TRUE SPACE JOCKEY! PLANET GYLFI IS SIXTH ON TH' RIGHT!
ALWAYS LET YOUR CABBIE BE YOUR GUIDE! SURE ENOUGH ...
ARE WE HERE?
THAT'S GYLFI, GOOFY! AN' TH' CRADLE'S ORBITING IT!
-URK!- RED-HOT METEORS ARE ORBITIN' IT, TOO!
WE'LL NEVER GET CLOSE!

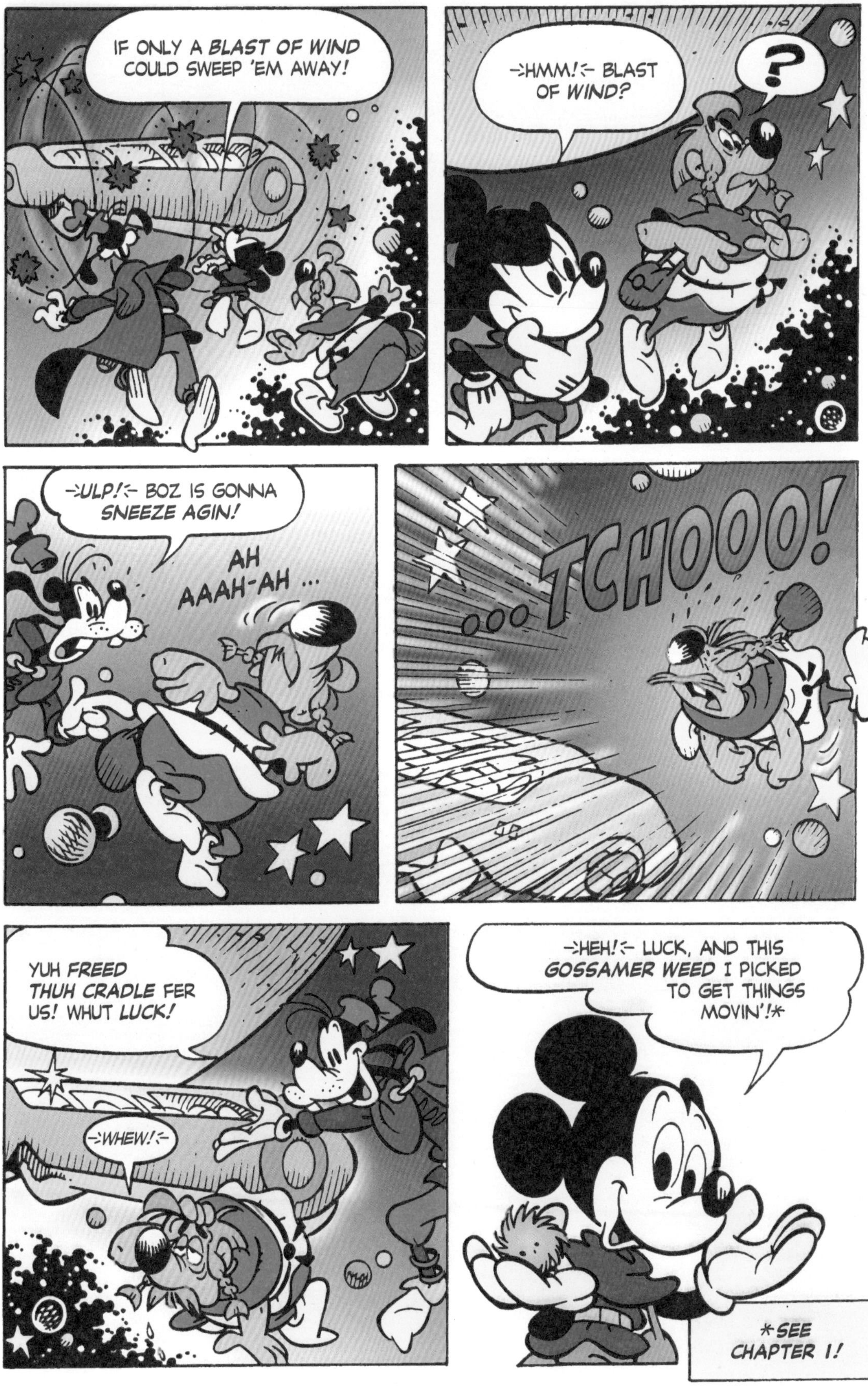
IF ONLY A BLAST OF WIND COULD SWEEP 'EM AWAY!
-HMM!- BLAST OF WIND?
?
-ULP!- BOZ IS GONNA SNEEZE AGIN!
AH AAAH-AH ...
...TCHOOO!
YUH FREED THUH CRADLE FER US! WHUT LUCK!
-WHEW!-
-HEH!- LUCK, AND THIS GOSSAMER WEED I PICKED TO GET THINGS MOVIN'!*
*SEE CHAPTER 1!

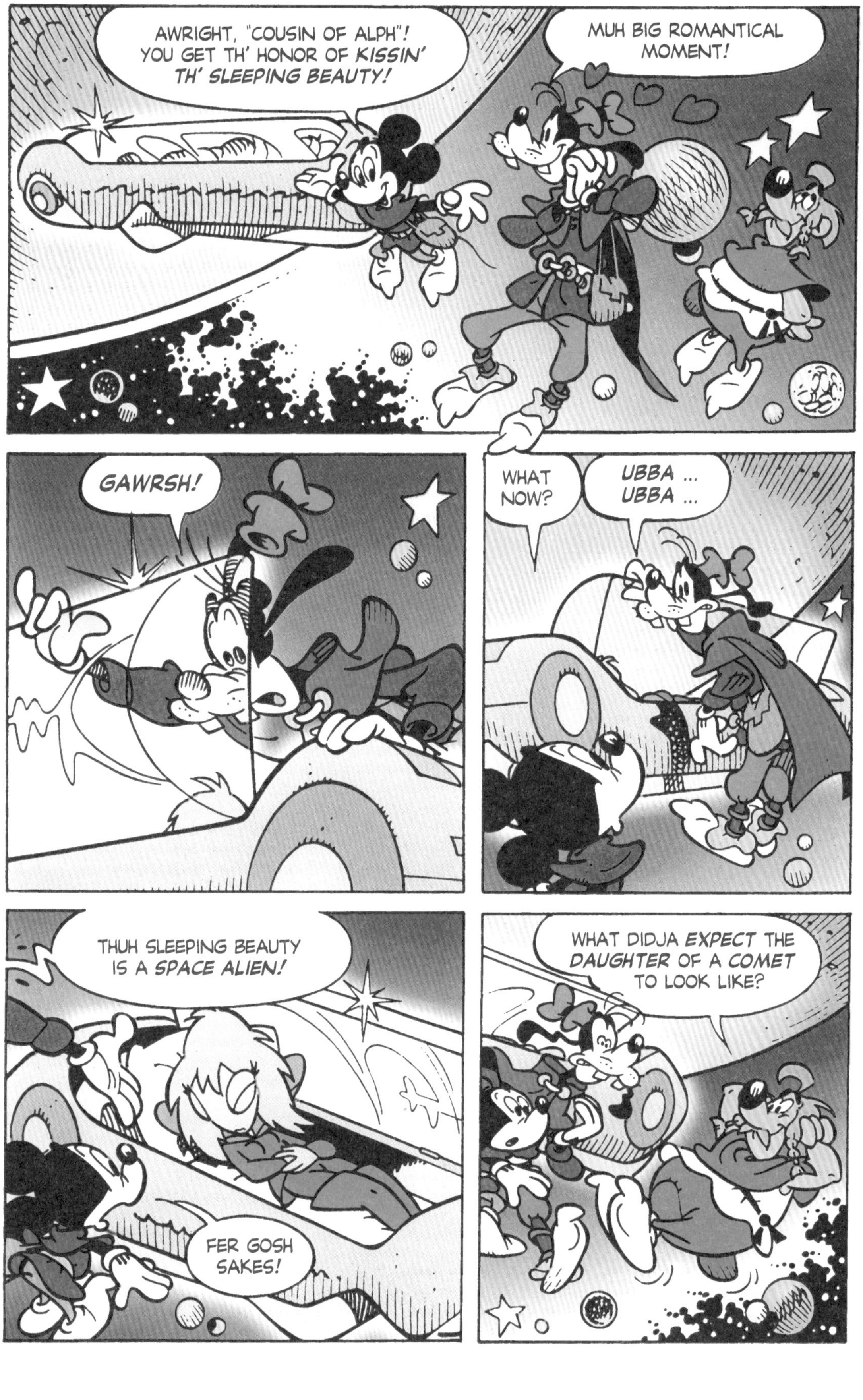
AWRIGHT, "COUSIN OF ALPH"! YOU GET TH' HONOR OF KISSIN' TH' SLEEPING BEAUTY!
MUH BIG ROMANTICAL MOMENT!
GAWRSH!
WHAT NOW?
UBBA ... UBBA ...
THUH SLEEPING BEAUTY IS A SPACE ALIEN!
FER GOSH SAKES!
WHAT DIDJA EXPECT THE DAUGHTER OF A COMET TO LOOK LIKE?

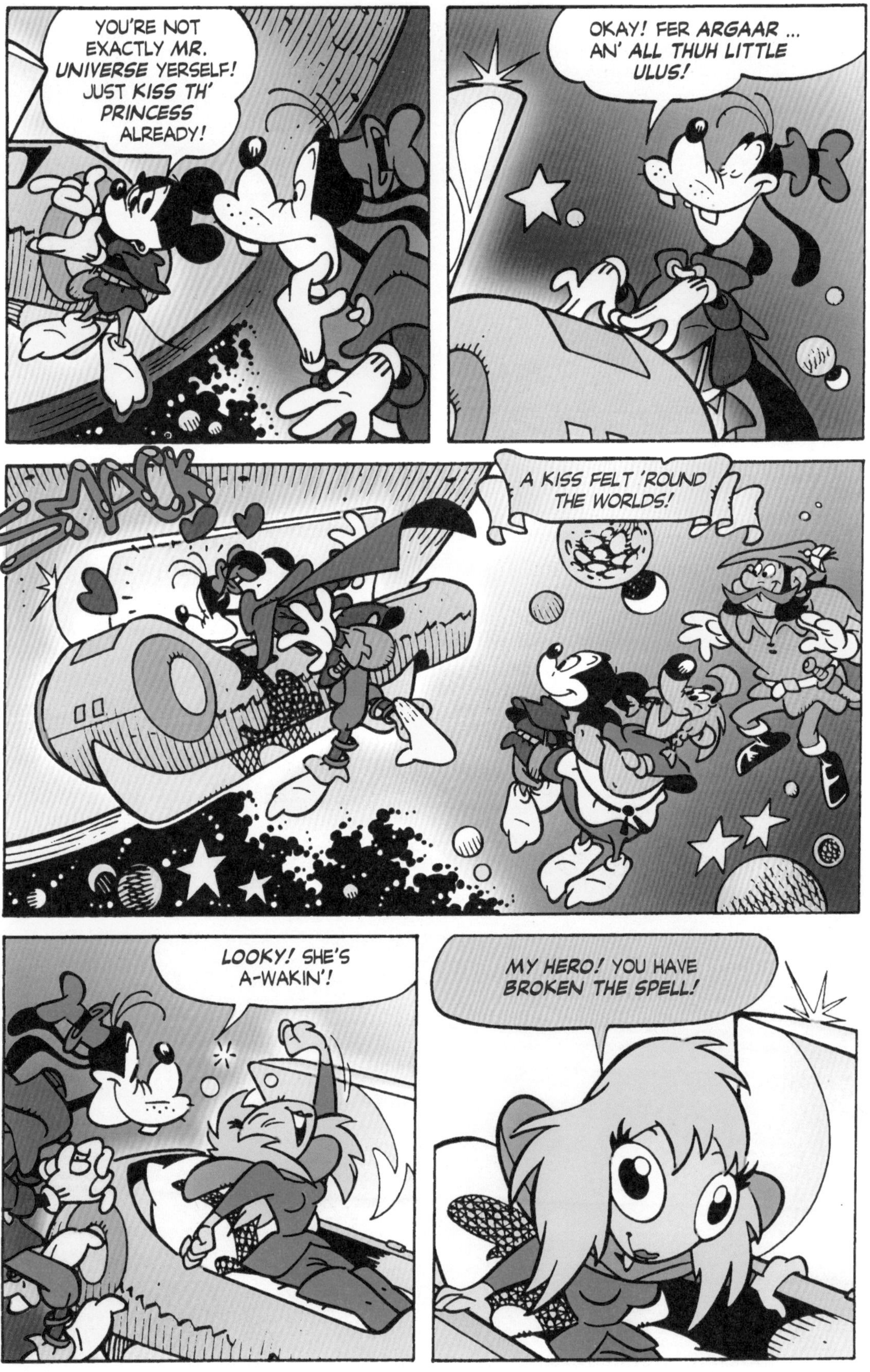
YOU'RE NOT EXACTLY MR. UNIVERSE YERSELF! JUST KISS TH' PRINCESS ALREADY!
OKAY! FER ARGAAR ... AN' ALL THUH LITTLE ULUS!
SMACK
A KISS FELT 'ROUND THE WORLDS!
LOOKY! SHE'S A-WAKIN'!
MY HERO! YOU HAVE BROKEN THE SPELL!

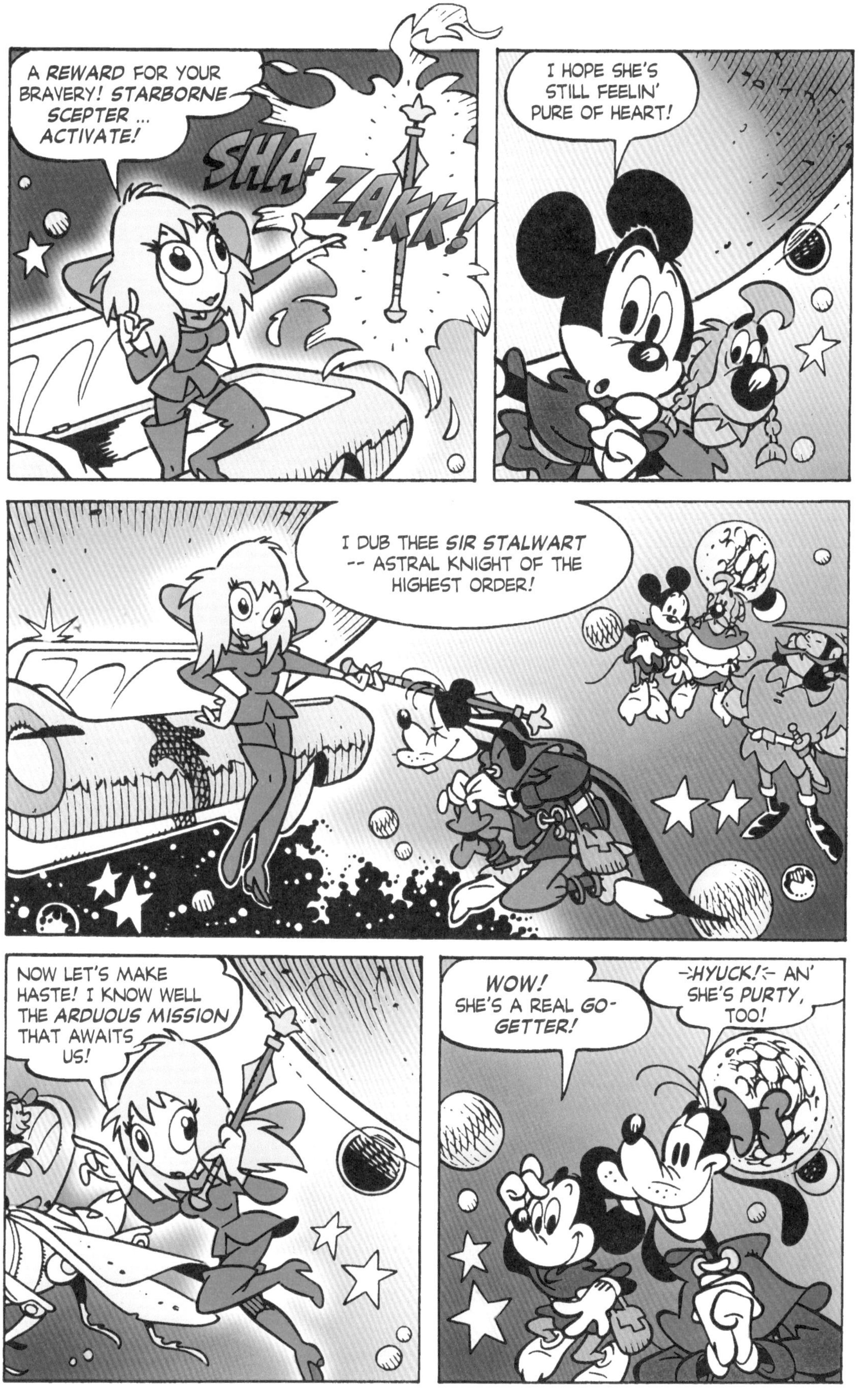
A REWARD FOR YOUR BRAVERY! STARBORNE SCEPTER ... ACTIVATE!
SHA-ZAKK!
I HOPE SHE'S STILL FEELIN' PURE OF HEART!
I DUB THEE SIR STALWART -- ASTRAL KNIGHT OF THE HIGHEST ORDER!
NOW LET'S MAKE HASTE! I KNOW WELL THE ARDUOUS MISSION THAT AWAITS US!
WOW! SHE'S A REAL GO-GETTER!
-HYUCK!- AN' SHE'S PURTY, TOO!

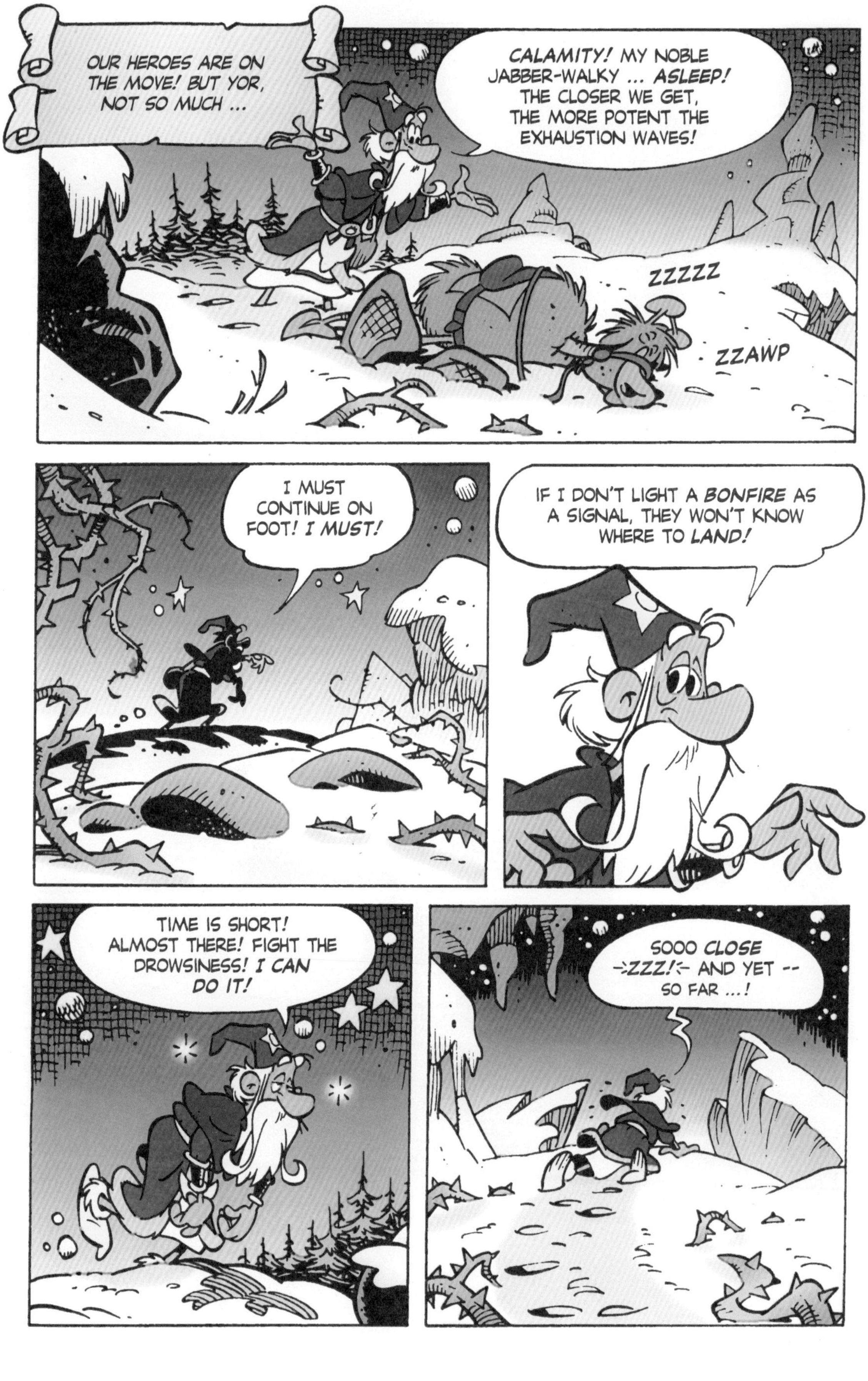

OUR HEROES ARE ON THE MOVE! BUT YOR, NOT SO MUCH ...
CALAMITY! MY NOBLE JABBER-WALKY ... ASLEEP! THE CLOSER WE GET, THE MORE POTENT THE EXHAUSTION WAVES!
ZZZZZ
ZZAWP
I MUST CONTINUE ON FOOT! I MUST!
IF I DON'T LIGHT A BONFIRE AS A SIGNAL, THEY WON'T KNOW WHERE TO LAND!
TIME IS SHORT! ALMOST THERE! FIGHT THE DROWSINESS! I CAN DO IT!
SOOO CLOSE --ZZZ!-- AND YET -- SO FAR ...!

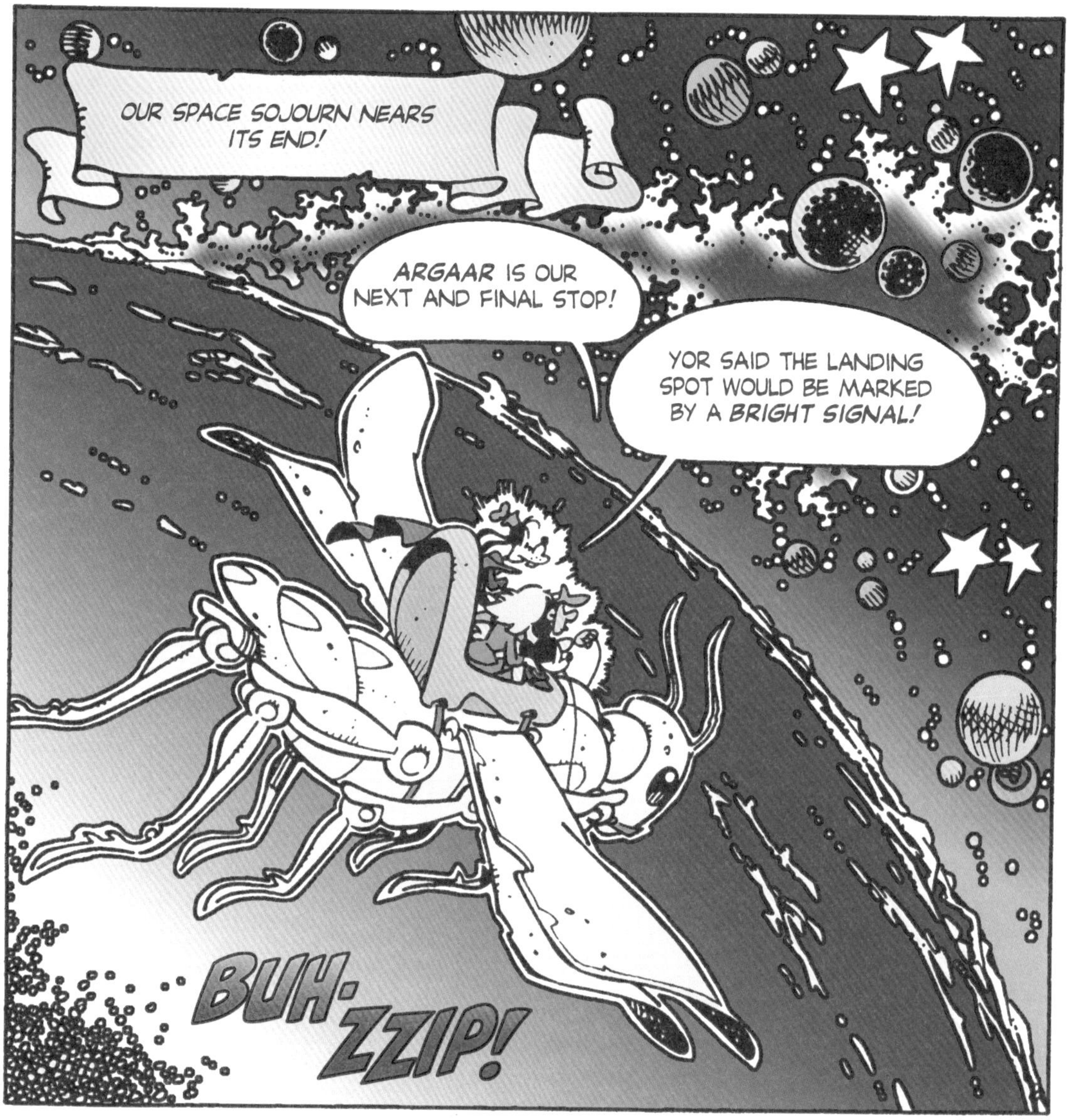
OUR SPACE SOJOURN NEARS ITS END!
ARGAAR IS OUR NEXT AND FINAL STOP!
YOR SAID THE LANDING SPOT WOULD BE MARKED BY A BRIGHT SIGNAL!
BUH-ZZIP!

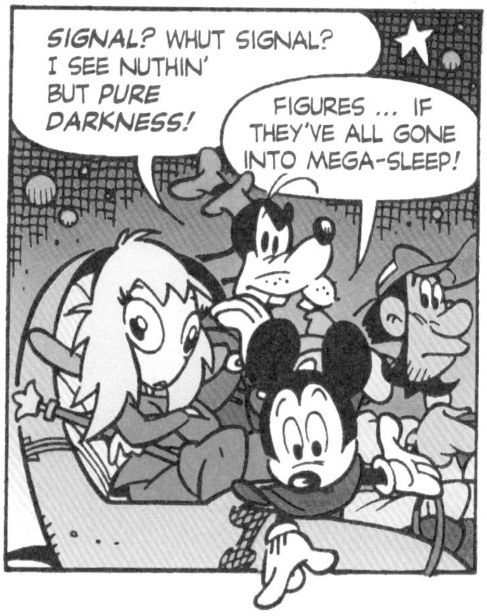
SIGNAL? WHUT SIGNAL? I SEE NUTHIN' BUT PURE DARKNESS!
FIGURES ... IF THEY'VE ALL GONE INTO MEGA-SLEEP!

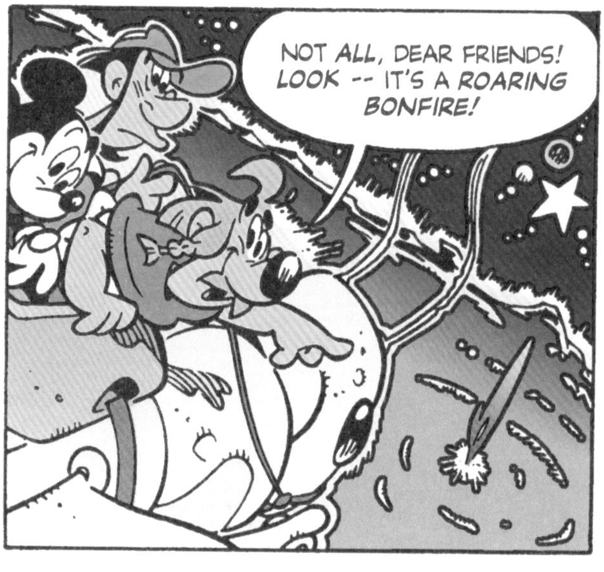
NOT ALL, DEAR FRIENDS! LOOK -- IT'S A ROARING BONFIRE!

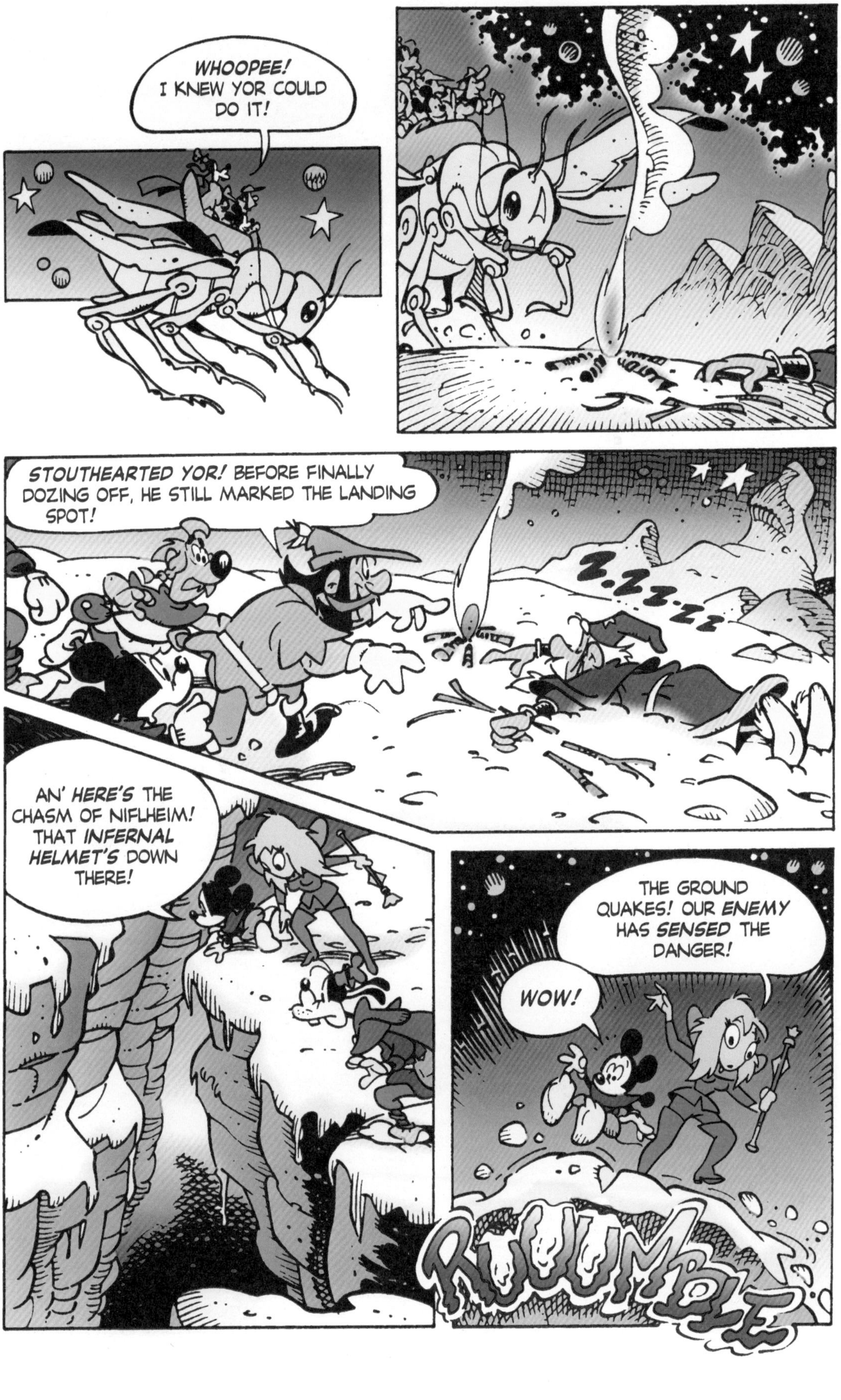
WHOOPEE! I KNEW YOR COULD DO IT!
STOUTHEARTED YOR! BEFORE FINALLY DOZING OFF, HE STILL MARKED THE LANDING SPOT!
AN' HERE'S THE CHASM OF NIFLHEIM! THAT INFERNAL HELMET'S DOWN THERE!
THE GROUND QUAKES! OUR ENEMY HAS SENSED THE DANGER!
WOW!
RUUUMBLE

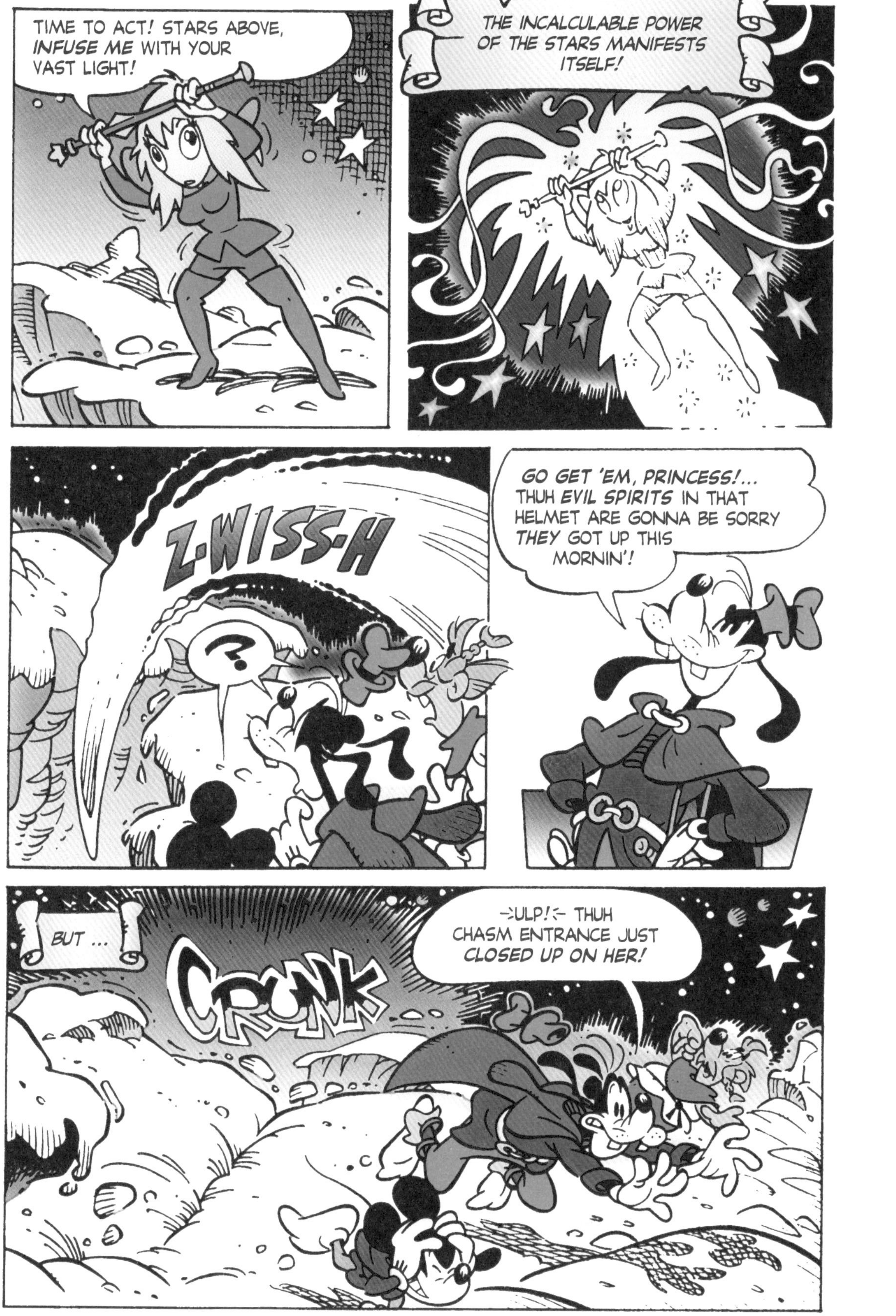
TIME TO ACT! STARS ABOVE, INFUSE ME WITH YOUR VAST LIGHT!
THE INCALCULABLE POWER OF THE STARS MANIFESTS ITSELF!
Z-WISS-H
?
GO GET 'EM, PRINCESS!... THUH EVIL SPIRITS IN THAT HELMET ARE GONNA BE SORRY THEY GOT UP THIS MORNIN'!
BUT ...
CRUNK
-ULP!- THUH CHASM ENTRANCE JUST CLOSED UP ON HER!

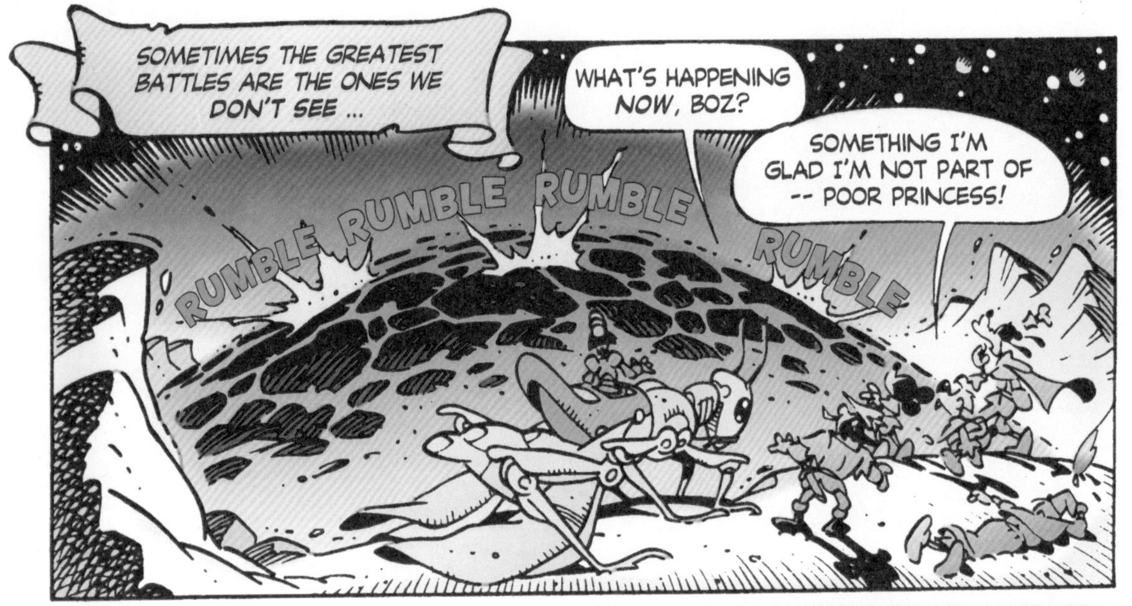
SOMETIMES THE GREATEST BATTLES ARE THE ONES WE DON'T SEE ...
WHAT'S HAPPENING NOW, BOZ?
SOMETHING I'M GLAD I'M NOT PART OF -- POOR PRINCESS!
RUMBLE RUMBLE RUMBLE RUMBLE
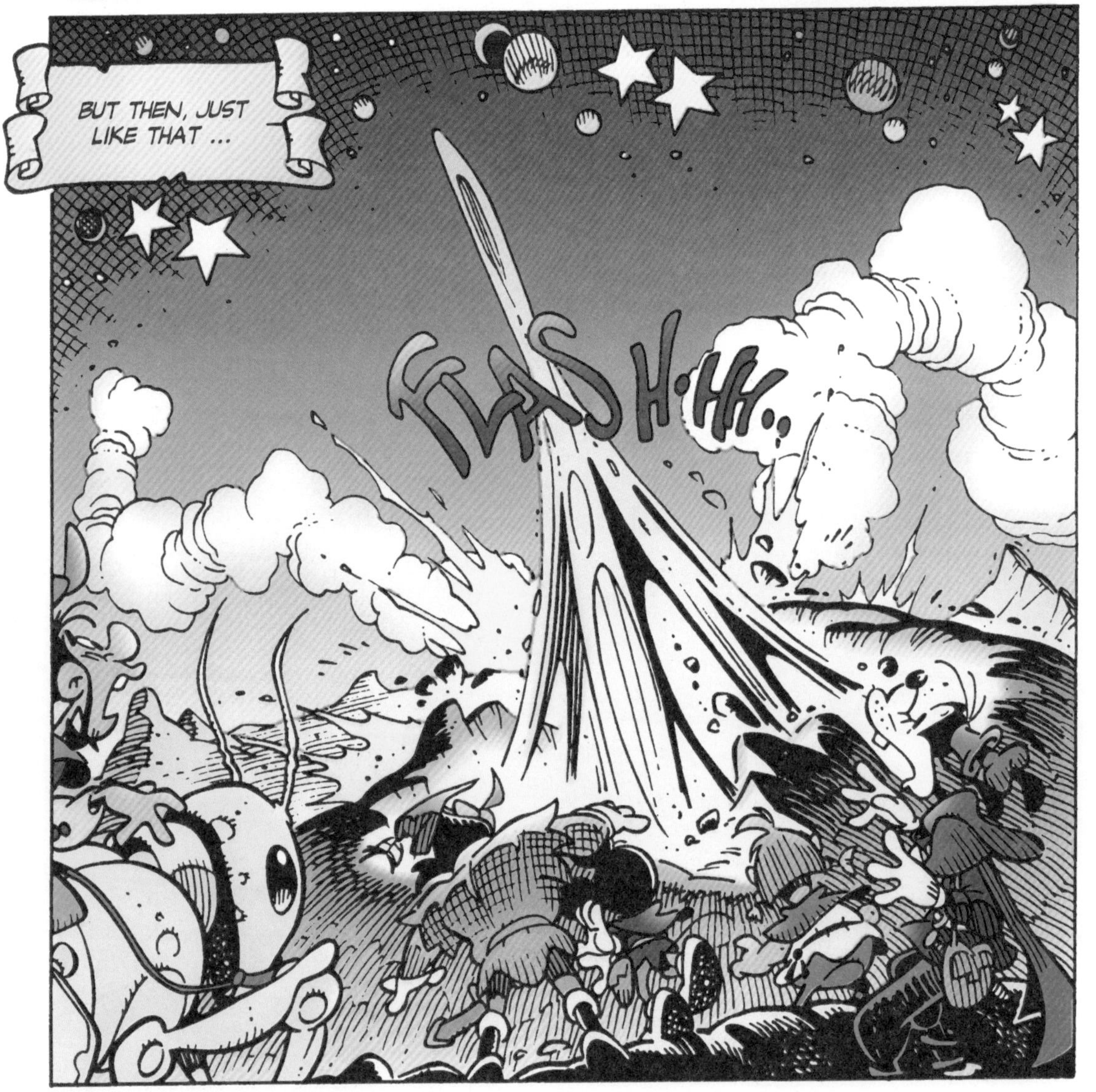
BUT THEN, JUST LIKE THAT ...
FLASH-HH...

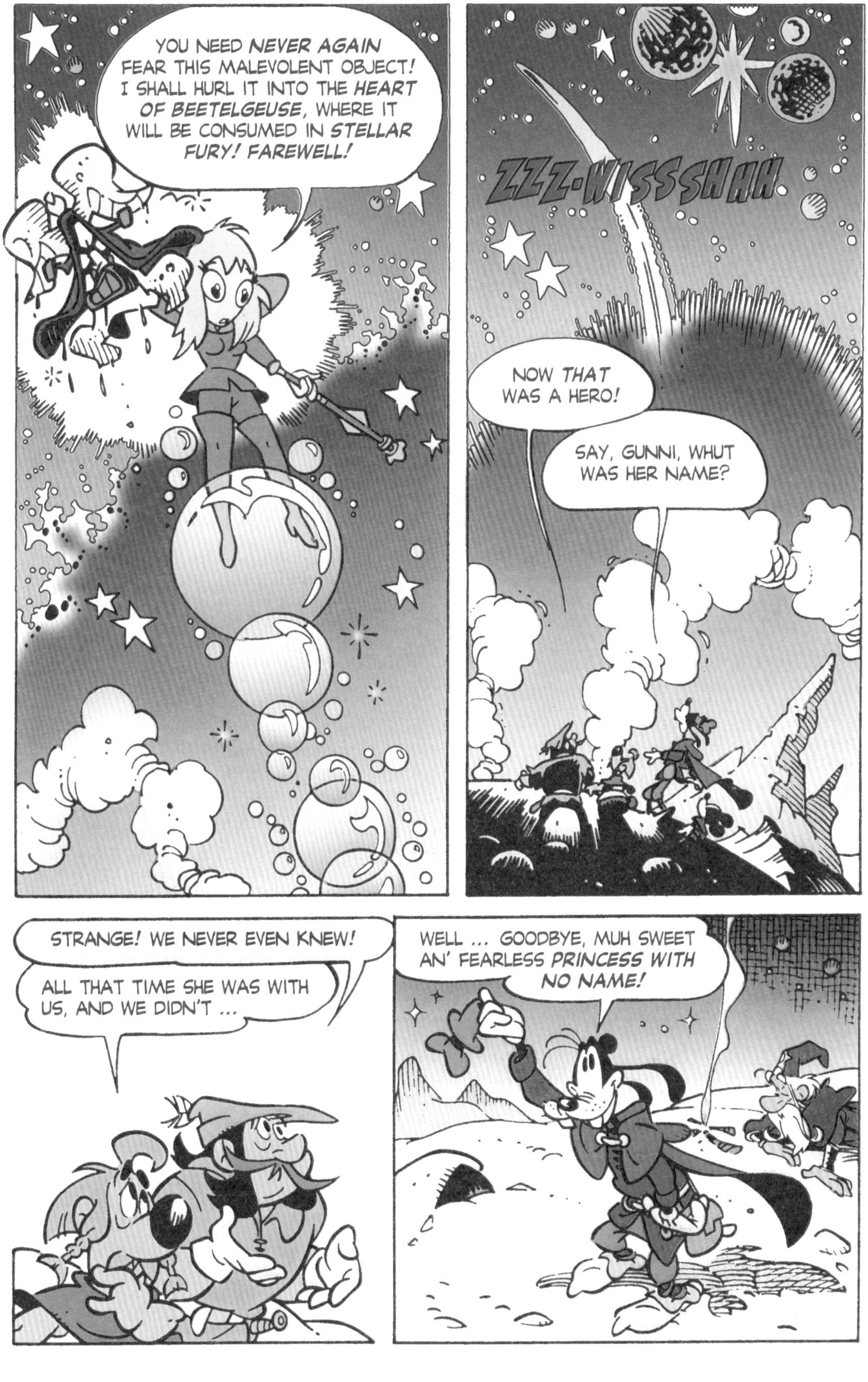
YOU NEED NEVER AGAIN FEAR THIS MALEVOLENT OBJECT! I SHALL HURL IT INTO THE HEART OF BEETELGEUSE, WHERE IT WILL BE CONSUMED IN STELLAR FURY! FAREWELL!
ZZZ-WISSSHHH
NOW THAT WAS A HERO!
SAY, GUNNI, WHUT WAS HER NAME?
STRANGE! WE NEVER EVEN KNEW!
ALL THAT TIME SHE WAS WITH US, AND WE DIDN'T ...
WELL ... GOODBYE, MUH SWEET AN' FEARLESS PRINCESS WITH NO NAME!

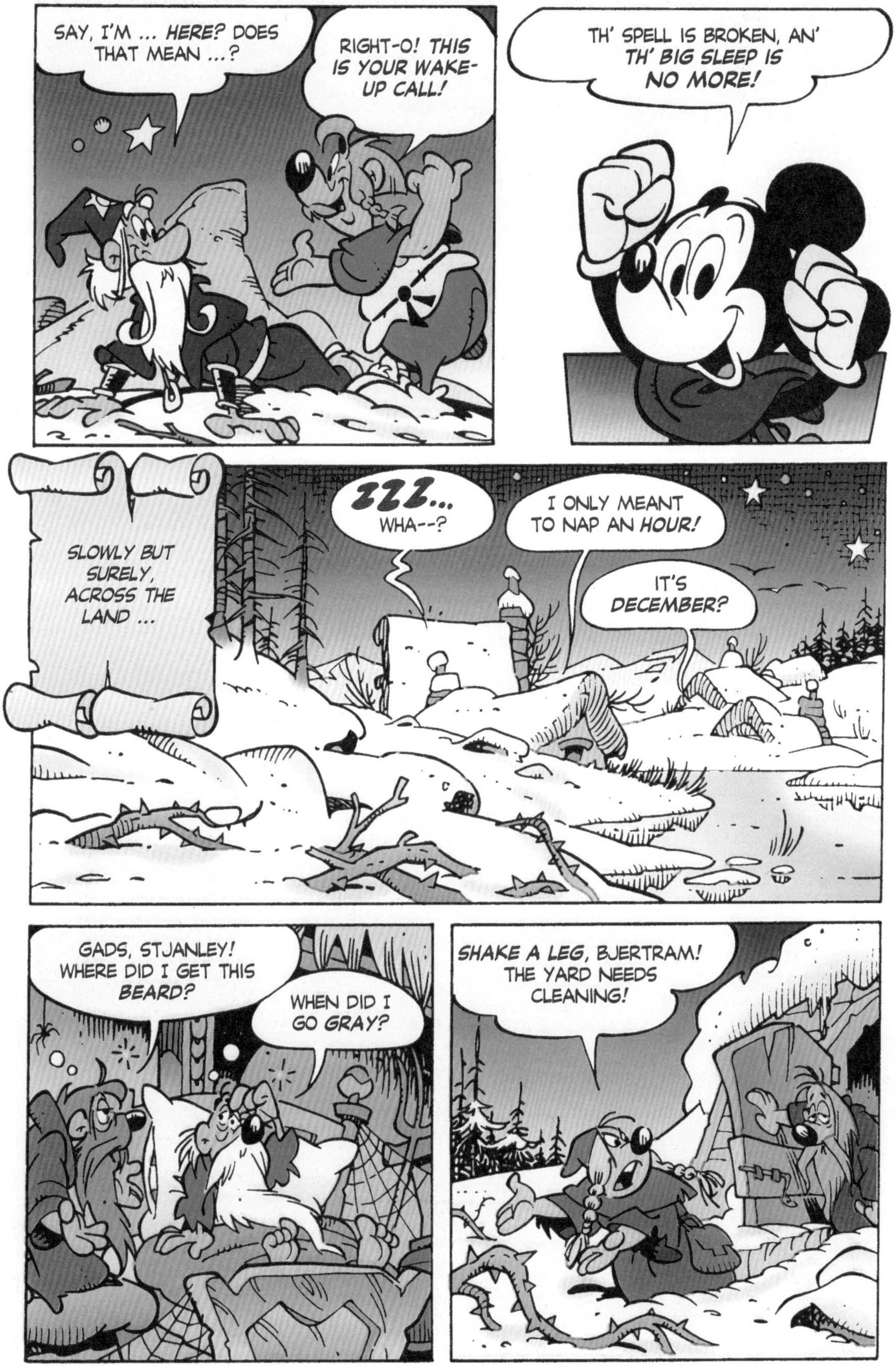

SAY, I'M ... HERE? DOES THAT MEAN ...?
RIGHT-O! THIS IS YOUR WAKE-UP CALL!
TH' SPELL IS BROKEN, AN' TH' BIG SLEEP IS NO MORE!
SLOWLY BUT SURELY, ACROSS THE LAND ...
ZZZ... WHA--?
I ONLY MEANT TO NAP AN HOUR!
IT'S DECEMBER?
GADS, STJANLEY! WHERE DID I GET THIS BEARD?
WHEN DID I GO GRAY?
SHAKE A LEG, BJERTRAM! THE YARD NEEDS CLEANING!

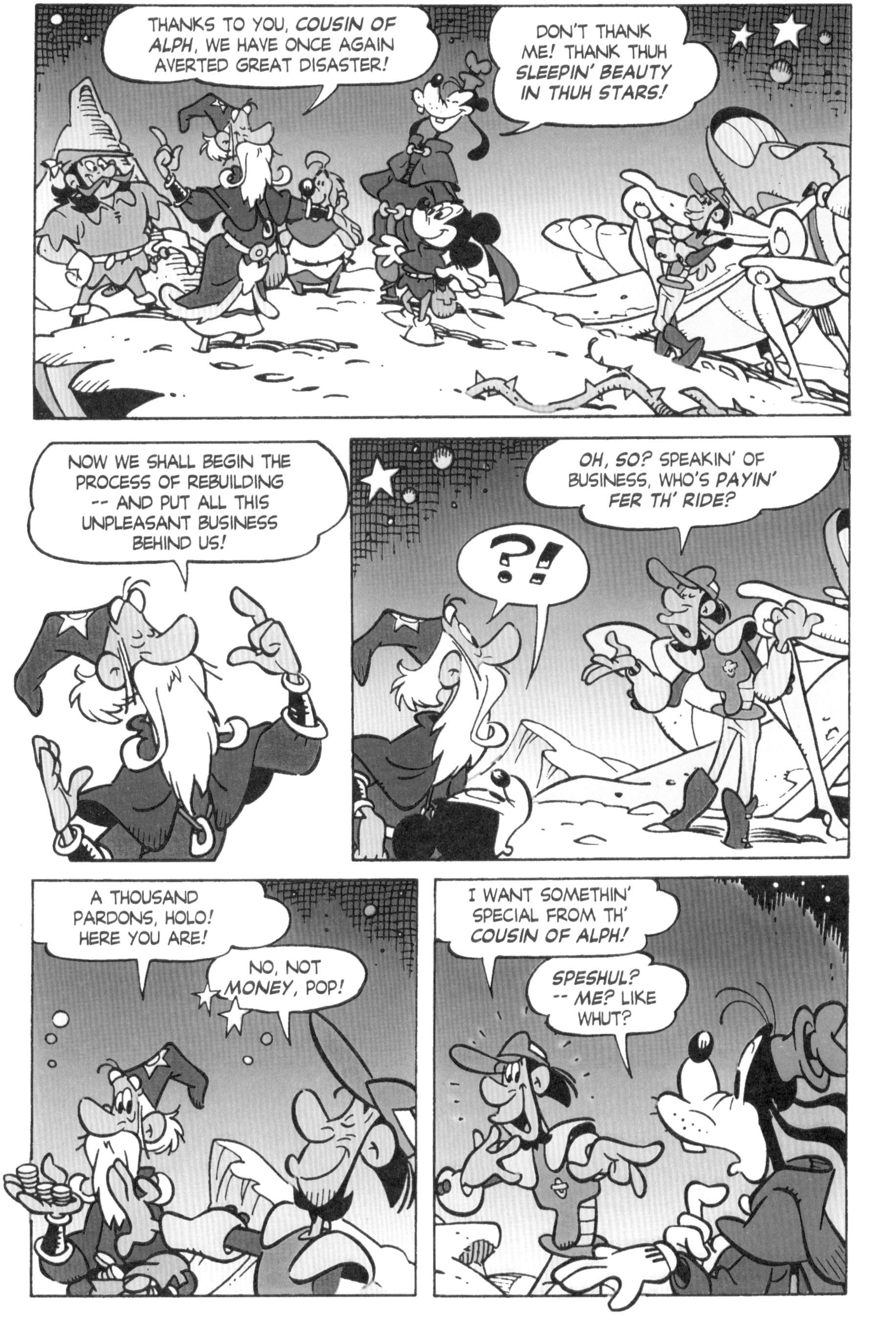
THANKS TO YOU, COUSIN OF ALPH, WE HAVE ONCE AGAIN AVERTED GREAT DISASTER!
DON'T THANK ME! THANK THUH SLEEPIN' BEAUTY IN THUH STARS!
NOW WE SHALL BEGIN THE PROCESS OF REBUILDING -- AND PUT ALL THIS UNPLEASANT BUSINESS BEHIND US!
OH, SO? SPEAKIN' OF BUSINESS, WHO'S PAYIN' FER TH' RIDE?
?!
A THOUSAND PARDONS, HOLO! HERE YOU ARE!
NO, NOT MONEY, POP!
I WANT SOMETHIN' SPECIAL FROM TH' COUSIN OF ALPH!
SPESHUL? -- ME? LIKE WHUT?

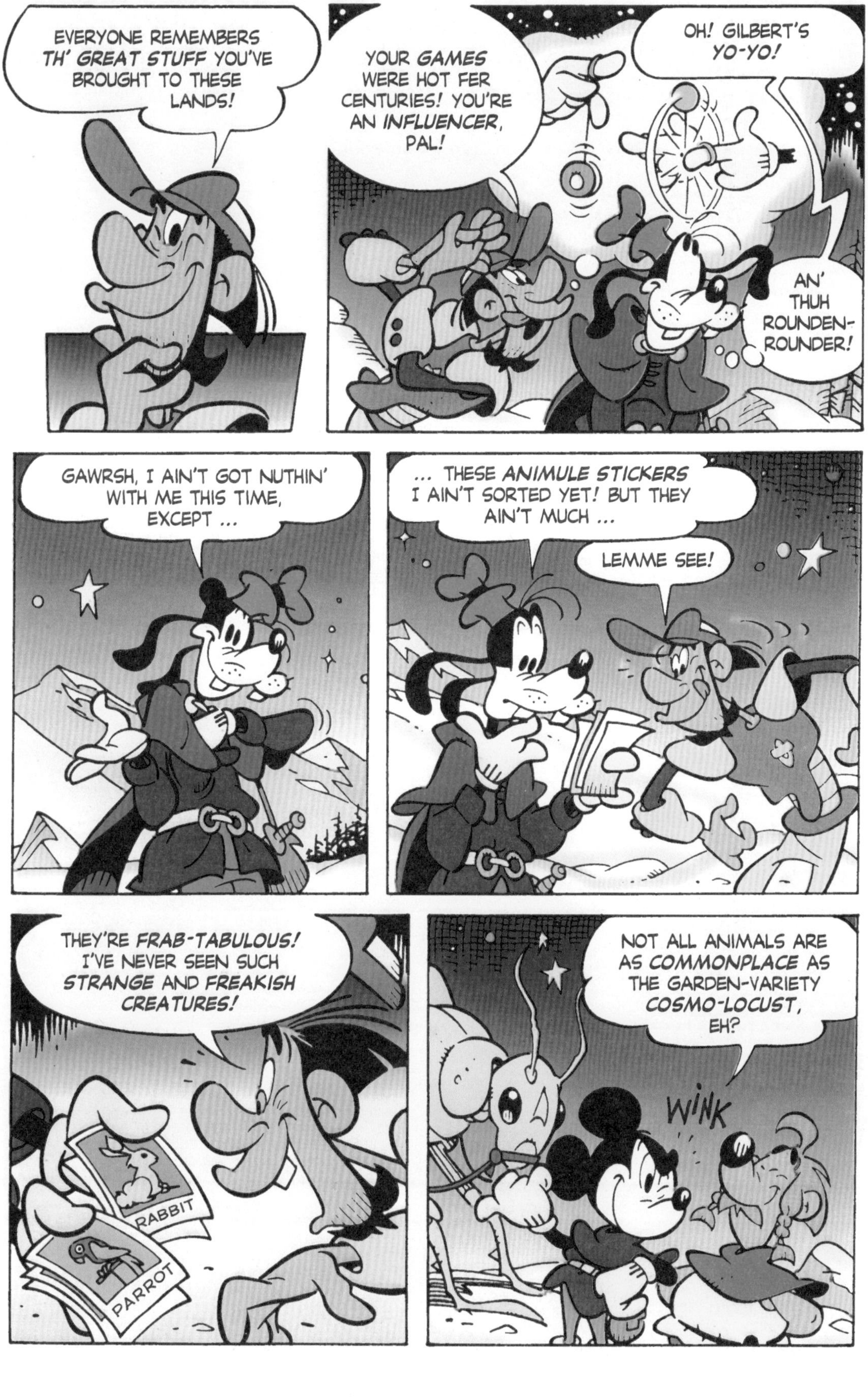
EVERYONE REMEMBERS TH' GREAT STUFF YOU'VE BROUGHT TO THESE LANDS!
YOUR GAMES WERE HOT FER CENTURIES! YOU'RE AN INFLUENCER, PAL!
OH! GILBERT'S YO-YO!
AN' THUH ROUNDEN-ROUNDER!
GAWRSH, I AIN'T GOT NUTHIN' WITH ME THIS TIME, EXCEPT ...
... THESE ANIMULE STICKERS I AIN'T SORTED YET! BUT THEY AIN'T MUCH ...
LEMME SEE!
THEY'RE FRAB-TABULOUS! I'VE NEVER SEEN SUCH STRANGE AND FREAKISH CREATURES!
RABBIT
PARROT
NOT ALL ANIMALS ARE AS COMMONPLACE AS THE GARDEN-VARIETY COSMO-LOCUST, EH?
WINK

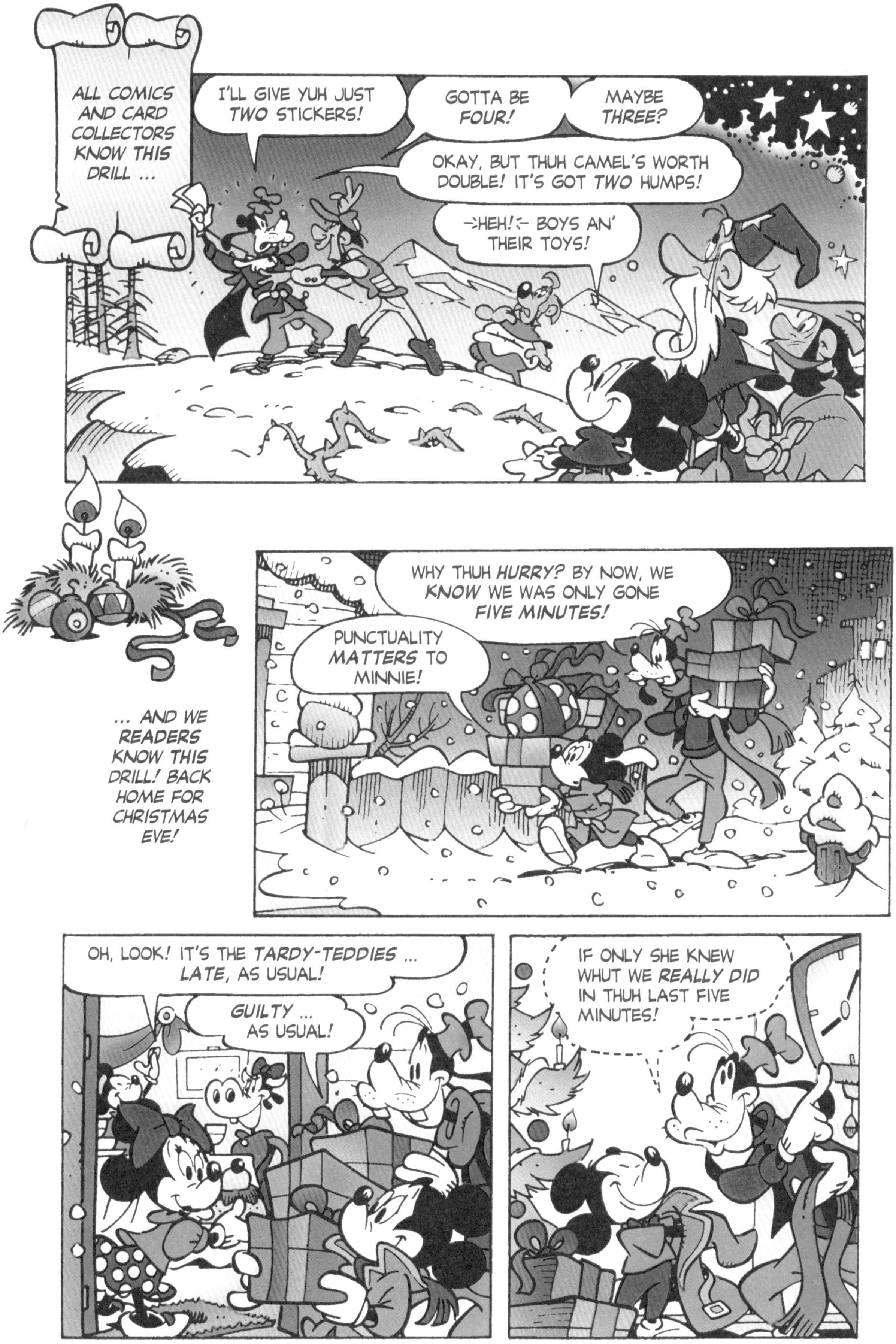
ALL COMICS AND CARD COLLECTORS KNOW THIS DRILL ...
I'LL GIVE YUH JUST TWO STICKERS!
GOTTA BE FOUR!
MAYBE THREE?
OKAY, BUT THUH CAMEL'S WORTH DOUBLE! IT'S GOT TWO HUMPS!
–HEH!– BOYS AN' THEIR TOYS!
... AND WE READERS KNOW THIS DRILL! BACK HOME FOR CHRISTMAS EVE!
WHY THUH HURRY? BY NOW, WE KNOW WE WAS ONLY GONE FIVE MINUTES!
PUNCTUALITY MATTERS TO MINNIE!
OH, LOOK! IT'S THE TARDY-TEDDIES ... LATE, AS USUAL!
GUILTY ... AS USUAL!
IF ONLY SHE KNEW WHUT WE REALLY DID IN THUH LAST FIVE MINUTES!

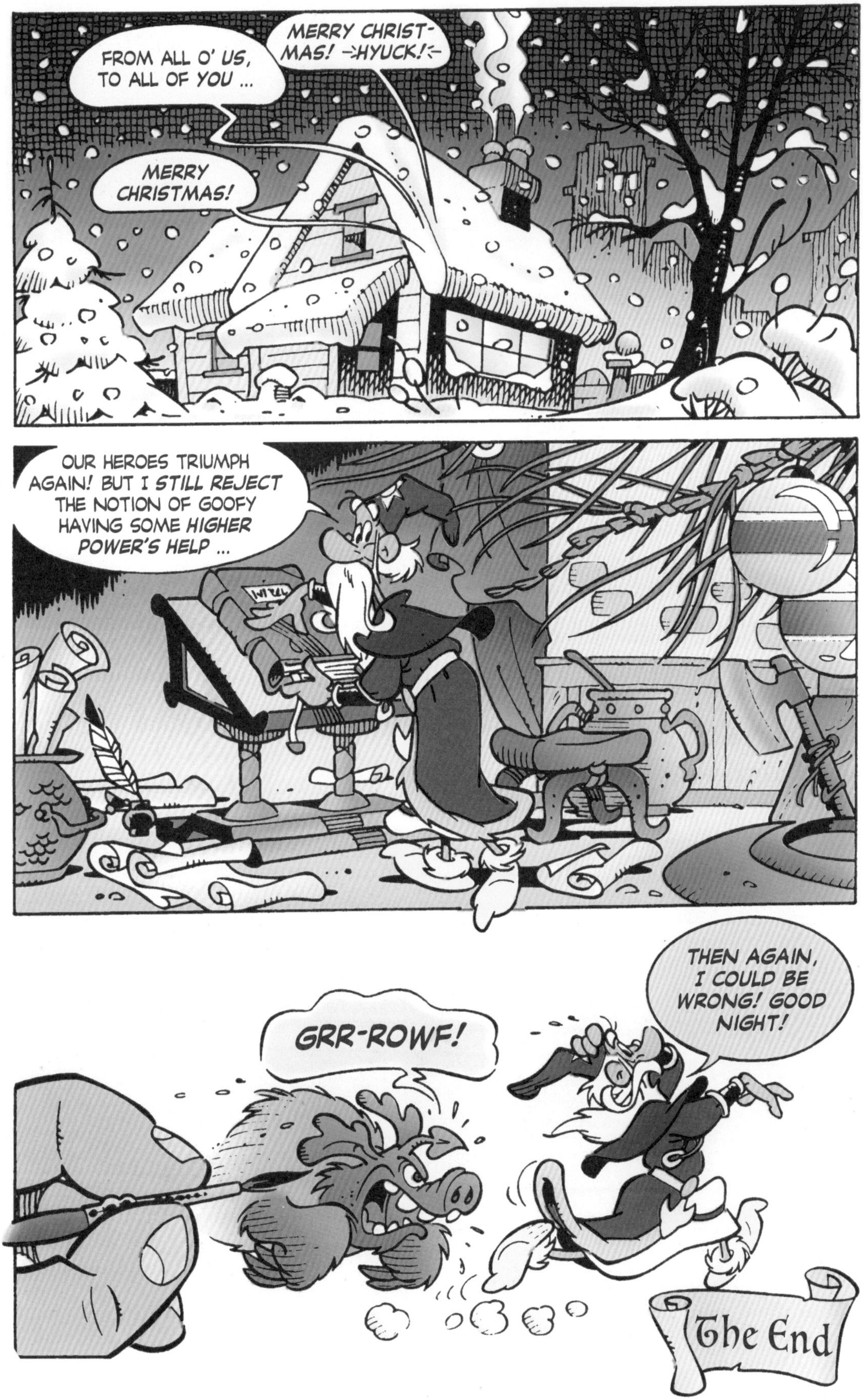

FROM ALL O' US, TO ALL OF YOU ...
MERRY CHRIST-MAS! -HYUCK!-
MERRY CHRISTMAS!
OUR HEROES TRIUMPH AGAIN! BUT I STILL REJECT THE NOTION OF GOOFY HAVING SOME HIGHER POWER'S HELP ...
GRR-ROWF!
THEN AGAIN, I COULD BE WRONG! GOOD NIGHT!
The End

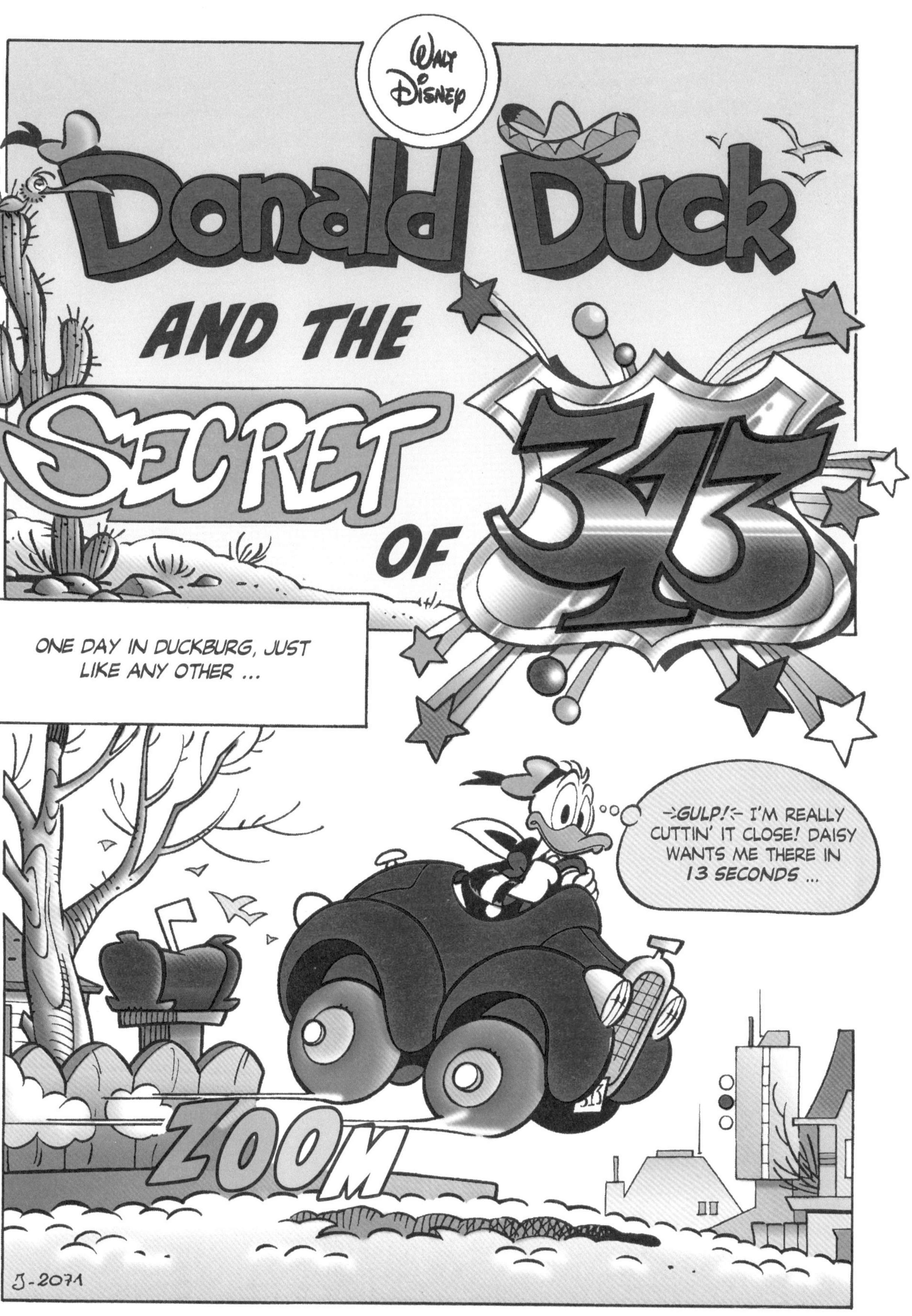
Walt Disney
Donald Duck and the Secret of 313
ONE DAY IN DUCKBURG, JUST LIKE ANY OTHER ...
–GULP!– I'M REALLY CUTTIN' IT CLOSE! DAISY WANTS ME THERE IN 13 SECONDS ...
313
ZOOM
J-2071

STORY AND ART BY MASSIMO DE VITA • TRANSLATION AND DIALOGUE BY THAD KOMOROWSKI • LETTERING BY PAUL BARESH AND CHRISTINA HWANG • COLORING: BY DISNEY ITALIA • EDITING BY DAVID GERSTEIN AND J. MICHAEL CATRON

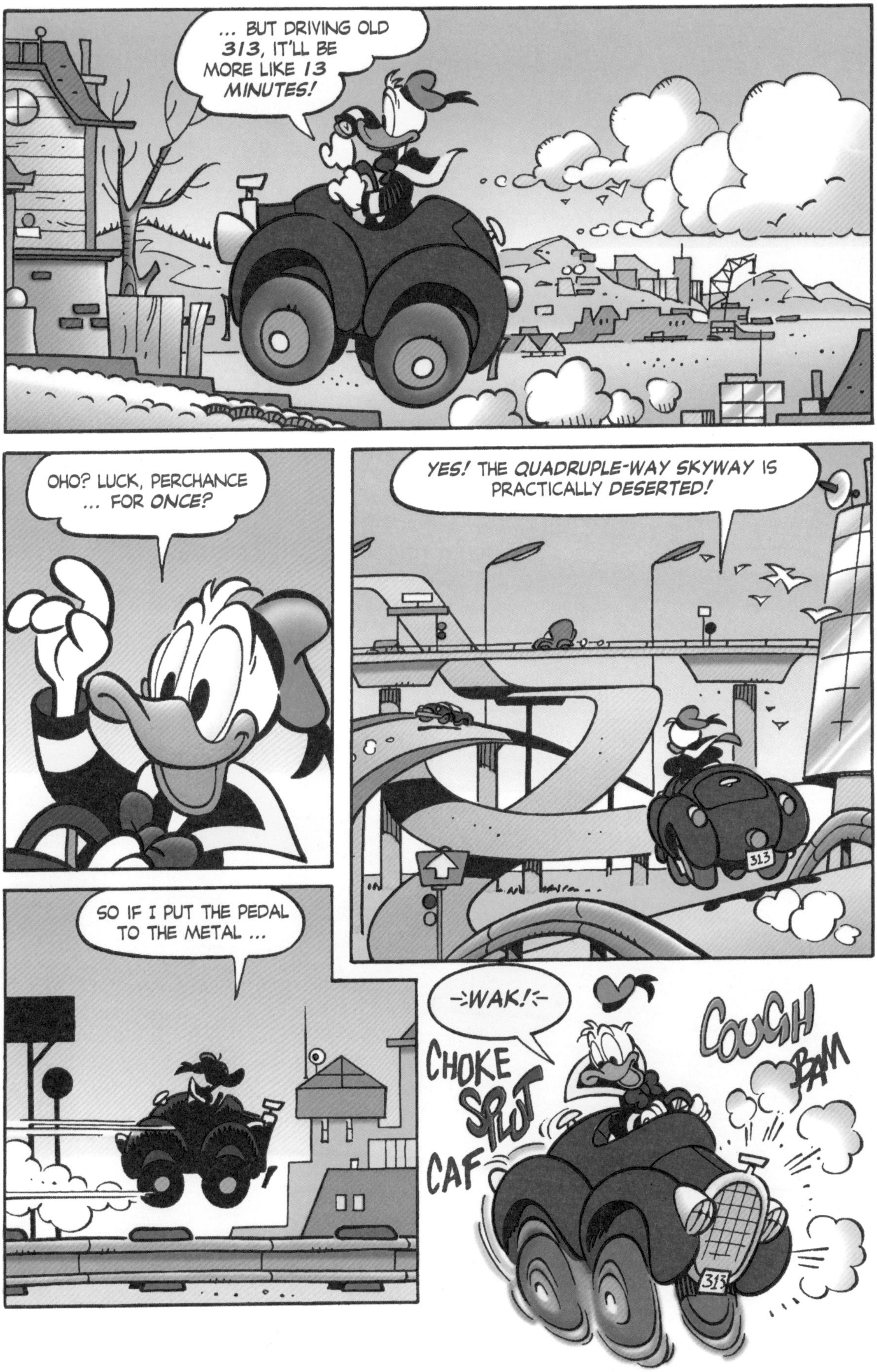
... BUT DRIVING OLD 313, IT'LL BE MORE LIKE 13 MINUTES!
OHO? LUCK, PERCHANCE ... FOR ONCE?
YES! THE QUADRUPLE-WAY SKYWAY IS PRACTICALLY DESERTED!
313
SO IF I PUT THE PEDAL TO THE METAL ...
-WAK!-
COUGH
BAM
CHOKE
SPLUT
CAF
313

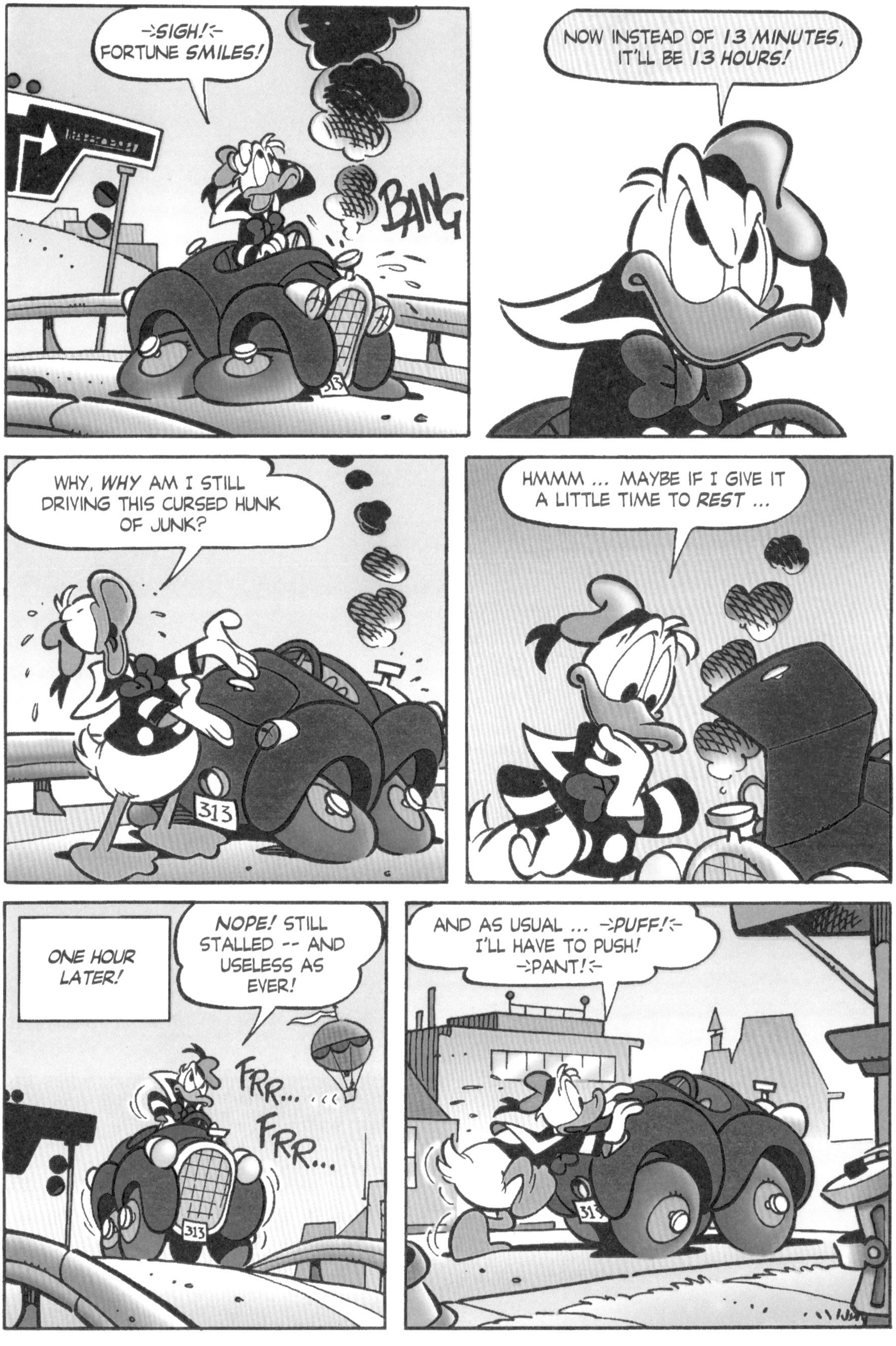
-SIGH!- FORTUNE SMILES!
BANG
NOW INSTEAD OF 13 MINUTES, IT'LL BE 13 HOURS!
WHY, WHY AM I STILL DRIVING THIS CURSED HUNK OF JUNK?
HMMM ... MAYBE IF I GIVE IT A LITTLE TIME TO REST ...
ONE HOUR LATER!
NOPE! STILL STALLED -- AND USELESS AS EVER!
FRR... FRR...
AND AS USUAL ... -PUFF!- I'LL HAVE TO PUSH! -PANT!-

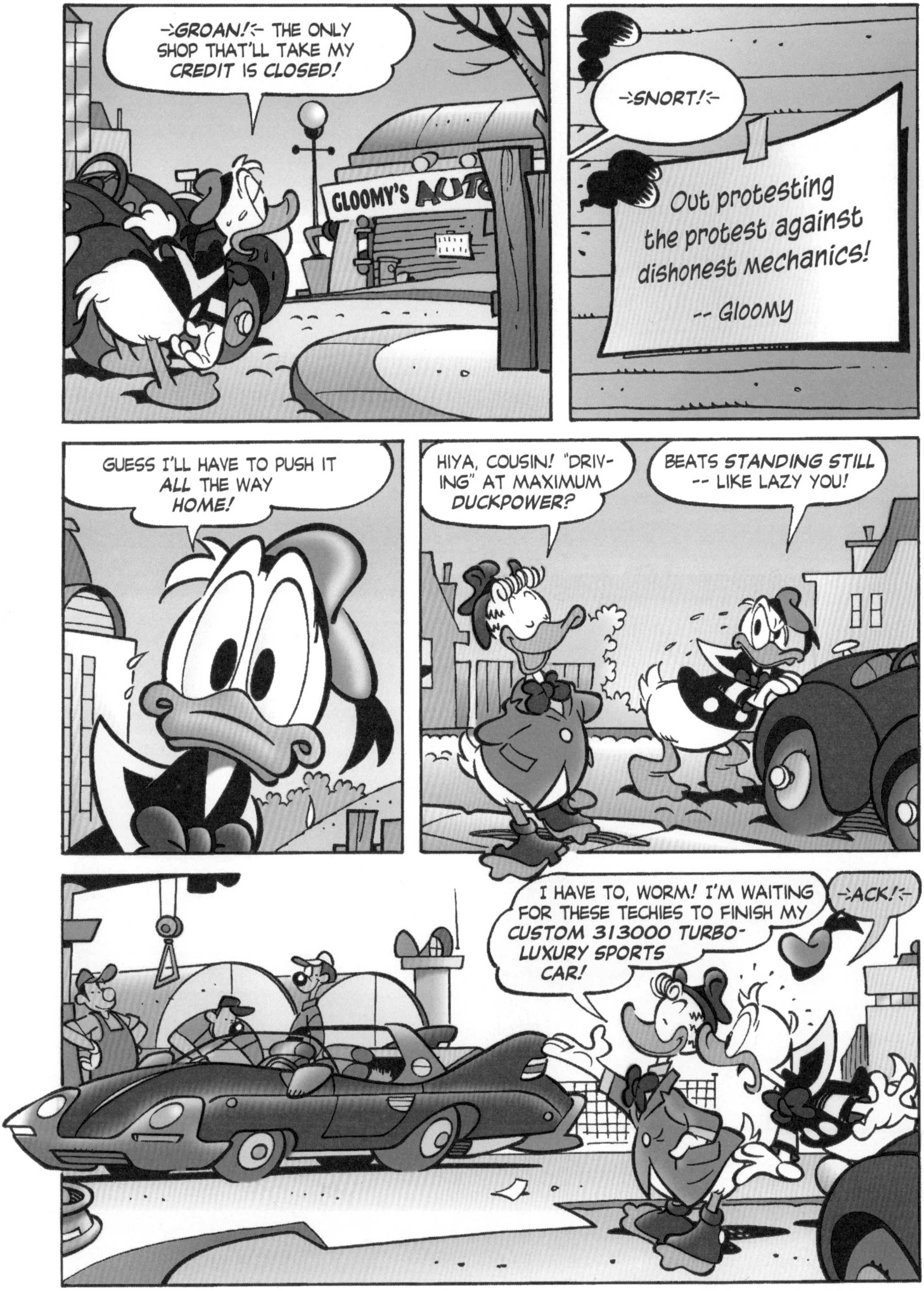
-GROAN!- THE ONLY SHOP THAT'LL TAKE MY CREDIT IS CLOSED!
GLOOMY'S AUTO
-SNORT!-
Out protesting the protest against dishonest mechanics!
-- Gloomy
GUESS I'LL HAVE TO PUSH IT ALL THE WAY HOME!
HIYA, COUSIN! "DRIV-ING" AT MAXIMUM DUCKPOWER?
BEATS STANDING STILL -- LIKE LAZY YOU!
I HAVE TO, WORM! I'M WAITING FOR THESE TECHIES TO FINISH MY CUSTOM 313000 TURBO-LUXURY SPORTS CAR!
-ACK!-

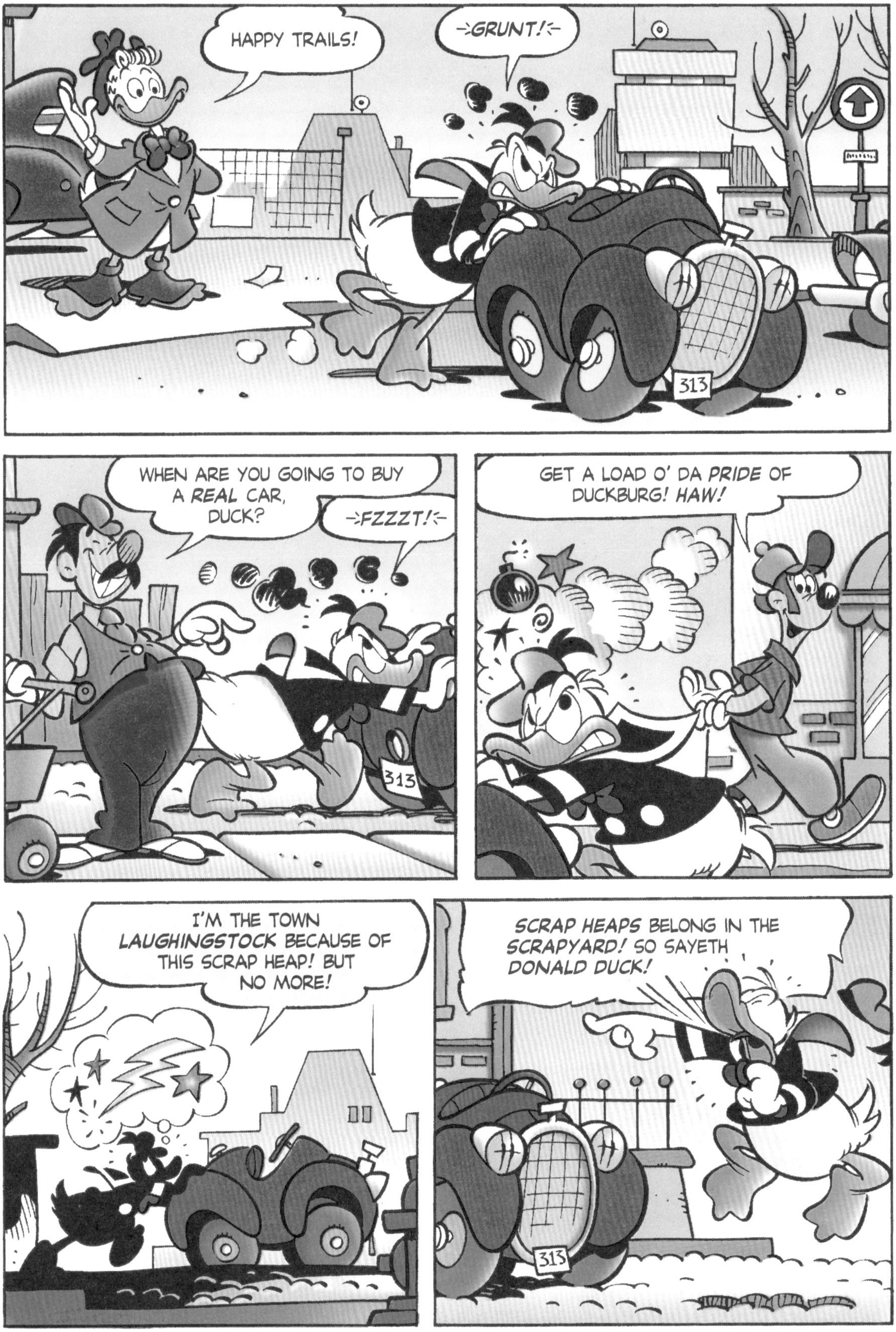

HAPPY TRAILS!
-GRUNT!-
WHEN ARE YOU GOING TO BUY A REAL CAR, DUCK?
-FZZZT!-
GET A LOAD O' DA PRIDE OF DUCKBURG! HAW!
I'M THE TOWN LAUGHINGSTOCK BECAUSE OF THIS SCRAP HEAP! BUT NO MORE!
SCRAP HEAPS BELONG IN THE SCRAPYARD! SO SAYETH DONALD DUCK!

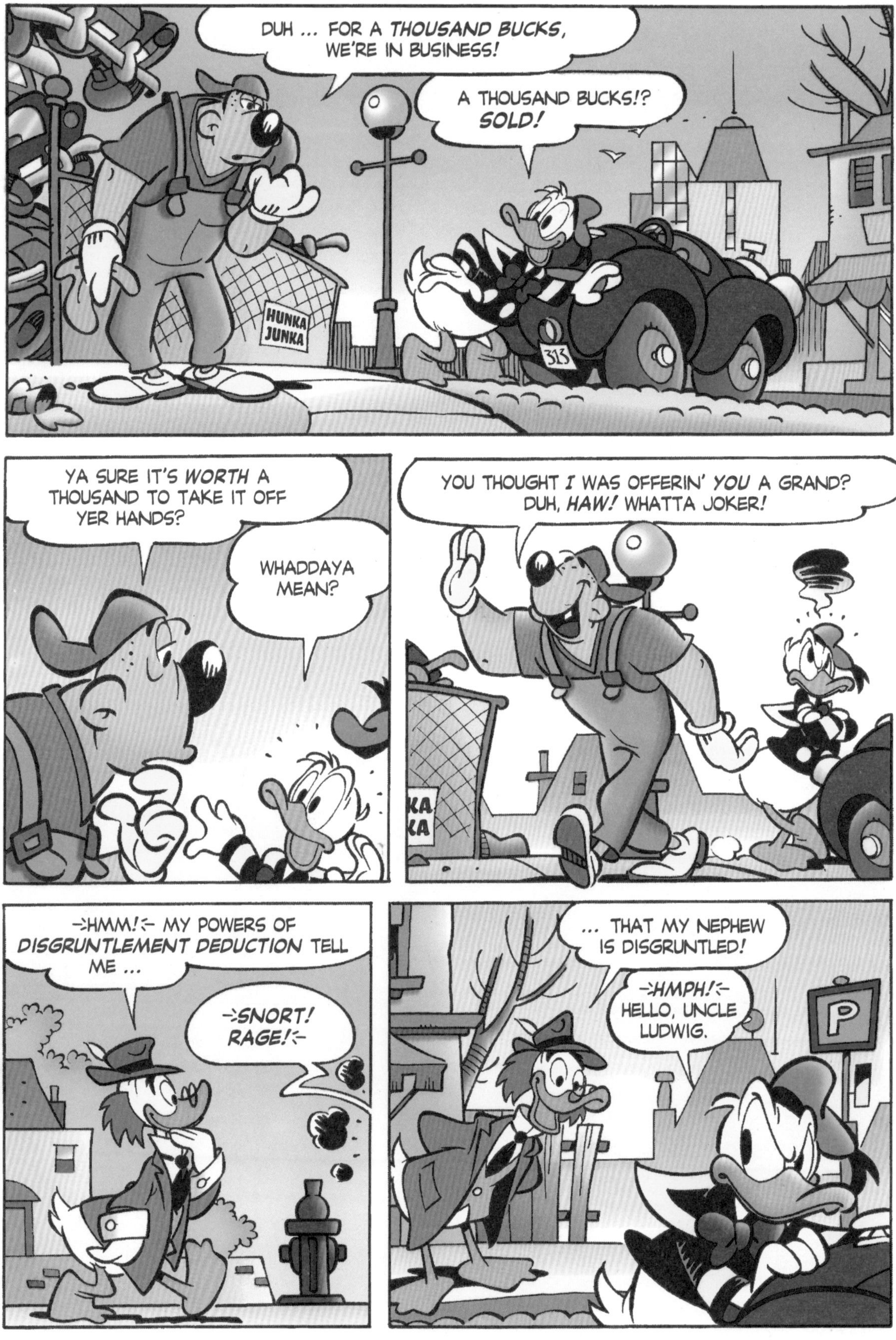
DUH ... FOR A *THOUSAND BUCKS*, WE'RE IN BUSINESS!
A THOUSAND BUCKS!? *SOLD!*
HUNKA JUNKA
313
YA SURE IT'S *WORTH* A THOUSAND TO TAKE IT OFF YER HANDS?
WHADDAYA MEAN?
YOU THOUGHT *I* WAS OFFERIN' *YOU* A GRAND? DUH, *HAW!* WHATTA JOKER!
HMM! MY POWERS OF *DISGRUNTLEMENT DEDUCTION* TELL ME ...
SNORT! RAGE!
... THAT MY NEPHEW IS DISGRUNTLED!
HMPH! HELLO, UNCLE LUDWIG.
P

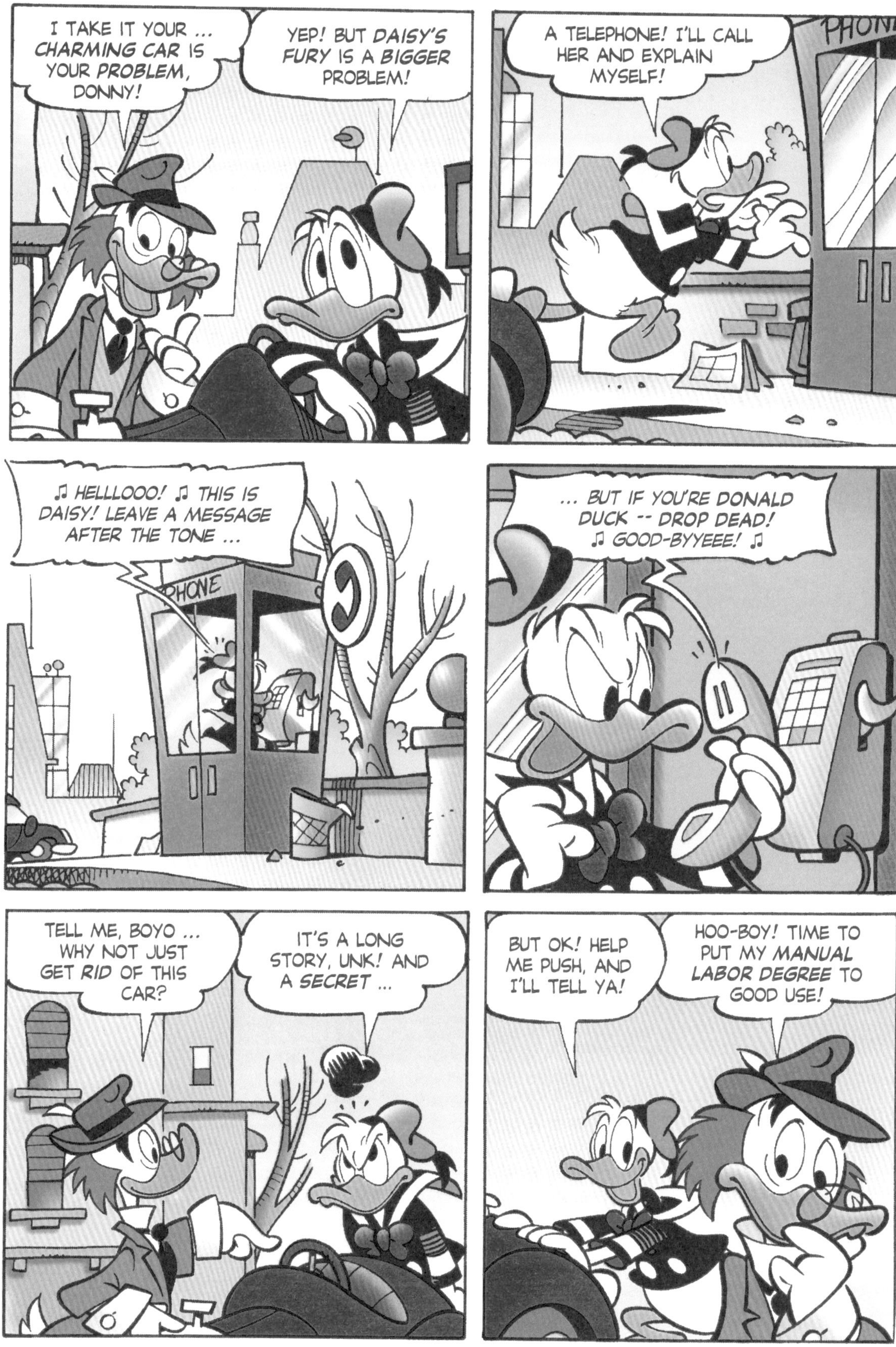

I TAKE IT YOUR ... CHARMING CAR IS YOUR PROBLEM, DONNY!
YEP! BUT DAISY'S FURY IS A BIGGER PROBLEM!
A TELEPHONE! I'LL CALL HER AND EXPLAIN MYSELF!
PHONE
♫ HELLLOOO! ♫ THIS IS DAISY! LEAVE A MESSAGE AFTER THE TONE ...
PHONE
... BUT IF YOU'RE DONALD DUCK -- DROP DEAD! ♫ GOOD-BYYEEE! ♫
TELL ME, BOYO ... WHY NOT JUST GET RID OF THIS CAR?
IT'S A LONG STORY, UNK! AND A SECRET ...
BUT OK! HELP ME PUSH, AND I'LL TELL YA!
HOO-BOY! TIME TO PUT MY MANUAL LABOR DEGREE TO GOOD USE!

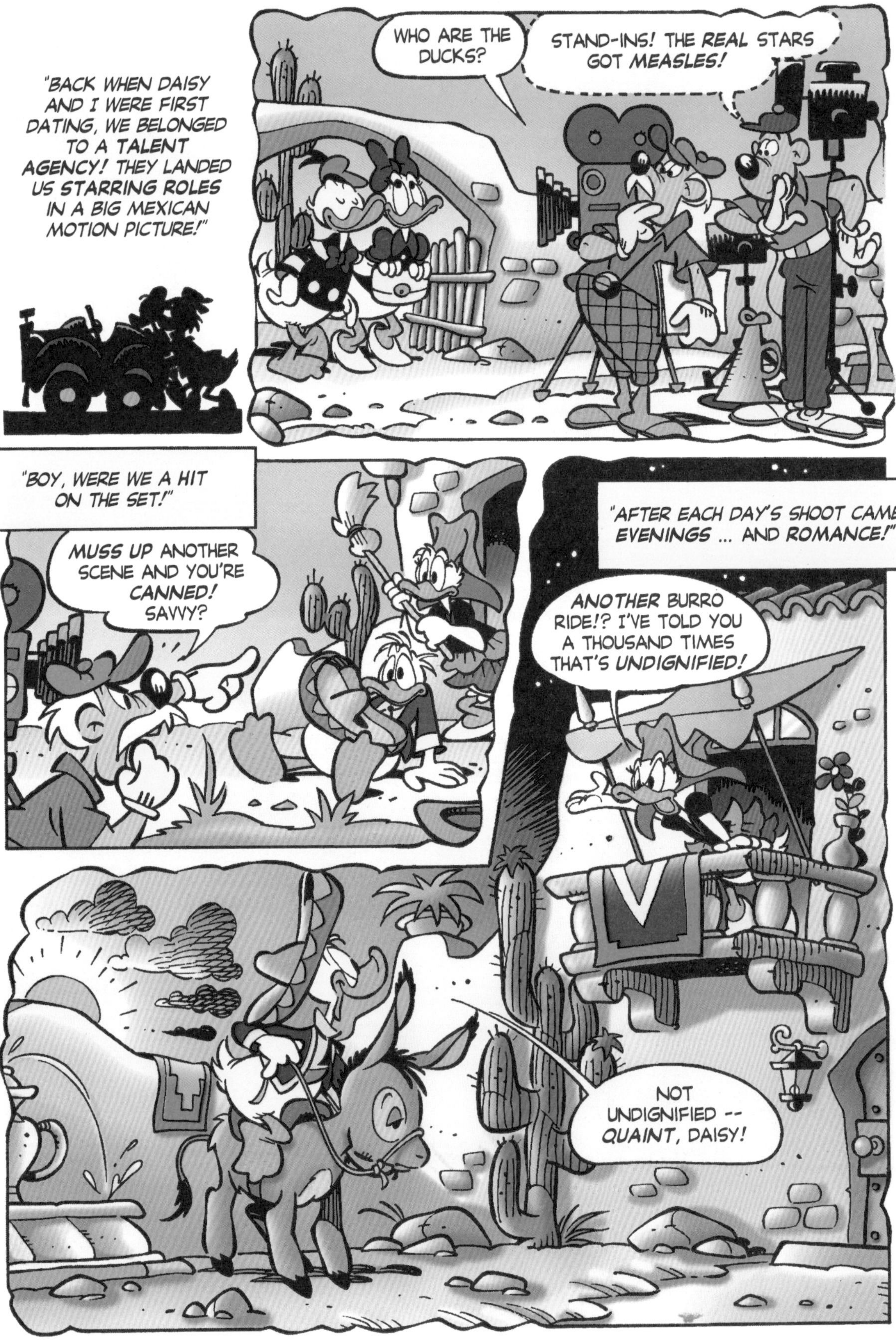
"BACK WHEN DAISY AND I WERE FIRST DATING, WE BELONGED TO A TALENT AGENCY! THEY LANDED US STARRING ROLES IN A BIG MEXICAN MOTION PICTURE!"
WHO ARE THE DUCKS?
STAND-INS! THE REAL STARS GOT MEASLES!
"BOY, WERE WE A HIT ON THE SET!"
MUSS UP ANOTHER SCENE AND YOU'RE CANNED! SAVVY?
"AFTER EACH DAY'S SHOOT CAME EVENINGS ... AND ROMANCE!"
ANOTHER BURRO RIDE!? I'VE TOLD YOU A THOUSAND TIMES THAT'S UNDIGNIFIED!
NOT UNDIGNIFIED -- QUAINT, DAISY!

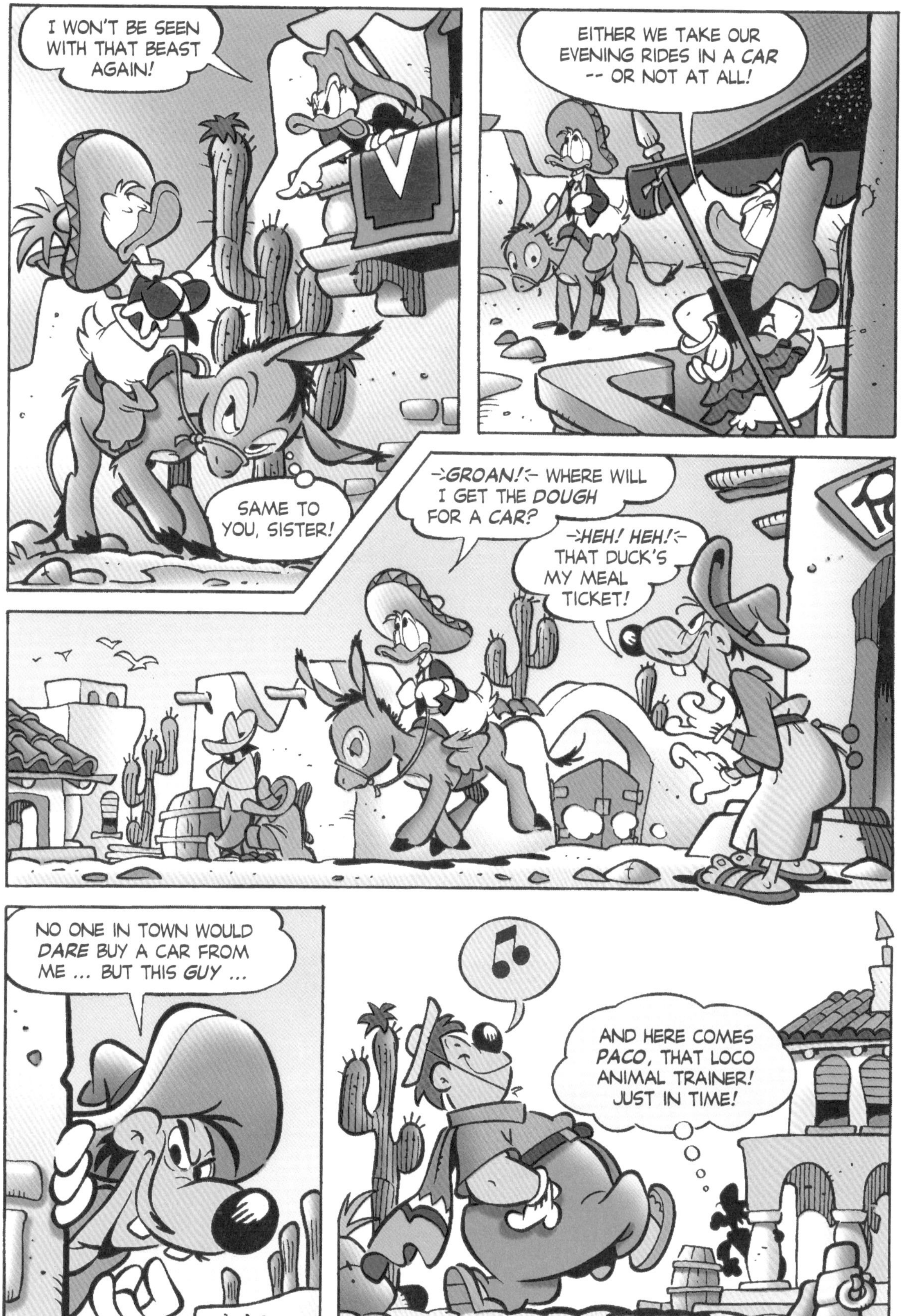
I WON'T BE SEEN WITH THAT BEAST AGAIN!
SAME TO YOU, SISTER!
EITHER WE TAKE OUR EVENING RIDES IN A CAR -- OR NOT AT ALL!
-GROAN!- WHERE WILL I GET THE DOUGH FOR A CAR?
-HEH! HEH!- THAT DUCK'S MY MEAL TICKET!
NO ONE IN TOWN WOULD DARE BUY A CAR FROM ME ... BUT THIS GUY ...
AND HERE COMES PACO, THAT LOCO ANIMAL TRAINER! JUST IN TIME!

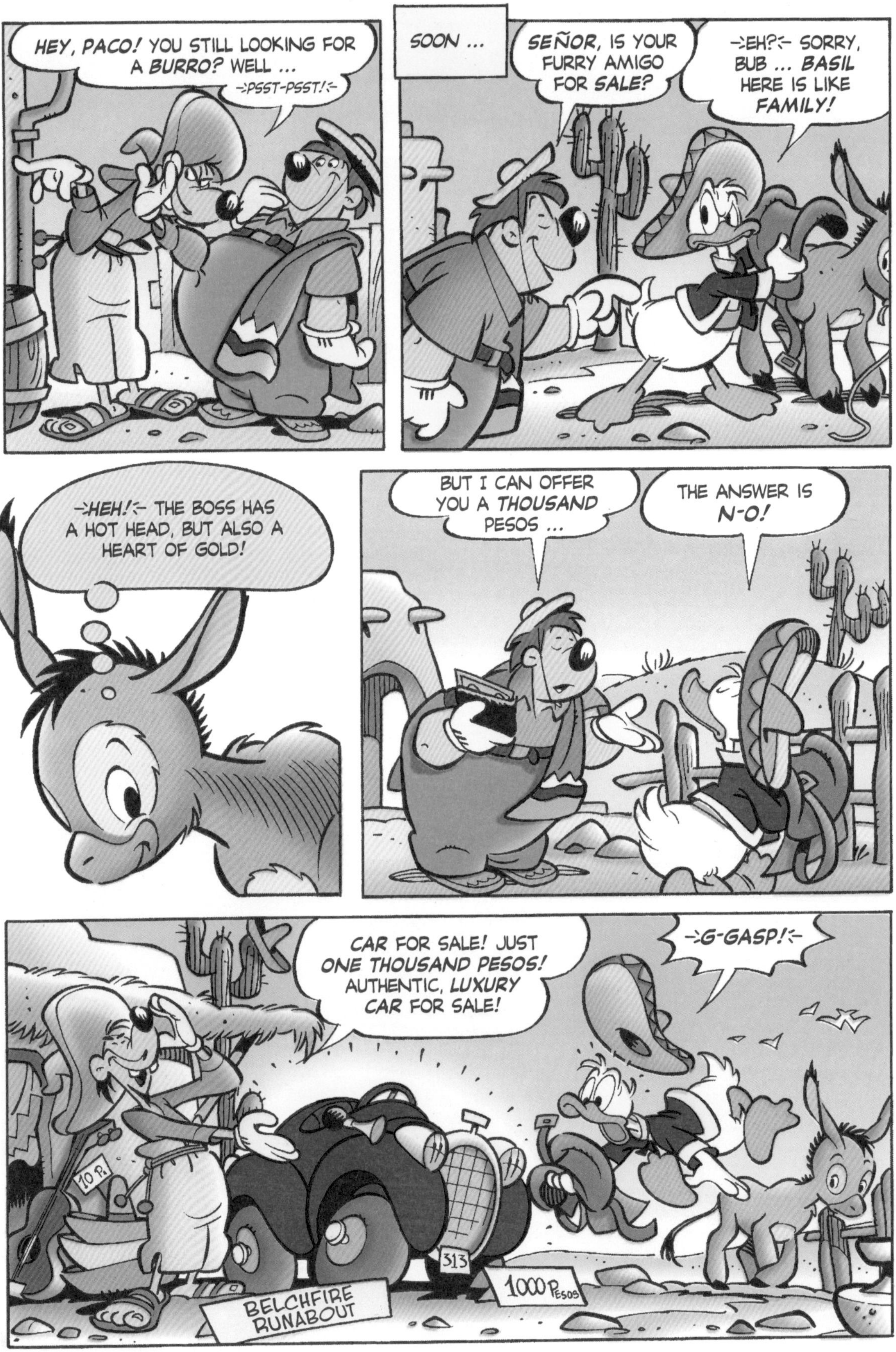
HEY, PACO! YOU STILL LOOKING FOR A BURRO? WELL ...
-PSST-PSST!-
SOON ...
SEÑOR, IS YOUR FURRY AMIGO FOR SALE?
-EH?- SORRY, BUB ... BASIL HERE IS LIKE FAMILY!
-HEH!- THE BOSS HAS A HOT HEAD, BUT ALSO A HEART OF GOLD!
BUT I CAN OFFER YOU A THOUSAND PESOS ...
THE ANSWER IS N-O!
CAR FOR SALE! JUST ONE THOUSAND PESOS! AUTHENTIC, LUXURY CAR FOR SALE!
-G-GASP!-
10 P.
313
1000 PESOS
BELCHFIRE RUNABOUT

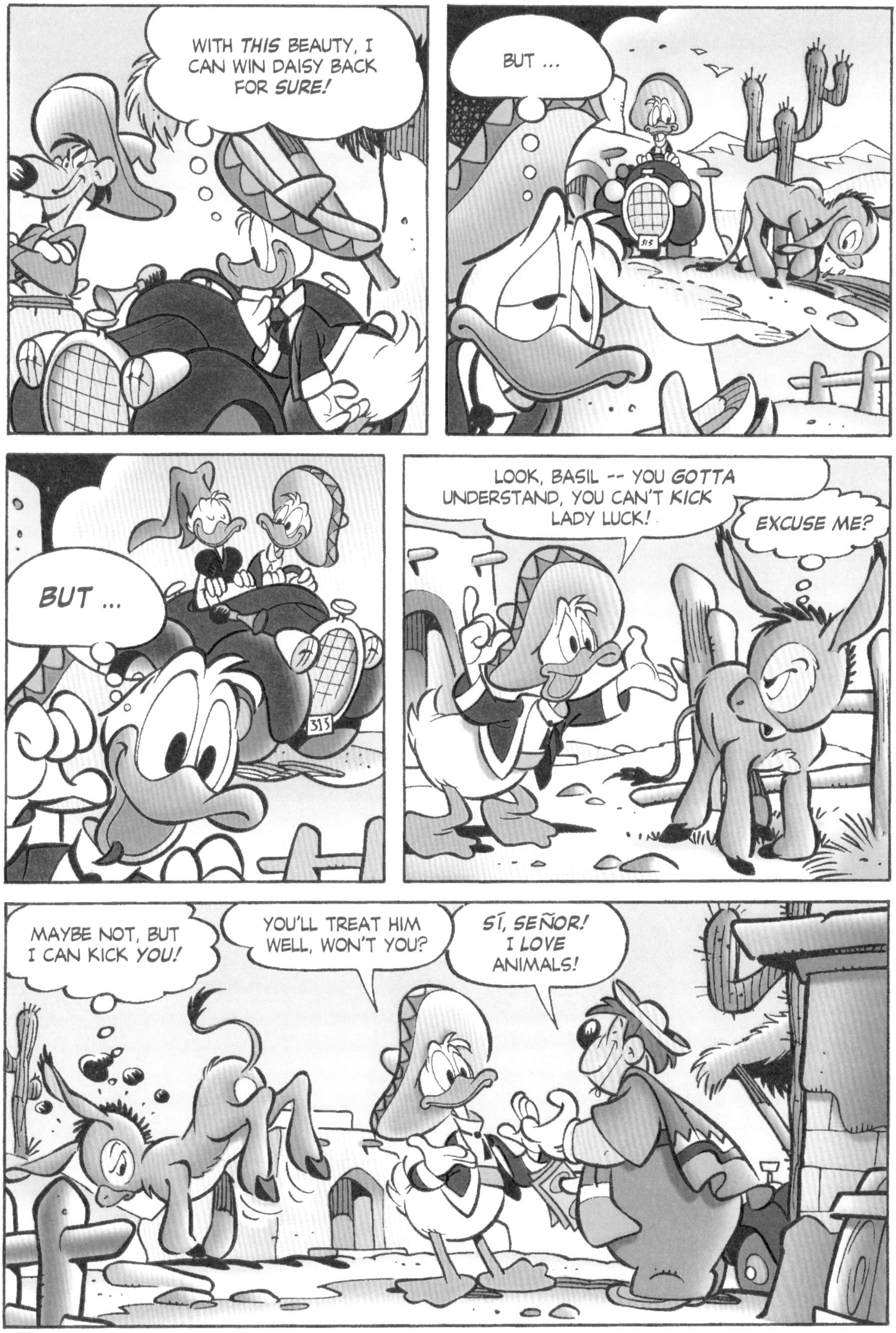
WITH THIS BEAUTY, I CAN WIN DAISY BACK FOR SURE!
BUT ...
BUT ...
LOOK, BASIL -- YOU GOTTA UNDERSTAND, YOU CAN'T KICK LADY LUCK!
EXCUSE ME?
MAYBE NOT, BUT I CAN KICK YOU!
YOU'LL TREAT HIM WELL, WON'T YOU?
SÍ, SEÑOR! I LOVE ANIMALS!
313

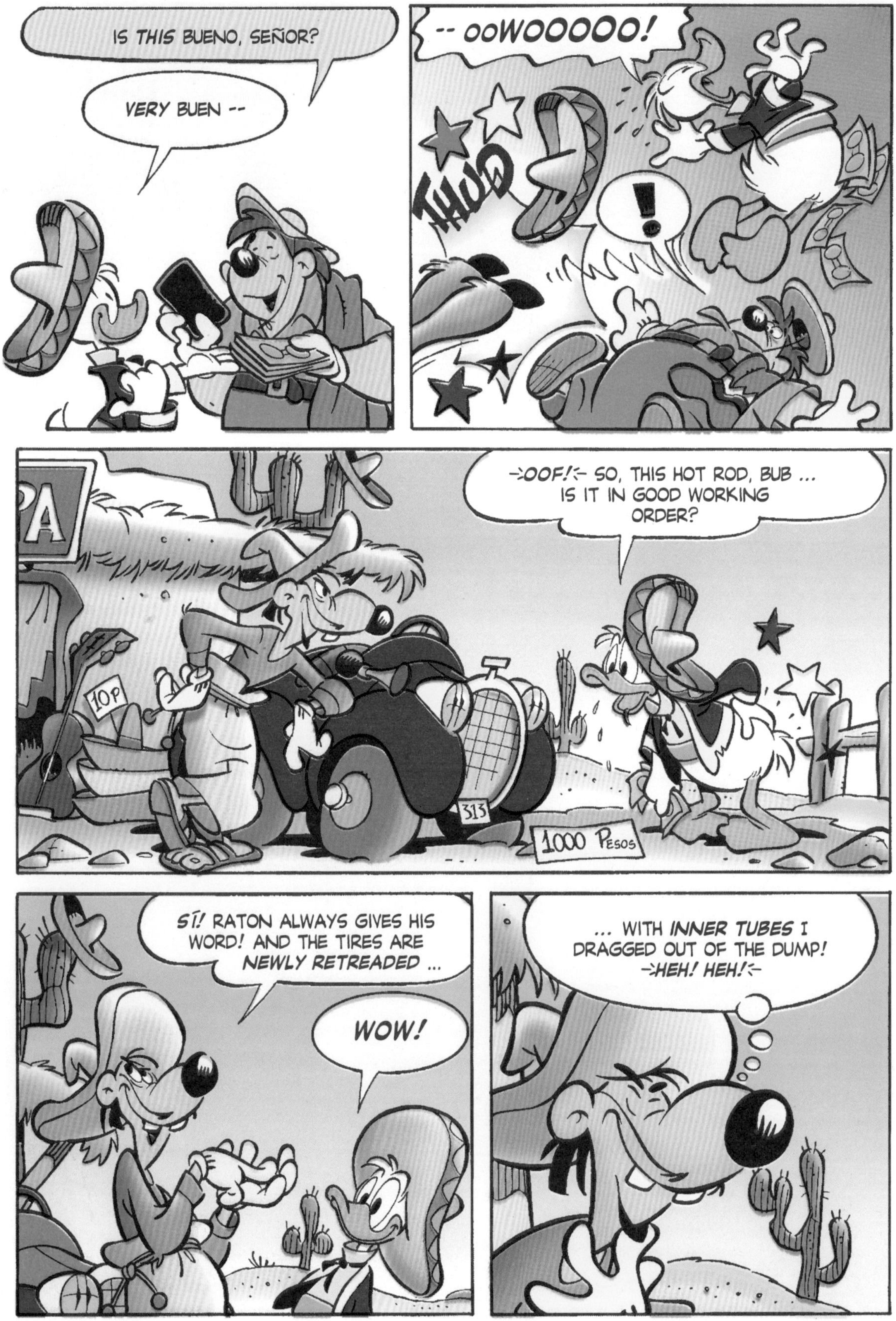
IS THIS BUENO, SEÑOR?
VERY BUEN --
-- OOWOOOOO!
THUD
!
-OOF!- SO, THIS HOT ROD, BUB ... IS IT IN GOOD WORKING ORDER?
PA
10P
313
1000 PESOS
SÍ! RATON ALWAYS GIVES HIS WORD! AND THE TIRES ARE NEWLY RETREADED ...
WOW!
... WITH INNER TUBES I DRAGGED OUT OF THE DUMP! -HEH! HEH!-

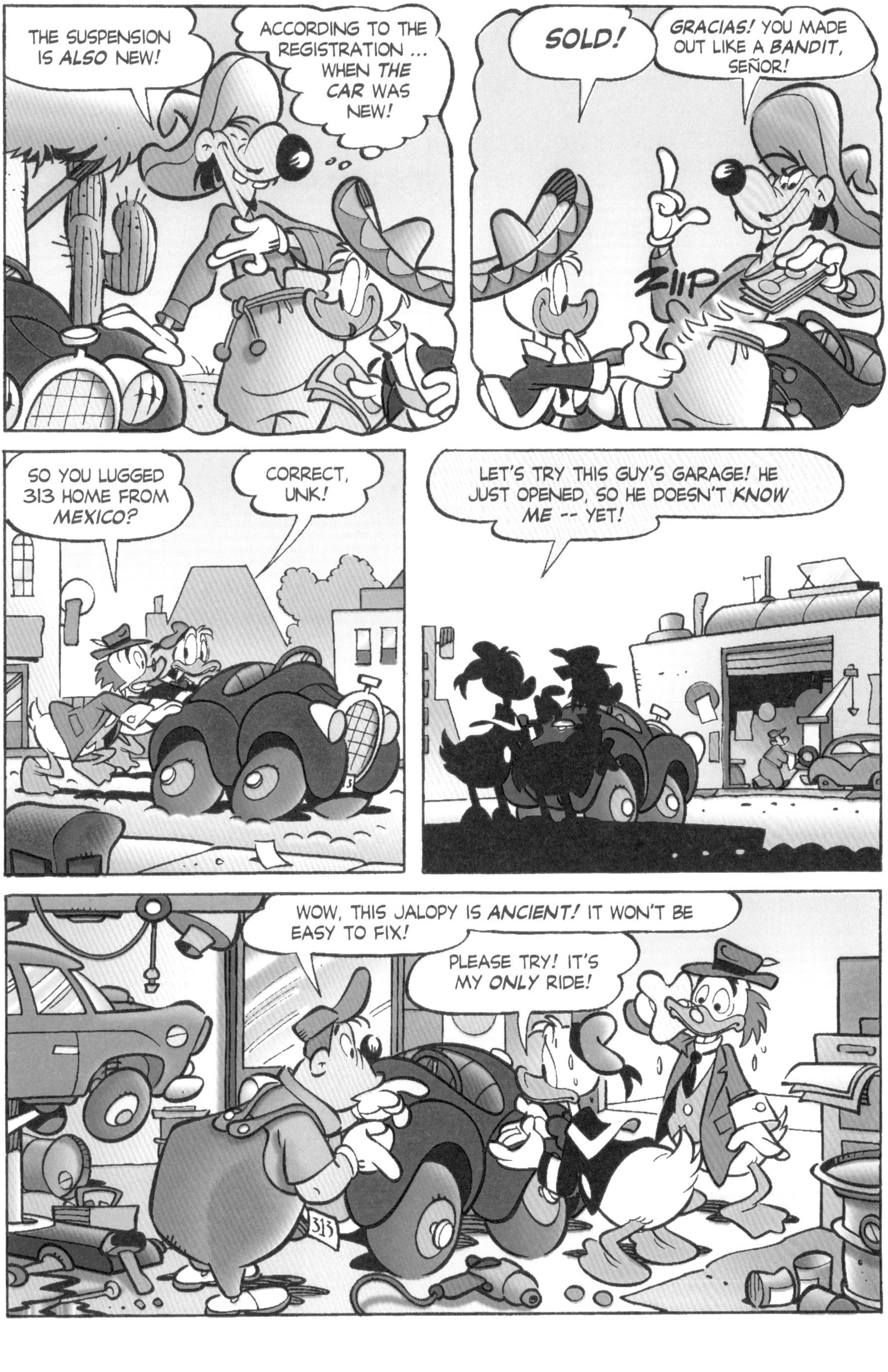
THE SUSPENSION IS ALSO NEW!
ACCORDING TO THE REGISTRATION ... WHEN THE CAR WAS NEW!
SOLD!
GRACIAS! YOU MADE OUT LIKE A BANDIT, SEÑOR!
ZIIP
SO YOU LUGGED 313 HOME FROM MEXICO?
CORRECT, UNK!
LET'S TRY THIS GUY'S GARAGE! HE JUST OPENED, SO HE DOESN'T KNOW ME -- YET!
WOW, THIS JALOPY IS ANCIENT! IT WON'T BE EASY TO FIX!
PLEASE TRY! IT'S MY ONLY RIDE!
313

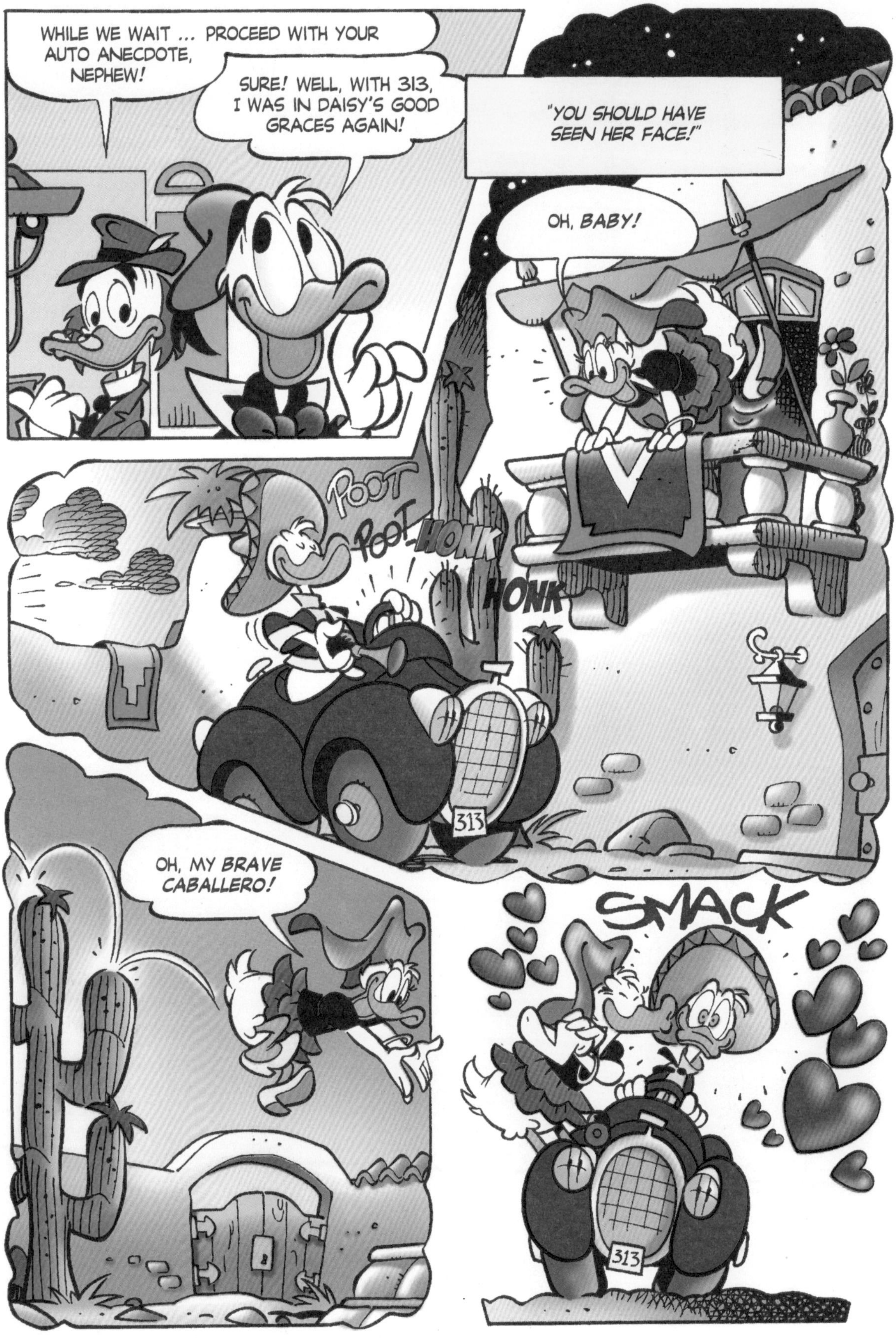
WHILE WE WAIT ... PROCEED WITH YOUR AUTO ANECDOTE, NEPHEW!
SURE! WELL, WITH 313, I WAS IN DAISY'S GOOD GRACES AGAIN!
"YOU SHOULD HAVE SEEN HER FACE!"
OH, BABY!
POOT
POOT
HONK
HONK
313
OH, MY BRAVE CABALLERO!
SMACK
313

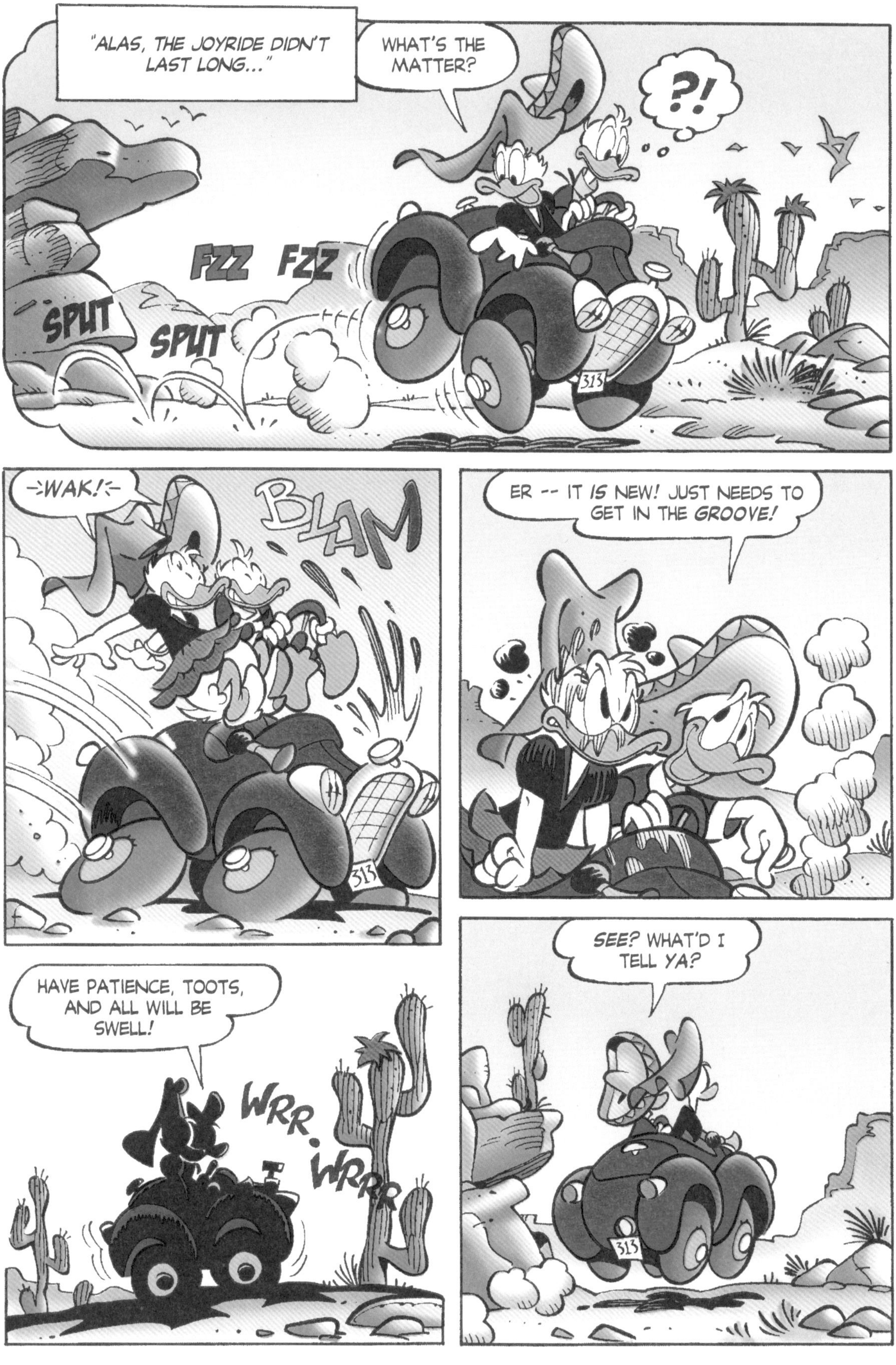
"ALAS, THE JOYRIDE DIDN'T LAST LONG..."
WHAT'S THE MATTER?
?!
FZZ FZZ
SPUT SPUT
-WAK!-
BLAM
ER -- IT *IS* NEW! JUST NEEDS TO GET IN THE *GROOVE!*
HAVE PATIENCE, TOOTS, AND ALL WILL BE SWELL!
WRR-WRRR
SEE? WHAT'D I TELL *YA?*

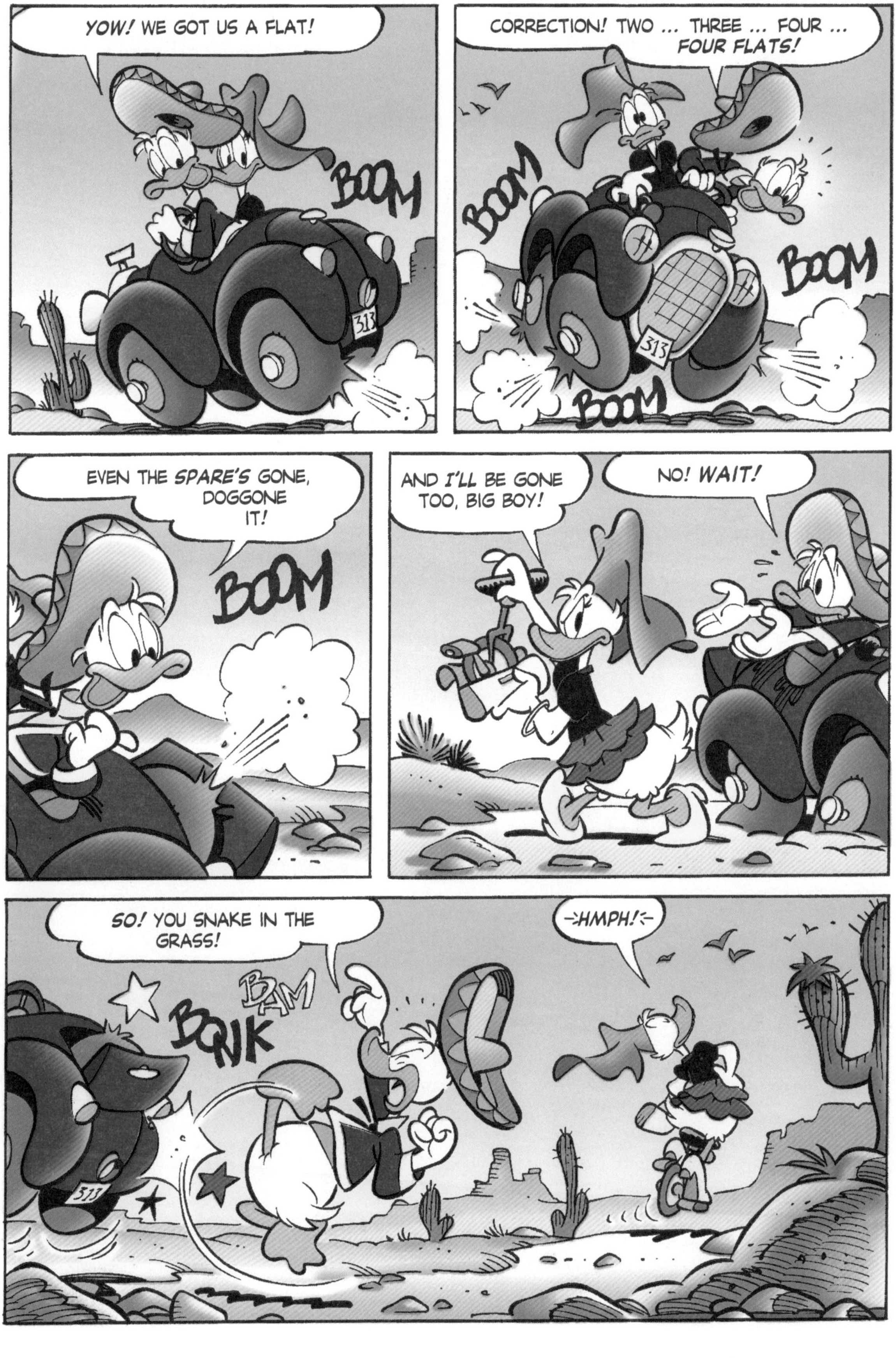
YOW! WE GOT US A FLAT!
BOOM
CORRECTION! TWO ... THREE ... FOUR ... FOUR FLATS!
BOOM
BOOM
BOOM
EVEN THE SPARE'S GONE, DOGGONE IT!
BOOM
AND I'LL BE GONE TOO, BIG BOY!
NO! WAIT!
SO! YOU SNAKE IN THE GRASS!
BONK
BAM
HMPH!

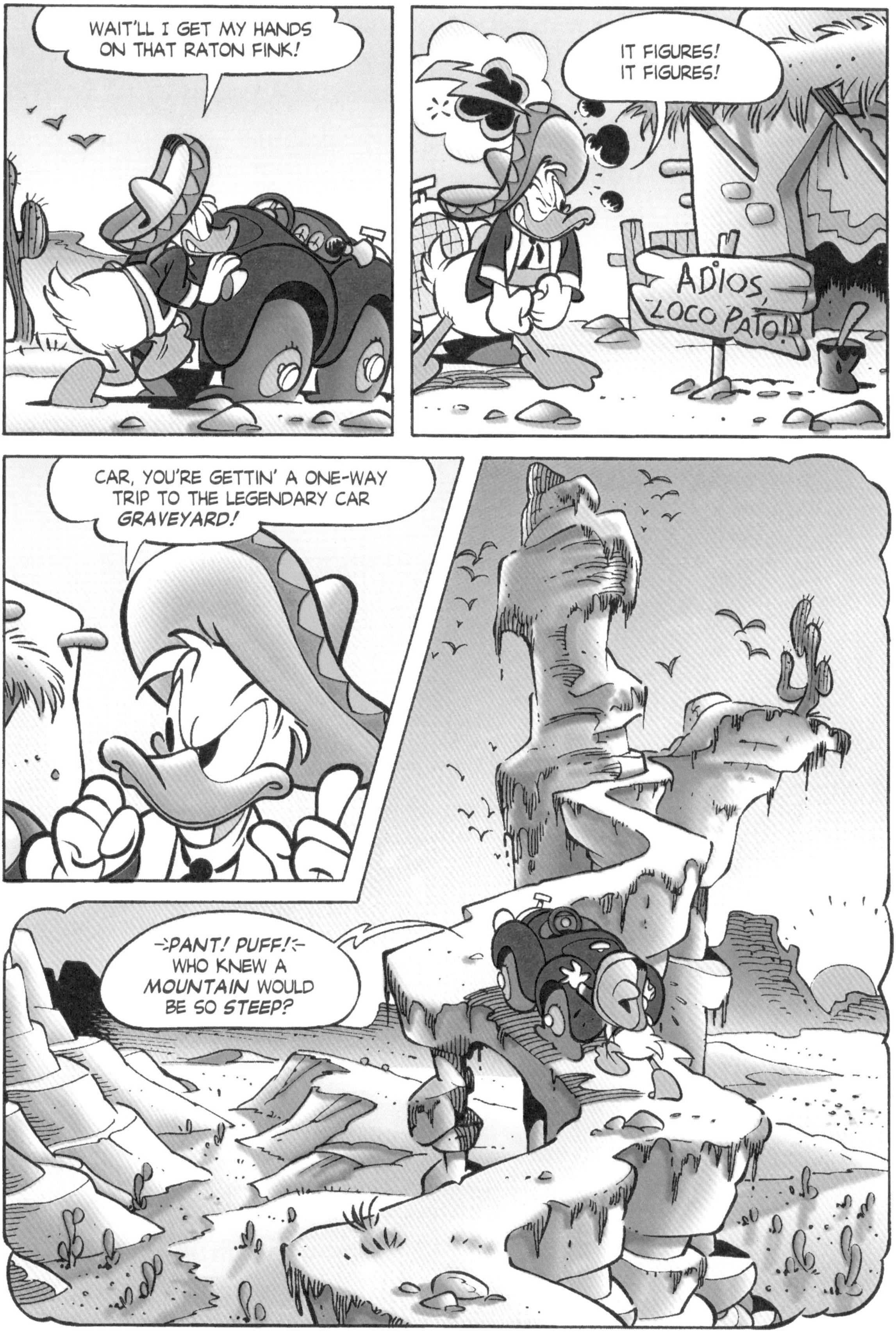
WAIT'LL I GET MY HANDS ON THAT RATON FINK!
IT FIGURES! IT FIGURES!
ADIOS, LOCO PATO!
CAR, YOU'RE GETTIN' A ONE-WAY TRIP TO THE LEGENDARY CAR *GRAVEYARD!*
PANT! PUFF! WHO KNEW A *MOUNTAIN* WOULD BE SO *STEEP?*

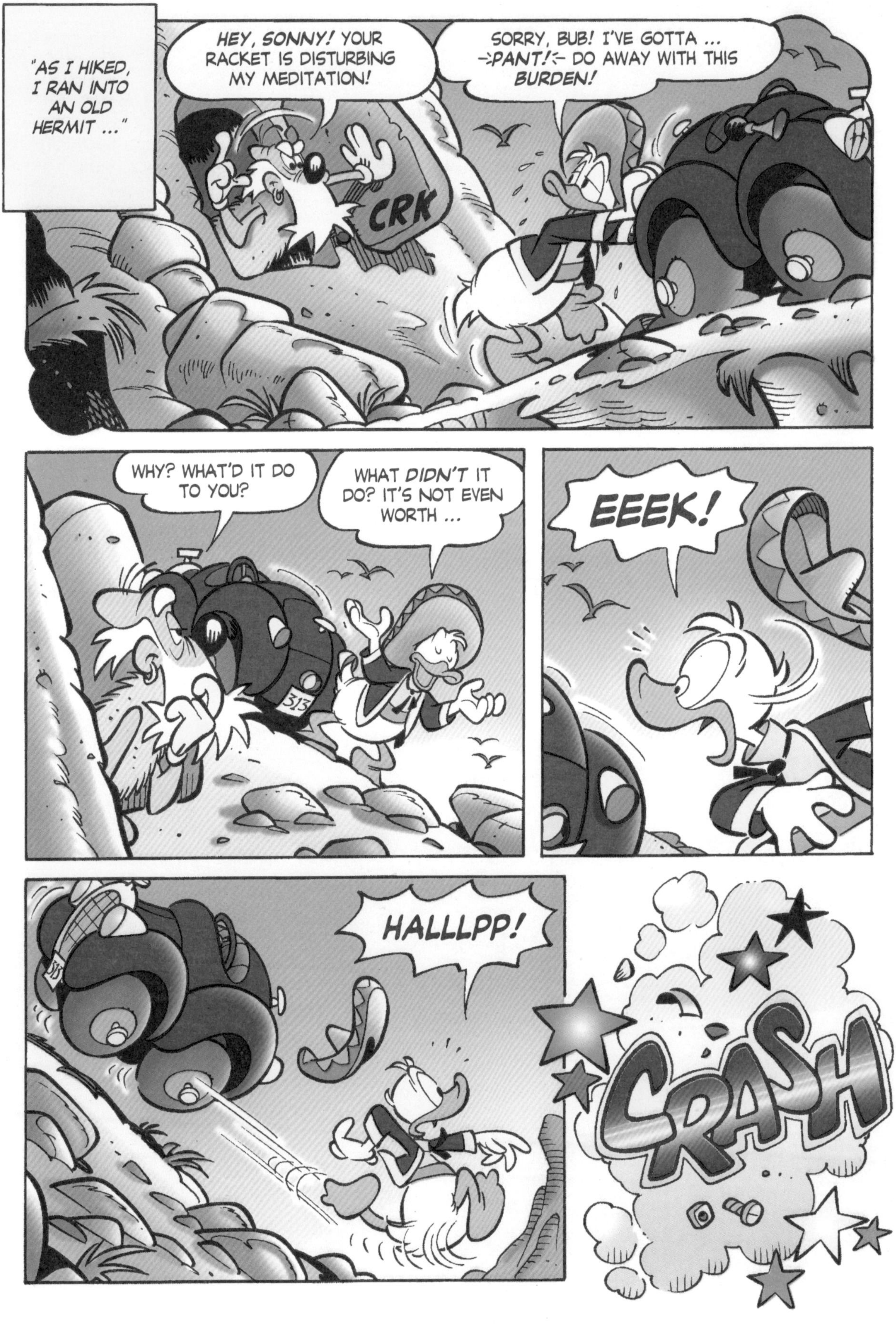

"AS I HIKED, I RAN INTO AN OLD HERMIT ..."
HEY, SONNY! YOUR RACKET IS DISTURBING MY MEDITATION!
SORRY, BUB! I'VE GOTTA ... –>PANT!<– DO AWAY WITH THIS BURDEN!
CRK
WHY? WHAT'D IT DO TO YOU?
WHAT DIDN'T IT DO? IT'S NOT EVEN WORTH ...
EEEK!
HALLLPP!
CRASH

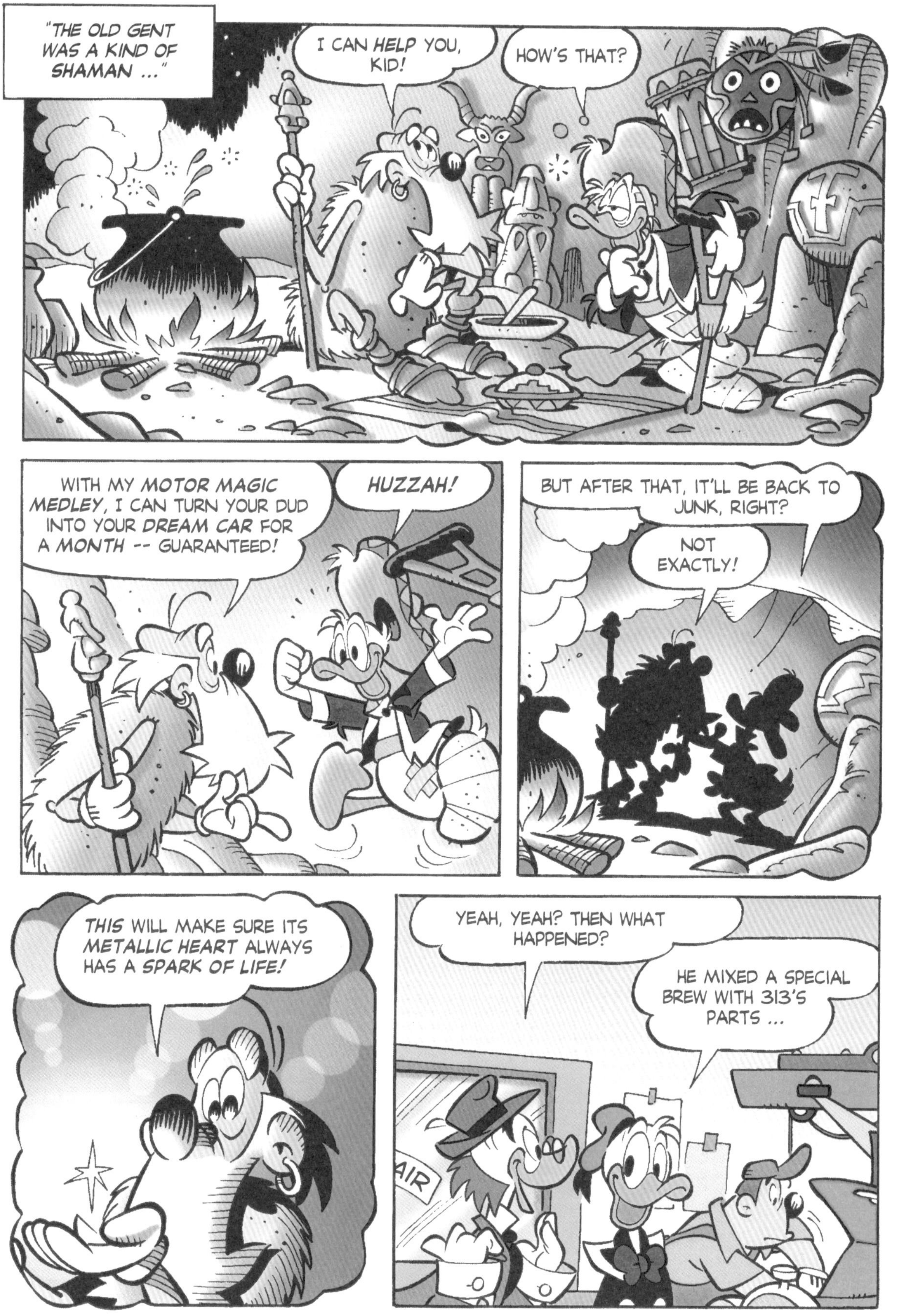
"THE OLD GENT WAS A KIND OF SHAMAN ..."
I CAN HELP YOU, KID!
HOW'S THAT?
WITH MY MOTOR MAGIC MEDLEY, I CAN TURN YOUR DUD INTO YOUR DREAM CAR FOR A MONTH -- GUARANTEED!
HUZZAH!
BUT AFTER THAT, IT'LL BE BACK TO JUNK, RIGHT?
NOT EXACTLY!
THIS WILL MAKE SURE ITS METALLIC HEART ALWAYS HAS A SPARK OF LIFE!
YEAH, YEAH? THEN WHAT HAPPENED?
HE MIXED A SPECIAL BREW WITH 313'S PARTS ...
AIR

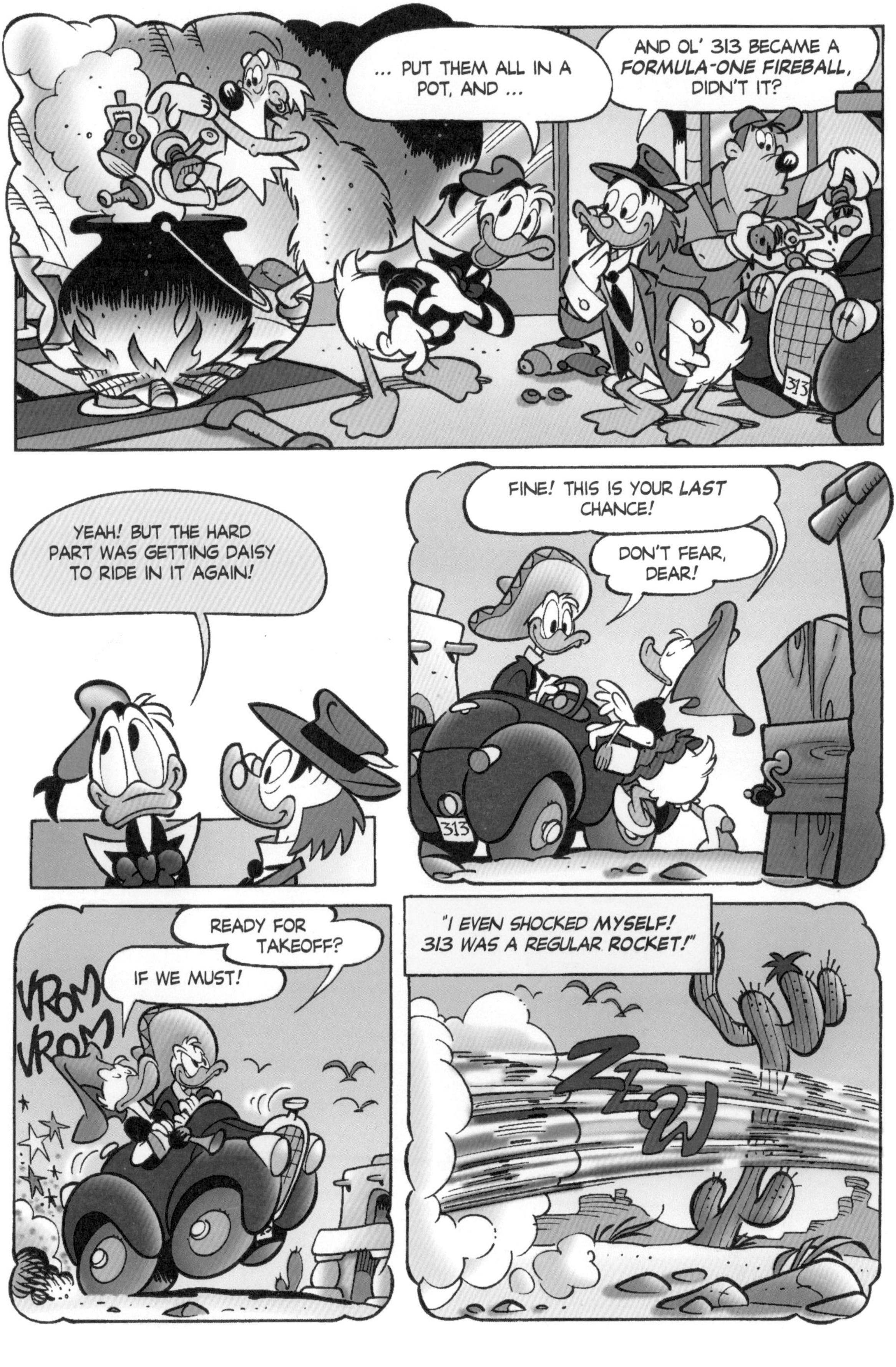
... PUT THEM ALL IN A POT, AND ...
AND OL' 313 BECAME A *FORMULA-ONE FIREBALL*, DIDN'T IT?
313
YEAH! BUT THE HARD PART WAS GETTING DAISY TO RIDE IN IT AGAIN!
FINE! THIS IS YOUR *LAST* CHANCE!
DON'T FEAR, DEAR!
313
READY FOR TAKEOFF?
IF WE MUST!
VROM VROM
"I EVEN SHOCKED MYSELF! 313 WAS A REGULAR ROCKET!"
ZEEW

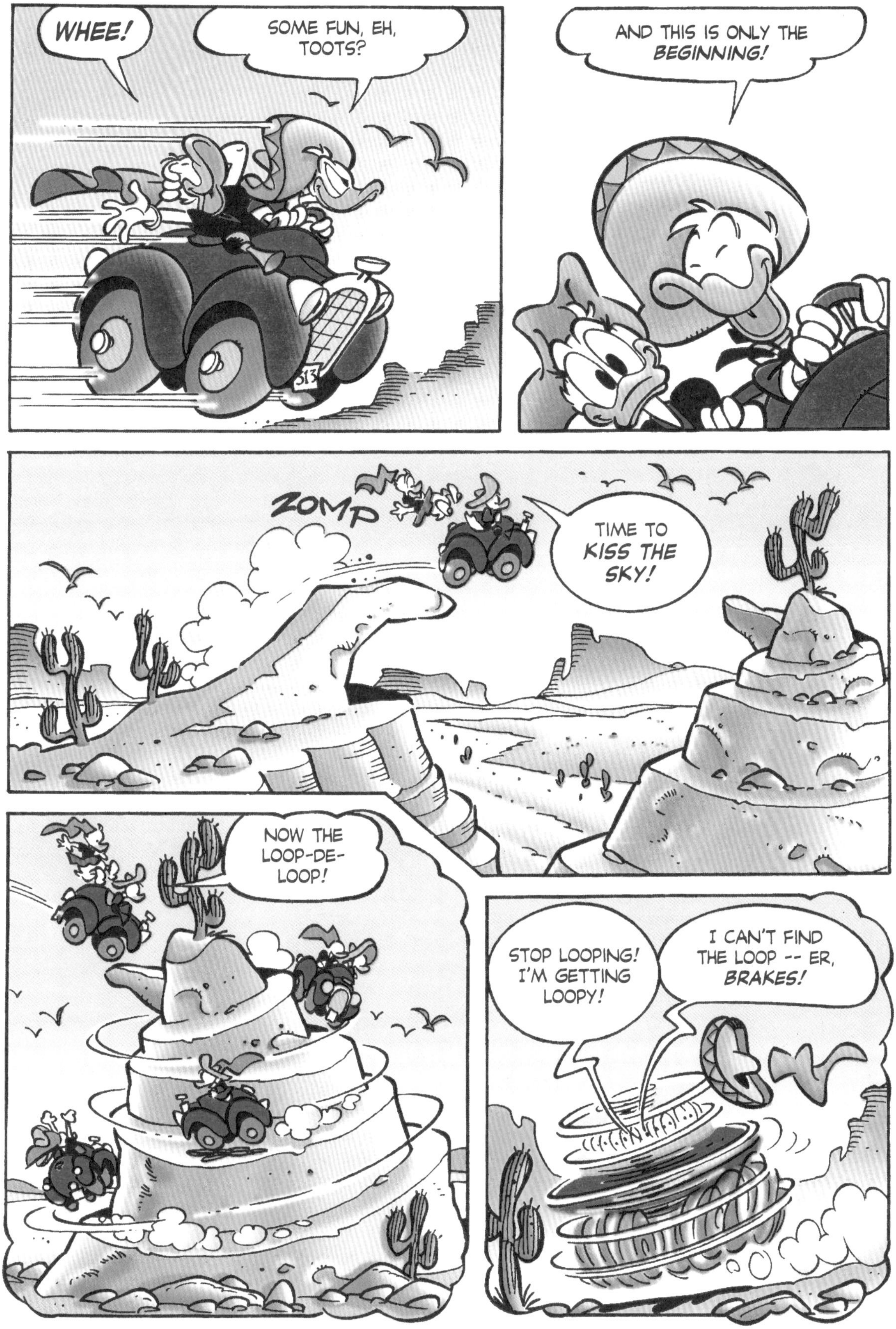

WHEE!
SOME FUN, EH, TOOTS?
AND THIS IS ONLY THE BEGINNING!
ZOMP
TIME TO KISS THE SKY!
NOW THE LOOP-DE-LOOP!
STOP LOOPING! I'M GETTING LOOPY!
I CAN'T FIND THE LOOP -- ER, BRAKES!

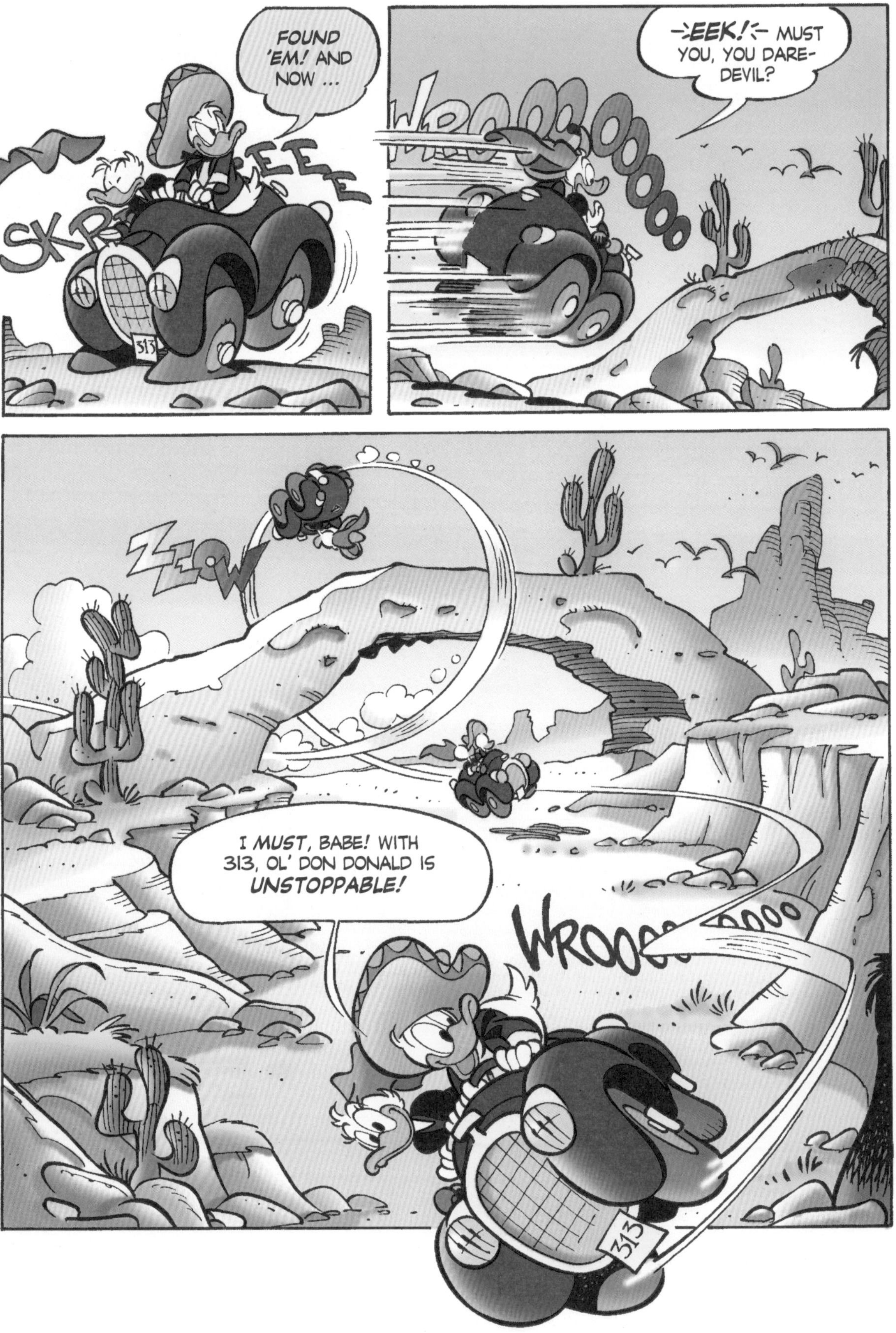
FOUND 'EM! AND NOW ...
SKR
EEEE
-EEK!- MUST YOU, YOU DARE-DEVIL?
ZEOW
I MUST, BABE! WITH 313, OL' DON DONALD IS UNSTOPPABLE!
313

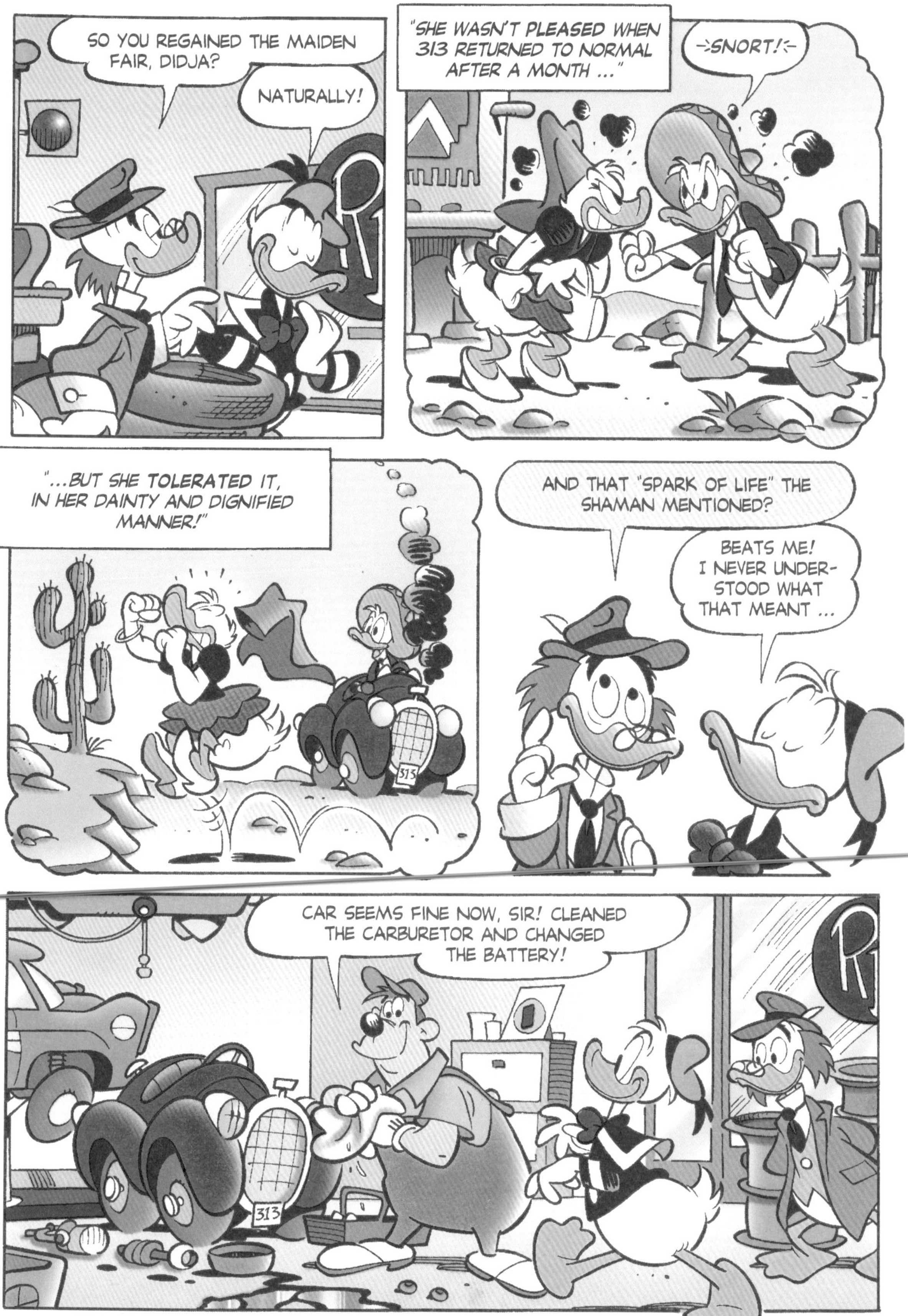
SO YOU REGAINED THE MAIDEN FAIR, DIDJA?
NATURALLY!
"SHE WASN'T PLEASED WHEN 313 RETURNED TO NORMAL AFTER A MONTH ..."
SNORT!
"...BUT SHE TOLERATED IT, IN HER DAINTY AND DIGNIFIED MANNER!"
313
AND THAT "SPARK OF LIFE" THE SHAMAN MENTIONED?
BEATS ME! I NEVER UNDER-STOOD WHAT THAT MEANT ...
CAR SEEMS FINE NOW, SIR! CLEANED THE CARBURETOR AND CHANGED THE BATTERY!
313

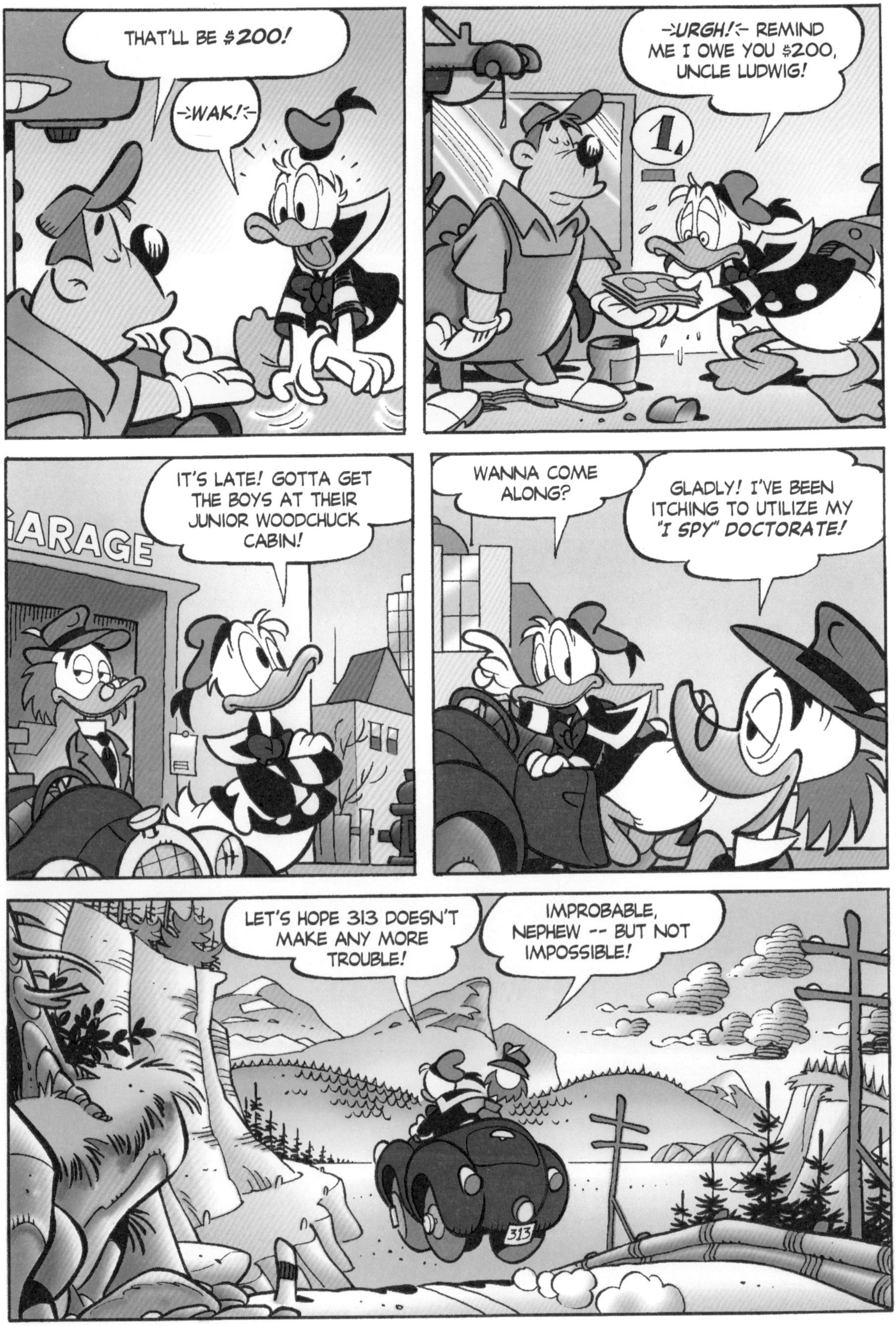
THAT'LL BE $200!
-WAK!-
-URGH!- REMIND ME I OWE YOU $200, UNCLE LUDWIG!
IT'S LATE! GOTTA GET THE BOYS AT THEIR JUNIOR WOODCHUCK CABIN!
GARAGE
WANNA COME ALONG?
GLADLY! I'VE BEEN ITCHING TO UTILIZE MY "I SPY" DOCTORATE!
LET'S HOPE 313 DOESN'T MAKE ANY MORE TROUBLE!
IMPROBABLE, NEPHEW -- BUT NOT IMPOSSIBLE!
313

AS 313 CLIMBS HIGHER, THE SNOW PILES UP ...
MAN, DID THE WEATHER GET BAD!
I SPY WITH MY LITTLE EYE ... AN AVALANCHE WAITING TO HAPPEN!
WOOO-OOO OOO OOO
WOODCHU
POST #37
313
-ULP!- NO, NO, NO ...
COFF COFF COUGH
313
I SPY ... A JALOPY IN NEED OF SERVICING! -HOO-HOO!-
NOOO!
313

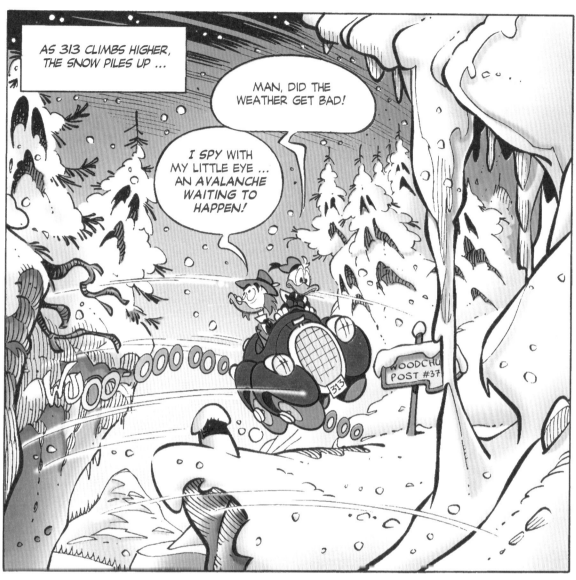

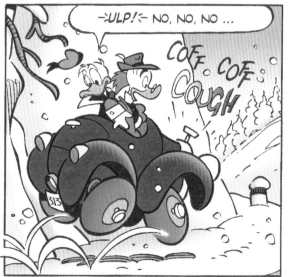

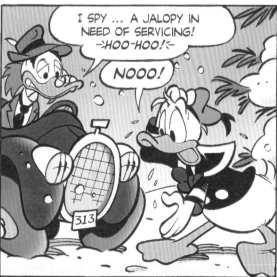

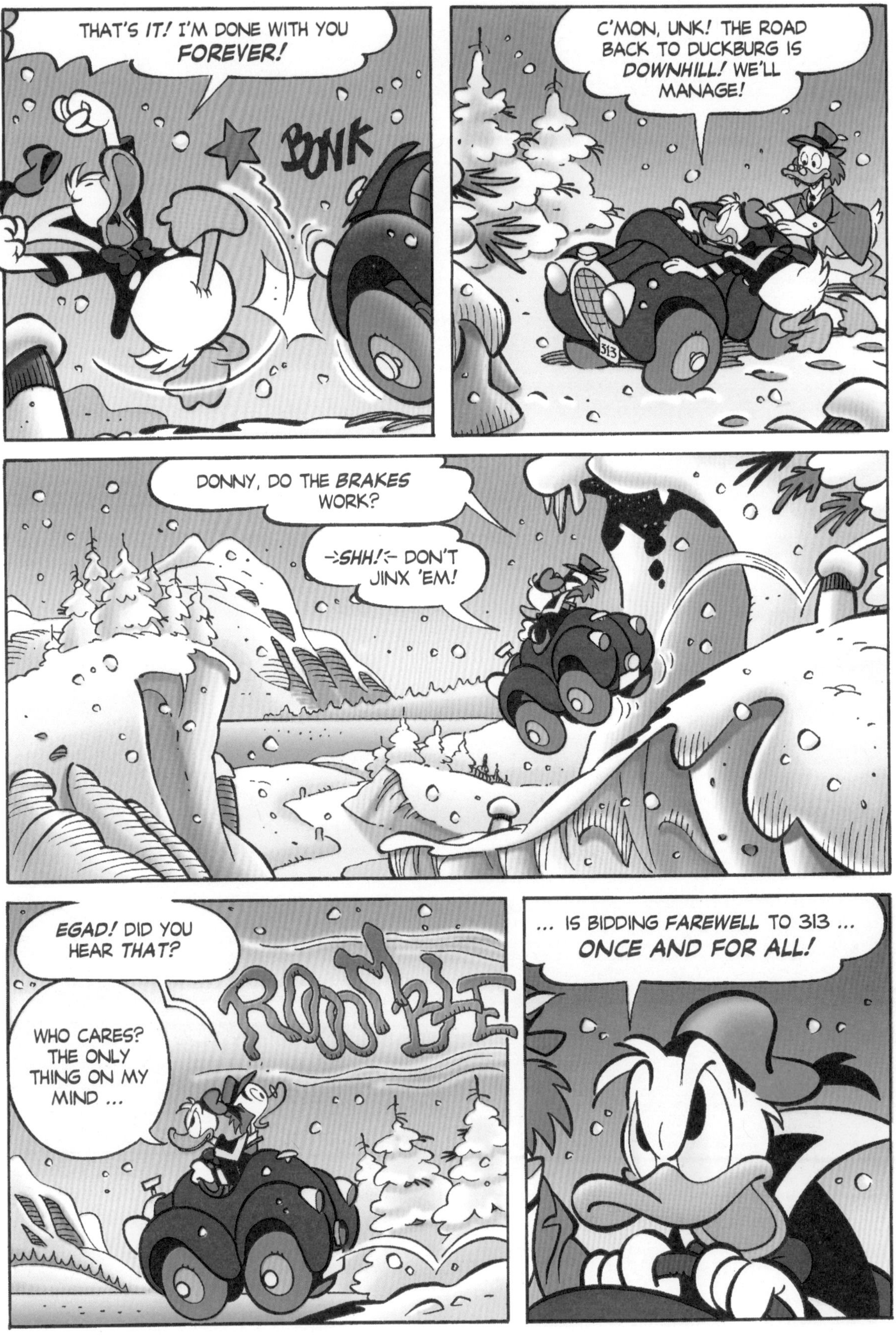
THAT'S IT! I'M DONE WITH YOU FOREVER!
BONK
C'MON, UNK! THE ROAD BACK TO DUCKBURG IS DOWNHILL! WE'LL MANAGE!
313
DONNY, DO THE BRAKES WORK?
SHH! DON'T JINX 'EM!
EGAD! DID YOU HEAR THAT?
ROOOMBLE
WHO CARES? THE ONLY THING ON MY MIND ...
... IS BIDDING FAREWELL TO 313 ... ONCE AND FOR ALL!

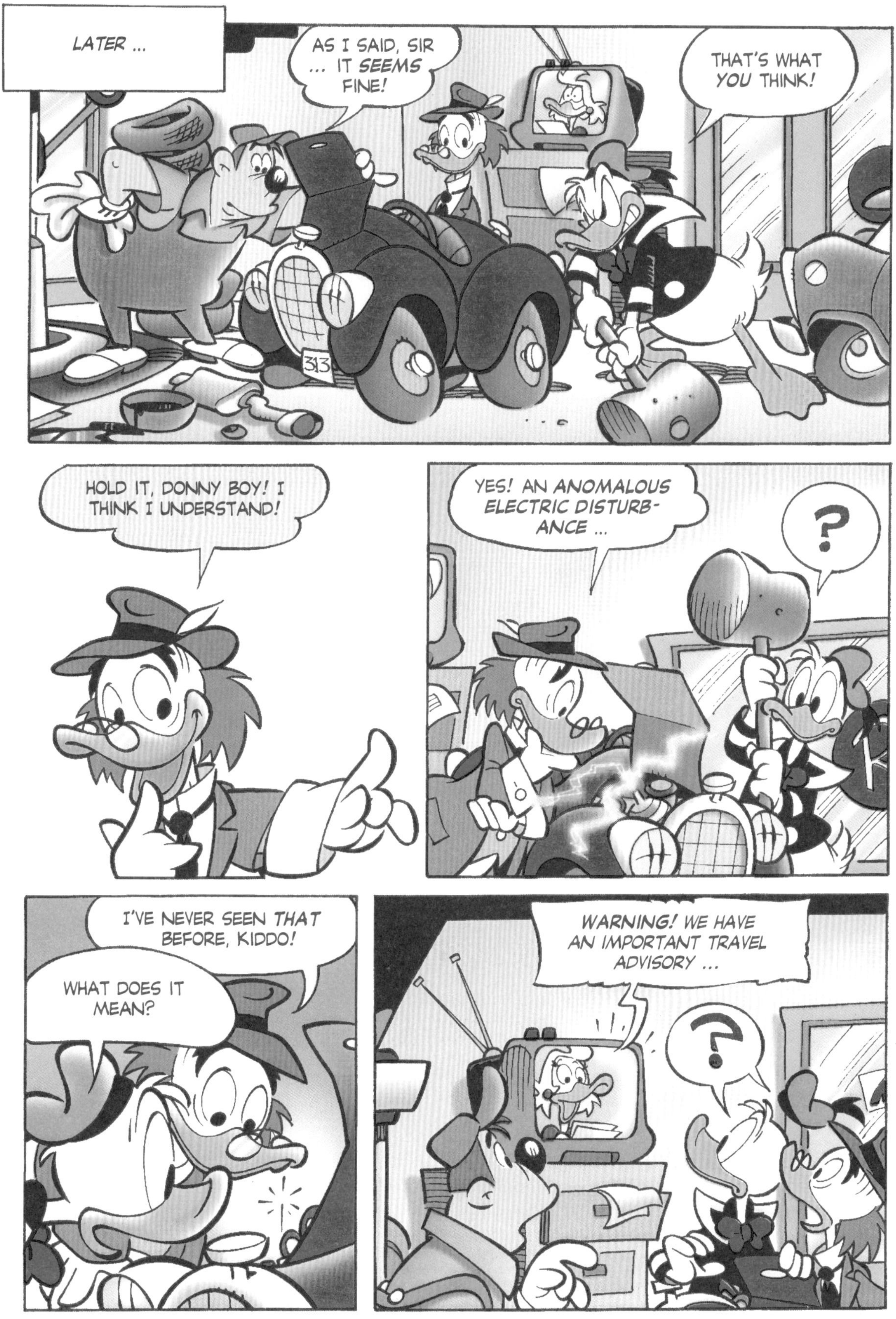
LATER ...
AS I SAID, SIR ... IT SEEMS FINE!
THAT'S WHAT YOU THINK!
313
HOLD IT, DONNY BOY! I THINK I UNDERSTAND!
YES! AN ANOMALOUS ELECTRIC DISTURB-ANCE ...
?
I'VE NEVER SEEN THAT BEFORE, KIDDO!
WHAT DOES IT MEAN?
WARNING! WE HAVE AN IMPORTANT TRAVEL ADVISORY ...
?

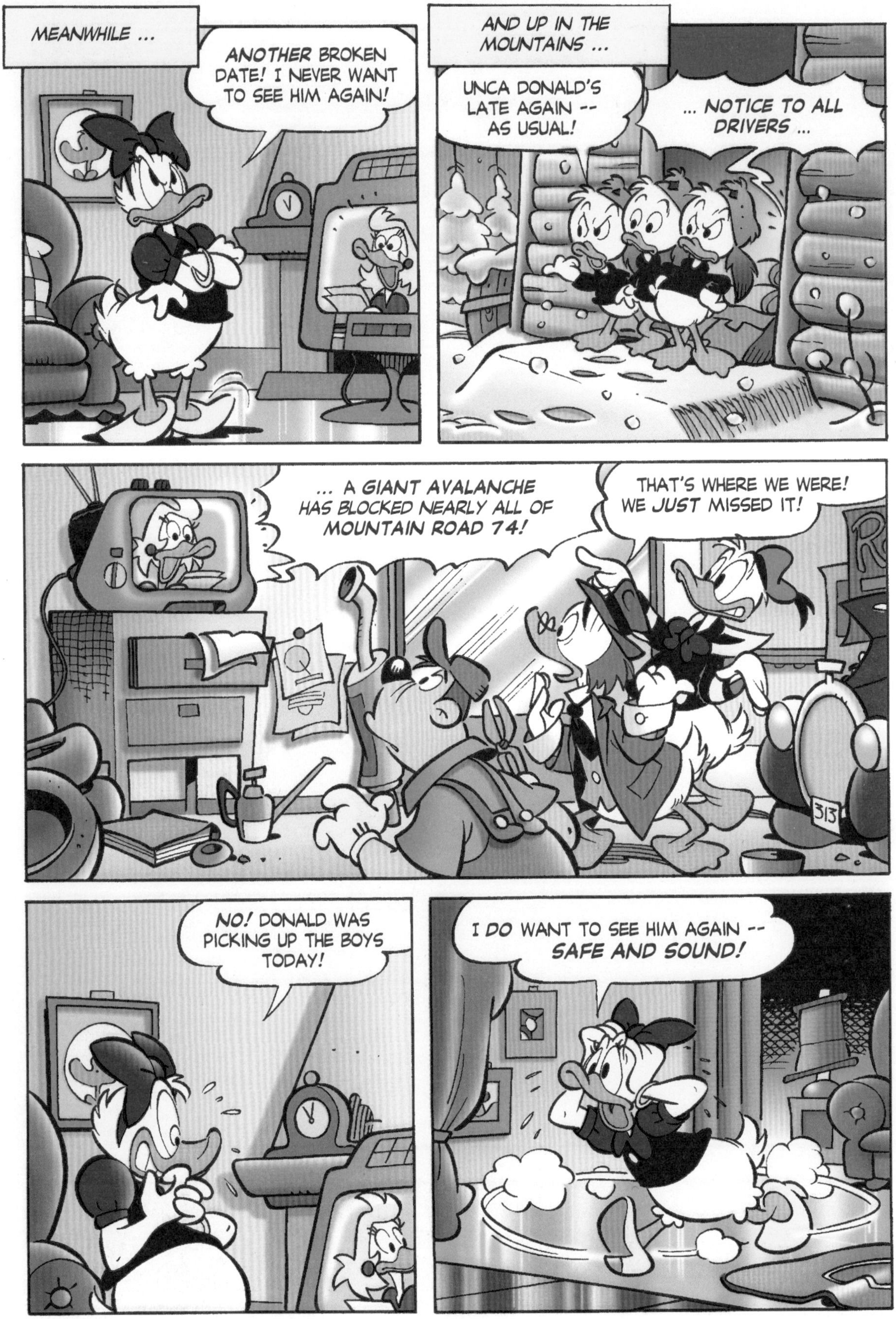
MEANWHILE ...
ANOTHER BROKEN DATE! I NEVER WANT TO SEE HIM AGAIN!
AND UP IN THE MOUNTAINS ...
UNCA DONALD'S LATE AGAIN -- AS USUAL!
... NOTICE TO ALL DRIVERS ...
... A GIANT AVALANCHE HAS BLOCKED NEARLY ALL OF MOUNTAIN ROAD 74!
THAT'S WHERE WE WERE! WE JUST MISSED IT!
313
NO! DONALD WAS PICKING UP THE BOYS TODAY!
I DO WANT TO SEE HIM AGAIN -- SAFE AND SOUND!

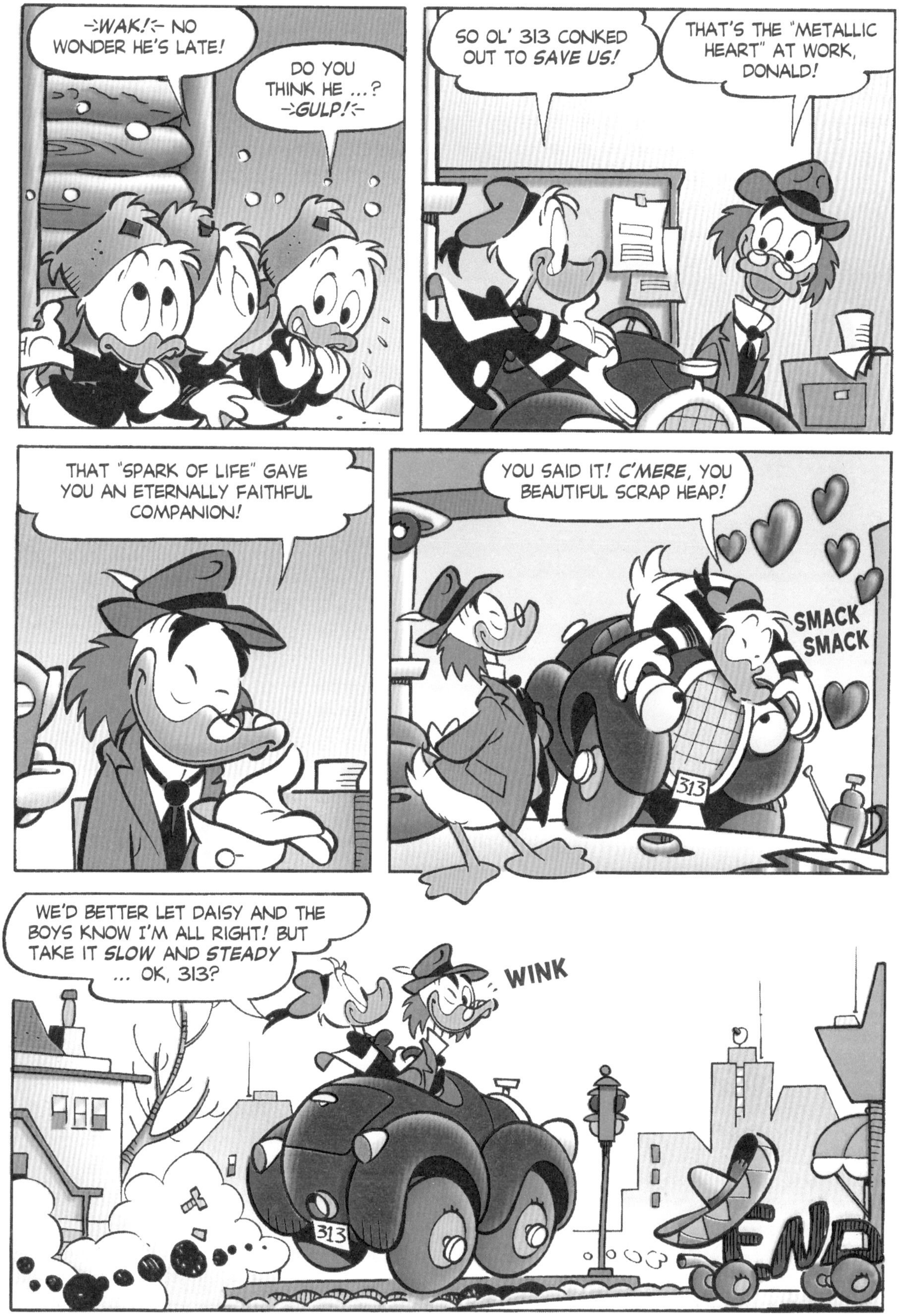
WAK! NO WONDER HE'S LATE!
DO YOU THINK HE ...? GULP!
SO OL' 313 CONKED OUT TO SAVE US!
THAT'S THE "METALLIC HEART" AT WORK, DONALD!
THAT "SPARK OF LIFE" GAVE YOU AN ETERNALLY FAITHFUL COMPANION!
YOU SAID IT! C'MERE, YOU BEAUTIFUL SCRAP HEAP!
SMACK SMACK
313
WE'D BETTER LET DAISY AND THE BOYS KNOW I'M ALL RIGHT! BUT TAKE IT SLOW AND STEADY ... OK, 313?
WINK
313
END

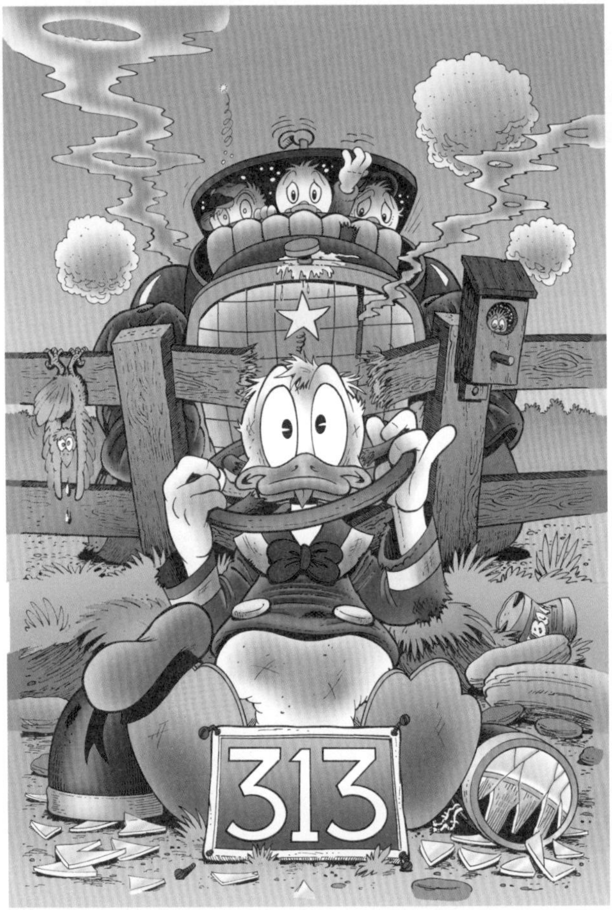
313

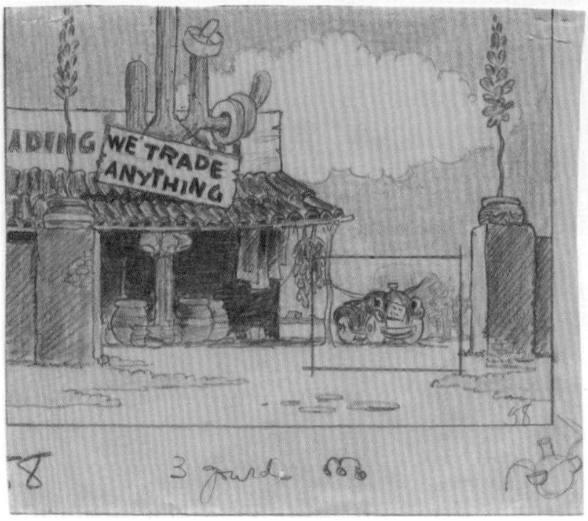
WE TRADE ANYTHING

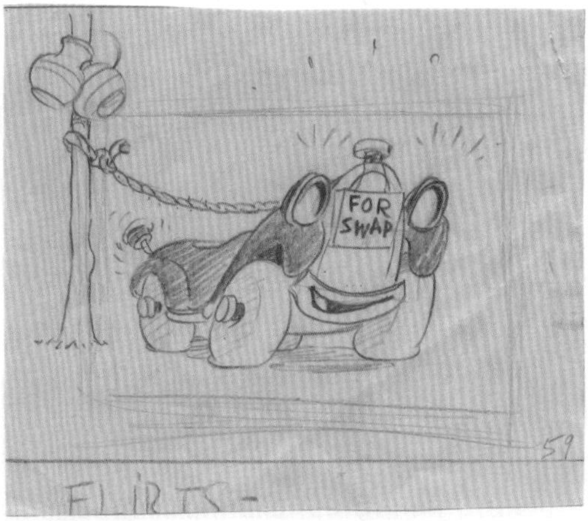
FOR SWAP

Storyboard drawings (top right and above right) courtesy Disney Publishing Worldwide.

Good Ol' 313

MASSIMO DE VITA'S "The Secret of 313" was inspired by *Don Donald* (1937), the animated cartoon that introduced Donald's beloved car, his burro Basil, and Donna Duck — the earliest version of Daisy Duck (though Donna was later rebooted in comics as a separate character).

These *Don Donald* storyboard drawings by Albert Hurter (above right) give the car an anthropomorphic "face" that it didn't have in the finished film but that De Vita briefly gives to it in his story. Meanwhile, a pin-up poster by Don Rosa (above right; *Walt Disney Uncle Scrooge and Donald Duck: "Escape from Forbidden Valley"*, The Don Rosa Library Vol. 8, Fantagraphics Books, 2017) shows the car as most often conceived by artists today: a non-anthropomorphic rattletrap prone to falling apart. *[DG]*

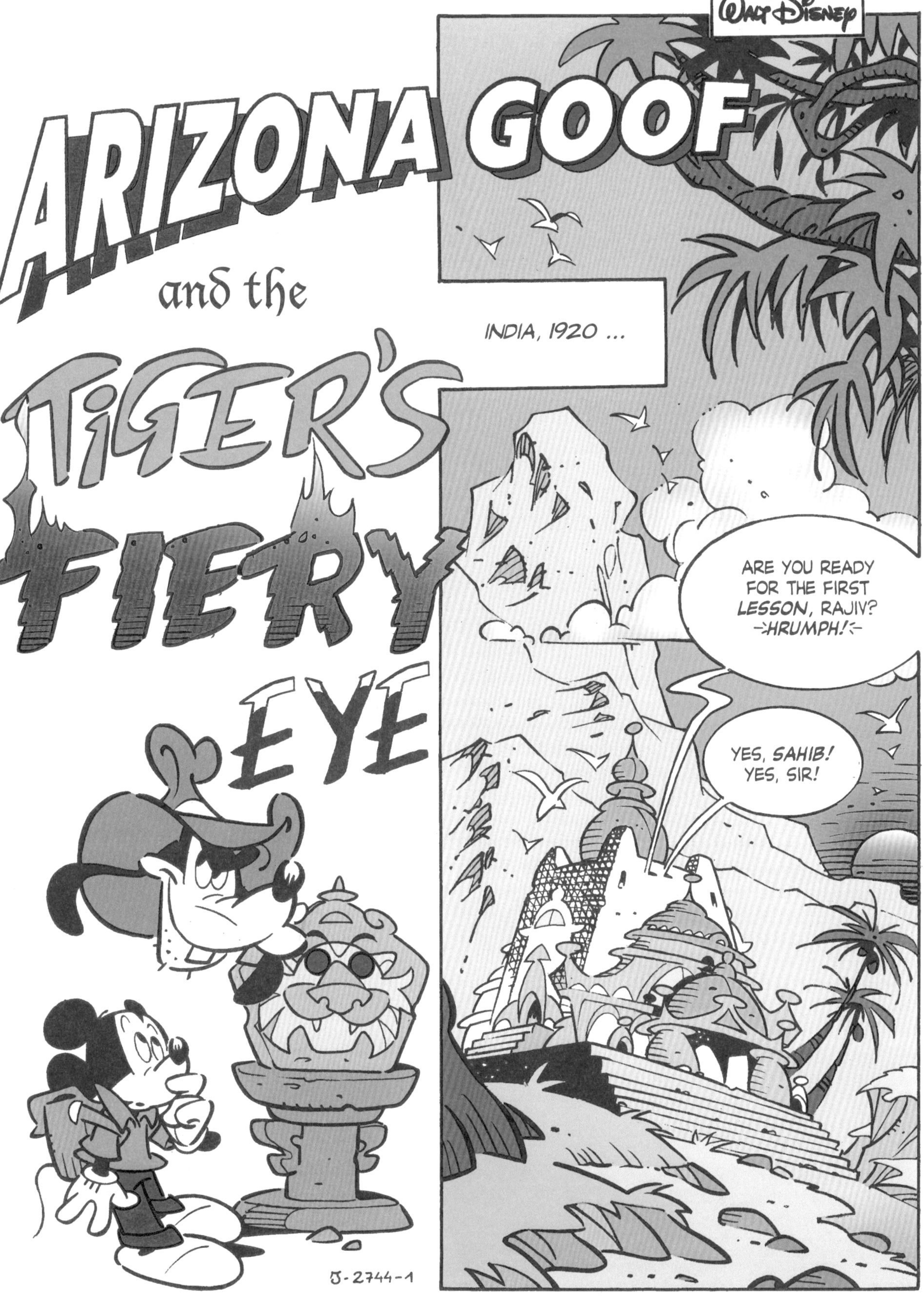
WALT DISNEY
ARIZONA GOOF
and the
TIGER'S
FIERY
EYE
INDIA, 1920 ...
ARE YOU READY FOR THE FIRST LESSON, RAJIV? -HRUMPH!-
YES, SAHIB! YES, SIR!
J-2744-1

STORY AND ART BY MASSIMO DE VITA • TRANSLATION AND DIALOGUE BY DAVID GERSTEIN • LETTERING BY PAUL BARESH AND CHRISTINA HWANG • COLORING BY DISNEY ITALIA • EDITING BY J. MICHAEL CATRON

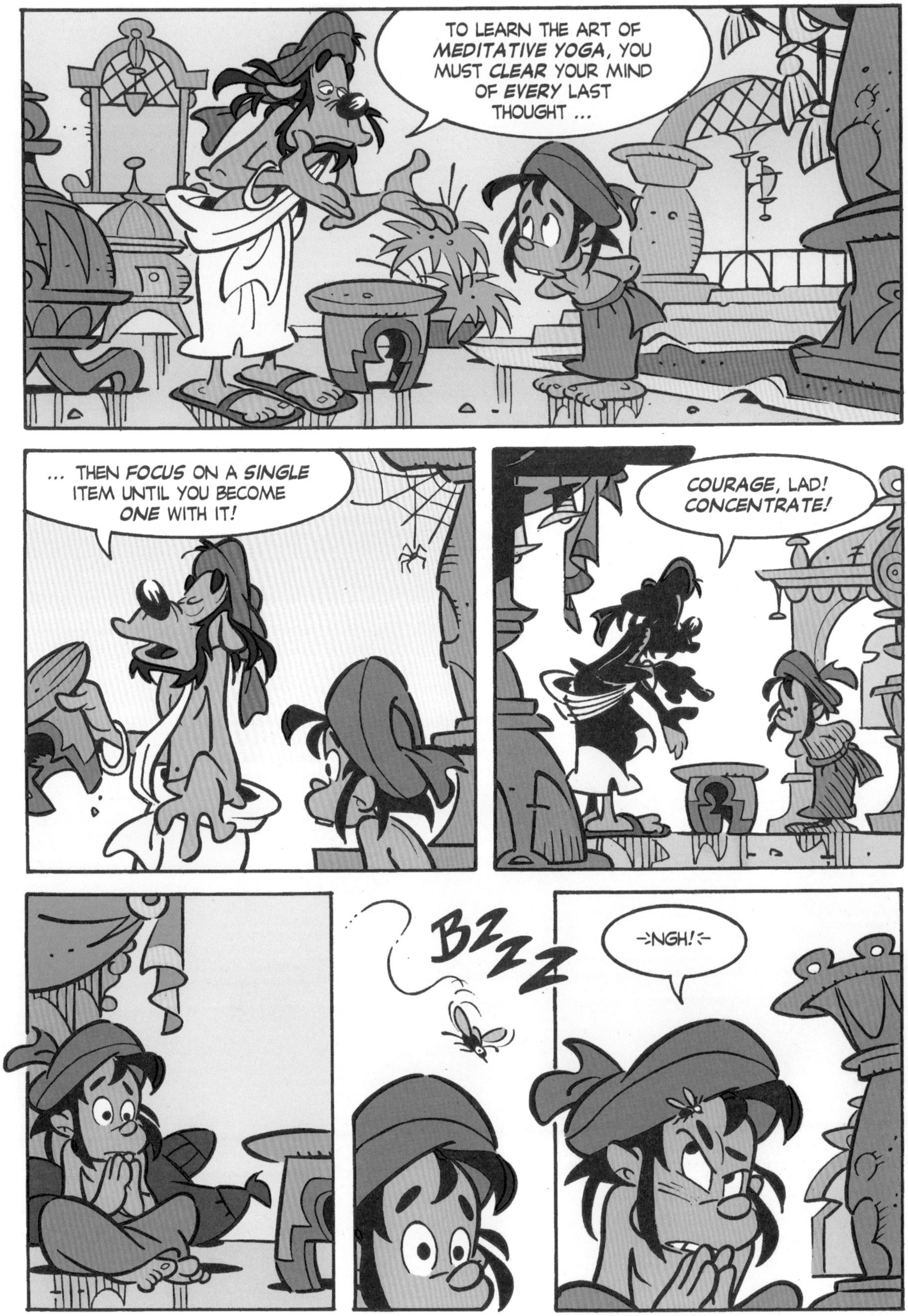
TO LEARN THE ART OF MEDITATIVE YOGA, YOU MUST CLEAR YOUR MIND OF EVERY LAST THOUGHT ...
... THEN FOCUS ON A SINGLE ITEM UNTIL YOU BECOME ONE WITH IT!
COURAGE, LAD! CONCENTRATE!
BZZZZ
NGH!

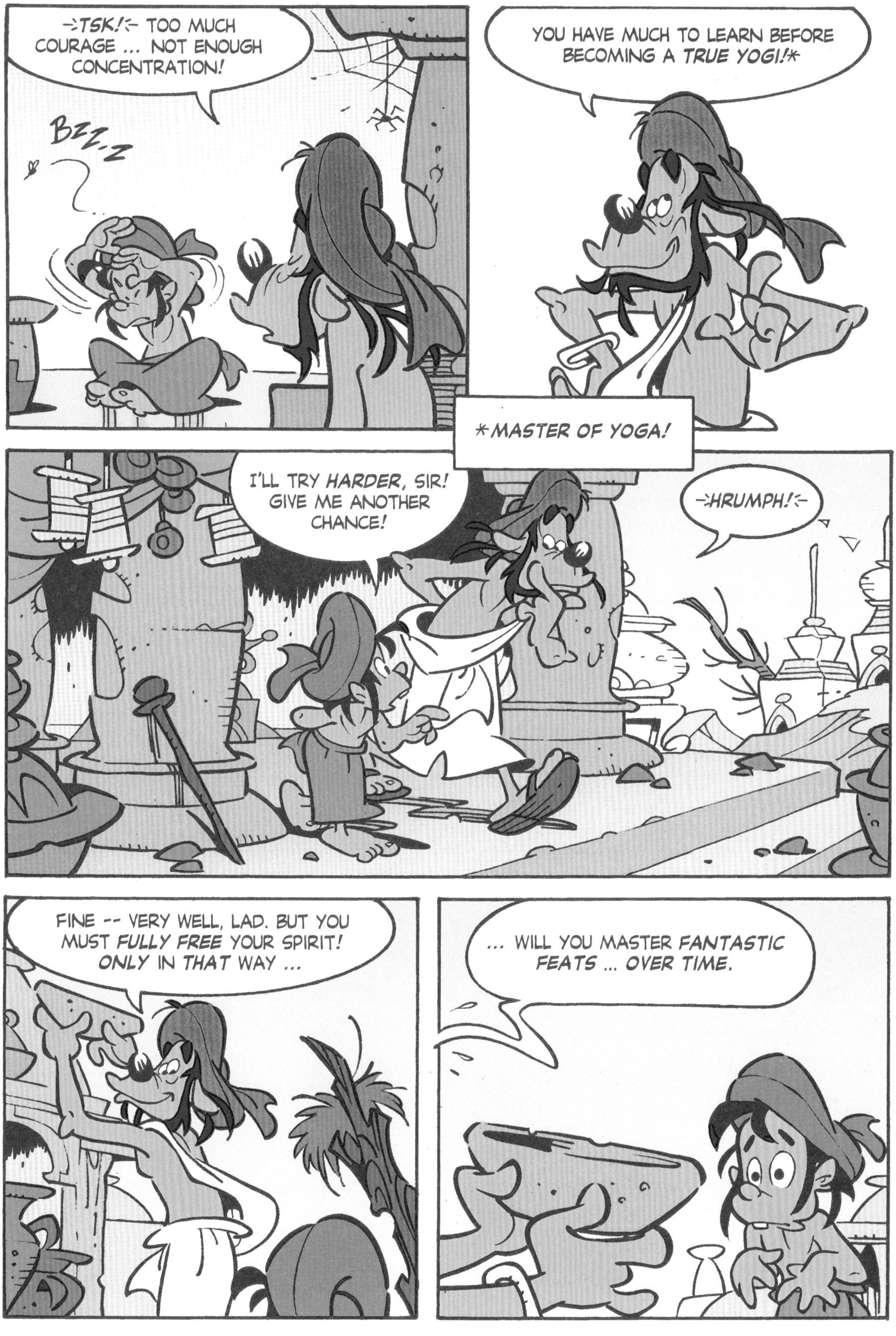
-TSK!- TOO MUCH COURAGE ... NOT ENOUGH CONCENTRATION!
BZZ-Z-Z
YOU HAVE MUCH TO LEARN BEFORE BECOMING A TRUE YOGI!*
*MASTER OF YOGA!
I'LL TRY HARDER, SIR! GIVE ME ANOTHER CHANCE!
-HRUMPH!-
FINE -- VERY WELL, LAD. BUT YOU MUST FULLY FREE YOUR SPIRIT! ONLY IN THAT WAY ...
... WILL YOU MASTER FANTASTIC FEATS ... OVER TIME.

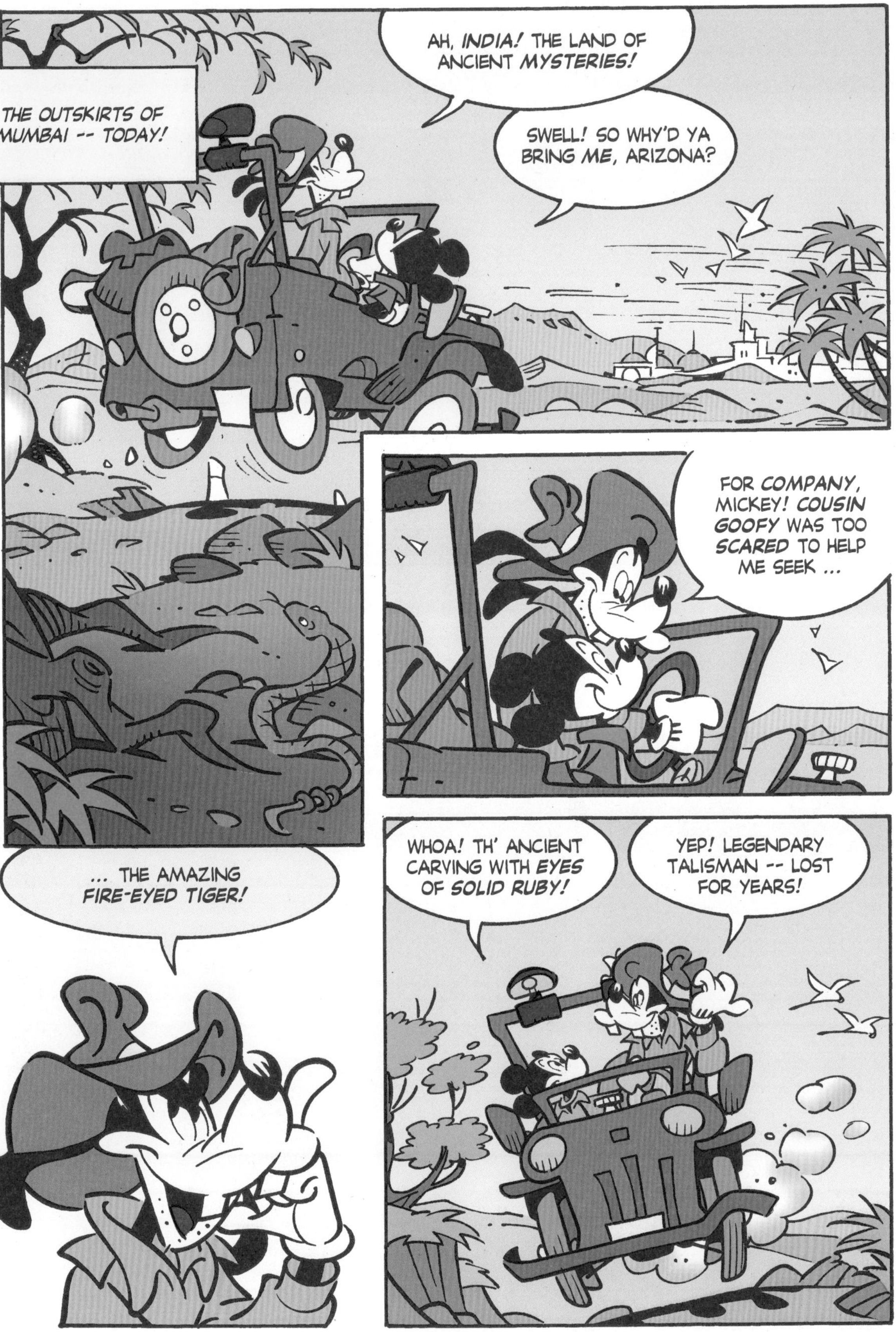
THE OUTSKIRTS OF MUMBAI -- TODAY!
AH, *INDIA!* THE LAND OF ANCIENT *MYSTERIES!*
SWELL! SO WHY'D YA BRING *ME*, ARIZONA?
FOR *COMPANY*, MICKEY! *COUSIN GOOFY* WAS TOO *SCARED* TO HELP ME SEEK ...
... THE AMAZING *FIRE-EYED TIGER!*
WHOA! TH' ANCIENT CARVING WITH *EYES* OF *SOLID RUBY!*
YEP! LEGENDARY TALISMAN -- LOST FOR YEARS!

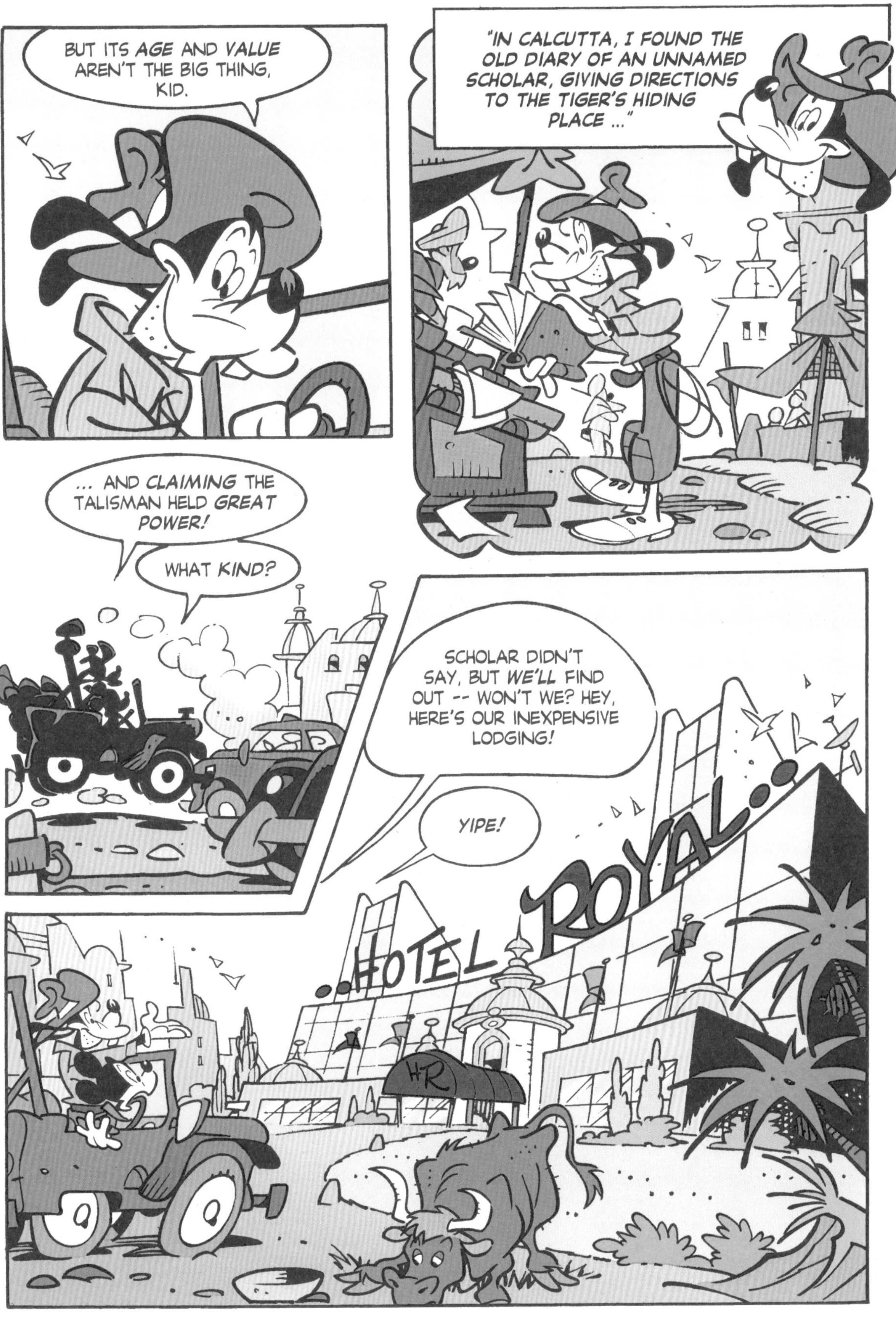

BUT ITS AGE AND VALUE AREN'T THE BIG THING, KID.
"IN CALCUTTA, I FOUND THE OLD DIARY OF AN UNNAMED SCHOLAR, GIVING DIRECTIONS TO THE TIGER'S HIDING PLACE ..."
... AND CLAIMING THE TALISMAN HELD GREAT POWER!
WHAT KIND?
SCHOLAR DIDN'T SAY, BUT WE'LL FIND OUT -- WON'T WE? HEY, HERE'S OUR INEXPENSIVE LODGING!
YIPE!
..HOTEL ROYAL..
HR

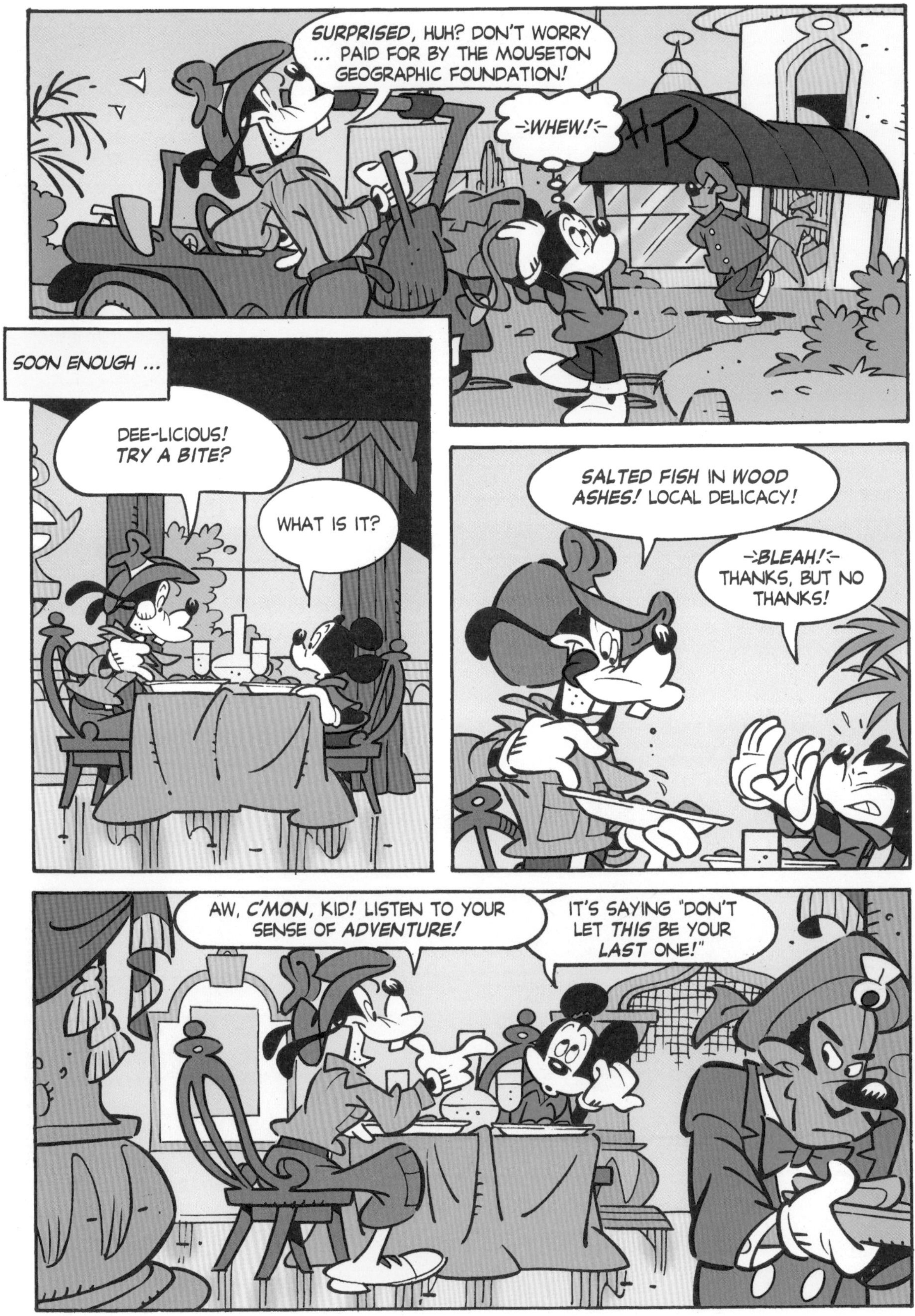
SURPRISED, HUH? DON'T WORRY ... PAID FOR BY THE MOUSETON GEOGRAPHIC FOUNDATION!
WHEW!
SOON ENOUGH ...
DEE-LICIOUS! TRY A BITE?
WHAT IS IT?
SALTED FISH IN WOOD ASHES! LOCAL DELICACY!
BLEAH! THANKS, BUT NO THANKS!
AW, C'MON, KID! LISTEN TO YOUR SENSE OF ADVENTURE!
IT'S SAYING "DON'T LET THIS BE YOUR LAST ONE!"

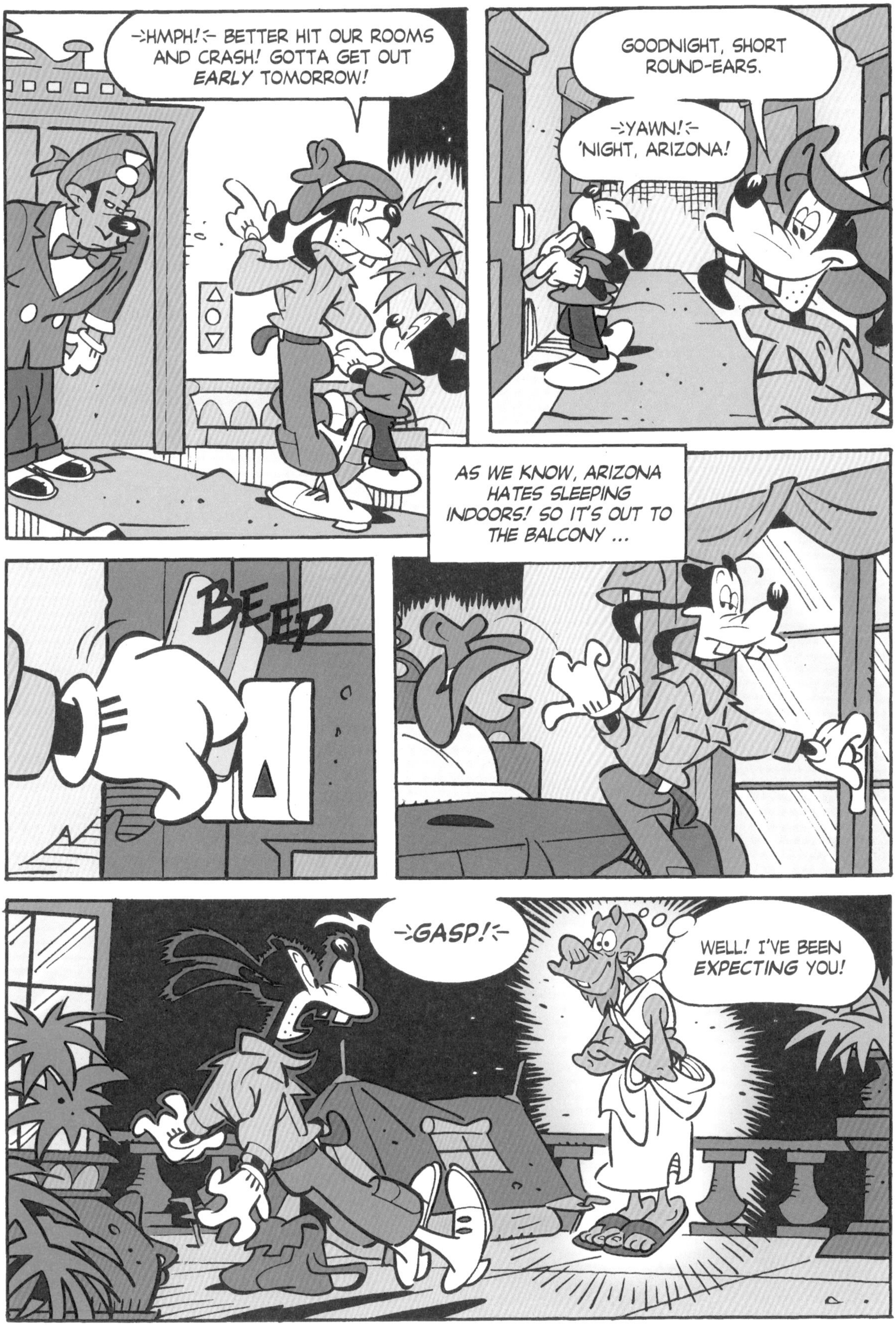

-HMPH!- BETTER HIT OUR ROOMS AND CRASH! GOTTA GET OUT EARLY TOMORROW!
GOODNIGHT, SHORT ROUND-EARS.
-YAWN!- 'NIGHT, ARIZONA!
AS WE KNOW, ARIZONA HATES SLEEPING INDOORS! SO IT'S OUT TO THE BALCONY ...
BEEP
-GASP!-
WELL! I'VE BEEN EXPECTING YOU!

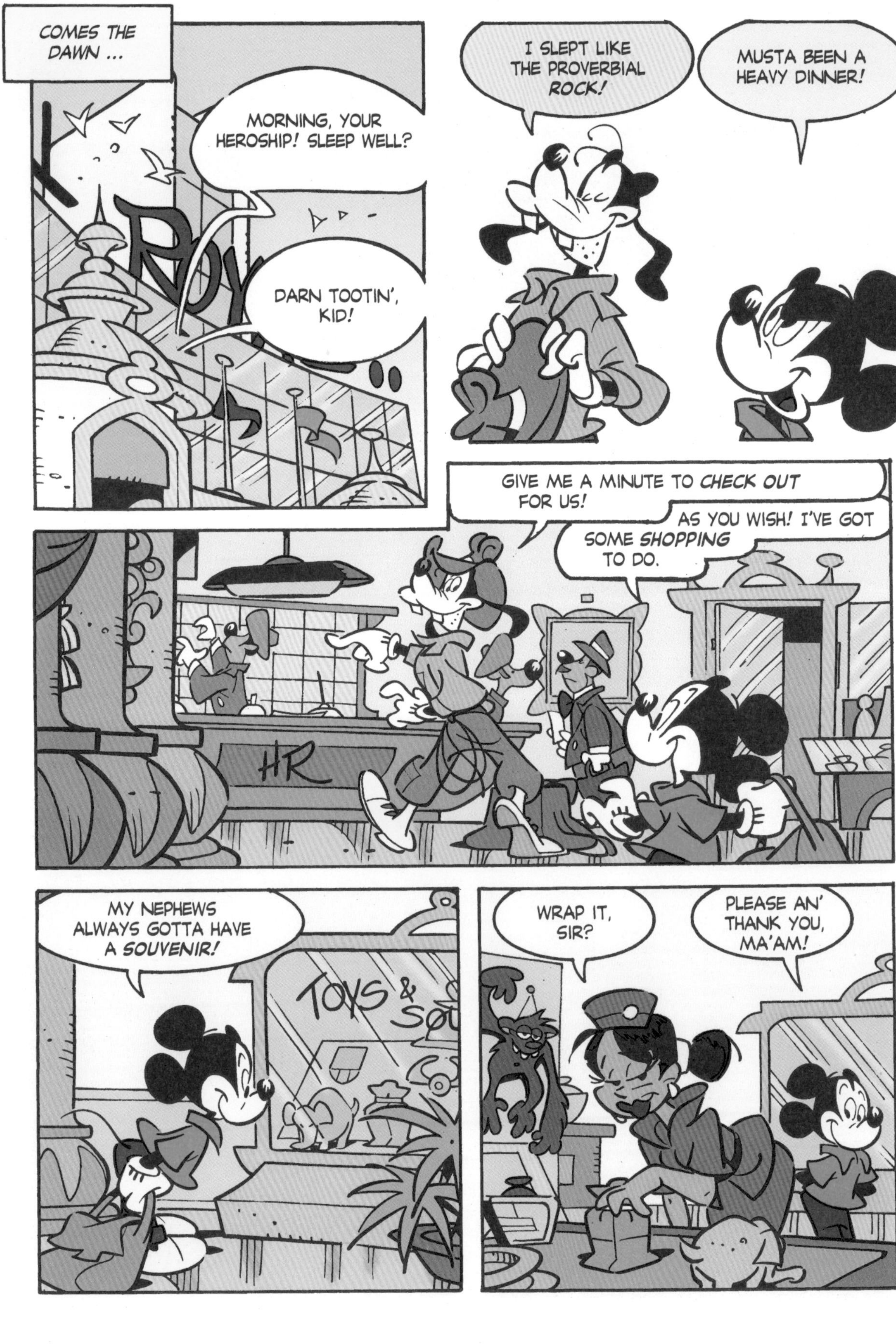
COMES THE DAWN ...
MORNING, YOUR HEROSHIP! SLEEP WELL?
DARN TOOTIN', KID!
I SLEPT LIKE THE PROVERBIAL *ROCK!*
MUSTA BEEN A HEAVY DINNER!
GIVE ME A MINUTE TO *CHECK OUT* FOR US!
AS YOU WISH! I'VE GOT SOME *SHOPPING* TO DO.
HR
MY NEPHEWS ALWAYS GOTTA HAVE A *SOUVENIR!*
TOYS &
WRAP IT, SIR?
PLEASE AN' THANK YOU, MA'AM!

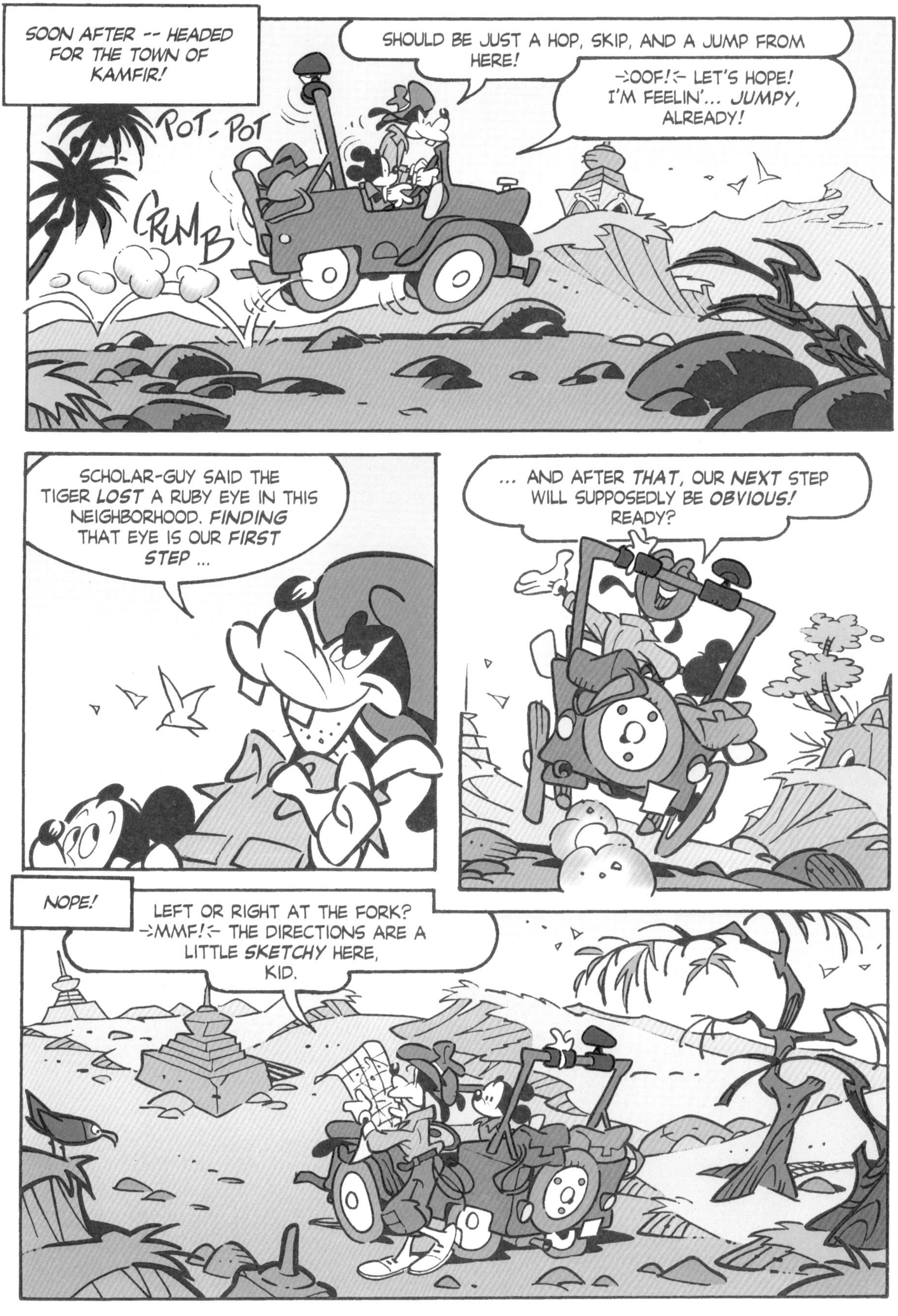
SOON AFTER -- HEADED FOR THE TOWN OF KAMFIR!
SHOULD BE JUST A HOP, SKIP, AND A JUMP FROM HERE!
-OOF!- LET'S HOPE! I'M FEELIN'... JUMPY, ALREADY!
POT-POT
CRUMB
SCHOLAR-GUY SAID THE TIGER LOST A RUBY EYE IN THIS NEIGHBORHOOD. FINDING THAT EYE IS OUR FIRST STEP ...
... AND AFTER THAT, OUR NEXT STEP WILL SUPPOSEDLY BE OBVIOUS! READY?
NOPE!
LEFT OR RIGHT AT THE FORK? -MMF!- THE DIRECTIONS ARE A LITTLE SKETCHY HERE, KID.

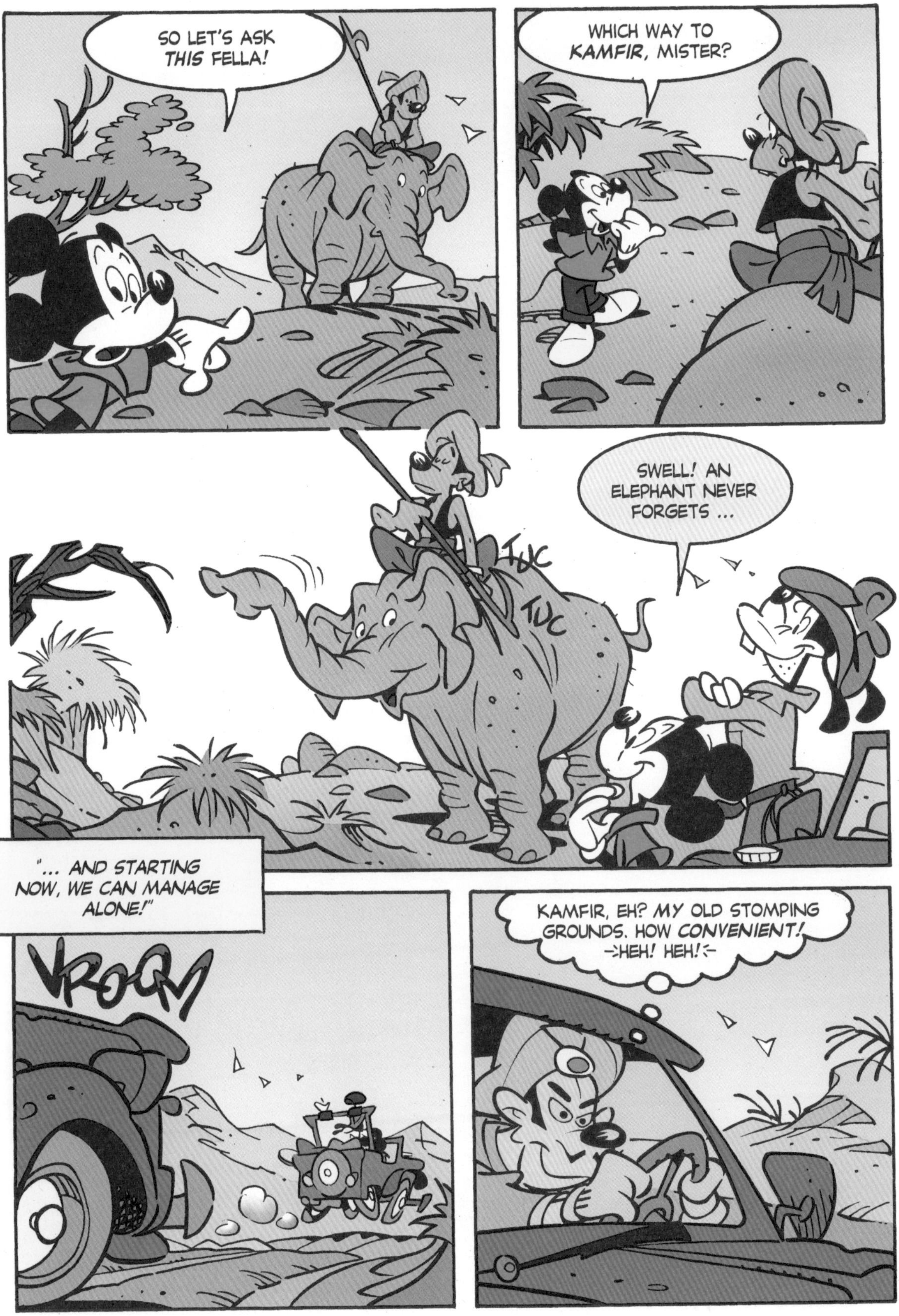
SO LET'S ASK *THIS* FELLA!
WHICH WAY TO *KAMFIR*, MISTER?
SWELL! AN ELEPHANT NEVER FORGETS ...
TUC
TUC
"... AND STARTING NOW, WE CAN MANAGE ALONE!"
VROOM
KAMFIR, EH? *MY* OLD STOMPING GROUNDS. HOW *CONVENIENT!* HEH! HEH!

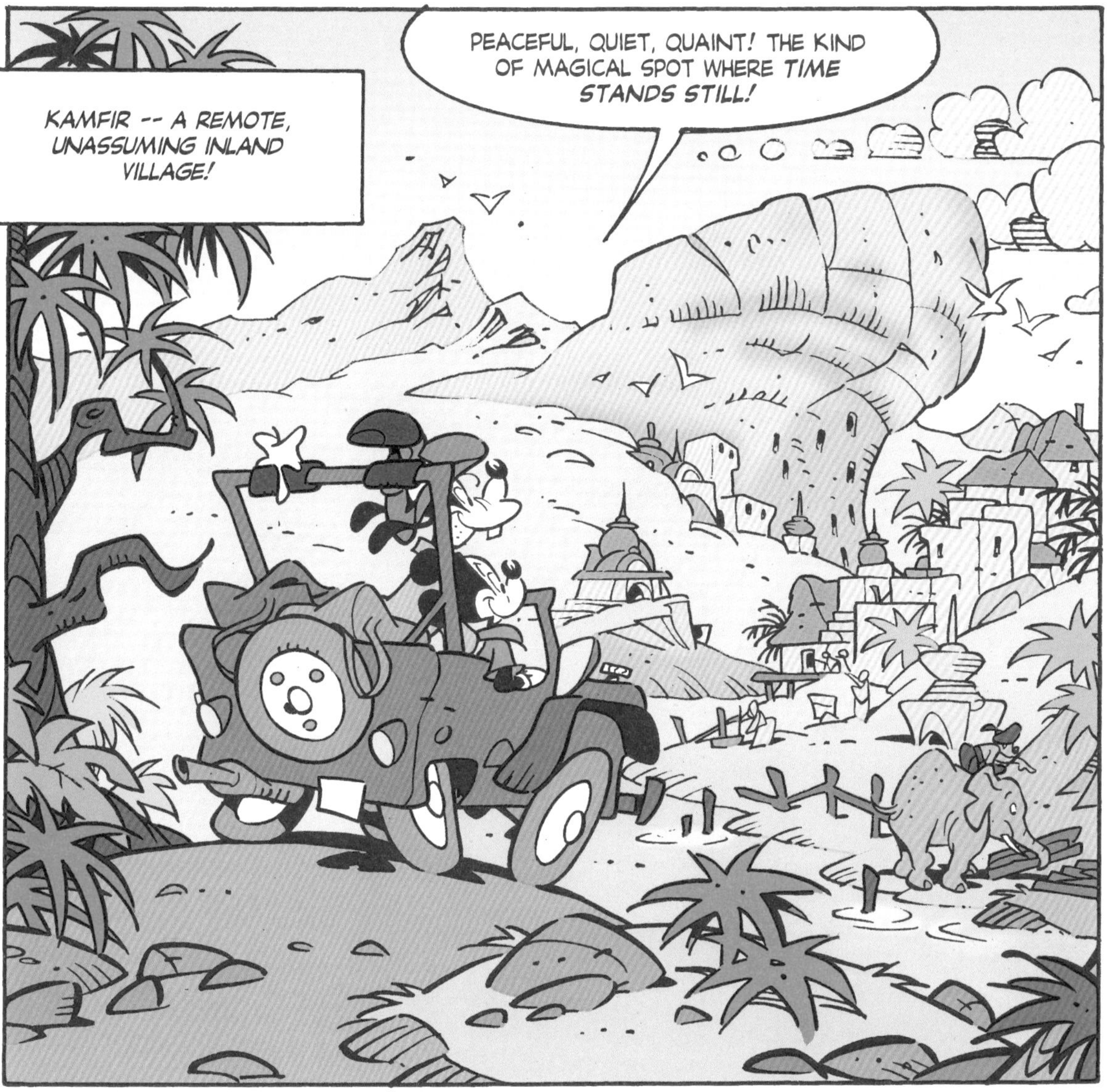
KAMFIR -- A REMOTE, UNASSUMING INLAND VILLAGE!
PEACEFUL, QUIET, QUAINT! THE KIND OF MAGICAL SPOT WHERE *TIME STANDS STILL!*

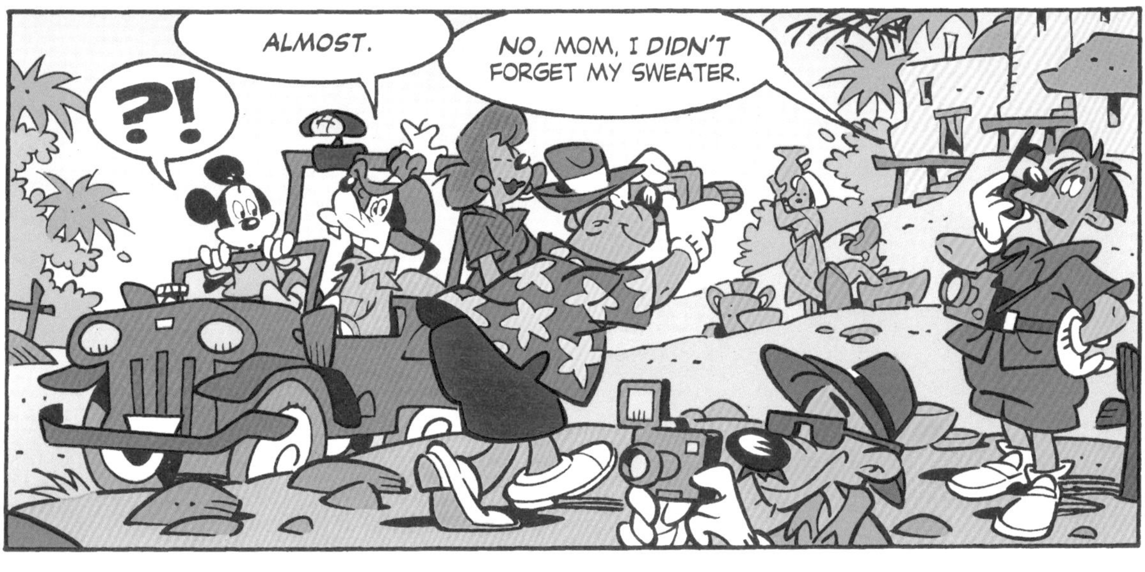
?!
ALMOST.
NO, MOM, I *DIDN'T* FORGET MY SWEATER.

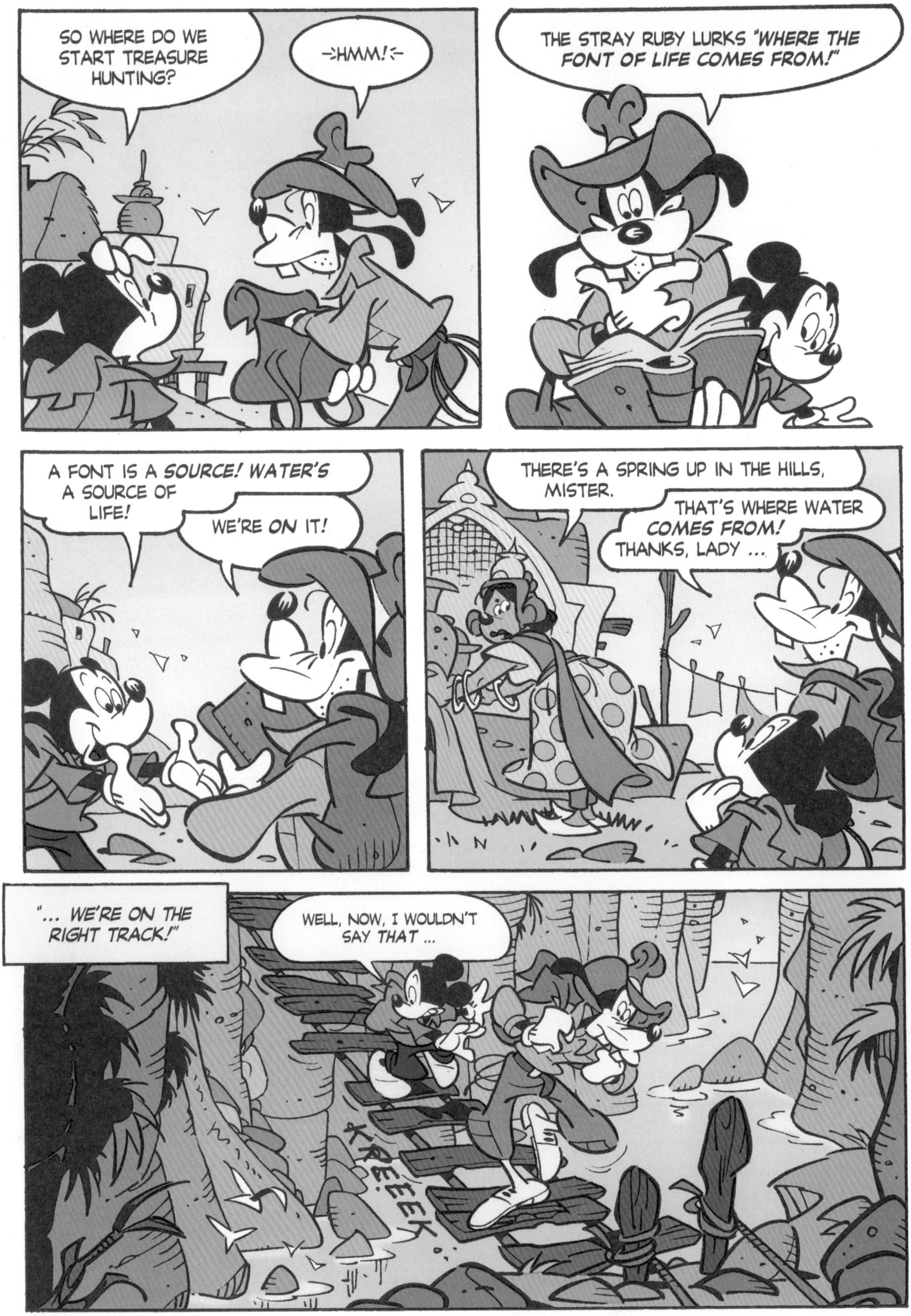
SO WHERE DO WE START TREASURE HUNTING?
HMM!
THE STRAY RUBY LURKS "WHERE THE FONT OF LIFE COMES FROM!"
A FONT IS A SOURCE! WATER'S A SOURCE OF LIFE!
WE'RE ON IT!
THERE'S A SPRING UP IN THE HILLS, MISTER.
THAT'S WHERE WATER COMES FROM! THANKS, LADY ...
"... WE'RE ON THE RIGHT TRACK!"
WELL, NOW, I WOULDN'T SAY THAT ...
KREEEK

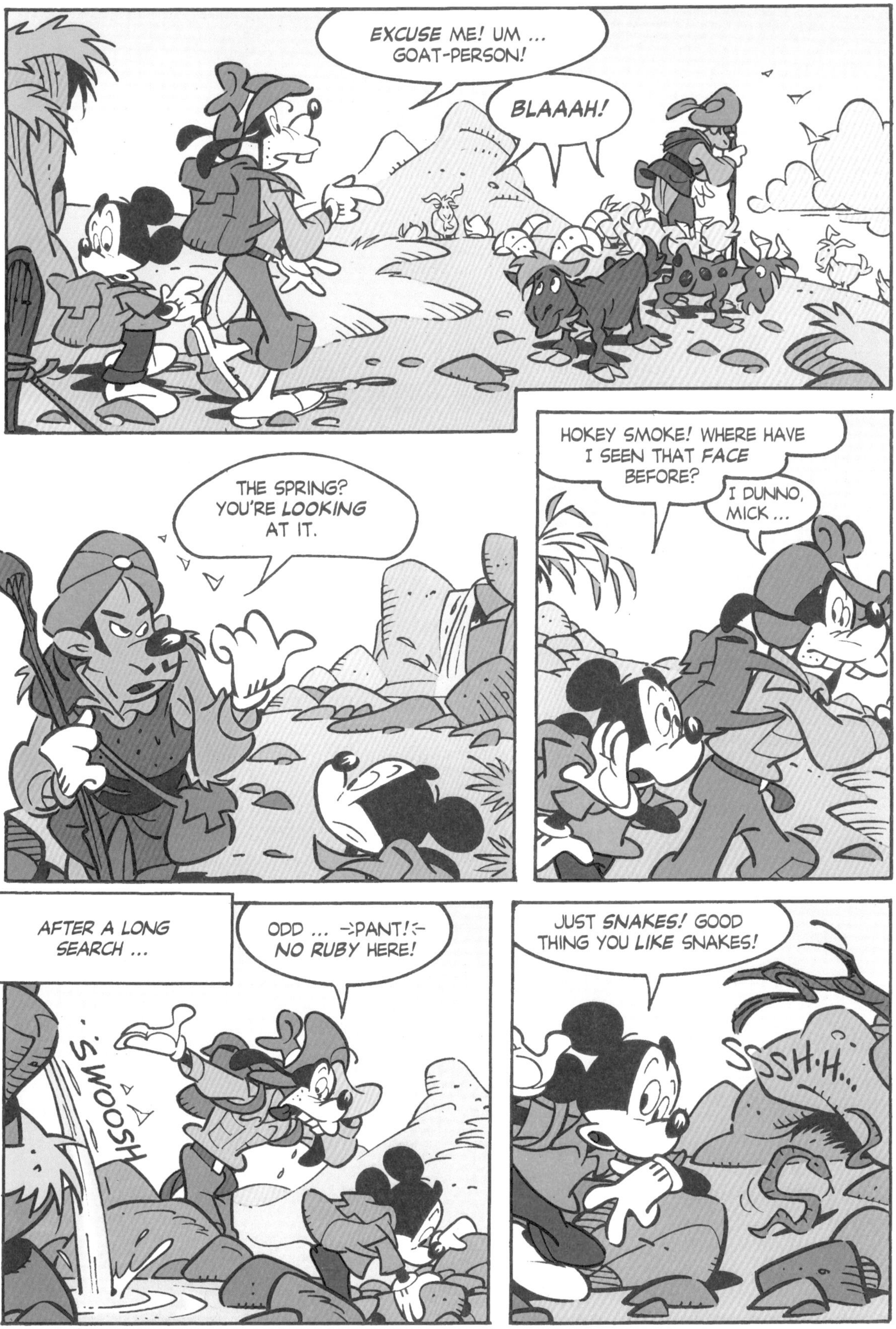
EXCUSE ME! UM ... GOAT-PERSON!
BLAAAH!
THE SPRING? YOU'RE LOOKING AT IT.
HOKEY SMOKE! WHERE HAVE I SEEN THAT FACE BEFORE?
I DUNNO, MICK ...
AFTER A LONG SEARCH ...
ODD ... PANT! NO RUBY HERE!
SWOOSH
JUST SNAKES! GOOD THING YOU LIKE SNAKES!
SSSH·H...

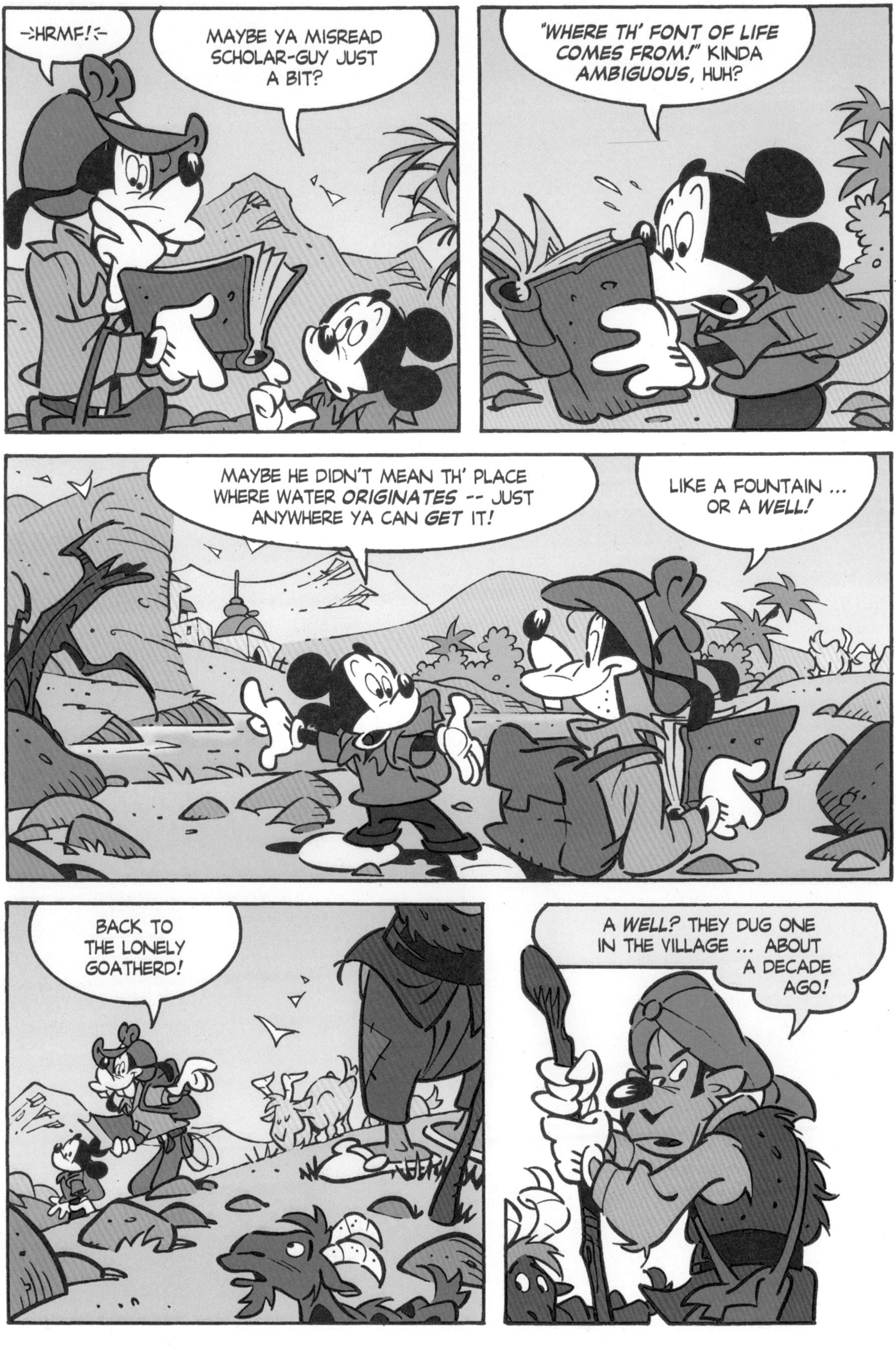
-HRMF!-
MAYBE YA MISREAD SCHOLAR-GUY JUST A BIT?
"WHERE TH' FONT OF LIFE COMES FROM!" KINDA AMBIGUOUS, HUH?
MAYBE HE DIDN'T MEAN TH' PLACE WHERE WATER ORIGINATES -- JUST ANYWHERE YA CAN GET IT!
LIKE A FOUNTAIN ... OR A WELL!
BACK TO THE LONELY GOATHERD!
A WELL? THEY DUG ONE IN THE VILLAGE ... ABOUT A DECADE AGO!

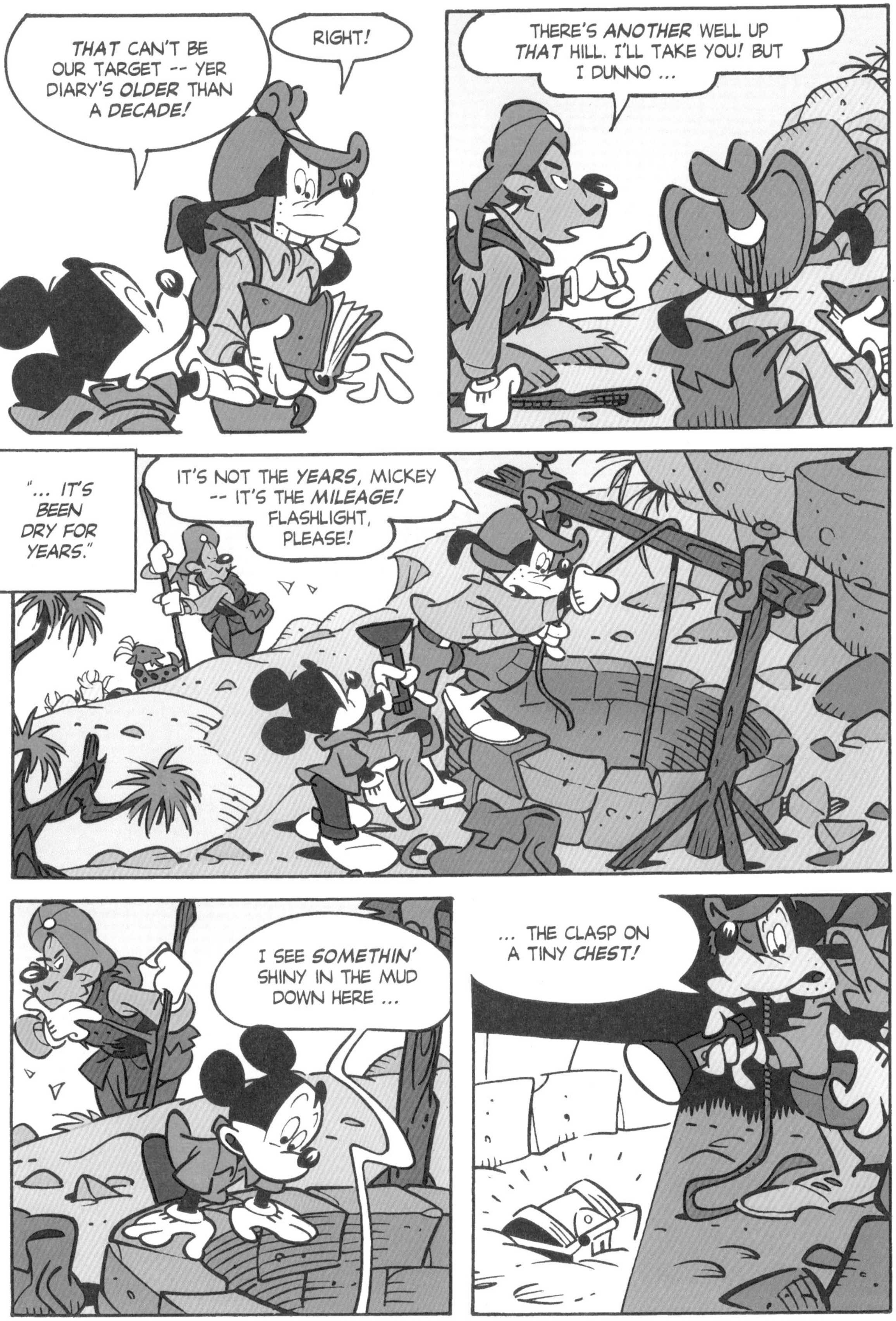
THAT CAN'T BE OUR TARGET -- YER DIARY'S OLDER THAN A DECADE!
RIGHT!
THERE'S ANOTHER WELL UP THAT HILL. I'LL TAKE YOU! BUT I DUNNO ...
"... IT'S BEEN DRY FOR YEARS."
IT'S NOT THE YEARS, MICKEY -- IT'S THE MILEAGE! FLASHLIGHT, PLEASE!
I SEE SOMETHIN' SHINY IN THE MUD DOWN HERE ...
... THE CLASP ON A TINY CHEST!

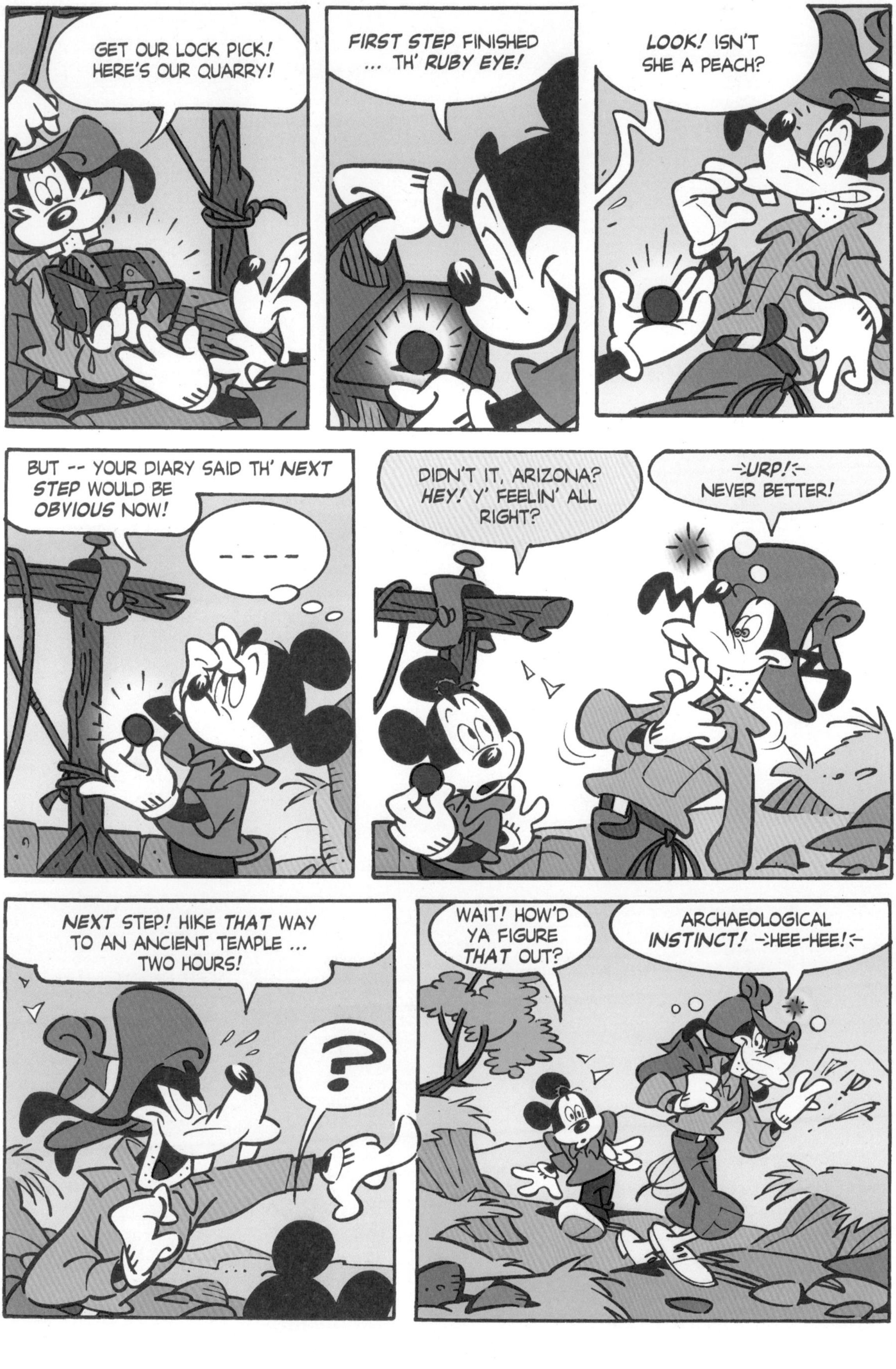
GET OUR LOCK PICK! HERE'S OUR QUARRY!
FIRST STEP FINISHED ... TH' RUBY EYE!
LOOK! ISN'T SHE A PEACH?
BUT -- YOUR DIARY SAID TH' NEXT STEP WOULD BE OBVIOUS NOW!
- - - -
DIDN'T IT, ARIZONA? HEY! Y' FEELIN' ALL RIGHT?
URP! NEVER BETTER!
NEXT STEP! HIKE THAT WAY TO AN ANCIENT TEMPLE ... TWO HOURS!
?
WAIT! HOW'D YA FIGURE THAT OUT?
ARCHAEOLOGICAL INSTINCT! HEE-HEE!

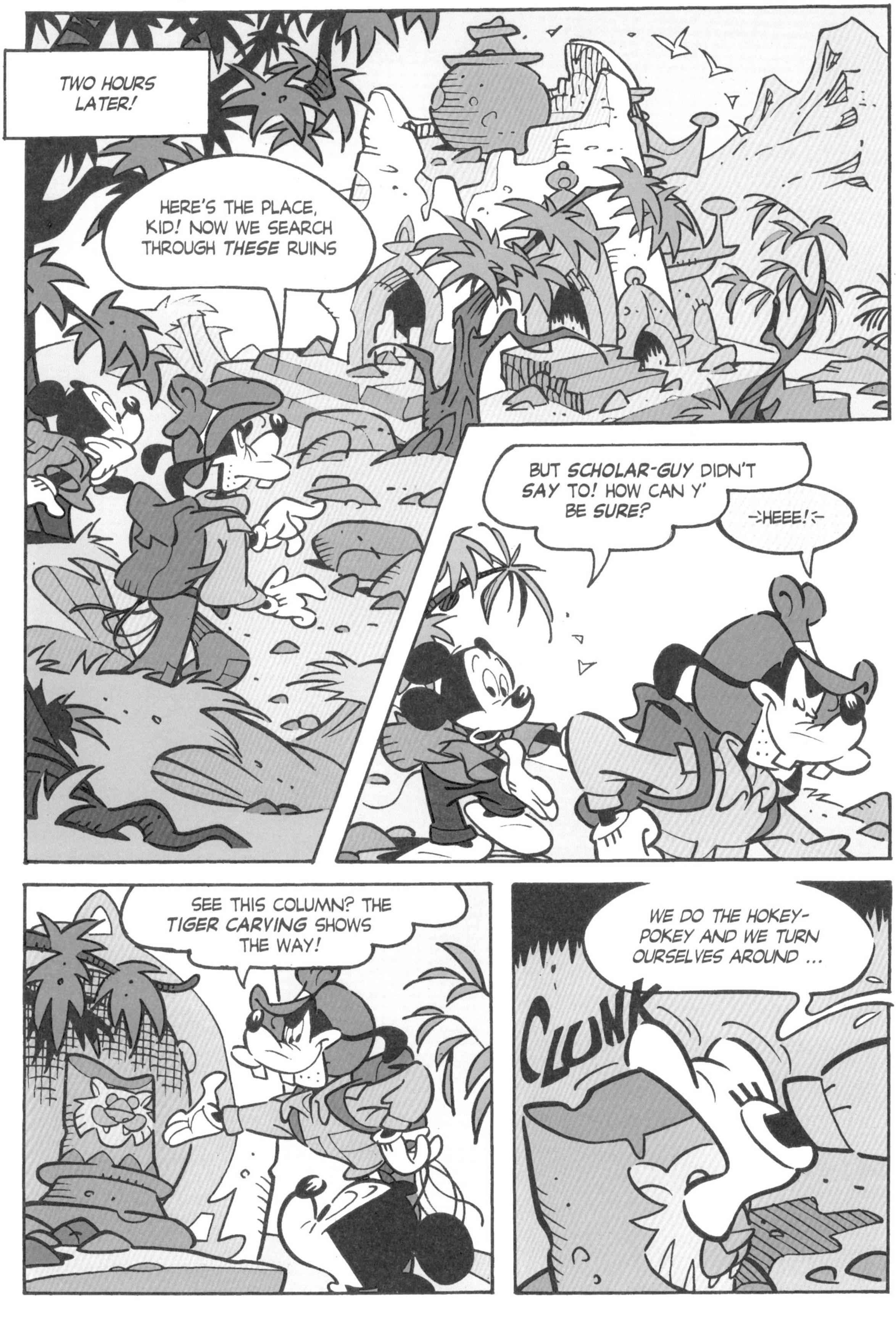
TWO HOURS LATER!
HERE'S THE PLACE, KID! NOW WE SEARCH THROUGH THESE RUINS
BUT SCHOLAR-GUY DIDN'T SAY TO! HOW CAN Y' BE SURE?
HEEE!
SEE THIS COLUMN? THE TIGER CARVING SHOWS THE WAY!
WE DO THE HOKEY-POKEY AND WE TURN OURSELVES AROUND ...
CLUNK

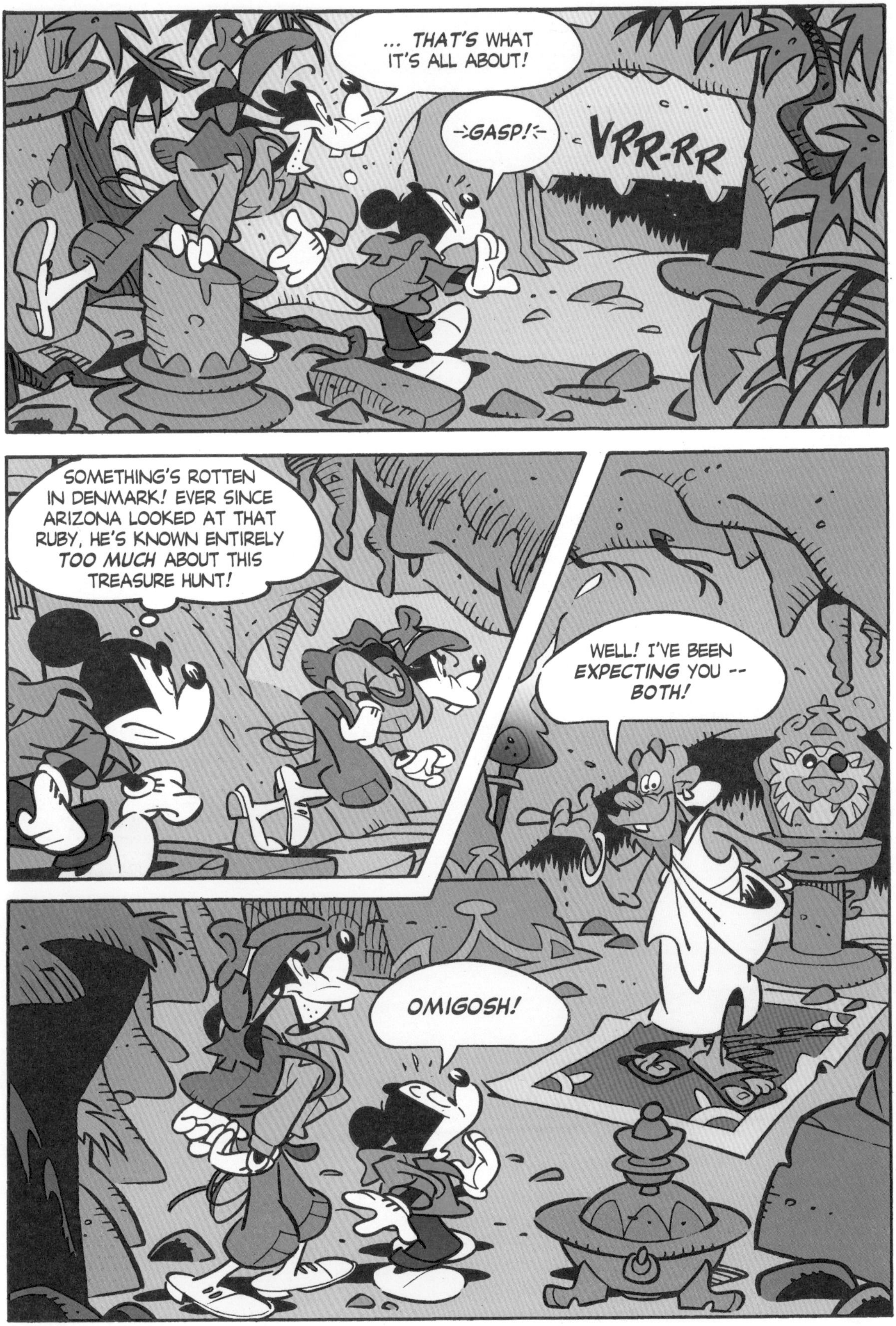

... THAT'S WHAT IT'S ALL ABOUT!
GASP!
VRR-RR
SOMETHING'S ROTTEN IN DENMARK! EVER SINCE ARIZONA LOOKED AT THAT RUBY, HE'S KNOWN ENTIRELY TOO MUCH ABOUT THIS TREASURE HUNT!
WELL! I'VE BEEN EXPECTING YOU -- BOTH!
OMIGOSH!

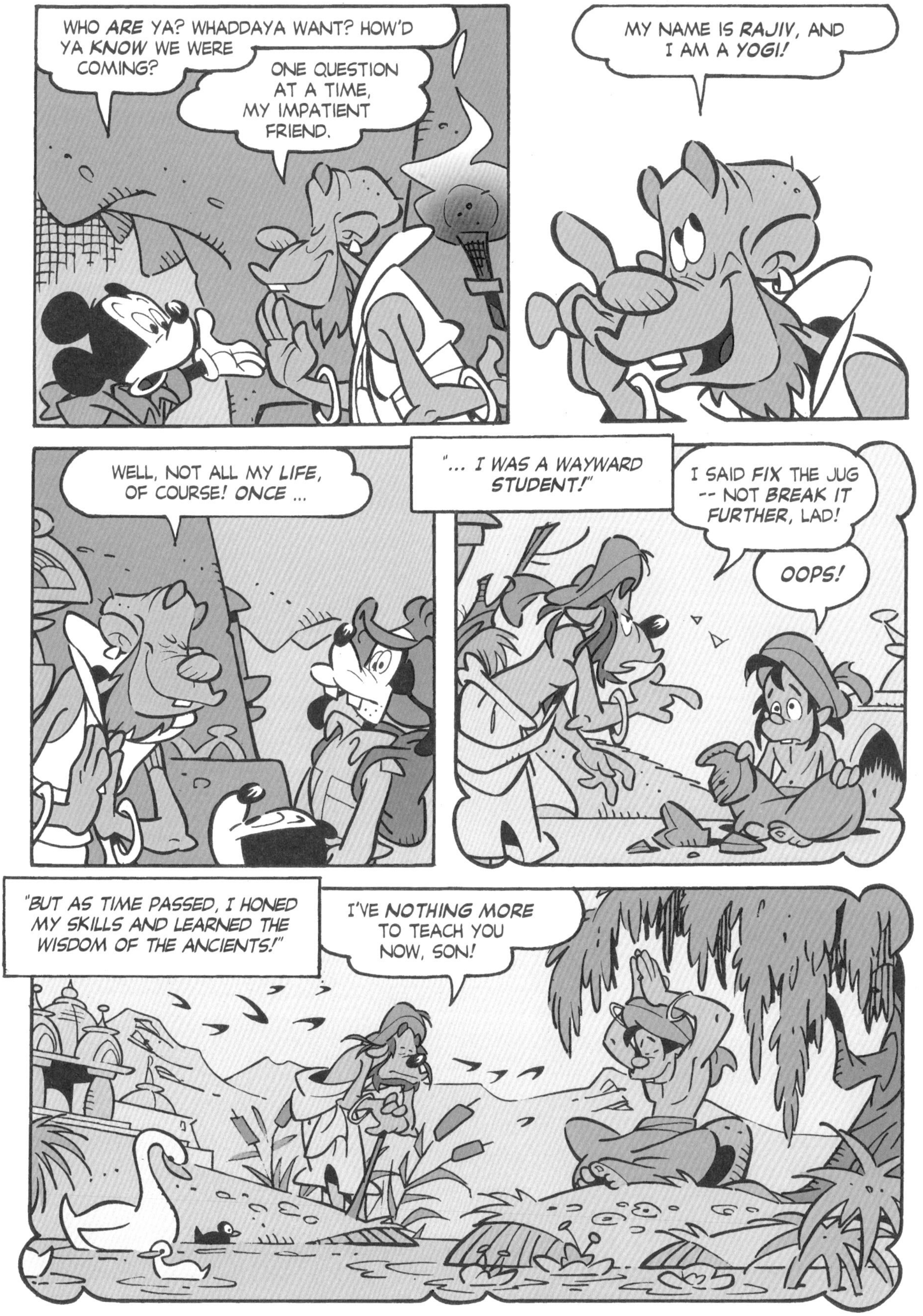
WHO ARE YA? WHADDAYA WANT? HOW'D YA KNOW WE WERE COMING?
ONE QUESTION AT A TIME, MY IMPATIENT FRIEND.
MY NAME IS RAJIV, AND I AM A YOGI!
WELL, NOT ALL MY LIFE, OF COURSE! ONCE ...
"... I WAS A WAYWARD STUDENT!"
I SAID FIX THE JUG -- NOT BREAK IT FURTHER, LAD!
OOPS!
"BUT AS TIME PASSED, I HONED MY SKILLS AND LEARNED THE WISDOM OF THE ANCIENTS!"
I'VE NOTHING MORE TO TEACH YOU NOW, SON!

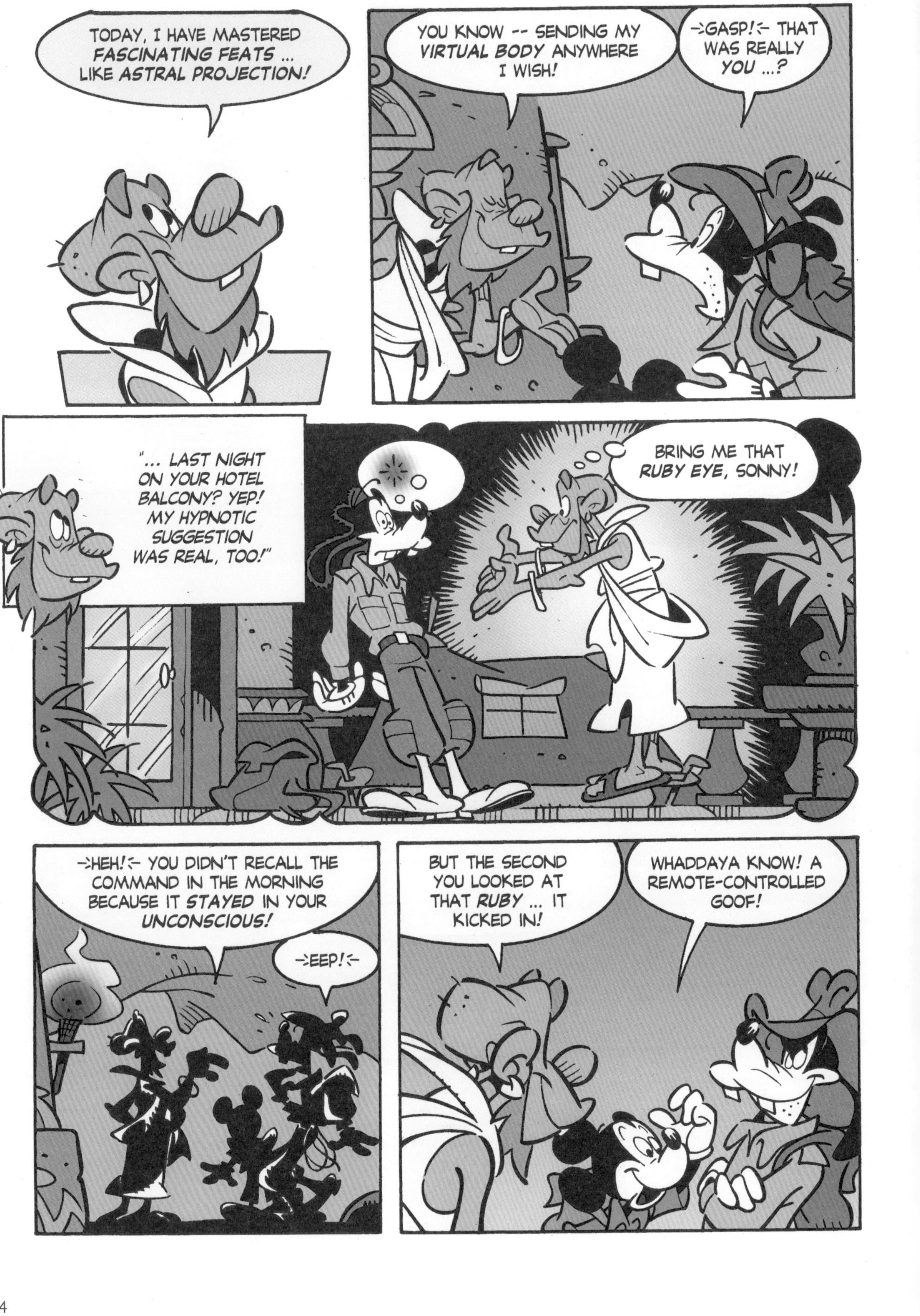
TODAY, I HAVE MASTERED FASCINATING FEATS ... LIKE ASTRAL PROJECTION!
YOU KNOW -- SENDING MY VIRTUAL BODY ANYWHERE I WISH!
GASP! THAT WAS REALLY YOU ...?
"... LAST NIGHT ON YOUR HOTEL BALCONY? YEP! MY HYPNOTIC SUGGESTION WAS REAL, TOO!"
BRING ME THAT RUBY EYE, SONNY!
HEH! YOU DIDN'T RECALL THE COMMAND IN THE MORNING BECAUSE IT STAYED IN YOUR UNCONSCIOUS!
EEP!
BUT THE SECOND YOU LOOKED AT THAT RUBY ... IT KICKED IN!
WHADDAYA KNOW! A REMOTE-CONTROLLED GOOF!

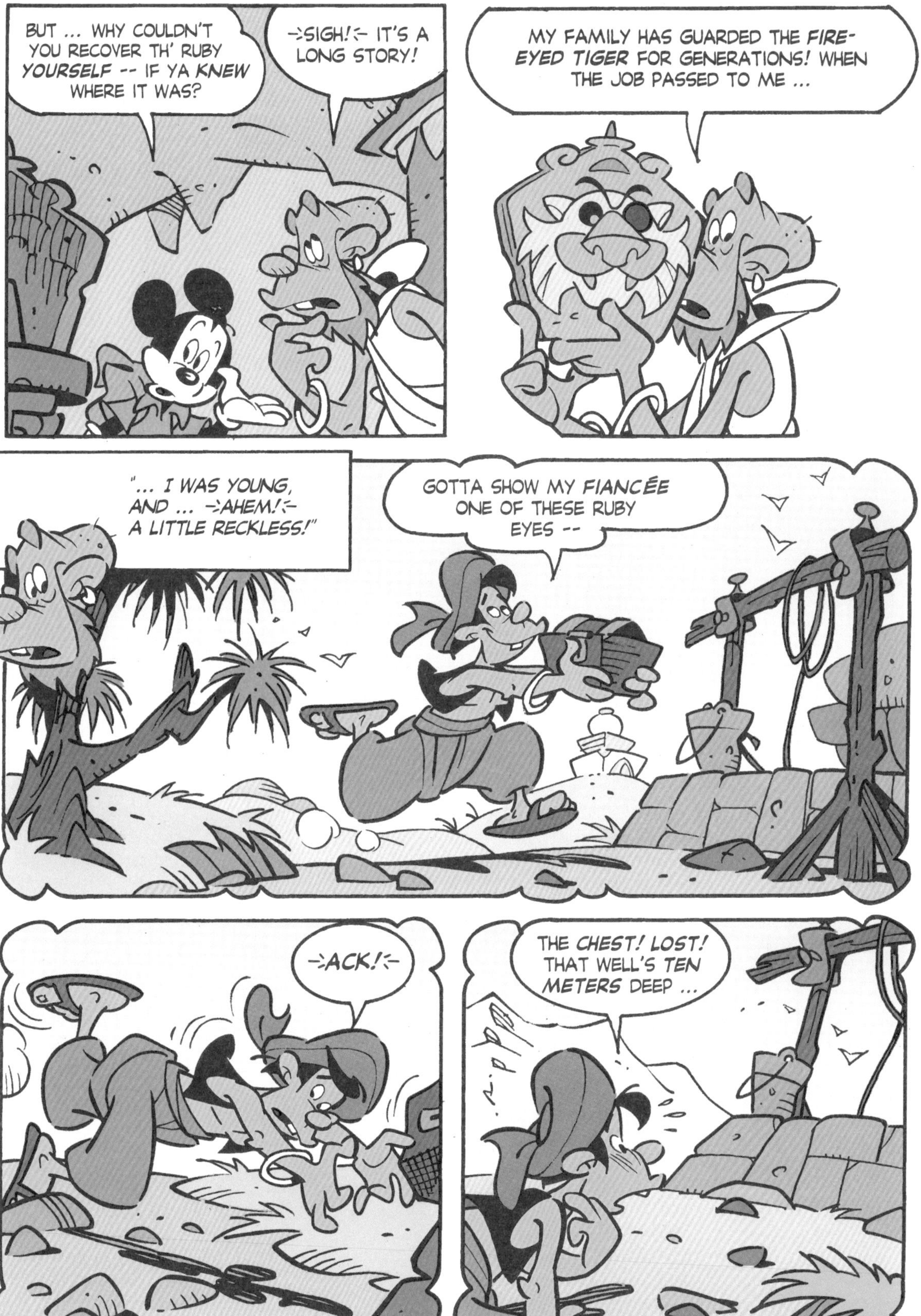
BUT ... WHY COULDN'T YOU RECOVER TH' RUBY *YOURSELF* -- IF YA *KNEW* WHERE IT WAS?
-SIGH!- IT'S A LONG STORY!
MY FAMILY HAS GUARDED THE *FIRE-EYED TIGER* FOR GENERATIONS! WHEN THE JOB PASSED TO ME ...
"... I WAS YOUNG, AND ... -AHEM!- A LITTLE RECKLESS!"
GOTTA SHOW MY *FIANCÉE* ONE OF THESE RUBY EYES --
-ACK!-
THE *CHEST! LOST!* THAT WELL'S *TEN METERS* DEEP ...

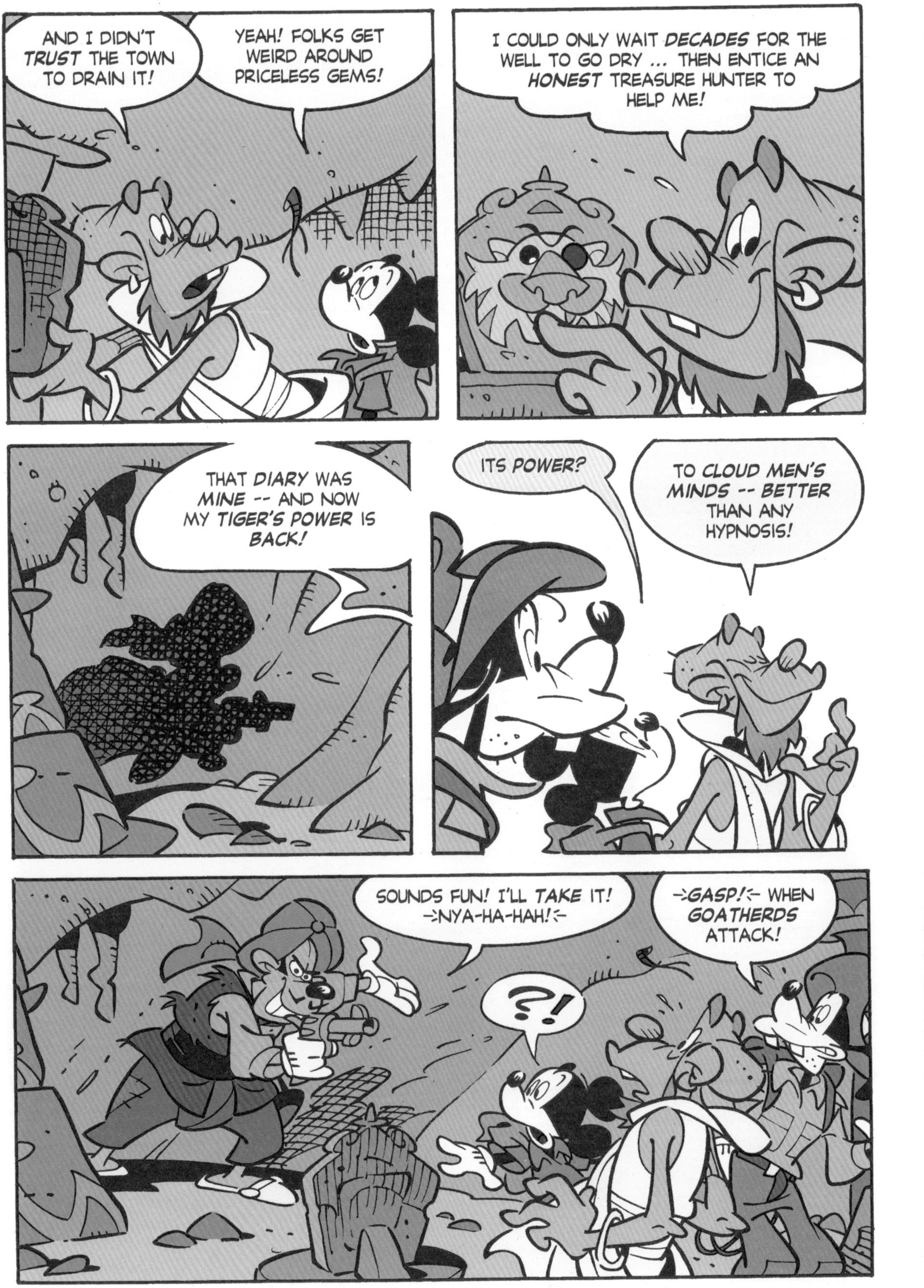
AND I DIDN'T TRUST THE TOWN TO DRAIN IT!
YEAH! FOLKS GET WEIRD AROUND PRICELESS GEMS!
I COULD ONLY WAIT DECADES FOR THE WELL TO GO DRY ... THEN ENTICE AN HONEST TREASURE HUNTER TO HELP ME!
THAT DIARY WAS MINE -- AND NOW MY TIGER'S POWER IS BACK!
ITS POWER?
TO CLOUD MEN'S MINDS -- BETTER THAN ANY HYPNOSIS!
SOUNDS FUN! I'LL TAKE IT! -NYA-HA-HAH!-
?!
-GASP!- WHEN GOATHERDS ATTACK!

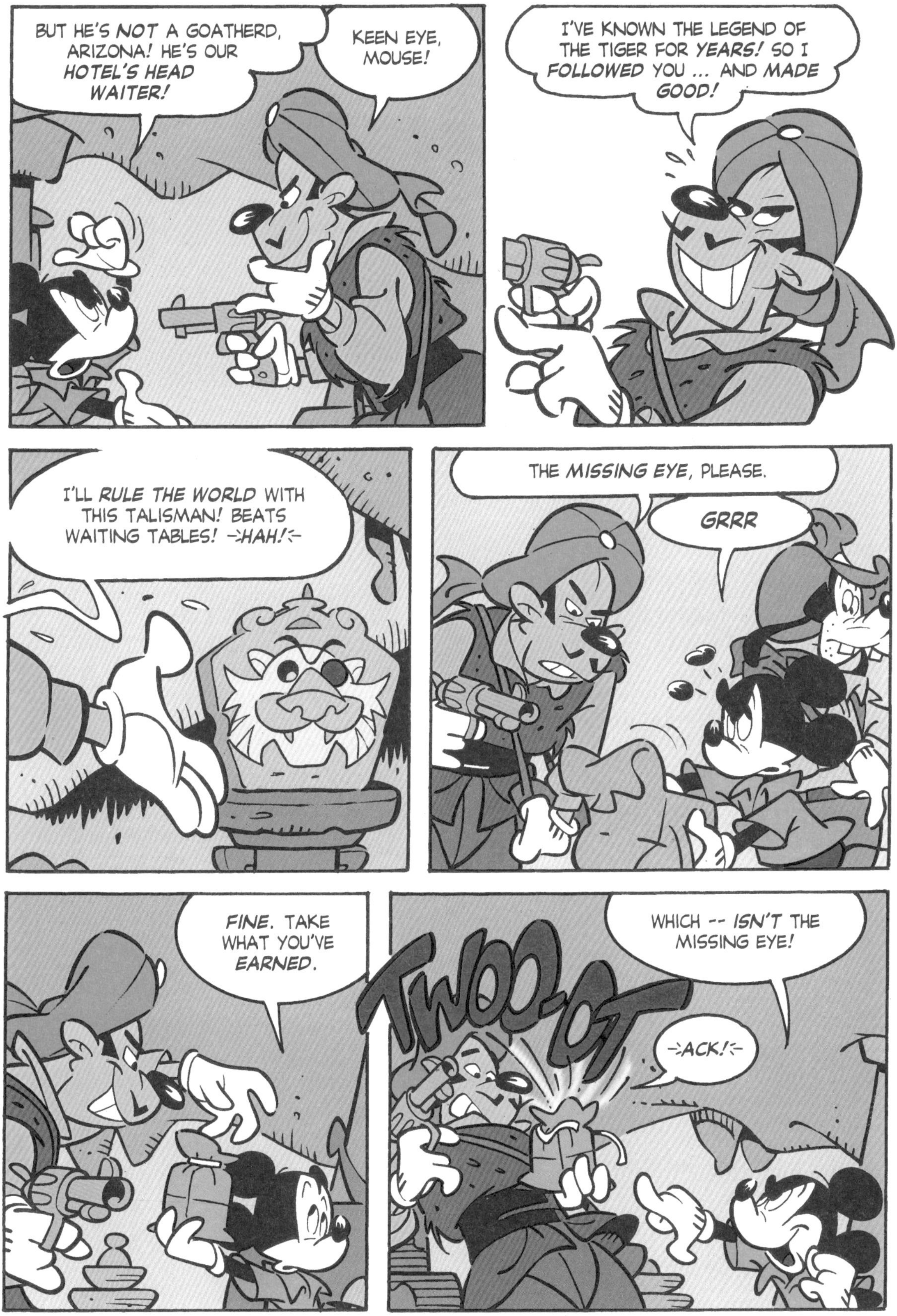

BUT HE'S NOT A GOATHERD, ARIZONA! HE'S OUR HOTEL'S HEAD WAITER!
KEEN EYE, MOUSE!
I'VE KNOWN THE LEGEND OF THE TIGER FOR YEARS! SO I FOLLOWED YOU ... AND MADE GOOD!
I'LL RULE THE WORLD WITH THIS TALISMAN! BEATS WAITING TABLES! HAH!
THE MISSING EYE, PLEASE.
GRRR
FINE. TAKE WHAT YOU'VE EARNED.
TWOO-OT
WHICH -- ISN'T THE MISSING EYE!
ACK!

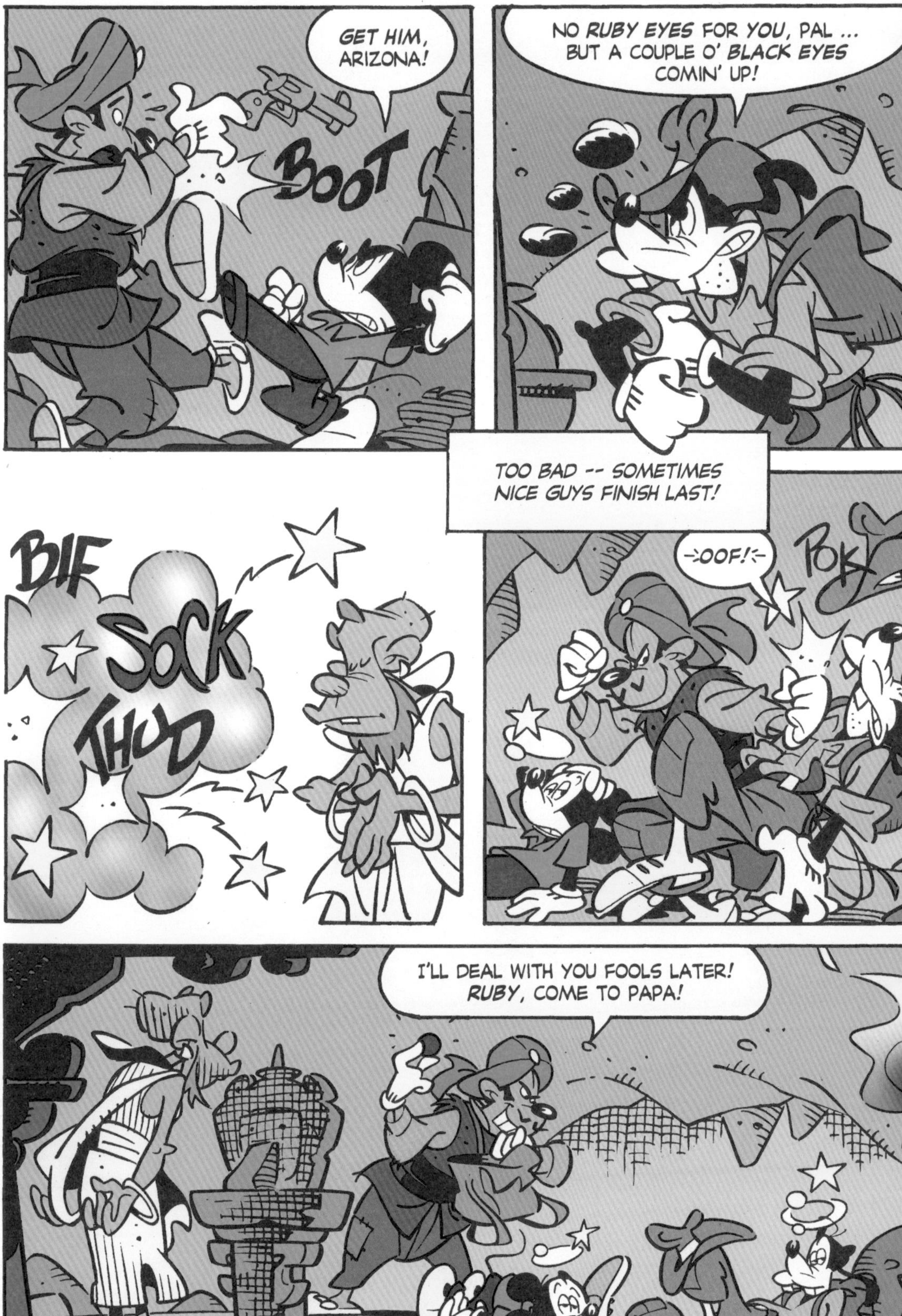
GET HIM, ARIZONA!
BOOT
NO RUBY EYES FOR YOU, PAL ... BUT A COUPLE O' BLACK EYES COMIN' UP!
TOO BAD -- SOMETIMES NICE GUYS FINISH LAST!
BIF
SOCK
THUD
OOF!
POK
I'LL DEAL WITH YOU FOOLS LATER! RUBY, COME TO PAPA!

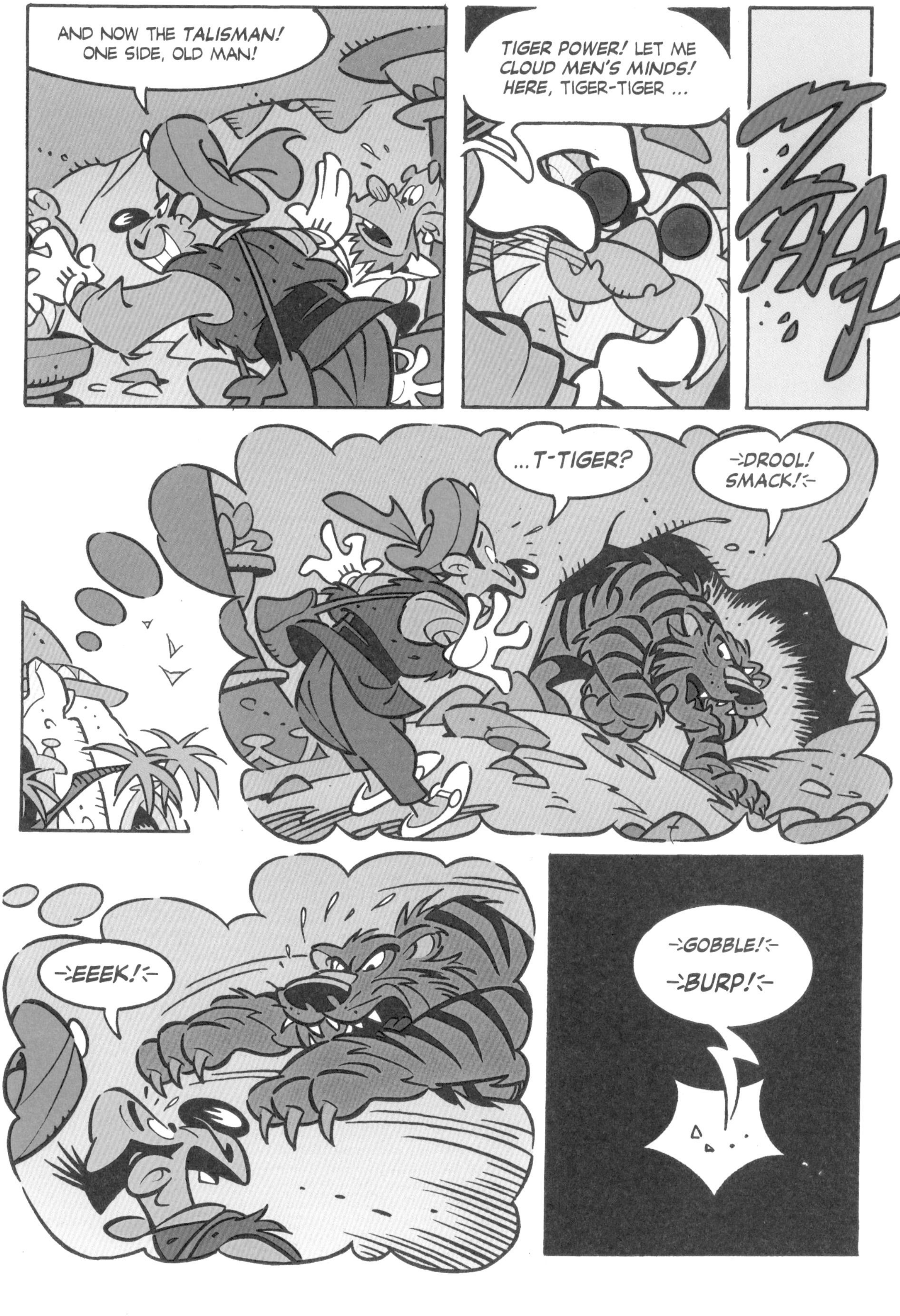
AND NOW THE TALISMAN! ONE SIDE, OLD MAN!
TIGER POWER! LET ME CLOUD MEN'S MINDS! HERE, TIGER-TIGER ...
ZAAAP
...T-TIGER?
DROOL! SMACK!
EEEK!
GOBBLE!
BURP!

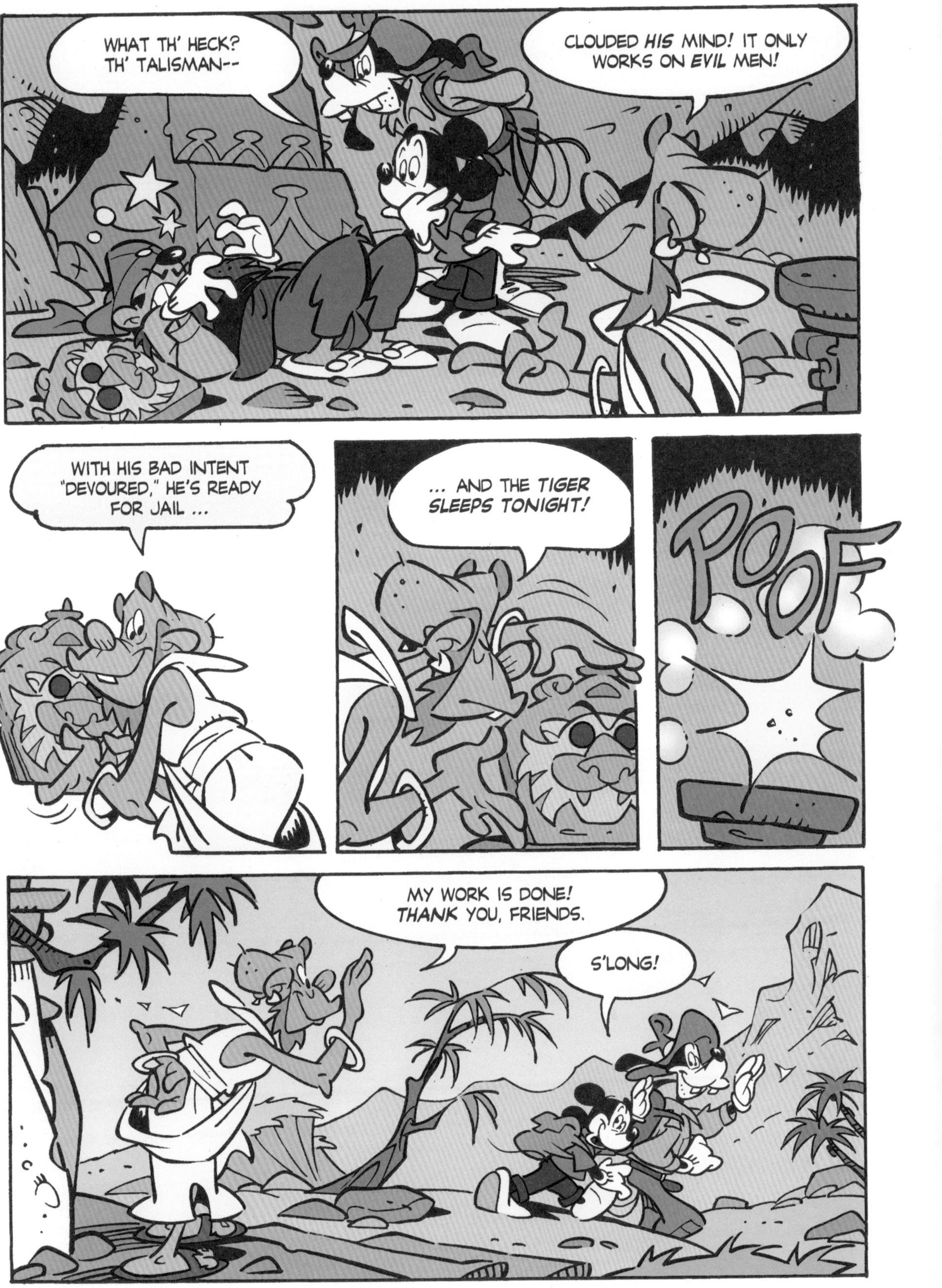
WHAT TH' HECK? TH' TALISMAN--
CLOUDED HIS MIND! IT ONLY WORKS ON EVIL MEN!
WITH HIS BAD INTENT "DEVOURED," HE'S READY FOR JAIL ...
... AND THE TIGER SLEEPS TONIGHT!
POOF
MY WORK IS DONE! THANK YOU, FRIENDS.
S'LONG!

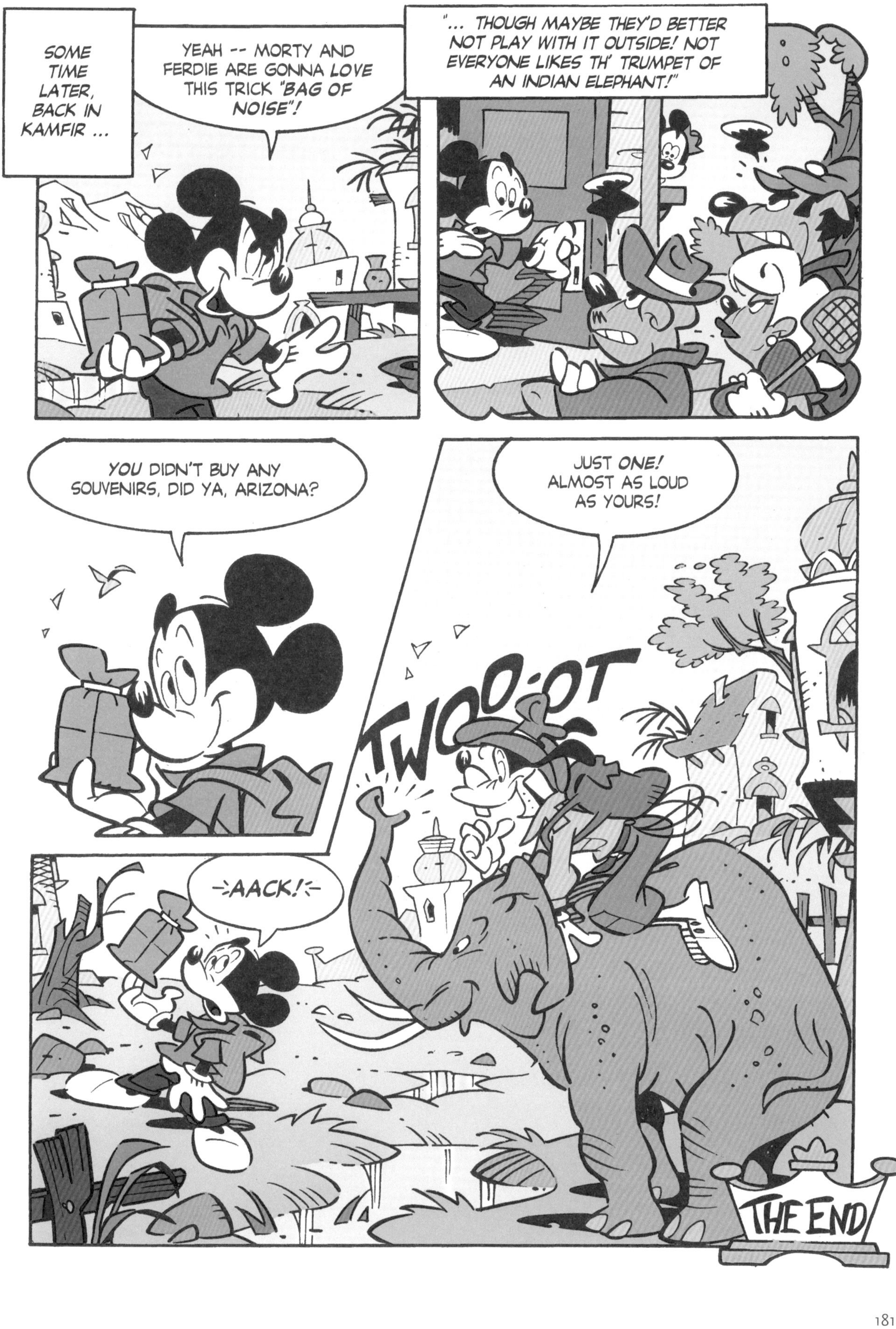
SOME TIME LATER, BACK IN KAMFIR ...
YEAH -- MORTY AND FERDIE ARE GONNA LOVE THIS TRICK "BAG OF NOISE"!
"... THOUGH MAYBE THEY'D BETTER NOT PLAY WITH IT OUTSIDE! NOT EVERYONE LIKES TH' TRUMPET OF AN INDIAN ELEPHANT!"
YOU DIDN'T BUY ANY SOUVENIRS, DID YA, ARIZONA?
JUST ONE! ALMOST AS LOUD AS YOURS!
TWOO-OT
-AACK!-
THE END

Song of the Sword

by ALESSANDRO SISTI and LUCA BOSCHI

Translation by David Gerstein

MASSIMO DE VITA had to choose: Ducks or Mice?

De Vita had established himself as an auteur producing Donald Duck and Mickey Mouse stories for Italy's weekly comic book, *Topolino* (*Mickey Mouse*), but now he had come to the point in his career where he felt he wanted to specialize and focus his efforts on one or the other.

It was a difficult decision to make, in part because Mickey can be difficult to write convincingly — suspended, as he often is, between the roles of boyish adventurer and Sherlockian detective. And yet, meeting that challenge makes every success all the more gratifying.

He chose Mickey.

De Vita had already begun the process of creating a Mickey Mouse that was distinctly his own by blending elements of previous Mouse masters — the comic strip work of Floyd Gottfredson and the comic book work of Paul Murry and Romano Scarpa — and adding new twists. One of De Vita's great strengths as a storyteller is his ability to create fully realized new worlds for Mickey and Goofy to explore — designed expressly to showcase important aspects of their personalities.

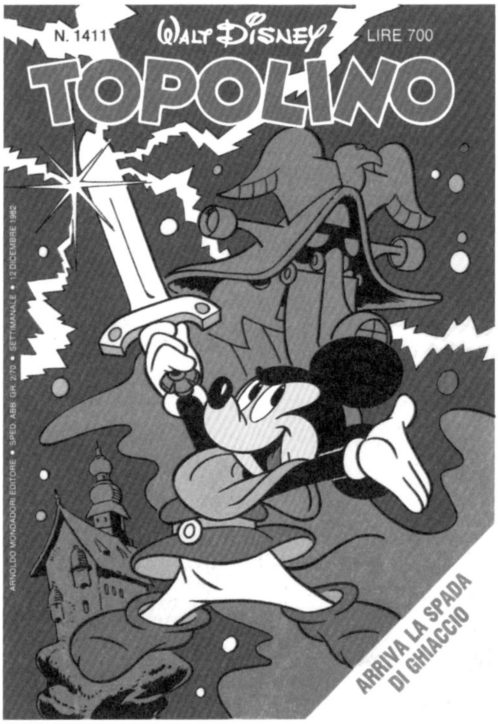
N. 1411
WALT DISNEY
LIRE 700
TOPOLINO
ARRIVA LA SPADA DI GHIACCIO

Marco Rota's cover for *Topolino* #1411, December 12, 1982, illustrates De Vita's first "Ice Sword" adventure. Rota is himself famous for a Disney comics fantasy series, the Viking Age tales of Donald's ancestor "Andold Wild Duck."

De Vita's Mickey, like the best Mickeys of his predecessors, is intrinsically good — honest, dynamic, skilled, and smart — but he is also hindered by youthful indecision and hesitation.

The place to test such a character, then, is a world in which exciting adventures come a little too fast. Such is the world of Argaar.

The term "saga" is too often carelessly applied to any long-form narrative, but it is justified in Massimo De Vita's case because of the epic scope and clever ways he combines familiar aspects of actual medieval sagas: the hero's journey, elements of witchcraft, swashbuckling battles, and valiant quests for magical objects.

Mickey and Goofy — with an emphasis on Goofy, for once an equal in his accidental knightly role — face very different challenges in Argaar than those of everyday Mouseton.

The realm of Argaar is a fantasy world worthy of its L. Frank Baum, J.R.R. Tolkien, and Lewis Carroll antecedents: full of elves, trolls, and giants, its relative believability compromised only by striking gusts of ironic humor. The Ice Sword Saga is unusually self-aware for a Disney comics story, deploying fourth-wall-breaking moments like few others.

That innovation was deliberate, as De Vita recalled:

> [Reading] a book on Nordic mythology ... I began thinking it would be interesting to try recreating the myths' atmosphere and narrative structures; in the script, I even took some character- and place-names directly from Norwegian folklore. My intention was to give ["The Secret of the Ice Sword"] a comical and joking flavor, rather than recreating the hifalutin tones of the original Norse sagas verbatim; I had seen some movies try to do this, but I didn't really appreciate how seriously they took themselves. Nevertheless, when I was later invited to Bergen, Norway, for a comics convention, I found myself in front of a queue of at least 200 people waiting for a drawing; the readers up there were literally crazy for Argaar, and the stories' parodic aspect was overshadowed by the fact that I was the first to translate Norwegian myths into Disney idiom.

Between the transposition of Scandinavian legends — not exactly widely known to the Italian public at the time — and De Vita's ironic storytelling tone, one might have expected the initial story in the Ice Sword Saga to have had trouble winning the approval of *Topolino*'s editors. But it didn't.

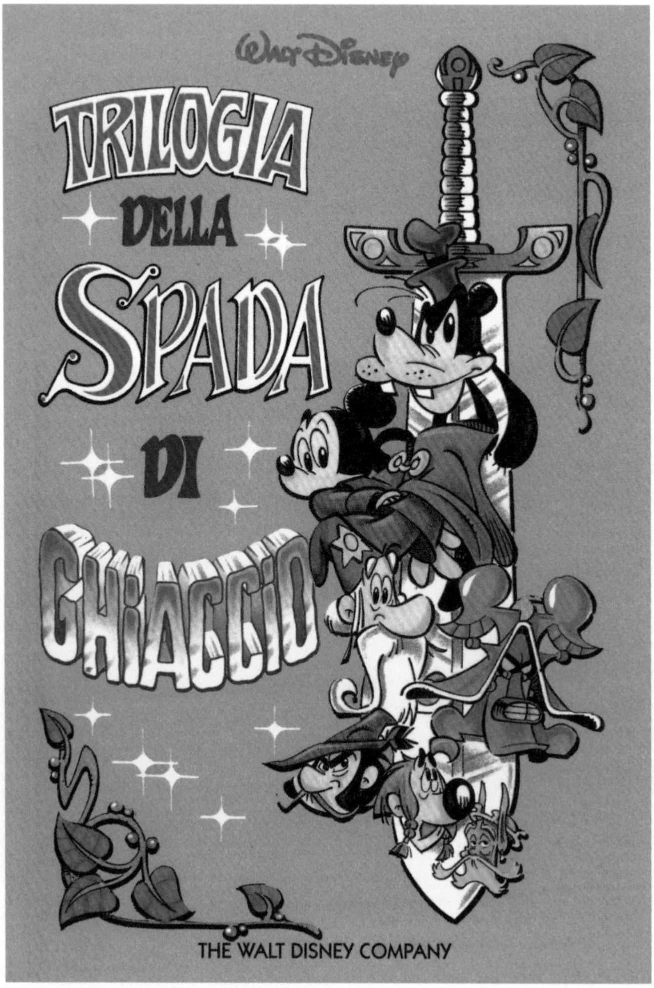
TRILOGIA
DELLA
SPADA
DI
GHIACCIO
THE WALT DISNEY COMPANY

Massimo De Vita's cover for a 1989 anthology collecting what was then the Ice Sword "trilogy." The fourth story's arrival in 1993 expanded the saga into a tetralogy — but you can just call it a "saga."

"I proposed the story to [editor] Franco Fossati," De Vita explains, "who at the time was responsible for [overseeing] scripts. Besides being a cartoonist, Fossati was a historian and an expert in pop culture, so he immediately understood [my aims]. If I had any trouble in getting approval, it related only to my having subverted the traditional use of Goofy as Mickey's sidekick. In 'The Secret of the Ice Sword' [*Disney Masters Volume 9, Mickey Mouse: The Ice Sword Saga Book 1*], Goofy is the true protagonist, with his refusal to believe in magic reflecting my own point of view."

Mickey and Goofy's first trip to the realm of Argaar was created by De Vita in 1982 as a self-contained story. It was not an obviously open-ended tale. Nevertheless, a year later, De Vita followed it up with a sequel, "The Grand Tournament of Argaar" (Book 1), framed, like its predecessor, as a Christmas story. It is Christmastime in Mouseton when the adventure kicks off, and it was Christmastime in our world when the sequel made its December 1983 appearance on newsstands.

"The Grand Tournament of Argaar" continues the first story's emphasis on Goofy, who returns to his role as the supposed "cousin" of a legendary hero — and wins the day with

E ORA OSSERVA SOT-TO DI TE! COSA VEDI?
UN MARE...UN MARE SCON-FINATO!
E' IL MARE DELLO "SPAZIO-TEMPO!" BUTTATI!
MA... MA...
E' UN'ALTEZ-ZA VERTIGI-NOSA!
PRESTO... PRIMA CHE SCOMPAIA TUTTO! BUTTATI!
MA SI'...TANTO E' SOLO UN SOGNO!
CREDI... TOPOLINO?
Fiiiii-iiii-iii-i
FLOP

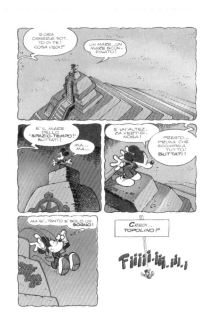

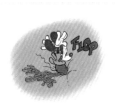

An original Italian spread from "The Prince of Mists Strikes Back" (p. 14-15) shows the unusual full-page presentation of Mickey's plunge into an empty white void.

his "rounden-round," a simple toy brought from Mouseton that De Vita himself actually conceived and created.

"I built one with a ping-pong ball and some rubber bands; it must still be in some drawer. I also proposed to Gaudenzio Capelli — the editor of *Topolino* at the time — to have [the rounden-round] manufactured and sold as a premium with the magazine. It was not possible," De Vita laments, "and even today I think it was a pity. I think readers would have liked to hold in their own hands the same game that Goofy uses as a problem-solver in the story."

Then, late in 1984, the Ice Sword series became a trilogy with "The Prince of Mists Strikes Back" (p. 1), in which the helmet of the villain from the first Ice Sword story is re-activated and sends out mental waves that sink Argaar's inhabitants into an amoral torpor. It was a plotline that De Vita hoped would deliver a powerful message, albeit sweetened with a spoonful of sugar.

"['The Prince of Mists Strikes Back'] was a metaphor for the consumer society of the time," explains the author. "I tried to convey that when mankind's critical spirit is lost, problem-solving becomes impossible. Of course, I meant this message for my more grown-up readers; I think it is essential that Disney comics speak to each portion of the audience in their own language."

For modern art fanciers, "The Prince of Mists Strikes Back" includes a page that no reader who has seen it will ever forget — entirely blank, apart from a corner in which Mickey dives into the white, empty surface. "The first to actually appreciate it was Elisa Penna, the assistant editor of *Topolino*," De Vita recalls. "[Editor]Capelli jokingly scolded me for trying to save work."

"The Prince of Mists Strikes Back" seemed to conclude the "Ice Sword" series, and for the next ten years, the stories were routinely referred to as a trilogy. But in January 1993, De Vita took us back to Argaar and its cast of characters in "The Sleeping Beauty in the Stars" (p. 59). The long delay was due to De Vita's hesitancy: "Editor-in-Chief Capelli had asked me several times to resume the series, but the theme grew tired in my mind. This is why each story in the cycle had a shorter length than the one before. But then screenwriter Fabio Michelini gave me his own idea for a sequel, which he cared about a lot — and I enjoyed the opportunity [the story gave me] to make fun of fairy tales and mix the genre with sci-fi."

And so, the famous Ice Sword "trilogy" became a "tetralogy," even if fans now prefer just to call the story arc a "saga." To this day, many readers hold out hope that De Vita will create new installments for the series, which fans around the world have acclaimed as the greatest fantasy work in Disney comics history.

"There are even those who, in praising the series, have told me that I perfectly understood and internalized the lessons of Tolkien," an amused De Vita recalls. "It's a pity that I've never read Tolkien."

DISNEY MASTERS

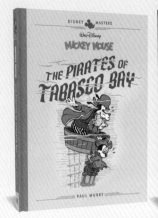

PAUL MURRY
Volume 7

ROMANO SCARPA
Volume 8

MASSIMO DE VITA
Volume 9

MAU AND BAS HEYMANS
Volume 10

Plus...

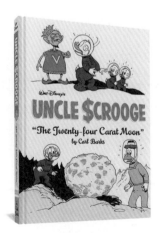

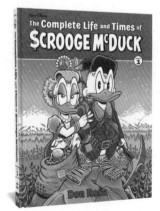

CARL BARKS

DON ROSA

FLOYD GOTTFREDSON

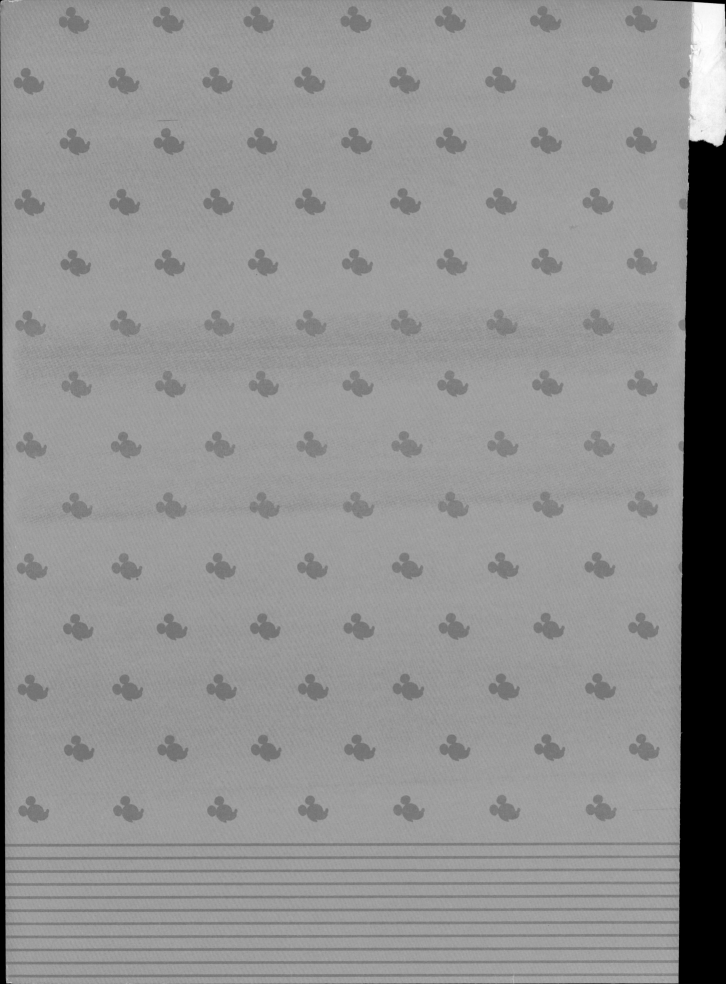